MANJA

Persephone Book N° 39
Published by Persephone Books Ltd 2003

First published in German by Querido Verlag, Amsterdam in 1938
Reissued by Persona Verlag, Mannheim in 1984
First published in English in 1939 by Secker & Warburg as
The Wall in a translation by Philip Owens

© Persona Verlag, Mannheim 1984
Translation © Kate Phillips 2002
Preface © Eva Ibbotson 2002

Endpapers taken from a Wiener Werkstätte fabric called 'Paul'
1927 designed by Clara Posnanski, reproduced by courtesy of
the Österreichisches Museum für angewandte Kunst, Vienna
and Dr Angela Völker

Typeset in ITC Baskerville by Keystroke,
Jacaranda Lodge, Wolverhampton

Colour by Classic Cheney Press, Banbury

Printed and bound by Biddles Ltd,
Guildford and King's Lynn

ISBN 1 903155 290

Persephone Books Ltd
59 Lamb's Conduit Street
London WC1N 3NB
020 7242 9292

www.persephonebooks.co.uk

MANJA

a novel about five children
by
ANNA GMEYNER

translated by KATE PHILLIPS

with a new preface by

EVA IBBOTSON

PERSEPHONE BOOKS
LONDON

PREFACE

I remember my mother writing *Manja*, in the sitting-room of a flat in Belsize Park. The year was 1938 and she had come to London as a refugee in 1935.

The story of *Manja* had its origin in a small piece, hardly more than a paragraph, in a newspaper, describing the fate of a twelve year-old girl in a German town. The book spans the period between 1920 when Germans were trying to forget the defeat and horror of the war and 1933 when the hopes and aspirations of decent people had suffered a second defeat in the triumph of Nazism.

It is the story of five children, their loyal and resolute friendship, their attempts to escape into a life of the imagination centred on a piece of waste ground with a crumbling wall, which is all that remains of a ruined house above the river. At the story's heart is Manja, the little Polish Jewess whose capacity for happiness and gift for life transforms the lives of the other children. She is the only girl, the other four are boys whose families represent the various political and social strands dominant in the foredoomed German Republic. Franz is the son of a Nazi, Karli of a proletarian activist, Heini of an idealistic doctor who represents the 'good'

German never quite forceful enough to prevail. Harry's father is a rich industrialist unable to believe that his money won't protect him from the consequences of a partly Jewish lineage.

The beginning of the novel attracted considerable attention, even criticism at the time, and gave it a cachet as a 'woman's novel'. It opens with the five nights on which the children are conceived. Born two streets away from where Sigmund Freud lived, my mother must have thought it evident that the sexual encounters of the five couples would presage the nature of the children that had been conceived. Franz is conceived as the result of a marital rape; Heini after a night of fulfilment and joy. . . . And for Manja's conception Anna Gmeyner produces a lyric, romantic conjunction, a 'one-night stand' taken to the heights after a performance of Mahler's *Das Lied von der Erde* which leaves the sad little Jewess Lea to face a pregnancy alone.

The children are born in the same hospital, gradually meet and intermesh. Only partly understanding, they are drawn into the destinies of their parents: the left-wing activist to imprisonment and flight, the Nazi from poverty and humiliation to power, the doctor compelled to defend his humanitarian stance in the hospital where he works, the financier in increasingly desperate attempts at assimilation.

But the boys have each other, and they have Manja. On Wednesdays and Saturdays when they can meet by the crumbling wall above the river they are safe. Manja is 'warmth, she is closeness, she has no room for hate'. It is Manja who evokes the five-pointed constellation Cassiopeia as their symbol – and it is Cassiopeia which is left shining over their ruined playground at the end.

Increasingly the boys are forced to pay for their friendship with her as anti-Semitism takes hold, yet they remain loyal. Only when the bullying Nazi youth, Martin, finds their sanctuary is she defeated. But if the book is a chronicle of tragic times, it is not depressing; nor is it a polemic with characters chosen only to represent creeds and points of view. Even the most unpleasant people in the book have redeemable virtues; the concierge who betrays Karli's father to the Nazis goes to the prison where he is held, leaving a pot of home-made jam. And because she brings to her work a poet's eye, the testimony of the author does not only embrace great issues and causes. Here we find the pattern of the wallpaper in a German pension, the corridors and doors of a maternity hospital, the pallid flowers on a tenement window box.

Manja was published under a pseudonym – Anna Reiner – to protect those of my mother's relatives who were still in Europe, notably her own mother, whose ancestors were re-arranged so that she emerged as only a quarter Jewish and was able to live unmolested in Vienna throughout the war. It could not of course be published either in Germany or Austria and a Dutch publishing firm, the Querido Verlag, brought out the German version. But the English translation quickly followed: the book was called *The Wall* in Britain and *Five Destinies* in America. It collected excellent reviews, not only in the *émigré* press, but in the mainstream papers. The *Manchester Guardian* called it 'a remarkable novel, a book of

truth and tenderness.' The *New York Times* referred to it as 'a
tale of a terrible beauty.' Berthold Viertel, the film director,
regarded it as 'the richest, the most beautiful, the most life-
enhancing novel to emerge from the experience of exile.'

The road which led Anna Gmeyner to Belsize Park was a
well-travelled one in the years after Hitler came to power. Its
streets abounded with Jewish doctors and lawyers and school
children; with Communists and Social Democrats, with actors
and writers and bankers of no particular political persuasion
who had spoken out against the Nazis. The war had not yet
come but these refugees saw its necessity as the English could
not yet do. They used their humour to keep the terror and
desolation at bay but it was always there.

My mother fitted well into this band of exiles who had
been deprived in a few years of the certainties of centuries.
She was born in 1902 in Vienna, the daughter of a lawyer
who belonged to that displaced group of Jews, created by
Hitler – assimilated, non-religious intellectuals, the backbone
of Austrian cultural life, many of whom had never set foot
inside a synagogue.

The family was prosperous; Anna was the eldest of three
daughters who went, as most Viennese children did, to the
local school but was followed each morning by a kind of
footman carrying her satchel.

She minded this; minded inequality, minded injustice –
asked from very early on the questions that Tolstoy asked:
'Why are we here?', 'Why is life not fair?', 'What is it that we
should do?'. Like him she often got the wrong answers but the
questions were right.

At six she was the acknowledged story-teller of the neighbourhood; at seven she dictated her memoirs to an aged relative; at thirteen she wrote a verse drama called 'Ideal and Reality'. Her precocity infuriated her aunt who lived with the family and was in love with Anna's father. The whole household might have been created by Schnitzler – my mother longed to get away.

She used the traditional method of escape. At twenty-two she met and married a young biologist, Berthold Wiesner, whom she had found weeping because he had just finished eating the last pot of strawberry jam made by his mother before she died. A mutual unhappiness, a longing to get away from home, was the bond between them and of course it was not enough.

I was born a year later and even then it was clear that the marriage was a mistake. They went to Edinburgh where my father took up a university lectureship and studied the maternal behaviour of rats, which he found, I think, more satisfactory than the maternal behaviour of my mother, who left for the Scottish coalfields to study the life of the miners and returned so horrified by their plight that she turned our house into a collecting centre for money and clothes. One of my earliest recollections is helping to cut out the sweat stained 'dress preservers' which the donors had left in the clothes they gave to 'the poor'. By now her left-wing sympathies and evident lack of interest in the bourgeois minutiae of Edinburgh academia could no longer be concealed. She went to Berlin, taking me with her, and my parents never lived together again.

Her success in Berlin as a playwright, a poet, a librettist, coincided with those years of the Weimar Republic which have become legendary. She worked with Bertolt Brecht; she wrote lyrics for Hanns Eisler, and film scripts for Pabst. Her experiences in the Scottish coal mines became a play, *Heer ohne Helden (Army without Heroes)* and her play *Automatenbüffet* was commended for the Kleist prize.

This success, which forced on her the independent 'feminist' life which women later had to fight for so hard, came at a price. Her marriage was effectively over; she was not able to keep me during the lean periods, and I was sent to my grandparents in Vienna and subsequently to board in the kind of *Kinderheim* so popular during the twenties and thirties. Later she told me that there were times when she had eaten potato peelings.

During this period, when concern for the underdog, for the oppressed and unemployed, for the sins of the rich, were in the forefront of her mind as in the minds of her fellow writers and artists, she travelled to Russia. The purpose of the visit was to make a film with Eisenstein, but the great director was already falling under a cloud and the film was never made. Nevertheless, her experience in Russia was seminal: her feeling for the 'Russian peasant', idealised or not, stayed with her all her life. In a remote village to which she was driven, the peasants brought hay and water to feed her car – this in the year of the hydroelectric dams and the Five Year Plan.

At the end of 1932 she moved to Paris and accommodated refugee poets and actors and musicians in her tiny Montparnasse flat. Pabst too had fled Germany and was making a film of *Don Quixote* starring Chaliapin, and she worked with him on the scenario.

One day the concierge brought up a note from the gentleman in the flat below. He was trying to write a book and wanted to know if Madame Gmeyner would permit him to buy her a pair of slippers. The noise she made walking up and down was making it impossible for him to work.

My mother raged. The concierge maintained that nevertheless the gentleman was very nice and they should meet. She was right. The man in the flat below, Jascha Morduch, was a philosopher, Russian and Jewish, tall, blonde and blue-eyed, the essence of integrity. He had fought on the side of Kerensky's Provisional Government in the revolution, led his troops in error into a Finnish bog and never returned to his native land.

They fell in love and married. My mother adored him for the rest of her life and never recovered from his death. Soon afterwards he made a disconcerting statement which nevertheless saved both their lives. 'Paris is for bachelors,' he said. 'London is for married men.'

So they went to London, where he revealed an unexpected brood of bourgeois sisters in Ealing and two brothers who owned a factory in Slough. My mother found this hard, and they moved to Belsize Park.

Thus she brought to her exile all the seeds that came to fruition in *Manja*. The knowledge of Central European politics, the experience of the Nazi menace at first hand, the literary sophistication and expertise she had acquired working with the best minds in Germany. And her own unquenchable emotionalism which annoyed some people but was as much part of her as her limbs. Bernice Rubens once said that 'a writer should write in yesterday's blood' and perhaps this is true. But *Manja* was written in fresh blood, in 'today's blood', as the author saw in the street she looked out on the victims of Hitler's deeds.

A second novel followed a year after *Manja*. *Café du Dôme*, is set in Paris and describes the life of the *émigrés* washed up like flotsam in the city my mother so much loved, but the story was overtaken by events. By the time the book was published, a very different clientele drank at the Café du Dôme: the Nazi Stormtroopers who had conquered France.

Britain was now at war. As the bombing of London intensified, my mother and her husband went to live in Berkshire, in a thatched cottage by the Thames. He began to write a philosophical work entitled *Terzium Datur*, made raspberry jam to put into his tea and ritually consumed a dried egg omelette every night so as not to trouble the meat ration. She developed a passion for gardening and helped him with his work. When she wrote now, it was in English. The change of language deprived her of the nuances and the facility she had had in German, but she was no longer interested in her past fame, and increasingly distanced herself from the life of her fellow *émigrés*. People making a pilgrimage to talk about her work in the Weimar Republic received short shrift. 'That's all over,' she said and led them to her herbaceous border. As far as anybody could be in those troubled times she was happy.

Her husband's sudden death in 1950 left her utterly bereft. She tried to pursue him through every religion and belief known to man: Sufism, spiritualism, Buddhism, anthroposophy. Her novels, her plays, and her poems in German were forgotten by others as they were forgotten by her.

She grew old and increasingly confused and eventually found refuge in The Retreat, a Quaker hospital in York.

Then at the beginning of the eighties a young German woman, Lisette Buchholz, decided to use a legacy from her parents to start a small publishing firm which would specialise in 'exile literature': in the books of the lost years when Hitler was in power. Looking about for suitable titles, she consulted Dr Landshoff, the veteran survivor of the Querido Press in Amsterdam, who unhesitatingly recommended *Manja*.

But the author was lost; it was known only that she had fled to England at the beginning of the war. On an impulse Ms Buchholz put an advertisement in the *Jewish Chronicle* asking if anyone knew of her whereabouts. I had long been married to an Englishman, never saw the *Jewish Chronicle* ... but a distant relative of my father happened to see it and got in touch with me.

Thus *Manja* was reborn. When Lisette Buchholz came to England to interview my mother she found an old woman in a wheelchair, her memory gone. She had brought a notebook, camera, tape-recorder ... but when I looked in to see how the interview was going I found Lisette in tears. 'I feel as though I am in the presence of the whole of exile literature,' she said.

Manja was republished in Germany in 1984 under the author's real name and was an immediate success. The reviews were excellent but more than that, this first product of the new Persona Verlag became almost a rallying point for women trying to understand the past. There were readings, discussions, meetings . . . When I visited Germany, which I had been afraid to do for fifty years, it was like coming home. And now nearly two decades later *Manja* has been republished in English and in a new translation by another publishing house dedicated to finding what was valuable and lost. Re-reading the book now what strikes me is its topicality, with its belief in 'the unsubduable heroism of the human spirit', independent of any religious or political creed.

There is a poem in *Manja* – *Tanzlied* or Dance Song which Lea, Manja's young mother, finds in the notebook of the musician with whom she spends his last night on earth. It is written with the cadence of the old shtetl songs; wistful, sad and probing, a last fragment left by a young man before he commits suicide, unaware that he has fathered a marvellous child. Like all poems this is in the end untranslatable, but the refrain goes:

> Who dances with the lame?
> Who walks with the blind?
> Who sings with the dumb?
> Where can we him find?

My mother was obsessed by this question all her life, but for me there was an answer. She did: she danced with the lame and walked with the blind or tried to, all her life. She really did.

Eva Ibbotson,
Newcastle, 2002

PUBLISHER'S NOTE

Manja begins in the early summer of 1920 when 'everyone wanted to make up for the four years when laughter had been a crime and pleasure a sin.' But Germany was still in turmoil following its defeat in the Great War and the punitive Treaty of Versailles imposed on it.

The Kaiser had abdicated, Germany had become a Republic, and there were a series of attempts to seize power by both right-wing and left-wing revolutionaries. Immediately after the War had ended German nationalists had started to spread the myth that the November 1918 Armistice was the result of a 'Stab in the Back' by so-called 'November criminals', that is politicians disloyal to Germany.

Germany faced the burdens both of its own war-debts and of enormous reparation payments demanded by the victors to punish Germany and to help compensate for the massive devastation it had caused in Northern France and Belgium (Germany itself had hardly been physically damaged).

There were many political murders, of which the best-known were those of Karl Liebknecht and Rosa Luxemburg (both left-wing revolutionaries) in 1919, of Matthias Erzberger (the Centre Party leader, who had previously sought a compromise peace) in 1921, and above all that of Walter Rathenau on June 24 1922 (not, as Chapter 9 implies, in 1920). Rathenau was Foreign Minister, and had been committed to trying to meet half-way the reparations demands of the victors; he was also a once-powerful industrialist, a forward-looking social theorist, and a Jew.

At the end of 1922 Germany defaulted on its reparations obligations, and in reprisal 70, 000 French and Belgian troops occupied the industrial region of the Ruhr. The economic consequences of this were catastrophic: during 1923 unemployment rose from 2% to 23%, the mark depreciated from 17,000 to the dollar to 4.2 trillion, wages were taken home in wheelbarrows, all accompanied in Berlin 'by a hectic gaiety . . . a rage for dancing . . . to the strident sound of American jazz and "Yes, We Have No Bananas"' (G.Craig *Germany* p452). In November 1923 Adolf Hitler made his first, unsuccessful, attempt at a 'national völkisch revolution' when he led 2,000 extremists through Munich and was dispersed by a few salvoes from the Bavarian state police.

During the 1920s the economy improved somewhat, Germany's debts were settled, and American money began to pour in. But politically the 'Weimar Republic' was always unstable, with much of the left and the right unwilling to accept parliamentary democracy and the nationalists obsessed with reversing Germany's humiliation at Versailles. Then, from 1930, Germany's short-lived economic recovery was destroyed in the Great Depression, and unemployment doubled to nearly 6 million by the end of 1931. More and more voters turned to Hitler's Nazi party, which by September 1930 had polled 6.4 million and become the second largest party. By July 1932 the Nazis had gained 13.7 million votes, and after months of intrigue Hitler became Chancellor in January 1933.

The Reichstag Fire of February 1933 gave Hitler his excuse to go further. He called elections in which he massively increased his vote to 17.2 million (43% of the vote), and then in March 1933 the Reichstag passed the Enabling Law which set the framework for the Nazi dictatorship. The two most spectacular acts of terror which followed were the boycott of Jewish shops at the beginning of April, enforced by the strong-arm tactics of the SA (Stormtroopers), and the public burning of 'unGerman' books a month later, presided over by leading professors and student unions. During the rest of 1933 Hitler consolidated his hold on the civil service, the judges and the trade unions, and banned other political parties.

The third and fourth parts of *Manja* take place in the period between the Reichstag Fire and the end of 1933 when violence 'was on a different scale from anything which had happened before . . . Men were beaten, arrested and murdered for no more substantial reason than to satisfy a private grudge, to secure a man's job or his apartment, and to gratify a taste for sadism. . . .' In parallel '1933, like other revolutionary years, produced great hopes . . . a feeling of exhilaration and anticipation after the years of hopelessness . . . Hitler succeeded in releasing pent-up energies in the nation, and in re-creating a belief in the future of the German people' (A.Bullock *Hitler* p278).

LIST OF MAIN CHARACTERS

Hanna (a piano teacher) = Ernst Heidemann (a liberal doctor); their son is HEINI

Frieda = Anton Meissner (who becomes a Nazi); their children are Tilde, Mariechen and FRANZ

Hilde = (1) Max Hartung (a half-Jewish businessman); ≠ (2) Walter von Adrian; their sons are HARRY and Hans Peter. Hartung's parents are Samuel and Matilde Hamburger

Anna = Eduard Müller (a Communist factory worker); their children are Hans, Hede, an un-named child and KARL

Lea ≠ (1) David Goldstaub = (2) Leo Meirowitz (a Jewish shopkeeper); their children are MANJA, David and Munio

CHRONOLOGY

The Prologue begins with the end in late autumn 1933. In Part One, Chapters 1-5 take place on 25 May 1920 and Chapters 6-12 during the months between July 1920 and early March 1921; Part Two, Chapters 13-19, between 1923 and 1929; the Interlude in 1932; Part Three, Chapters 20-28, between March and September 1933; Part Four, Chapters 29-36, in October and November 1933.

CONTENTS

MANJA

PROLOGUE
BEGINNING WITH THE END

The five bright stars of Cassiopeia could, for a moment, be seen above the church tower. Then they disappeared behind scurrying black clouds.

It was dark now, apart from the lamps along the bridge and the lights of the town reflected in the river. The sloping field was invisible in the darkness, the trees black and strange, and the four children sitting on the wall could not see each other's faces.

All that was visible of Heini's lowered head was his fair hair. Harry, with his large nose and spectacles, looked like some strange night-bird. Karl propped himself on his fists, his round head resting like a big black globe on two smaller ones. Franz was the only one who moved, his heels kicking against the wall, breaking off bits of stone. Manja was not there. But she had tied her torn scarf to the little birch tree growing on the wall. It was sodden after four nights of rain.

The children suddenly had no idea why they had come to the wall as usual that Wednesday evening – as if what they were looking for could be found there.

They had once been like kittens snuggling together for warmth. Now their childhood nest had been destroyed and they would never climb into it again.

1

Even though they were sitting so close together, as if it were a comfort just to be near each other, they were quite alone. The old 'we', 'us' and 'together' had become part of the past, like outgrown clothes.

Each in his different way realised they could only help one another if they separated, only stay together when apart. For a moment, before going back to their everyday lives, they were wrapped in the aura of what had been lost; then they parted. They did not say the usual 'See you on Wednesday, see you on Saturday', but went quietly across the rain-drenched fields.

Every moment grows, like a plant with tangled, hidden roots, out of the soil of the past, and is invisibly shaped by it. What these children had suffered, uncomprehendingly, reached back further than their memories, back into the time before they existed and before their lives began.

And even that was not the beginning.

PART ONE

CHAPTER 1
HEINI

The cuckoo-clock struck loudly in the hall of the Pension Heinzinger, Luisenstrasse 4. Ten times. It could be heard in every room, although very few people were in at that hour. Most were out and about on the streets, in cinemas, or in cafés and restaurants, where laughter and excitement was finally making everyone realise that the War was over at last. Lost or won, it was over, it was the spring of 1920 and now everyone wanted to make up for the four years when laughter had been a crime and pleasure a sin. Light flooded the streets; dazzling advertisements latched onto the passers-by as if with hooks, forcing the names of bars and chorus girls' legs into their brains and anyone who could not drink cocktails or buy the women knew at least that they existed and where. Bright lights had replaced the dim street-lamps, which had been covered by ghostly anti-aircraft shields in darkened streets.

So it was not surprising that the light was on in only one room in the pension, a room just like the others with its wall-paper of purple roses and green parrots round the walls and a brass bedstead beneath a pink overhead light with red plush tassels – the same plush that covered the sofa, table and bed, and the curtains that prevented the inquisitive across the street from seeing in.

The pattern of purple roses repeated itself six times – the parrots five and a half – in the strips of wallpaper. Eight strips, and therefore forty-eight roses and forty-four parrots on each wall, roses and parrots alternating. But because of the two windows and the wardrobe, some of the wallpaper was missing. Thus, forty-eight times four (not quite) is one hundred and ninety-two roses and one hundred and seventy-six parrots. Behind the wardrobe, if one moved it, there must be the same pattern, its colours bright, not dusty and worn; but that can only have been seen at spring cleaning.

Hanna Cornelius approaches the wardrobe and is about to push it away from the wall, but pauses, takes fright and withdraws her hand. That way madness lies. Two paces to the table, two paces back, and to the bed. Counting flowers on the wall-paper, being aware of every ugly detail of your surroundings. Listening to every sound, every car horn, every voice. Waiting when there is no point, no hope. But waiting with every fibre of one's being.

It would be better to go to bed and read, at least to undress. She sits on the edge of the bed and undoes her shoe-laces, picks up a newspaper, puts it down again. In the mirror opposite she can see a girl in a white silk blouse with two of its buttons undone and a smooth black skirt, a very pale face framed by brownish hair. She sits quite still holding a shoe in her hand.

Downstairs the front door opens. Hanna jumps up. With one shoe in her hand, the other on her foot, she runs to the door and listens. Steps come up the stairs and pass; a key is put in a lock, a door opened. Silence. Nothing. Again a car horn outside, deep male laughter. Under the tread of feet in the room above her the lamp sways. A water pipe in the wall moans and gurgles. The clock strikes a quarter-past ten. Again the front door opens. Voices are heard. A woman giggles and is silenced by her companion, who whispers so that every word can be heard through the walls, 'Don't make such a row. Does everyone have to know that I'm taking a girl up to my room?' On tiptoe, the stairs creaking. Then all is quiet again. And from walls and furniture, from street and staircase, noises pierce the nerves like needles, cling like poisonous arrows; the pattern on the wall-paper dances, the wardrobe cracks like gunshot.

Two paces to the bed, sit down, stand up. Two paces to the table, to the door, and back. And to the wardrobe. Half of its front is a mirror. Hanna stands before it. Her face is colourless and dull; the brown eyes are dull, the skin slack, the nose red from weeping. Random thoughts flutter about inside her head. No wonder people are indifferent to her. No wonder Ernst Heidemann is in a train going home. No wonder he does not like her – for everything else is pretence and self-deception, the bullet in the lung and that he is not healthy enough and that nowadays it's almost impossible for a young doctor to find a post and that it's his decision to live alone. The curtains move as if someone has tapped on the window. If only he was standing in the street, looking up at the window. He would not dare to wake anyone up at night. He would never ring. Perhaps he was indeed standing in the street. He could be . . .

She draws the curtains, opens the window wide, leans out. The street is in semi-darkness. In the light of a gas-lamp a few spindly little chestnut trees gleam an eerie green. A girl is tugging at a dog, a couple squeezes together into a dark porch. Otherwise the street is empty. Of course it's empty. How could it be anything else but empty? She had gone with Ernst Heidemann to the station at midday. She had shaken his hand, his and hers in gloves, and looked past him and yet knew every feature of his face. Farewell. In the many years they had known one another she had often said farewell to him. Grievous farewells during the War. But now, farewell for ever.

Half-past ten. She sits on the bed. The pillows are dirty. Impossible to lie down. The linen is not clean, even though recently changed. A bed in a third-rate pension, two large pillows with their hideous lace edges touching. One can imagine the faces of commercial travellers, officials, trainee teachers, sleeping with their mouths open on these pillows, next to their wife, or some pick-up they had embraced for three minutes before they started to snore next to her. The green parrots on the wall are cut in two by the corner of the room.

In two. No longer two, nor alone, but in two. In two! Her heart aches. No mere phrase this. It hurts. It is in two. A step towards the table. A cigarette. The box is empty. Too late to ring. What will happen? What ought to happen? A calendar hangs on the wall. Thursday, the twenty-fifth of May. A quite ordinary day, nothing special. One is unhappy. But there are worse things in the world, far worse in these days when people collapse in the street and children go hungry. What does one person matter? Of what significance is she in the world? A day, an ordinary day, Thursday, the twenty-fifth of May and tomorrow is Friday, the twenty-sixth of May. Just as it should be. Fräulein Cornelius will give her lessons. She will sit down calmly at the piano, quite calmly she will say: 'C sharp and *piano* and pedal.' And everything will be the same as usual. Yet it won't be. Lies. Humbug. Of course famine exists and the world is in flames and normal life is in flux; but doesn't everyone have the right to their own despair even if that is the only right they have?

And so? Should one jump out of the window? One would only break a leg and be sent to the general ward of a hospital. There it would heal and then everything would go on as before – except one would limp as well! One could hang oneself on the curtain-cord. But it would undoubtedly break in half. Because it's frayed, like everything else in the Pension Heinzinger. Foolishness. Childishness. She is twenty-five years old, has lived a little, is a grown-up, earns a living and has to go on existing.

The clock strikes a quarter to eleven. But why? For whom? Forty-eight roses and forty-four and a half parrots. Why don't people know, why won't they admit, that love is an illness, a grave, dangerous, skulking fever? And worse. After all, the sick have doctors, nurses, hospitals. Why don't they build hospitals for those in love? Large white peaceful houses where they could be cured of illness, of dizziness, of heart-ache, of fever? In which they would be tied to their beds, kept till they were better and sent away cured – calm, cleansed and smiling in gratitude.

The gentleman above pours out water to wash in, knocking his jug against the basin. He gargles. Now his spit falls into the empty bucket. How nice to have someone so clean living overhead. Now he walks to and fro and the tassels on the lamp shake menacingly. Then his bed creaks. The gentleman has settled down for the night.

If you have been shot in the lung you need someone to take care of you even more. 'It might come back again.' Anything can. But Ernst Heidemann won't come back again because he's in the train and he'll write and tell her that he's had a good journey and he'll regularly send his best wishes at Christmas and on her birthday, because they have been friends since childhood.

This day has been a turning-point, and there are very few of these. From them threads are spun that form the web of the years to come, and a day like this determines whether everything one touches turns to gold or to tar. The gentleman above coughs self-pityingly.

Miracles don't happen. Doors don't fly open as they do in fairy-tales. People don't come along at the very moment another's heart opens up to them, when each understands the other without speaking and can embrace without touching. Stones don't speak and stars don't fall out of the sky. You are alone in Pension Heinzinger, 4 Luisenstrasse, and you will go on being alone, whatever happens, whether you have lovers or not, whether you give yourself to everyone or to no one – you will remain alone.

Eleven o'clock. Eleven 'cuckoo!'s and again someone opens the door downstairs. Foolish to listen out. Pointless to be startled. You may not know who is coming upstairs, but you can be quite certain who is not. Miracles don't happen.

Doors don't fly open. 'Excuse me,' says someone below, 'I've forgotten my key. Will you let me in with you?' A mistake. A fantasy. It's not Ernst's voice. A mirage. The same mirage all evening. A voice answers, dubious and nasal: 'I don't really know if I ought to . . . You must excuse me, nowadays there are so many people who . . . Here, this is all very well but . . .' The intruder, it seems, pays no attention whatever to these remarks, and comes upstairs impatiently, stopping in front of Hanna's door. Unmistakably at her door. But the person does not knock. He just stands there and holds the handle, which Hanna is holding from inside, and it is a peculiarly long time before she opens the door. Meanwhile the indignant gentleman has stormed up the stairs. 'May I . . .' he says, and then looks completely taken aback at the woman standing in the doorway, frozen with joy, as the tears flow slowly down her flawlessly beautiful face and disappear into the neck of her silk blouse.

'My apologies,' is all the gentleman says, pushing Ernst Heidemann into the room and shutting the door behind him. Then, without noticing what he is doing, he tiptoes in his old-fashioned boots across the corridor, into his own room.

The man and the woman stand without speaking, Heidemann holding her cold hand in his. Any other gesture would be too much for him. It's as if they are on a mountain top with the vastness of the ocean and sky all around them; although in fact they are standing by the table, under the pink lamp, in the shabby room with its atmosphere of unwashed people and cheap romance. Happiness has a sound similar to the distant murmur you hear when you hold a sea-shell to your ear. It is heavy, it falls in languid drops. In its presence one is as silent as the pious in church. A miracle is not the unexpected, the unpredictable: a miracle is when what is longed-for, what is most deeply desired, happens at the moment it is most awaited and most wanted.

'I was frightened you would throw me out, Hanna. Really. That you would say: "What are you thinking of, coming here in the middle of the night?"'

'Were you?' She wipes away her tears with her hands and takes hold of his head. 'You are so stupid, so stupid. Always the same.' Suddenly there are no words. Her laughing face touches his. His eyes are so near hers that they merge into one large blue eye in the middle of his forehead. Then he takes her in his arms – one hand still holding onto his suitcase – and very gently kisses the wonderfully bright eyes, her neck, her cheeks, her mouth.

'The case.' Hanna cannot breath, for his mouth will not release hers. She speaks into his lips. 'Put it down.' Her right hand strokes his hair, then seizes his hat and throws it onto the bed. Without letting go of her he simply drops the case with a crash behind her. Immediately there are several knocks on the ceiling and the lamp swings to and fro. In an indignant but mostly unintelligible rush of words 'lack of consideration' and 'shocking' can be heard.

Without removing their lips from each other, the pair laugh like children, and he says into her mouth: 'Shocking.' Then both become serious. He lets go of her and, gazing at her, whispers: 'I'm staying here.' It was hardly a question, more a statement, and she replies, her face lifted to his, 'Of course.'

Once more the lamp shakes violently. Overhead the bed creaks. Irritably the gentleman tosses from side to side.

'You must be tired, darling. Let's go to sleep. You can tell me everything in the morning.'

Extraordinary how this small pretence helps them to behave as if they were an old married couple who, for years, have lain side by side in bed – as if he were her husband returning home from a journey; and even more extraordinary that this should be the truth.

Very slowly and calmly she unbuttons her white blouse and sits on the bed, as if she did this every night, and takes off her stockings and shoes. But there is excitement and joy in each trivial movement, the murmur of the shell in her ear, the music of happiness. Her wedding night. The tide is in.

He too begins to undress, no more quickly than usual, unhurriedly, calmly. This is no adventure, no orgy. This is reality. There is the gurgle of water down the wall – someone is using the lavatory. Yet they are as happy in this room as they would be in a springtime wood full of young beech trees or by a lake gleaming with water-lilies and gliding swans or in a summer meadow covered in flowers. Pension Heinzinger, Luisenstrasse 4.

They look at each other with eyes which are darker than usual. For a moment they hold back, like people who have been out in a storm but hesitate at the doorway to their home, the better to savour the light and warmth waiting for them when they go in. In their ears the sound in the sea-shell roars like surf. Again they put off the final moment.

And then there is only touch and nearness and a homecoming as extraordinary and as overwhelming as death; and the great miracle of life – that two people become one at the very moment that each desires the other.

That night, in a womb that was fertile and ready, not withered and parched, a boy was conceived. Later they would call him Heini.

CHAPTER 2
FRANZ

On the same night, in the same town, at almost the same time, Frau Frieda Meissner was woken because her daughter Mariechen, whose cot stood at the foot of her bed, cried out in her sleep. Used to the child being a light sleeper, she merely asked, without opening her eyes, 'What is it, Mariechen?'

'Mother – there's a black bear!' came the child's sleepy whimper.

'There's no black bear. It's night-time. Go back to sleep.'

The child seemed reassured by this. There was still a whimper or two, and the sound of the little body tossing restlessly in the cot; then everything was quiet, except for her even breathing. Frieda Meissner, however, though she kept her eyes closed, could not sleep any more. Anton Meissner was still with his friends in the beer cellar, so the bed was empty beside her. On the two evenings he went out, Wednesday and Saturday, she went to bed as early as possible, straight after the children, and enjoyed a few hours' sleep undisturbed by her husband's snores – to which nine years of marriage had not accustomed her. I shall get back to sleep again straightaway, soon, if I don't think about anything at all. How much did the butter cost? Sixty-five or seventy-five? But won't it go bad in the heat? It ought to have been put in water. Should she get up? But then she would not be able to sleep at all. She would lie awake till morning, and at half-past six she had to get up and wake Tilde so that she would get to school on time, and, most importantly, so that the room could be tidied. Her husband did not like it if there was any evidence that Tilde slept in the dining-room. That was never mentioned. The unspoken assumption was that somewhere there was another room for a child – as there should be – separated from the front rooms by a long corridor. Officially, too, Mariechen was sleeping with her parents only temporarily, because she was so delicate. For this reason there couldn't be any clothes in the dining-room, and the sofa had to be covered with the smoothed-out cloth and its row of three green cushions. And if Anton Meissner happened to see a child's stocking on a chair, he would advance on it as if it were a rattlesnake, pick it up and say: 'What's a child's stocking doing in the dining-room?' On those mornings Mariechen sicked-up her milk and Tilde got four out of ten at school.

Better not to think. You don't sleep when you think. And sleep was like a wonderful warm coat in which to wrap yourself, a beautiful deep valley between the bleak mountains of her everyday life. There are said to be people who like waking up but Frieda Meissner is not one of them. Eggs are getting dearer again; she won't be able to manage if eggs get dearer, and probably flour will go up too. 'I don't understand, Frieda, what you do with the money!' How many times has she heard this sentence! But only once has she replied to it, indignantly, 'Well, I certainly haven't bought myself a hat with it!' Never again. For she has not forgotten the flushed, swollen face, with the red veins in his eyes and Anton Meissner's voice as he bellowed that afternoon: 'Are you trying to suggest that I don't support my family? That I don't give you enough money, regularly?' And after every sentence he banged on the table like a hammer. No, since then she has never replied to that question. Sleep, not think. One, two, three, four, five, six, seven, eight.

Then the door opens. The woman buries her face in the pillow. She can count up to ten once more, one, two, he turns on the light and hangs his overcoat up, three, the bowler hat on top of it, four, he turns out the light and opens the dining-room door, five, six, seven, he gropes along the wall through the dining-room, there where the sideboard is, not by the chaise-longue where he would knock against the sleeping child who, of course, is not sleeping there. Chairs have been pushed well under the table so he doesn't knock against them. With any luck there is nothing in the way. No. Eight, the bedroom door now, nine, his hand goes to the switch, ten, presses it down. Brightness stabs the woman's eyes through lids she does not open. The child tosses restlessly in her cot.

Meissner turns his back on his wife and whistles while he undoes his shoes. Sitting on the chair he bends down with a groan and pulls them off, laboriously. She peeps across at him between anxious eyelids. Above his belt his shirt slowly rises up, a band of soft plump flesh becoming visible, then, lit-up, the large expanse of fleshy back, the hairy arms and, now that the shirt has been drawn up over it, the head again emerging on its powerful red neck. A short-fingered hand scratches the cropped hair as he yawns loudly and pleasurably. Frieda Meissner shuts her eyes. Once the cherry trees were in blossom, white sweet-smelling clusters under a deep blue sky, an entire island of such clusters, towards which one went up the river on a boat with music playing. Under those clusters they sat on wooden benches, Anton in uniform, herself in the light-blue dress that Tilde and Mariechen, after they had worn it on Sundays, now went to school in. *I'm off to see Frieda today* the band had played. And Anton had pressed her hand under the wooden table and whispered in her ear: 'I am too, if I may.' His eyes had been so twinkling.

'Well, Frieda?' The woman starts and opens her eyes. Under the white lace cover his fleshy red hand reaches for her arm. He is wearing his nightshirt with the blue border. He has two of these with red and two with blue. How often has she washed, ironed and patched them! His face is red, his eyes are shining, the sword-cut on his cheek looks like a brand-mark. He looks at her as she lies there, at the thin blonde hair done in a plait, its little mouse-tail hanging down over a corner of the pillow, at her pale, tired face, the careworn mouth with its thin lips, the long mournful nose which looks to him like a hen's beak, and the pale eye-lashes and wide-open blue eyes with which he had once fallen in love. He turns out the light. Pulling the cover up under her chin, the woman folds her hands over her body. 'Did you have a nice time, Anton?' she asks hurriedly.

'Splendid. There's a magnificent atmosphere, you know. We spoke our minds politically, too. Well, there's no point my talking about that, you don't understand these things.' He gets into the bed, which creaks. Meissner laughs. 'Something damned funny happened. While we were sitting together and von Pless was letting fly at the Republic and the Jewish racket, who do you think comes in? My colleague, Herr Rosenstock! Goes up to the bar, gets a beer and has the cheek to come over to our table. But we soon put him wise. There he was standing with his hand out and we – no one looked at him, just as if he was air. No one said a word. Pale as death he was, let me tell you. Turned round and cleared off.'

'Rosenstock?' Frieda asks, startled. She knew the stoutish, good-natured salesman in the same firm as her husband who manages (because of his dog-like fawning, Meissner says) to get three times as many orders as anyone else, who is so efficient that he's their employer's right-hand man.

'Yes, Rosenstock,' repeats Meissner irritably. 'Who else? Why do you ask in such a stupid way?'

'But supposing he tells the boss? He thinks such a lot of him.'

'Let him! I don't mind if he does. As far as I'm concerned he's welcome,' shouted Meissner, but becoming immediately calmer. He's in a good mood, he won't let himself be upset – and he reaches out his hand to her. But Frieda's hands lie folded over her body.

'You always look on the bad side, you're always grumbling, Friedchen. Aren't you? When there's nothing I like more than to come home to some fun and laughter! Well, can't you say anything? Aren't you always turning the tap on, always sulking? What man likes coming home to that?' She swallows down her answer.

'Did you hear what I said, Frieda, or are you deaf as well?'

'I hear you, Anton,' she whispered.

'To hear you laugh again, I've got to tickle you, eh?' And, sniggering, he starts to try. Across her face glides the warm beery smell of his mouth. He pulls back the cover and thrusts his hand through the neck of her nightdress into the armpit.

'Go on, laugh, laugh a bit, do!' Her knees pressed together in a spasm of defenceless misery, she lies rigid.

'Anton, leave me alone, please leave me alone!' Her voice is choked, almost mute; he thinks she is laughing. 'Don't make such a fuss! Be a little nice to your husband. Eh, Frieda?' Cold shudders run down her spine. 'Eh, Frieda?' His tone is threatening. Anything in the world but that. Mariechen needs shoes, Tilde must have schoolbooks, the nursing-home costs a fortune, then one had to have help in the house. Anything rather than that! Beneath his grasp her gaunt body becomes hard as a board. This makes him angry; at the same time the resistance of her otherwise apathetic body excites him.

'You won't? You don't want your husband? You refuse me, eh? Are you a virgin or what?' He sniggers. 'You still owe me a son and heir, Frieda, you know.' And while hissing these words into her set face and tight lips, he seizes her clenched hands and wrenches her legs apart. He hurts her. But she gives in – as she always does.

Once, nine years ago, the cherry trees were in bloom. Now there is no more cherry blossom. She must ask Frau Binder; she knows a herb drink which helps. My God, supposing it's a girl again? How he looked at her when Mariechen was born! Dear God, so many bad women don't have children nowadays, they sin and don't have children. Dear God, not another baby! Is that sin? Am I sinning now? *I'm off to see Frieda today* . . . the cherry trees have blossomed . . . white clusters of flowers . . .

Anton Meissner breathes evenly again, turning his back on her and immediately falling asleep. Frieda lies awake, listening to the snores of her husband resounding as if they were the last trumpet. She dares not keep still. Frau Binder says that if you move you don't have a baby. So, silently under the cover, she moves her legs back and forth, up and down, up and down, until, tears of exhaustion in her eyes, she gives up, as she always does, and falls asleep.

And out of this mixture of lust and fear a boy was conceived, whom they later called Franz.

CHAPTER 3
HARRY

The last guests were leaving Kommerzienrat* Hartung's villa. The staircase, as was fashionable, was lit by bulbs which did not shine down directly but were projected onto the ceiling from discreet glass squares. Two men still stood beside their host who, a cigar in his mouth, was telling them one last anecdote. His dinner-jacket was cut from the most expensive cloth by the most exclusive tailor, but even this could not give him an athlete's flat stomach. A giant dressed in black, he stood by the banisters; his sparkling little eyes, sunk into the cushions of his cheeks, reflected both his cheerful mood and his delight at his own joke. Both men had heard it before; nevertheless, they laughed. But although Herr von Adrian, standing very blond and slender beside his stout host, moved his lips, his eyes did not lose their nervousness. The older of the two men, the professor and director of the municipal hospital, roared with laughter. 'Excellent.' His hand, with its closely cut nails, played with his beard. He was in a hurry to get home to his young wife, whom he had excused on the

* title conferred on a distinguished businessman

grounds of indisposition. He had no wish to bring her along to these *parvenus*. Nevertheless, he had not yet broached his real business and the whole evening would be wasted if he could not get things settled.

'By the way, I have an important request, Herr Kommerzienrat,' he began without preamble. 'I had no opportunity to mention it during the delightful meal.'

'How much?' asked Hartung with twinkling eyes.

'You're a marvel, Kommerzienrat, one certainly can't fool you!' He laughed again. 'It's about the hospital. It's in a bad way. The State's contribution, well, you know all about that, and so I thought of you, as a friend in need.'

'And what did you hope for?' asked Hartung unpleasantly.

'I leave that to your well-known generosity.'

Hartung frowned. Generosity was the most expensive thing of all. 'Send someone to the bank tomorrow,' he said. 'I'll write out a cheque.'

'Thank you very much,' cried the professor, and held out his hand. Hartung kept hold of it for a moment. 'And next time,' he said with an ironical smile, 'let us hope your wife will not be indisposed. Goodbye, my friend.'

The professor hesitated, then regained his self-possession. 'Of course,' he said, picking up his hat and gloves, 'and give my regards to your lovely wife.' Then he shook Adrian's hand and went to the door.

Adrian stayed. Hartung offered him a cigar. He refused it, taking a cigarette from his own case. His hand shook. Hartung bit his cigar and lit it; he waited; there was no need to make things easier for Adrian, whatever it was he wanted. As he gave him a light he brought his face and his glowing cigar close to Adrian's. Hartung's face almost touched his and an uncontrollable antipathy, a physical disgust, made him recoil. At that moment Hartung remembered how, after dinner, Adrian had bent over his wife to light her cigarette, and the smile with which she had thanked him.

He stood and puffed on his cigar. He was not going to lift a finger to make speech any easier for this young man who felt physically sick at his nearness and yet kept on coming to his house, silent, nervous, immaculate, in what was certainly not a new dinner-jacket. Good manners, Hartung thought, while, uninhibitedly, he scrutinised the face and figure of his guest; hysterical, proud, far from stupid. He remembered the expression with which Adrian had looked at him when he introduced him to his wife, as if searching for some explanation as to why Hilde should actually be married to him. It was amusing. But if his guest did not hurry he would have to go away again without having had his say, for Hartung had no wish to spend the night on the landing.

'I have a proposition to make to you, Herr Hartung.' Adrian avoided the title of Kommerzienrat as being too sycophantic. He spoke very quietly.

'A proposition?'

'We have a family property, Bucheneck, two hours from town, of eighty acres.' Adrian stopped and moistened his lips. 'I would like to mortgage it.'

'Hmm.' Hartung smacked his lips and looked at him. 'A second mortgage.'

'Yes, indeed,' cried Adrian, flaring up, his face crimson.

'Yes, indeed,' repeated Hartung. He blew smoke through his nose. 'You said a proposition. A second mortgage is certainly a proposition, but only for the person taking it up. Let us talk frankly. You have debts, liabilities, and you want me to help you.' Adrian tried to reply, but Hartung would not let him speak.

'Wait,' he said. 'You don't want to be obliged to me, so let's not have any philanthropy between us – let's stick to business, Herr Adrian.' He dropped the 'von', just as Adrian had dropped his title.

'I think I may be able to do something to help you. If you come and see me in the bank tomorrow morning at ten I might do a deal – though I'll probably regret it. Now, good night.'

'I shall think it over,' said Adrian, with a curt military bow that restored the distance between Hartung and him. 'I must go now, if you permit me.'

'Of course, my dear fellow, I'll see you tomorrow.' They did not shake hands.

Max Hartung stood in the brightly-lit hall, seeing himself reflected from the front, from the right and from the left – these last in profile – in the triple-framed mirror: the stubble on his right cheek and the stubble on the left, the large ears with tufts of hair in them, and the faun's mouth with its yellow teeth. He was certainly not handsome. Which made it all the more admirable that he had got where he had. No one could have anticipated this at his birth. They were all reluctant enough to concede him his place in the world, yet they had been forced to concede it, even though, behind his back, they called him a shark, a cut-throat, a war profiteer. He was well aware of the comments his guests made about him on the way home; however, there was not one who would dare to turn down an invitation. These well turned-out puppets, with manners any chimpanzee could learn – that is, if someone took the trouble to teach them! He had no manners himself. If one was the son of a Jewish watchmaker, Samuel Hamburger, and a Christian carpenter's daughter from Vilna*, whose family frustrated his timid father's every step out of spite, then one had no time for manners. Max Hartung had come a long way from the childhood which he concealed from everyone but thought about in private, gloatingly, to remind himself of the intelligence and iron-will needed to get where he had.

He went up the stairs, carpeted with grey felt, chewing his cigar, and opened the door to the drawing-room on the first floor. As he walked past he glanced at the large portrait on the grey-blue wall, the only picture in the room. It was of a fair, blue-eyed woman with the sad face of a nun. 'My mother,' was all Hartung would say if someone asked him about the picture, which was painted and hung so that it could not help but attract attention. It had been done by a famous painter from the little photograph taken in Vilna, that showed Samuel and Matilde as a married couple. But instead of her limp hair the artist had painted golden locks; instead of the large, worn-out hands crossed in a forlorn pose on her breast, he had

* now Vilnius

26

given her a slender hand with a valuable ring; he had then filled out the worn, shabby figure and given her a dress which the poor woman had never even dreamt of while she was alive. Yet, though flattered and softened, her face still had something of that monastic quiet and childlike apprehension which it had carried to her early death. Hartung never passed the picture without greeting it with at least a glance. But he did not have a portrait of Samuel Hamburger there.

He got undressed in his bedroom. There were ladders, poles, a cross-bar and a punchball fixed to the walls of the large, whitewashed room. He never used them. In the morning he was in too much of a hurry, in the evening he was too tired and on Sunday he wanted a rest. But there they were, and he could start training whenever he wanted. He took a pair of green pyjamas out of the wardrobe, sprinkled them with lavender water and went into the bathroom in his vest and slippers.

A few minutes later he entered his wife's bedroom, where she sat in front of the mirror in a white dressing-gown. Her black hair was loose and fell round her like a gleaming shawl. She was sitting quite still, comb in hand, not using it, looking with wide-open sea-blue eyes through her reflection in the mirror and at the same time seeing herself from behind in the large crystal mirror hanging on the wall over the four-poster bed. Her husband stopped and his eyes took in the perfect, doll-like beauty of that face, the low flawless forehead, the flower-like skin, the very long arching eyelashes, the curved mouth. Between her two mirrored reflections she saw him come towards her in Nile-green pyjamas, his hair stuck down

27

on his temples with a wet brush, and she looked through him as she had looked through her own reflection before. He came a step nearer and laid his hand on her neck. 'Are you tired, darling?'

'No, Max.'

'Aren't you going to bed?'

'Yes, in a minute.'

'I'll keep you company for a little, darling, shall I?'

'Please do.'

'So, did you have an amusing day? Everything went off well this evening, didn't it?'

'Yes, very well.'

This kind of conversation with his wife was nothing new for Hartung. He rarely heard more from her. Her response always sounded like the memorised birthday poem of a small girl reciting, in an unemphatic high-pitched voice, something she has not quite understood. Usually her *naïveté*, her refreshing silliness, as he thought of it, charmed him. But at other times her dreaminess, her self-absorption, aroused in him intense anger or lust.

'You were enchanting tonight, everyone said so.'

'Really, Max? I'm so glad.' Hartung, autocratic and aggressive to everyone else, was unsure with his wife, incapable of penetrating behind her mask, of knowing whether she, in inspired coquetry, guessed that it was only her coldness that held him.

The terrible mirrors, in which he saw himself interminably in the most comic distortions both from the front and behind, disconcerted him. They had been a crazy idea of his, put in in order to capture and multiply his wife's beauty, of which he could never have too much; an idea to which she obstinately clung, while he found it more and more upsetting.

'I'll take off your shoes, so you needn't bend down, shall I?' And, kneeling, he could see himself from behind, the green stripes of his pyjamas like hoops round a barrel. He brushed the silk of her stocking with his lips. Pulling her foot away, she tried to stand up.

'Max, please leave me alone tonight.'

'Why?' He let go of her at once and stood up.

'I'm tired.'

'That's not true,' he said in a low voice, 'you weren't tired just now.' He took hold of her shoulders, brought his face close to hers and tried to hold her evasive glance. As he touched her mouth with his, for the second time that night he saw a flinching, a dread of him; and their common abhorrence united Adrian and Hilde just as if he had discovered them in some obscene embrace. He was stabbed by the memory of their two faces in the light of the match.

'What did you talk to Adrian about?'

'Nothing in particular, Max. Why do you ask?'

Hartung does not reply. He stands, with the mirror exaggerating the profile of someone angry and watchful, the lacklustre mien of a jealous man, Othello's unquiet eyes. But how can one use a pillow to smother a woman who is sitting quietly in front of the mirror plaiting her hair? He is utterly helpless. Bit by bit that evening's triumph disappears. Intelligence, irony, laughter, are gone and only mirrors remain! Once there was a whole house of them. A room with

girls laughing and dancing . . . slowly it lit up like a stage . . .
a house of mirrors . . . His pockets were full of banknotes. He
was in an odd mood after the strain of being so much alone
. . . throwing around the money which he had demeaned
himself to earn. There was a girl, with whom he went upstairs.
He could not remember her name, or her face; only the
mirror, a black plait, a white arm, and her thighs reflected in
the mirror on the wall. Seize her, take her, possess her at any
cost . . . Murder is also a kind of possession. But now he knew
that one could possess anything – except what one loves.

'It's two o'clock, Max; you have to get up early in the
morning.' The large eyes stare at him out of the white face
she is slowly rubbing with cream.

'No, darling, I'm not going to go. Sometimes you're tired
and at other times you're ill. Today I'm staying.'

She makes only one gesture, both pathetic and shaming,
which is reflected in all the mirrors – she presses both hands
to her temples, her mouth very slightly open, in the gesture
of a frightened child. At that moment Hartung is ready to
slink away like a dog. But immediately he is flung with
enormous force back into a buried experience of childhood.
Hungry and dirty, he stands before the plate-glass of a
delicatessen where hams, cheese and plump geese are piled up.
His mouth waters, tears are in his eyes, there's a burning ache
in the pit of the stomach. Then everything dissolves in the
great joy of bending down to pick up a sharp brick – and this
despite a policeman being on patrol not far away.

'Max, what's the matter?'

Hilde's startled cry whips him forward thirty years. He
looks at his raised arm and at the cut-glass bottle of eau-

de-Cologne, and then sees the way out – the light switch on the wall. An enormous transition from brightness to utter darkness.

'Max ! Max ! What are you doing?'

He stands quite still, she can only hear his breathing. The thought that she could simply touch the same switch does not occur to her.

'Max, why don't you say something?' She stands up, her chair scraping on the floor, and gropes her way towards him, touches him.

'Why are you standing like that?' She clutches his hands and he draws her slowly towards him. Fear bridges the distance between them. Her childish dread of him and horror of the unknown, and his cold dread faced with the real, the inexorable, form a brief understanding between them.

For a second her hands reach for his; she was grateful and relieved when he grasped and held her. For a second it was possible for him to say to her: 'You will never love me, I know, but if you were ever to love someone else . . .'

'I love nobody, Max, no one at all.' Already reassured, she was trying to tear herself away from him, he clinging to a new hope. The fragile bridge collapses, darkness remains. It was as if a warm sponge was being wiped over flayed skin; it was the opposite of that sinister clarity in the mirrors; it was oblivion. He did not let go of her, but carried her to the bed, where she lay with wide-open eyes and gazed up at the ceiling as though he was unreal, a phantom, a Golem, carrying her in her dreams over moonlit roofs. Just as children hear the howling of the wind at night and are frightened by it but feel that they are protected by locks and walls, so she heard his feverish voice; far away, many rooms away, someone whispered: 'Sweetheart, my sweet.'

And so, incomprehensibly and quite unintentionally, a child was created in the womb of a woman whose body was alienated from her lover, whose thoughts took flight from him, whose soul crept behind walls out of his sight. They were to call him Harry.

CHAPTER 4
KARL

Two evenings later, on the third floor of a red-brick tenement-building on the outskirts of town, Eduard Müller's family were waiting for him to return, but in vain. Usually he came home from work punctually, back at half-past six like the Amen in a prayer; so if he was not home by eight o'clock, there had to be a reason.

'Perhaps he's gone to a meeting,' said ten year-old Hans.

'Then he'd come home first and tell mother,' replied his younger sister, using a check tea-towel to dry the plates which her mother lifted, dripping wet, from the washing-up bowl onto the kitchen table.

'Shall I run across and ask at the works, Mother?' Hans already had his hand on the latch. Anna wiped her arms, which were red from the water. 'No, dear, there's no sense in that. He will have left long ago.'

'But what if something's happened, Mother?'

'If something had happened we should have heard long ago. Go and do your homework and then go to bed.'

'Mother, please let me run across. Please! I'll be back in ten minutes, word of honour.'

It was difficult to refuse the boy something when he pleaded in that tone and with those eyes. 'Well, off you go then, but be quick!' The kitchen door slammed behind him: he did not waste a second in shutting it properly.

Anna Müller carried the plates to the dresser and stacked them up carefully; but it seemed to little Hede as though this took her far longer than usual. Kneeling in front of the open cupboard, her mother looked like a great mountain of blue and white stripes. She did not move. There was only the rattling of the plates in her large plump hands, and then that stopped as well. This stillness on her part was something so alarming and so unusual that Hede took a step nearer.

'Perhaps he's only been run over by a bus,' said the child consolingly. 'Perhaps he's only lost a leg and everything else is fine.' The blue and white mountain jerked round and turned into her mother again – her large, round face, her eyes which, when they laughed, as they did now, almost disappeared in a circle of little wrinkles. She stood up and stroked the child's head. Her large capable hand almost covered it.

'You've cheered me up very nicely, Hedelchen! Now, get some hot water from the kettle and wash yourself properly. And see if baby's covered up.' Relieved and proud, the child obediently went into the bedroom, fetched an empty jug and put it under the spout of the kettle, while her mother went to the hearth, where the fire was slowly dying, laid a log of wood on it, lifted the lid of the saucepan in which Eduard Müller's supper had been keeping warm for the last two hours, and put it back again. Just then the door burst open with a crash similar to that with which it had slammed earlier. 'He left for good at six o'clock.'

His mother turned round quickly. 'Who did you speak to?'

'The night-watchman.'

'Did he say anything else?'

'I didn't ask him anything else,' said the boy sullenly. Anna Müller looked at him and did not ask any more questions, knowing that his rudeness was not meant for her. Probably the watchman had said something derogatory about his father, or had been pleased he had been sacked.

'Well then, that's not so bad,' she said. 'Father will find something else, something better perhaps. Thank you, Hans.'

So that was it. And although Anna knew what it meant when her husband was out of work, and she had to do the washing in other people's houses all day, while the neighbours kept half an eye on the children, and Hede took care of the baby, and she herself, after coming home, had to prepare meals for the next day – in spite of all this she was very glad it was only that. This was nothing new. It had happened before and, after a few difficult weeks or months, they got over it. This was not irrevocable, certainly not as bad as she had been imagining: a man smashed to pulp in the roadway, a bullet fired by a political opponent from a dark street corner, a fight with knives – none of this was that rare nowadays. He'd got the sack, then. Just that. And he didn't come home because he was afraid of her reaction – no other reason. Suddenly she laughed her deep infectious laugh and the children, after a moment's surprise, laughed too.

'What do you think, shall we bake some apples before going to bed?'

'Bake some apples?' Both children shouted together, unable to believe it, because baked apples meant a celebration

35

or a holiday, made them think of Christmas, changed the day from something ordinary into a birthday or the last day of term. So their mother was pleased that their father had lost his job; which meant, contrary to what they thought, that this was something to celebrate. With smiling faces they watched her get things ready, saw her go into the larder and come out with the large, green apples. They could have happily eaten them uncooked on such a mild evening. But then they would have been ordinary and sour, not something for a special occasion, filling the kitchen with their delicious smell.

As Anna wiped the apples and pushed the baking tin into the black jaws of the oven, she was amazed by her decision. She would have preferred to reverse one action after the other – just as if she were winding a film backwards – up to the moment when the green apples were lying on the shelf in the larder again. For, if Eduard came home now when the children were standing by the hearth so expectantly, how would he be able to tell them what had happened? But he did not come: during the crackling and hissing, the opening of the oven, the devout consumption of the bronzed, sweet-smelling apples, the washing of the children in the round wash-tub with much howling and splashing, and saying good night at their bedside, the last calls back and forth – daily forbidden yet daily attempted, just for the reassurance that their mother was washing or sewing in the kitchen, and that her warmth filled the room, even if she only said: 'But now not another word, or else . . .!'

Anna takes the overflowing work-basket, brings a chair up to the table, pulls the lamp down and sets to work. Her husband's black sock, drawn over her large hand, has another hole next to the circle of darns on the heel, another worn place where her white skin gleams through. And, noticing this, she remembers that something has happened and feels enormously tired; she visualises the long line of days in which she battles, like a general, against disintegrating socks, breaking glasses, damaged and dirty furniture. And now, to this campaign, which consumes all her energies, will be added the fight for a living, with chaos not far away because she is out all day.

She glances angrily at the plate that has been on the table for three hours – knife to the right, fork to the left – as if Eduard's head is already bent over it, as if he is already wiping his soft brown moustache with the back of his hand, a thing he always does when uncertain and embarrassed. And to this Eduard Müller she says: 'One loses all patience with a man who won't let himself be told anything, a man with wife and children.' And the defiant Müller replies: 'I am more than just a family man.' And, furious with this reply, she retorts: 'Really? And who will support you if you get sacked all the time, when no one wants to take you on any more?' She asks him why he doesn't think of his children and hears the answer that, just because he does think of the children he's got to fight for things to be better, so that they can have a life fit for human beings. And she shouts at him that they will starve till then, if he goes on like this, and that she's had enough of it, she can't stand it any longer, he's kept on promising to keep quiet at the works and to be cautious. But he can't keep his mouth shut. That's got nothing to do with his principles. He's just a gossip

... And at this Eduard falls silent, puts his hand over his forehead and raises his eyebrows, looking under his hand at her with eyes just like the boy's.

But at this point she hears the real Eduard coming upstairs very slowly. He coughs, and opens the door. He stands with the light falling on his face, twisting his moustache and saying, without looking at her, 'Hello, Anna.' He goes to the stove, opens the oven door where his food is being kept warm, lifts up the lid and says: 'Good. Peas and bacon.' And this is done so clumsily, so oddly, that she smothers a laugh. For Anna knows that this is a dish which he usually gulps down without comment, because it's cheap and filling, qualities she has often praised in the past since it's not a favourite dish of his. 'Any news?' he asks, taking the plate from the table and filling it.

'Nothing special.' She does not look up from the sock and does not ask any of the questions he expected.

Eduard Müller, holding the plate carefully in both hands, stands for a moment behind his wife and looks fixedly over the broad shoulders at her hand which, inside the black sock, looks like the paw of a beast of prey. Pulling himself together he says rapidly: 'I have to tell you, Anna. I'm out of work again.' Then he puts the plate down and waits, is ready to listen to all her reproaches and to counter them, to tell her everything he has resolved on. But his cue does not come: Anna has not the slightest desire to repeat her imaginary conversation. Slowly she turns round. There he was, exactly as she had imagined, holding his hand across his forehead – his eyes the same as the boy's when he's done something wrong and is ready to defend himself – waiting for her to be angry with him. And instead she smiles, and this smile becomes broader, since she no longer fights against it, no longer forces herself to feel angry, when she has already forgiven him. Incredulously Eduard Müller stares at his wife's face, the broad moon-shaped childish face with its strong cheekbones framed in two margins of wispy brown hair – increasingly thin and grey on top – a face in which the splendid teeth suddenly flash and the eyes almost disappear into her smile.

'Chucked you out, have they, Father? It's taken them a long time to do something sensible. I wouldn't have let you come in to begin with!' And now Eduard Müller really is speechless, twiddling his moustache as though he didn't mean a single hair to be left; but finally has to laugh too, and his eyes became moist, which he puts down to the beer he drank to prepare himself for a quarrel. It's inconceivable that she has not the slightest reproach to make; and the wives of all his workmates come to mind, blonde and brunette, lean and fat. There isn't one of them who would not, in the same position, greet her husband with reproaches and wailing and keep him up all night with her chatter. And here sits his Anna, a blue-striped mountain of a woman with a black sock over her big hand; and so much stability and so much warmth radiates from her that, if he were not a class-conscious proletarian who was opposed to romance, he would have pulled her hand out of the sock and kissed it. But he decides to shake off these unmanly feelings and says:

'Didn't we have peas on Saturday?'

'In future we'll have peas quite a lot, my dear, and we'll be glad enough of them,' replies his wife placidly. And that is the only allusion she makes to what has happened.

It is the usual evening routine once more. They sit opposite one another, he eating, she sewing, the flickering lamp hanging just over their heads. Eduard is telling her how it happened. There was a young workmate who had to have sick-leave, quite suddenly – a consumptive. He could not stay a day longer. And they had whittled down his pay and didn't want to give him his full week's money. The lad was easily swayed, nearly agreed to it. But then he himself had jumped in and told the foreman something, something he wouldn't brag about. And so once again he'd lost control of himself. And Anna would have been the first to have talked the same way if she had been there. His mates said, there's no one like you for telling them what's what, Eduard. But he had got the sack on the spot.

He talks volubly, and she sits and sews and sometimes asks a question and sometimes merely listens. And while he talks, peering into her pale, broad face lit up on the surface by the lamp and in its depths by goodness, tenderness and gratitude continue to burn in him like a small flame. But not till later, as they lie in bed, does he conquer his shyness. Not till darkness covers his face, and hers, can he say: 'My good Anna, my dear Anna.' And with a longing he has not felt for a long time, suddenly turning from deep emotion into desire, he presses himself against his wife's warm body, just as a child, when something has happened, huddles in the protection of the lap which held it for the very first time.

And thus the father of her three children – who was also her eldest child – produced, at a time in their life when there was not even enough bread for the others, a fourth, a son. They called him Karl, in honour of Marx.

CHAPTER 5
MANJA

That same spring, in a Polish town not far from the frontier, a well-known orchestra gave the last concert of the season, Gustav Mahler's *Das Lied von der Erde*. In the crowded prom section of the stalls a girl and a man, who were strangers, stood next to each other squeezed against a pillar. Of all the faces lost in the music – eyes shut, staring into space or bent over a score – these two were the most intensely involved. The man's face was pale and somehow burnt out, his heavy eyebrows furrowed as if in anguish. The girl, uncomfortably pressed against the pillar and squashed by the large score of her small neighbour on the left, held her bent head in thin, badly manicured hands, over which fell a mane of chestnut hair; tears ran down her long fingers, into the sleeves of her dark dress. Locked in their private emotional turmoil, neither noticed the other, until the neighbour on the left turned over her score, and in so doing struck the girl awkwardly on the face with her elbow, so that she jerked back and thus brushed a damp cheek against the drooping hand of the man on her right. He, opening his eyes, saw in the half-darkness of people's backs and low-cut dresses a face wet with tears. Without missing a note of the music he stretched his arm out so as to protect her from the hard column and her neighbour's elbow, and she snuggled into it like a cat on a pillow.

And now her attention was divided between the man and the music, her tears drying as every now and then she stole a glance at him; whereas his face kept its forlorn expression. 'Eternal, eternal are the white clouds. Eternal, eternal.' He had come to hear this, to hear these unearthly yet human voices, this tune and those words, sung to be understood by him alone among the listeners in the hall. He trembled all over, as if touched with exquisite tenderness. Eternal, said the voice. And again, softly: Eternal – bringing him back from the depths of anguish and wrapping him in a stillness like a swoon. And the woman who lay in the hollow of his arm, pressing herself closer and closer, felt this shudder pass through him and die away in peace.

The last notes of music faded away and people, as if released from a ghostly and somewhat disquieting embrace, cried 'bravo' and clapped, while others scurried like fugitives to find the trusty embrace of an overcoat; but the man and the girl stood linked together in a strange enchantment till she, noticing the glances of those who were leaving, said: 'Now we must go.' Only then did he take his arm from her shoulder and realise with a belated start, and with a pleasant feeling of arousal, that the person whom he had been embracing with such intimacy was an unknown woman.

They went out together. He had no hat and she no coat. His black hair was uncut and fell raggedly onto his coat collar. With dark, searching eyes she scrutinised him from head to foot, and decided he looked interesting, had very little money, and was a Jew. And since he stood helplessly watching her with peculiarly large, unhappy eyes, saying nothing, she tried to help him by talking.

'Are you an artist?'

He did not answer at once. For a moment he studied the picture she made, or rather the several pictures: her white face framed by thick brown curls, the full mouth, shining black eyes, her curved figure in a worn black silk dress. And he marvelled at this chance meeting on this particular evening of his life. Since, however, everything was settled and his purpose fixed, he could allow himself to drift and take whatever came as a gift.

'I am a composer,' he said, 'my professional name is Gold.' Walking silently beside her he was astonished at this remark. What would it have mattered had he given her his real name? Simply said: David Goldstaub. And why had he said composer when none of the music he had dreamed about had ever found its way onto paper? He had only ever sold a single dance tune, to a night-club owner in exchange for lunch. Lying was a bad habit . . . a leftover from the old days . . .

'How interesting,' said the girl. 'I am a singer.' David smiled. That she should lie, just as stupidly as he had, filled him with tenderness and brought her closer to him. She, surprised by the kindness which lit up his smile, responded brightly, putting her arm through his. Thus they walked with bare heads through the town's most elegant streets. Over the houses, stretched from roof to roof, hung a wonderfully star-lit sky. And David was by now convinced that her appearance on that evening was wonderfully right and of special signifi-

cance. Entranced, he walked along the pavements beside her
as if on air, and, still overwhelmed with emotion, listened to
her animated chatter. Music meant more to her than anything
else, was he the same? It always made her cry terribly when
she heard it. Did he know 'Santa Lucia'? Whatever had he
thought about her bad manners during the concert? But she
could not help it, she had been so desperately sad today. By
the way, her name was Lea.

And if this evening had been like any other evening David
would have abandoned her on the spot, for her prattle would
have jarred his nerves like a bucket of dirty water dousing a
festive candle. But tonight, which was so different from all
other nights, he was not annoyed by her, and he asked why
she had been so dreadfully sad and discovered that she had
left home six months ago. Her father, a priest in a small town,
was opposed to her artistic career. She had run away in the
middle of the night, and come to the town. Now she had a job;
but her father did not answer her letters; and there was
someone after her, a prosperous business man, a certain
Meirowitz, who wanted to marry her, but she would not sell
herself, no, she would rather drown or take poison. And her
job was unbearable. Meirowitz was a monster, with a face like
a cowpat with a moustache on it! She laughed when she said
that. And with friendly amusement he listened to her high,
eager, childish voice as if it were the song of a bird or the cry
of an animal, as grateful as a sleepless person who hears the
sound of voices or the barking of dogs. He reassured and
comforted her, heard his voice speaking kindly, meaningless
words as they strolled along the white paths in a park where

beds full of summer flowers could just be seen and smelt in the darkness. A fountain could be heard splashing somewhere, and the crackling of branches from an animal moving in the bushes. Suddenly Lea put her arms round his neck and her warm, wet lips kissed him on the mouth, and the tenderness which he had felt for her the whole evening grew stronger. Stroking her hair, he returned her kisses. Since tonight's events were decided, pre-determined, he had only to obey pre-determined laws.

They agreed to stay together, left the park and went across the large square to an elegant white hotel. Lea stood still, terrified.

'We can't go to the *Goldene Krone*!'

But David took both her hands and laughed. 'Of course we can! A composer and a singer together!'

He entered the brightly-lit lobby as though he had just stepped out of a royal coach and the girl at his side wore ermine instead of a cheap black dress. The stare of the uniformed porter, which would otherwise have seemed like a stab, glanced off him. Pressing a coin into the man's hand, the last he possessed, he said with the voice of a general in the field: 'The best room available.' And, miraculously, the paunchy fellow did not ask about luggage, nor did he demand that the room be paid for in advance, but simply handed over the keys.

Upstairs Lea, with delighted little cries, admired the four-poster bed, the mahogany furniture, the embroidered Japanese screen on which deer grazed among pale green grasses. 'Smart, fit for a prince.' And the little spark of childish pleasure made her beautiful and animated. What did it matter if she gabbled away, put on airs with clumsy little lying tales, boasted how all the men were in love with her and how she had sung a Schubert song in a charity concert? What did it matter that the song was not by Schubert at all? That excited, flushed face, with its warm shining eyes, was beautiful, and that comforting voice, which meant he did not have to talk, and indeed allowed him no opportunity to talk, was wonderful. In the middle of her chatter, however, sitting near him on one of the gilt chairs she had liked so much, she broke off, and her eyes became darker and larger. Seizing his hands, she brought her face close to his, so that he smelt the strong scent of her hair. 'You will be very happy with me, happier than with all other women,' she said very softly.

Then, while he washed his hands and face, she undressed behind the Japanese screen, like a *prima donna*, revealing, as she had seen on the films, a little bit of her shoulder and a bare arm. She omitted to hang her clothes over the screen, however, because the shoulder-straps of her petticoat were fastened with safety pins. Wiping his hands, David looked across at her. Beneath the deer grazing at the bottom of the screen he saw her bare, white legs standing in the green pile of the carpet as if in a meadow. And he went over to her, snatched away the screen and took hold of her shoulders. She did not move, only folded her hands over her breasts and, strangely transformed and silent, let herself be led almost humbly to the bed, where she wrapped herself protectively in the cool sheets and waited for him while he undressed in complete darkness. When he approached her, groping blindly in the dark, she stretched out her arms, drew him down and clasped her hands behind his head.

And for her too this night was different from all other nights, arousing her, taking her out of herself, so that her body perceived physically what was not comprehensible intellectually, felt anguish and passion and mortality streaming from him into her, realised for the first time how close the ecstasy of coupling is to the torment of death. Trembling with David in the lust which tore at him, she was more than simply a girl, Lea, but became a woman without a name, a vessel capable of limitless giving, turning into whatever he wanted her to be, a warm, pliable animal, tender and soft or quiet and satiated, listening only to him, receiving him.

And when, with his arms still round her, he lay breathing deeply beside her, and she, because the intensity of the moment disconcerted her – she was quite unused to her own pleasure – told him, murmuring indistinctly into the pillow, that everything would be all right and that she was so tired and that it had been the most wonderful night of her life, and fell asleep, David was left alone again, thrust back into solitude as into an abyss. He would have liked to shake her by the shoulder and implore her not to sleep, not to leave him; but he did not move. What right had he to wrench little Lea from her sleep and make her share his anguish?

She was a stage on his journey, she had given him consolation and tenderness. Now she slept and the night was taking its course.

The four-poster was like a tomb, arched over by black, shadowy beams, a box made of strips of shadow. Would his gold watch be enough to pay for the room?

It was a vault. Like the vaults in his body. Caves full of darkness. The cave of his mouth, his brain, his stomach, inhabited by monsters. His bowels were white, writhing dragons, his heart a quivering monster. And somewhere, hiding in some cavity, snugly behind his bones, was his soul, he, David Goldstaub, the man himself, the revolutionary among the bourgeois, the milksop among revolutionaries, the critic among artists. David Goldstaub, a spider's web stretched between earth and heaven, frail as a breath, torn by every fly, meditative where others feel, hesitant where others do things, passive where others act. Perhaps he might have lived as the son of a rich father, wrapped in the warm coat of a prosperity which the present times withheld from him. But what could become of this David Goldstaub, who, at the age of seven, during a pogrom, was hidden for a day and a night in a wine-crate, his hand over the mouth of his four year-old sister who was on the point of bawling, waiting until the soldiers, who were looking for someone whose name no one knew, had gone away; while his father and mother and the older children were screaming as they were being beaten? What could he be, the David Goldstaub who had never escaped from that hiding-place, whose back was still curved by it, whose vision was still obstructed by it as if by iron bars? A fighter? Too frail, too cowardly, too tolerant. A preacher? Too sceptical, too sensitive, too damaged. A racketeer? Too kindly, too self-aware, too detached. What could one do with the David Goldstaub who, for two years during the war, had been moved in every direction in large cattle trucks, in crates that grew as he grew, but whom they never succeeded in turning into a soldier? The crate had changed, that was all. But it never let him out. Until yesterday, when a student at the university had boxed his ears, and this trifling event had suddenly given him the emancipating idea that he could break out from his prison, his crate. He understood, then, that this resolution had already been taken in the night, long ago, and had been waiting within him until the right moment. And once he had realised that, he felt the stillness around him, and the peace, and life had a sharpness it had never had before, music affected him as never before. 'And eternal, eternal, are the white clouds.'

Quietly David Goldstaub got up and dressed. Once again he was tempted to wake up Lea. As he sees her face in the faint light of dawn, her thick hair spread over the pillow, she looks very childlike. He looks at her with both gratitude and tenderness; however, he does not either disturb her, or desire her any further. He must go on. She is the last stage, consoling as the beam of a lighthouse on some final point of land, a light which cannot restrain a ship from the voyage into darkness on which it has already embarked. On tiptoe he goes to the door, smiling. For the grey morning has transformed the room into a square crate barred with shadows. This time he will escape from it for ever. Not until he is outside, separated by a long corridor from the sleeping girl, does he take hold of the little pistol in his pocket and perform one last, unimportant act.

But before David Goldstaub, whose moment of dying had been growing in him for twenty years, finally broke out of his prison, he left in the unknown girl who had shown him a last kindness, a fragment of his life, a child, a daughter – Manja.

CHAPTER 6
THE SEARCH FOR A FATHER

Leo Meirowitz sat in his shop and dipped a thickly-buttered French roll into his coffee, with its dismal globules of fat swimming on the surface. In the warm summer sun spirals of dust danced through the air. The shop was full of dust. It had settled on trousers and sports clothes, on checked aprons and piled-up cardboard boxes of lace collars, buttons and lingerie – though exactly where any of these were to be found even Meirowitz did not know.

At this time of day he was rarely disturbed by a customer, so when the bell rang he started. He straightened his tie, put what was left of the roll in his mouth and got up. The door opened slowly. Lea, twisting her shabby little hand-bag between her fingers, stood there in her black dress and cotton gloves, a little bonnet on top of her brown hair.

'Good morning, Herr Meirowitz.'

'Good heavens! Fräulein Lea! This is a surprise. What a pleasure!' He advanced on her with outstretched hands, his face a deep red. 'But what a long time it's been since I saw you last! Let me think. Months! Well, what does it matter? The important thing is, here you are! Let's have a look at you. You're a little peaky, and very thin. So what's been happening, how are you?'

'Thank you, I am well,' said Lea.

'And where have you been all this time? What have you been doing? I was amazed when I heard you had left your job and no one knew where you had gone.'

'What did the old girl tell you about why I went away?' asked Lea quickly.

'She was abusive. Said you had been out all night.' He blinked at her sideways. 'Why shouldn't you stay out all night for once? A lovely girl, and in springtime too!' He had his large hand on her arm.

'I was with a girl friend,' said Lea. 'I missed the last tram.'

'It can happen,' agreed Meirowitz, stroking her arm gently. 'Like silk,' he said. 'And what gives me the pleasure, my dear Fräulein Lea? Can I get you a small collar, a pair of stockings?' His face was very close to hers and his breath smelt of chicory; the little brush of hair over his lips almost touched her cheek. A cowpat with a moustache, she thought, and felt sick. Quickly, keeping her eyes on a checked trouser-leg on which a golden patch of sunlight played, she said: 'If you meant what you said about marriage, Herr Meirowitz, I am willing.'

For a moment he was speechless, wavering between his delirious joy that at last he could have the girl whom he had desired for so many months, and the sudden suspicion that there was something not right. Had he been offered particularly good articles at a very low price, Meirowitz would have turned them over and over at this point, looking for hidden holes and damaged places.

'And how is it, Lea, that this has occurred to you so suddenly? How is it that Meirowitz is all of a sudden good enough to marry?' There was a malicious undertone in his voice. Lea supported herself on the edge of the counter. She was imagining the face of a film star as she lifted weeping eyes to an angry lover. She said with that tear-filled glance: 'I don't want to be alone any longer. In every job I do the men are after me.'

'That I can believe,' giggled Meirowitz, and laid his hand on her warm, downy neck. She allowed this and, as if the words sprang from her and she had to chase after them, said quickly: 'You were always so good to me, Herr Meirowitz. And a girl does need protection in life.' Then, forgetting the image of the film star, she said very softly, with her head bent and large tears hanging onto her lashes: 'I will be a good wife.'

Leo Meirowitz's disbelief and resistance collapsed. Taking her face in his great hands he drew it towards his. He could smell the scent of her hair. With his fat forefinger he wiped the tears from her lashes, approached his toothbrush moustache close to her mouth, and seized her lips with his as though he meant to gulp her down as he had done his coffee. Lea kept quite still; with her eyes shut endured his caresses as he became aroused, leaning with one hand on the counter and the other pressed against her body, as if this contact with herself gave her the strength to put up with his breath and nearness and insistent embrace. But when she opened her eyes for a moment and saw the round disc of his face, terrifyingly red and close, his eyes bulging, she shuddered, and he let go of her at once.

'May I ask why, if Leo Meirowitz is so disgusting, Fräulein Lea has come to him now, given that she never used even to glance at him?' His suspicion, stronger than both his desire and the magic of her body, broke out again, narrowing his eyes and making his face greenish. Lea, her hands pressed to her body, thus completing the circuit which gave her strength, said: 'Don't be angry, but I was so startled.'

'Oh?' growled Meirowitz. 'I'm not a wild beast.'

'I know, I know, that's why I came here.'

'That was very sensible of you, my little Lea. Nothing will happen to you here. I, Meirowitz, will not hurt you.'

'No,' said Lea, 'you are not like the others.' She took a step towards him and shut her eyes, because the room swam a little and his face, green and flattened, loomed like a moon, while aprons and bits of cloth looked like ragged clouds.

'One must be patient,' said Meirowitz, 'with a little girl who gets so frightened. But nothing will happen to you here.' Having covered her face and neck with hearty kisses he suddenly let her go, pulled out the small step-ladder which was used to reach the boxes on the higher shelves, climbed up and, balancing precariously on one leg, pulled down a pile of boxes, which he then emptied onto the counter: green and red glass beads, bracelets and buckles and belts made of paste, glittering brooches and ear-rings.

'Pick out something that you like, little Lea!' Clumsily he put a shining glass necklace round her throat. 'Choose, little bride! So – how does that brooch look on your black dress?' On her breast he fastened a round ornament, a glittering pair of turtledoves. Her face flushed with pleasure as she looked down at herself. Her cheeks and eyes became warm. 'Thank you very much, Herr Meirowitz.'

'Herr Meirowitz!' He clapped his hands together. 'She calls her bridegroom Herr Meirowitz! Leo's my name.' And, delighted with the similarity in the sound of their names, convinced of the fateful resonance which this must carry, and completely reassured by this, he said softly and almost solemnly: 'Leo and Lea. Well, how does that sound? As if made for one another.' He lifted her onto the counter, among the stuff which lay there, sat beside her and, his arms round her, said excitedly that he would sell the shop, they would go abroad, they would travel. Then he talked about the wedding, which was to take place as soon as possible, because why wait? They would have music. And he described the feast, the goose with tiny potatoes and the nut fritters and the almond biscuits, and the musicians would play and dance. And when, as he was talking, he turned a little away from her and she could no longer see his face, she felt the tears rise in her throat and would have liked more than anything to lean on his shoulder and tell him the truth and beg him to help her. But when he turned his face towards her again she knew she must never do that and there was no other way for her but the way she was going. She would be good to him and take care of him and she would keep still when he embraced her, and at night when it was dark, thank God, she would not be able to see his face. She would be obedient. She would be a good wife to him.

'And we'll move away from here,' said Leo Meirowitz eagerly, 'this is no place for us, there are no opportunities. A cousin of mine by marriage, old Samuel Hamburger, he has a son – what a career he's had in Germany! Why shouldn't Leo Meirowitz do just as well? That's the place for a man like me. You'll like it there, little Lea, living in a house full of glass and marble! And our children will eat with silver spoons and wear embroidered clothes, embroidered on the front and back!' Lea nodded. It seemed to her quite right that her child should eat with silver spoons and wear things embroidered on the front and back. And since Leo Meirowitz wanted to make all this possible, her heart filled with grateful fondness. Turning her head away and looking at a dozen mother-of-pearl buttons lying on silver paper next to her, she stroked his great paw, her first gesture of affection. Enchanted, Meirowitz fondled her little hands; he held them and gazed at the slender wrists.

'Like a little bird,' he said, very moved, 'like a princess!' He laid down his fat paw beside them. And suddenly reminded of something by the disparity, said:

'That night, Leachen, when you didn't go home, were you with the fat blond goy* with the gold chain on his belly, from the delicatessen across the road?'

'No,' said Lea.

'Swear,' pleaded Meirowitz, 'then I'll never say another word about it.'

And Lea, one hand pressed against her body, said with a sigh of relief: 'I swear it.' Silent and happy, he nodded.

Both reassured to the bottom of their hearts, they sat for a long time on the counter, dreams of the future binding them together as if they had come home.

*slang word for non-jew

CHAPTER 7
AN UNWANTED FATHER

Since his son had gone abroad fifteen years before, Samuel Hamburger had not left his small shop in the dingy side street. There was a camp-bed, a chair and a table in the room at the back, and if once a day someone came into the workroom to have a watch mended, and if once a month he sold a watch, then he made enough to live on.

It was very quiet in his room, as it always was in the evening. The old man was reading, his spectacles on his nose; in front of him the great book lay open on the table; he hunched over it, his shadow huge on the sloping wall. The knock on the door startled him. It was unusual for a person to knock at this hour. When it came again, he took the candle from the table and, carefully shielding the flame with his waxy yellow hands, went through to the shop. 'Who is that?' he asked.

'Meirowitz. Am I disturbing you so late?'

Hamburger took a bundle of keys from his pocket and unlocked the door. 'Late guests are welcome guests.' He took the visitor into the bedroom, pushed the chair towards him and sat down on the bed.

'You've been reading?' asked Meirowitz, pointing to the book.

'One has to do something, I didn't know I was having a visitor. It does not happen often.' He smiled. That part of his face not covered by his beard was older and more infirm than his years; he looked like an apple which has been in a warm place for a long time. But his eyes were strangely young, though hovering between boyish laughter and profound sadness. He sat and waited. He felt no need for entertainment, did not expect other people to take an interest in him, but was nevertheless delighted to have company in his quiet room: it felt like a holiday even though the two men had very little in common. Meirowitz, rather awkwardly putting his hand into his pocket, brought out his wallet and put two notes on the table.

'Here is the money back again, and many thanks for it.'

'There was no hurry,' replied the old man.

'Business is one thing and friendship another,' declared Meirowitz. The old man nodded. Although money borrowed without interest was a debt of honour to be settled as early as possible amongst respectable Jews, Leo Meirowitz had surely not come here at ten in the evening for that. Meirowitz did not keep him waiting long.

'I'm getting married.'

'My congratulations! Who is the bride?'

'A very beautiful girl. A real beauty.'

'But with no money?' said the old man.

'No,' admitted Meirowitz sheepishly.

'Well, you'll be all right. When you're young and healthy and try hard . . .' His head was sunk, his eyes faraway and sad. He too had been young and healthy and had had good intentions, yet he had not been successful. But perhaps the other was more capable, more full of life, and one mustn't discourage someone if he didn't have anything else.

'Your son has got on, though, eh?' said Meirowitz, slapping his thigh. 'Not a bad career!' Here he had touched on his subject; his head on one side, he looked over at the bed and the gaunt old man who, hands clasped in his lap, did not move. 'Oh yes, my son,' he said quietly. And Meirowitz felt deeply wounded by the words, as though they hid an insult. 'Well I'm not a complete failure!' he shouted.

The old man looked at him. 'My son was lucky,' he answered calmly. 'And why shouldn't you have the same luck? I wish it you with all my heart.' Leo Meirowitz, at once mollified, partly because it was not in his interests to quarrel, asked: 'Does he write to you much, your son?'

'Where is he going to find the time with all his affairs? I did have a letter last week. There's good news!' He smiled. 'They are going to have a child. I will be a grandfather. That's why my son wrote to me, even though he has so much work he can't sleep.' He stood up, stretched across Meirowitz to the drawer in the table and took out a yellow folder in which he kept his papers, letters and notes. In it there was the wedding photograph of Samuel and Matilde Hamburger, and the card of the Vilna photographer who had taken the portrait on which the famous painting in his son's house had been based; this was not on the wall, because the old man thought it dishonoured the dead to turn them into a lifeless object, to hang them up like a map or a bookshelf; he also thought it blasphemed God, Who had given and Who had taken away and Who had forbidden an image of Himself to be made. Removing a typewritten letter from the folder, he handed Meirowitz a photograph tucked inside it, which showed a smiling Max Hamburger arm in arm with his wife in the sitting-room of his villa. 'He has become fat, has Max,' said Samuel Hamburger. His white head and Meirowitz's black one bent with interest over the little snapshot. 'His house,' said Meirowitz, 'is hardly cardboard.'

'You can see they are happy.'

'It must be a palace.'

'He only had ten marks on him when he left here fifteen years ago,' said the old man with pride.

'There, you see,' cried Meirowitz, 'and I shall have far more than that when I have sold the shop.' And he put his hands on Samuel Hamburger's jacket.

'If you give me a letter for him, then won't he do something for me, seeing as he has business all over the country, like Rockefeller? He surely won't have forgotten his old father now he's so successful?'

Hamburger held the photograph between his fingers. 'If he had forgotten his father would he have sent this, and a letter, when he has such a lot to think about?'

'No, of course not,' said Meirowitz, satisfied. 'Have you answered the letter yet?'

Samuel Hamburger shook his head. 'I don't like writing – my son knows that. Thoughts are alive, words are dead. And how many letters get there safely, all that way?' Sadly, he added: 'It's a long time, fifteen years: life doesn't stand still.'

'Why don't you go to your son?' asked Meirowitz. 'Why doesn't Max have you to live with him? It's unkind of him, I must say.'

For the first time that evening the old man was annoyed. 'Why doesn't he have me to live with him? Because he understands his old father, because he knows I won't give up my business and be a burden on my son!' And he waved his hands about in front of Meirowitz's face.

'Why are you cross?' asked Meirowitz, putting his hand pacifyingly on the old man's sleeve.

'Yes, why am I cross?' repeated the old man, bewildered. 'You don't know Max. Perhaps one day, when the grandchild is born and my eyes are too bad for work, though God forbid, then I might go and live with my son. But an old person is like a plant in a pot. If you leave it where it is, it thrives; transplant it to fresh soil and it dies. It suits the young but kills the old.'

Meirowitz decided to pick up the thread of the conversation, which had somehow slipped away from him. 'And the letter?' he asked.

'I shall write soon,' muttered the old man.

'Supposing you wrote now? I could help you. I've got a good style and you could add a few words about me.' But the old man shook his head.

'I must write the letter on my own,' he said, 'even if I haven't got a fine style. Don't be angry, but there oughtn't to be a third person coming between father and son. I'll write tomorrow.'

Hurt, Meirowitz got to his feet. 'Then I'll not disturb you any further,' he said.

'If you come back again, tomorrow or the next day, I'll have done it. I'll tell my son about you, and if there's anything I've left out we can add it together.'

'Fine,' said Meirowitz, 'just as you like. But you'll be sure to write?'

The old man nodded and smiled. 'It will probably all come to nothing – the letter might never arrive as it's such a long way.'

'Do you know what?' exclaimed Meirowitz. 'I'll deliver the letter myself, so you needn't worry. And that will save you the postage. I'll go straight after the wedding, a week from now. Take your time and I'll come and fetch the letter.'

But Samuel Hamburger wrote the letter to his son that same night. He sat over it until the candle had burnt right down and the wax, dripping over the holder, congealed in delicate little whorls and sheets over the table and on his hands. In his misspelt Polish-Yiddish he wrote the following letter:

'My dear son,

Your letter warmed my heart. Your poor mother ought to have been alive today, she would have been so happy. A son is a great blessing. A man with no child is like a withered tree trunk. May the Almighty give you a good son, one who is a joy to his father, so that you will look after him and wrap him in love and never leave him out in the cold like a stranger. I know you have a lot to do, my son, and I am glad your affairs prosper; which is why you could not write the letter to

62

your father in your own handwriting, with every word clear and transparent – a stranger's hand wrote the letter to your father and held it before he held it himself. Tell your good, dear wife that she is only to have happy thoughts and not to look at any ugly pictures until after the child is born. It will not be granted to me to see my grandchild when his eyes open, nor will it be my good fortune to hold the child in my arms. My business is not going badly, one mustn't complain, since bitterness devours the heart and clouds the sight. I also wish you good fortune in your business and peace and happiness in your home.

Your loving father.'

Then he left half a page blank and wrote:

'I recommend to you, my dear son, Leo Meirowitz, who brings you this letter. He is a competent young tradesman in the clothing business, but could turn his hand to anything, and if you were able to give him a job in one of your many enterprises you would be rendering a great service to your Father, Samuel.'

When Meirowitz read this part of the letter a few days later – while vainly attempting to see the beginning, which the old man had covered with blotting paper – he made various suggestions and objections that the other would not accept. All he achieved was to add the word 'outstandingly' to qualify 'competent'. He also dictated a final sentence which outlined his qualifications. Then the old man sealed up the letter and wrote the address on it.

Only after Meirowitz had left did it occur to Hamburger that he might abuse his trust and open the letter before handing it over. He reached for his hat to run after him, but then felt ashamed of the suspicion with which he had wronged him. (By that time Meirowitz had sealed the letter again.)

* * *

When Lea, a few days before the wedding, was sorting through her belongings, she came across the little notebook that had been found in one of David Goldstaub's pockets after his death. Among all sorts of entries, notes, and addresses, it contained a hastily written-down song. It was called *Tanzlied*, and this was the text:

Had I strong legs
Oh, how I would have sprung.
Had I a voice
Oh, how I would have sung!

Had I not a weak eye
What would I have seen.
If I was not so stupid in the head
What would I have been!

If I had had a pen
What words would be mine.
Had I only one girl
Oh, what love would be thine!

(Refrain: softly but vigorously)

Who dances with the lame?
Who walks with the blind?
Who sings with the dumb?
Where can we him find?

When I look round in the spring
The surface grows dim.
When I look at the sun
Clouds cover him.

When I am pleased with a star
It ceases to shine.
A child's eyes have tears
When they look into mine.

(Loudly)

If I met myself in the dark
I would not be able to see.
Even if the moon was full
I would not know me.

(Refrain: very quietly)

Who dances with the lame?
Who walks with the blind?
Who sings with the dumb?
Him we won't find.

She ought to have burnt it now that she was going to marry
Meirowitz. But she loved it. Certainly she did not understand
it properly and it seemed a strangely unhappy text for a dance
song, but it made her pleasantly sad, and when she read it she
could see David's face. So she kept it although she was about
to marry Leo Meirowitz.

CHAPTER 8
A STEP INTO THE FUTURE

Kommerzienrat Hartung had given a large sum of money to the Municipal Women's Hospital. He hoped, he wrote to the director, to alleviate as far as possible the pains of childbirth for all women, irrespective of their station in life or their religion, and to provide them with all the attention and care a young mother required. The letter was printed in every one of the town's principal newspapers.

The director had entrusted his assistant, Dr Ernst Heidemann, with cataloguing the most essential requirements for the women's clinic and drawing up a list of improvements that would make the patients' stay more pleasant. Thus it was that Heidemann, though it was his afternoon off and his wife had come half an hour ago to fetch him, still sat at his desk, busily writing on a large sheet of paper.

'What sort of books would you want to read?' he asked, looking up.

'Well, I can think of a bookshelf-full that would be enough to sour the milk of a woman lying in,' said Hanna, frowning.

He got up and put an arm round her. 'I'll stop now, shall I?' She nodded. 'We have the whole afternoon to ourselves; doesn't that please you, sweetheart? As much as it does me?'

She shook her head slightly, a smile in her eyes. 'More.'
She leant backwards so that he could kiss her on the mouth
from behind.

'A thousand times more,' she said softly.

Heidemann put his papers in the drawer. 'That's it for
today.' His wife remained seated, her hands on her belly;
the child moved about inside her, swam up to her hands. It
wriggled and kicked and pushed. Hanna turned her slender,
open face towards her husband, her eyes full of happiness.

'He's dancing,' she said. 'Heini's dancing. Come and feel
– here!' She put his hand on hers.

He helped her up and gave her her hat, which she put on
in front of the mirror, shaking her head as she looked at
herself. 'Aren't you embarrassed, truthfully, to be seen out with
someone in my condition?' He stroked her hand. 'Leave the
boy alone,' he said. She leant against him for an instant and
held his hands. In happy moments, and there were a good
many of these, waves of warmth went from one to the other
as though some electric current of mysterious power and
strength ran through their hands.

'It's like lightning,' said Heidemann.

'Yes.' Her cheek was against his. 'Sometimes I could scream
with happiness, just scream.'

'Well not here, this is a hospital. Let's go, madam!' And he
propelled her through the doorway, holding the door open.
She was used to this sudden modulation into joking, this
dislike of sentiment: they were both the same. Arm in arm
they went along the disinfectant-smelling corridor. A nurse
came out of a side-door and pushed a case of instruments past

them: scissors, scalpels, forceps, tweezers. Heidemann took hold of his wife's arm more firmly.

'I'm all right, darling,' she said, but was paler. From the direction of the labour-room at the end of the corridor came a long moaning scream, shrill, choked, agonised. Heidemann pulled Hanna along but her legs buckled under her, the whole weight of her body slumped against him. 'Come along, Hannalein, come, you mustn't faint. Pull yourself together, darling. One, two, one, two – there. We'll be at the front door in a moment.' They almost ran along the corridor. The screams stopped. Then a child could be heard crying quietly.

They stood outside in the cool sunshine of early spring; then walked silently along the gravel path in the hospital garden. Not until they had sat down on a bench, facing a large field bathed in the brilliant but soft light, did Heidemann speak. 'Were you very frightened, my poor little darling?'

'Only for a second. She screamed so terribly.' The sun shone on her face, bringing colour into her cheeks again. Every moment took her further away from the recent night-mare, deeper into the quiet of the sunlit garden, into the profound joy of being together.

'At any rate, I shan't scream, darling,' she said.

'Are you afraid of it, my dearest?'

'No, I'm not. I was a little frightened just now. But I can say quite truthfully that I haven't been afraid for a single minute.'

He lifted her hand and kissed it. 'I'm frightfully curious about the little boy or girl, aren't you?'

'Yes, madly curious.' Her eyes grew moist, as they often did when something he said moved her very much. 'Everything has been so wonderful since we've been together. Everything came right. Your job in the hospital, the flat, every little thing. Like suddenly finding the solution to some mathematical problem one's been struggling with. And then it's simple: the problem came out, as we used to say at school.' With great tenderness she added: 'It's coming out for us, too. Only sometimes I'm frightened because it's too wonderful and the gods are probably a jealous lot.'

'They've been good to us so far.'

'You'll definitely be with me when he's born?' she asked suddenly.

'Of course, sweetheart.' Surprised, he saw that her face had become strained and worried. 'Hannalein, what is it?'

'Do you know what I was thinking about when the woman screamed so terribly? Not so much about the pain I'll have.' She drew a deep breath. 'But I wished the boy wouldn't have to come into the world, that I could keep him in me for ever. Because once he's born then he's no longer mine, and I feel as if I shall have to be responsible for everything that happens to him, but without being able to protect him from it.'

'Sweetheart, thoughts like that are medically forbidden! Look at me!' He held her head firmly between his hands. 'Who just spoke about a problem which suddenly comes out? Hannalein, when everything is as right between two people as it is between us, so wonderful, simple and good, then the boy should be all right.' He shook her head gently to and fro between his hands. 'Have the silly thoughts gone?'

'Almost,' she said.

70

'Shall I tell you about him?' She nodded. 'Well then, he'll be blond, I think, with your eyes.'

'I'd rather they were blue!' she pleaded.

'Don't argue, Hanna! At five he'll start writing poetry, at ten he'll write his university dissertation. At twenty he'll be a professor, at twenty-five he'll get married.'

'Too young,' said Hanna.

'At twenty-five he'll get married,' he persisted. 'At twenty-six he gets divorced.'

'Oh, why?'

'Don't interrupt me with details. They don't get on together or he's got a mother-fixation.'

'That sounds pleasanter to me; go on, darling.'

'At thirty it is suggested that he represents his Fatherland politically. He rejects this, saying he will remain an honest man till his death. At forty he's made President of the Academy of Poets. At fifty he'll discover the causes of cancer. At sixty he'll gather a community round him and found a new religion. At seventy he remarries.'

'He shouldn't do that, it's most unwise for a man of his age.'

'Don't interfere, Hanna dear, children must have their own way. Every Sunday he visits the grave of his beloved parents and lays a wreath on it. At eighty he has a son.'

'All honour to him!' said Hanna.

'At ninety he dies painlessly of old age and in every town in the world at least one street is called after him. There, will that do?'

'Silly one,' she said, drawing his face very close, 'silly fellow!'

The sun, low in the sky, gave no more warmth.

'Come along,' said Heidemann. Each in step with the other, they went quietly through the garden and out into the darkening streets; they said little, but were very close to one another.

CHAPTER 9
HONOUR AND A CHILD

When Anton Meissner, back from his Berlin business trip and preoccupied by the murder of Rathenau* – which everyone was talking about, in every café, in every railway carriage – went into the office, he found it was the subject of heated debate between those present – the secretary Fräulein Susanne, the office boy, and his colleague Rosenstock.

'You can say what you like, Herr Rosenstock,' said Fräulein Susanne, 'he wasn't a German and had no right to represent Germany.'

'And you can say what you like, Fräulein Susanne,' Rosenstock shouted, 'he was the cleverest Foreign Minister Germany has had for years and it's a shame and a scandal that such a thing could happen.'

Meissner had washed his hands outside and put down his sample case. He had travelled all night in order to stay in Berlin as long as possible, and came straight from the station, unshaven and without a clean collar. Coming in, he nodded at his colleagues. Rosenstock, with his back to him, was just

* although the chapter is meant to take place in early July 1920, Rathenau was in fact murdered on 24 June 1922

73

saying angrily, 'When I was travelling, I kept on seeing a slogan on the walls:

> Strike down Walter Rathenau,
> That God-damned Jewish sow.

I felt sick. But I never imagined that something like this was possible in a so-called civilised society!'

Fräulein Susanne was about to retort again, but Meissner went up to the desk with a typewriter where she sat and said: 'Don't waste your time, Fräulein Susanne, how can you expect Herr Rosenstock to understand what national honour is?' Encouraged by this unexpected support, she expressed her silent approval with a shrug of the shoulders, from which Rosenstock was excluded.

At this tense moment the telephone rang. Fräulein Susanne picked up the receiver. 'Yes?' she asked in a friendly tone. 'This is Herr Gottlieb's secretary speaking. No, he is not here yet. Certainly, Herr Kommerzienrat, I'll see to it. No trouble at all, Herr Kommerzienrat Hartung,' she said and made a note on her pad. Then she looked up, anxious to know if the dispute, cut short by the call, would be continued. But Rosenstock had turned his back on her and Meissner and was looking through the morning's post, bending low over it so that nothing but his back could be seen. Meissner took no notice of him. He told Fräulein Susanne how Berlin was celebrating. His words, aimed like arrows at Herr Rosenstock's back, were loudly emphasised. But Rosenstock, rustling his papers, did not react. Finally, he picked up the letters file and opened the door. 'Fräulein Susanne, please take dictation when you are ready.'

Half an hour later the owner of the business came in. While he was taking off his coat, Fräulein Susanne got through on the telephone to Kommerzienrat Hartung and put him through to the inner office. Herr Gottlieb spoke with respectful interest. At the end he said: 'Send the young man to me, of course. What's his name? Meirowitz? Not his fault. Good foreign connections are everything nowadays. Always at your service, Herr Kommerzienrat.' Then he rang for Fräulein Susanne, dictated a letter, and sent first for Herr Rosenstock and then for Herr Meissner.

Meissner came into the room holding himself even more upright than usual, his eyes shifty, the scar on his cheek a fiery red. He looked at the suave little man at the desk with distaste. He was not invited to sit down.

'I should be glad of your report, Herr Meissner.'

Meissner, standing just in front of the desk, reported briefly. He had visited various firms and private individuals on his list, but had not returned with a single important order.

'Not very impressive, Herr Meissner,' said his boss, gently tapping his pencil on the table. Meissner's face grew red; the veins on his temples swelled.

'However, I have sent for you in another connection,' the other went on without looking at him, and held up a letter. 'How is it that the deliveries for Dombrowski in Warsaw have not been sent? As far as I remember I entrusted you with this two weeks ago. Today I received a very unpleasant letter from which I learn that there has been no delivery.'

Meissner gave a start. So that was it. On any other day he would have given a cautious reply since, according to the rules of the firm, he was in the wrong. But today, the day when Rathenau had been shot and a pillar of the Jewish Republic had fallen, he said: 'I do not approve of your efforts to barter good German goods for worthless marks abroad.'

'I'm sorry?' said his employer, very quietly.

Meissner replied more loudly: 'We should not give presents to foreigners, even if some people profit out of it. I refuse to take part. Do you think no one notices that your whole business is going over to this corrupt kind of export?'

'Please leave the room immediately!' said his employer, almost inaudibly. But Meissner, now that everything was lost, was not to be silenced so quickly. Conscious of representing his country's cause, that same cause for which today men had found the courage to shoot down a minister of the state right in the heart of the city, and convinced that he spoke for universal justice and not just for himself, he freed himself in one bound from all the humiliations and degradations of offended vanity that had been bottled up in him for years. Everyone knew about the international Jewish conspiracy. These gentlemen need not think that no one saw through their tricks. Banging his fist on the desk he bellowed so that Rosenstock, ashen-faced, appeared in the doorway. 'One day you are going to get a surprise, you and your Herr Rosenstock! Real men still exist in Germany.' He banged on the table again, and the ink-pot rattled. 'You'll be put in your place.'

Horrified, Rosenstock stared from one to the other. Herr Gottlieb, white as the paper in front of him, rang his bell, and

Fräulein Susanne's dumbfounded face appeared in the door-way where, up to then, she had been eavesdropping. In the instant when Meissner paused to take breath, his employer said with all the calmness of the man in command who doesn't need to shout: 'Let the boy show Herr Meissner down the stairs. He is not well. If he does not go away voluntarily, inform the nearest policeman.' But Meissner had started to shout him down again. 'Don't bother. I'll leave this dirty hole myself, this pigsty. I'll tell the Press about it, I'll take care that this place is cleaned up, you may depend on that.' And with one last furious glance at the desk, as if he were pointing the muzzle of a pistol at it, he went to the door and slammed it with a crash like an exploding bomb. Outside in the corridor he roared: 'What happened to Rathenau could easily happen to the rest of you!'

'Can you believe it?' said Rosenstock.

Herr Gottlieb, proud of his composure, cut all discussion short with a gesture. 'What do you expect? However, we have dealt with Meissner once and for all.' And, wiping his fore-head, he locked the letters up in the drawer. He too anticipated a higher power, some kind of retaliation. He did not think of himself as the boss who, with the easy superiority of the stronger, dismisses a useless and disobedient subordinate, but rather as the one exercising retribution – just as though it was not the troublesome, long-disliked Anton Meissner he had deprived of his daily bread, but the unknown murderer of Rathenau.

* * *

Meissner went home on the tram. His hat pushed down over his unshaven face, he stood on the overcrowded platform being pushed about. Deprived of either the need for deference or an outlet for his anger, his rage grew from minute to minute.

Meanwhile Frieda Meissner sat alone in the flat she had tidied so carefully, re-knitting an old jersey into a child's dress. On the table lay the freshly wound balls of brown wool. The four long needles moved leisurely, two knitting, two softly clinking against them. Beside her was a half-empty glass of some dark infusion from which she now and then took a gulp. If one drank it regularly it was meant to do the trick. And she had, even though all it had done so far was give her a stomach-ache and make her feel terribly sick, and if Meissner had not noticed anything it was only because, once asleep, nothing ever woke him up. He did not notice her pale face or her changed figure. But she was oppressed by fear of the squalid, gossiping women whom many of her acquaintances had visited, of the neighbours' tittle-tattle, of the law and prison. In her frightened dreams she saw herself in a cell with clipped hair eating murky soup from a tin bowl. But what if the drink did not help after all? Then there were the knitting-needles, the four long knitting-needles. If she had a haemorrhage, the doctor would help. But if she was found out! Here her thoughts broke off as if cut in two by scissors. Anton was coming home at eleven o'clock in the morning! Putting her knitting down she stared at the door. He kept his coat on and threw his hat on the chair, something he never did usually. She wanted more than anything to be able to hide her face in her arms like a child.

'I gave it to him!' he shouted. 'They won't forget what I said in a hurry! They won't have heard anything like that before, that lot.' Frieda licked her lips, opened her mouth and shut it again.

'I told the boss what I thought of his business methods. He hadn't got a word to say. He was as white as a sheet.'

'Yes, but . . .' Slowly and inescapably the knowledge of what had happened penetrated her consciousness through his torrent of words.

'Then you won't be able to stay there now?'

'Wild horses wouldn't drag me back into that den of thieves! Not if Gottlieb went down on his knees to me!'

'And what's going to happen? With everything, butter and meat, getting dearer?' she wailed.

'How should I know? Something or other! For God's sake don't go and start crying! Take a grip on yourself.' She swallowed her tears. Her face twitched.

'This eternal, trivial whining! You moan on about food, you can't think about anything else! You aren't a bit interested in Rathenau being shot.'

'In the office?' asked Frieda, horrified.

Meissner laughed scornfully. 'There you are! You don't even know who Rathenau is! You can't even take a look at a newspaper; you aren't even interested in that!'

'When do I have time to read the paper?' she asked plaintively. 'With all this worry from morning to night.' That was one of the remarks that slipped out thoughtlessly and which, as soon as she said it, she would have gladly taken back. Had it not been for her disturbed nights, and the sickness caused by the drink, she would have kept silent, as she almost always did. He came quite close and stood in front of her, as he had before his employer. But here there was no table to form a barrier.

'Are you trying to say that you have not had what you needed? Have I let my family starve? Have I provided for you all, you slanderer? Or have I not provided for you all, liar?' He seized her by the shoulders, his rage growing with every sentence, as though she offered a desperate resistance, instead of which she remained motionless, with pinched lips, silent.

'Let go, Anton.' But he would not let go. Her hunched figure merged into that other figure behind the desk, into countless figures sitting small and bowed over desks, laying waste the country and treading honour underfoot. There was always a barrier between him and them; never could he get hold of them as they deserved, shielded as they always were. But here there was nothing between him and them; he could grab and shake what maddened him.

'There must be an end to it. It must stop! We've been patient long enough!' In a fury beyond words he shook the cringing, the perfidious, the wretched object of his fury, who was no longer the real object; seized it by the throat as if he wished to strangle it; but was startled when Frieda's gurgling voice said:

'You're killing me!' His grip loosened and she screamed out:

'I'm having a baby.' Immediately his hands fell away. It wasn't Rathenau flopping there in the chair, nor his boss, Herr Gottlieb, it was his wife – his Frieda. And her face was purple, her lips bloodless. He turned deathly pale. However violent his fits of temper, never before had he laid a hand on her. Running into the kitchen, he tore the towel from its holder, damped it, wiped her face, smoothed her hair, picked up the fallen knitting and put it in her lap. Then he stroked her hands and patted her cheeks. 'Is that true, Frieda, what you've just said? You didn't say it just to make me let go of you?' His voice was shaky and hoarse. She lowered her eyelids in answer.

'Why didn't you tell me, Friedelchen? Then I wouldn't have let myself go like that. I'm at the end of my tether. And you irritate one so, you can drive the calmest person mad.' She did not reply. The damp towel slid off her forehead. He bent down and replaced it. Her face was now deathly pale, the nose sharper than ever. 'Go to bed for a little, Friedelchen, it'll do you good.' He lifted her to her feet and, since she almost fell, put his arms round her and led her to the bed.

'I must go into the kitchen.'

'No, Friedelchen, you lie down here now.' He pushed her down on the bed. 'I'll fetch you something cold. And don't worry at all. I'll speak to a regimental comrade of mine, Herr von Adrian, he's got so many connections. He's sure to find something for me. I'll go and see him straightaway and hurry home to my little wife.'

But from the door he went back to the bed again and passed a hand over his wife's damp forehead, to which the hair was clinging. 'This time it'll be a boy, eh, Frieda? And he will love his Fatherland once more. And one day he'll be proud to be a German.'

He took her hand. With her tired, expressionless eyes she looked into his face and saw how he struggled for words and tried hard to excuse himself and could not do so. And she said: 'It's all right now, Anton, don't you worry.'

'So then everything's perfectly fine, Friedelchen,' he said gratefully. 'Mind you stay in bed till I come back! I'll bring something nice with me.' He put her knitting on the bedside-table. 'Here, so you don't get bored.' Then he picked up his hat and left.

She turned her head to one side. Entangled in the brown knitting were the four long needles. She picked them up. They felt icy cold in her hot hand. If she did it now, Anton would believe that it was his fault. And that wasn't right, given that he had brought her her knitting so she shouldn't get bored. But supposing it was another girl? She gave the needles a little tug. The knitting was strong and resistant in her weak hands; and if she took out the needles, then all the work she had done would be spoilt and she would have to count the stitches again. And perhaps it would be a boy after all and perhaps Anton would always behave to her as he had done just now, after he had tried to throttle her. She put down the needles, and the knitting slipped to the floor.

Ten minutes later she got up, put the knitting in the sewing-basket, poured the mixture down the sink, and began to prepare lunch.

CHAPTER 10
THE OTHER HEIR

Adrian walked nervously to and fro in the waiting-room at Hartung's bank. The place was like an art gallery, and Adrian felt annoyed by this demonstration, this proof – transformed into art – of the bank's solvency. He tried to concentrate on the conversation he was about to have, and almost bumped into a little man sitting with crossed legs on one of the vast leather arm-chairs, whose lively little eyes were transfixed by the splendid limbs of a 'Susannah Bathing'. He seemed over-whelmed by what he saw, his large head wobbling from side to side loosely. 'Sorry,' said Adrian, not stopping his pacing.

The man immediately looked away from Susannah. 'No doubt you are also here to see the Kommerzienrat.'

'I am,' replied Adrian curtly.

'He's very busy, the Kommerzienrat.'

'Yes.'

'As a matter of fact this is the third time I have been here today. Well, it's not surprising he's only just arrived, considering his wife is . . .'

'What?' asked Adrian in a low voice. He had stopped, his nails digging into his palms.

Meirowitz giggled. 'A happy event approaches and it's not going too well, the poor woman; I have it from a most reliable source. Let's hope to God nothing bad happens.'

Adrian turned his back. He felt sick and almost choked. That woman, that beautiful woman, was giving birth to Hartung's heir. No wonder that nature rebelled, that her womb refused to let the child out. Perhaps it would die. But she mustn't die. Why not that fat murderer instead? Fool. What possible interest had he in Kommerzienrat Hartung's wife? She was having a difficult time, and it was to be hoped everything went well. He would send some roses. Or rather, whether he did or not depended somewhat on Hartung and the talk they were about to have and which he wanted to think about ... At that moment an office boy opened the door. Meirowitz sprang up and snatched at his hat. 'Herr von Adrian' the boy called out in his thin voice and Leo Meirowitz sat down and went on looking at Susannah's legs resignedly.

Going into Hartung's office Adrian saw, separated from him by the whole length of the room, the large figure sitting at his dimly-lit desk, while he himself advanced as if on a brightly-lit stage. A theatrical trick, which put him at a disadvantage from the start. Hartung, even though his wife was possibly dying, sat there like some fat, indifferent monument. He did not appear to notice Adrian and was opening a pile of letters. The only sound in the room was the sharp hiss of the paper knife.

'Good morning,' said Adrian, coming up to the desk. A moment passed; then Hartung turned as if, interrupted in the middle of an important task, he had realised that someone had come in. Holding out his hand he stared uninhibitedly at the face in front of him. Adrian looked ill and much older; his blond hair now looked white against the wrinkles on his forehead and his balding head.

'Take a seat,' said Hartung. 'I have not seen you for a long time.'

'That is so,' replied Adrian, sitting down in the arm-chair furthest away from Hartung, 'I have been travelling.'

'Travelling, the whole time? You are a lucky man.'

'Not the whole time. I was on my estate; my father has died.' Hartung now noticed the mourning band on Adrian's arm. 'My condolences,' he muttered.

'Thank you.' This was said very dismissively, as though he would not allow Hartung to show any sympathy.

'And what are you going to do with the estate? Were you able to get a mortgage that time?'

'No.'

Hartung lifted his fingertips from the back of his hands and let them slowly sink. Though it ought really to have irritated him, he was again amused by the dislike in Adrian's face. Once again, at the wrong moment, he felt a liking for the man who sat opposite, so elegant and proud, almost bursting with loathing for him and yet in his power. 'I soon gave up the idea,' began Adrian, tearing his glance from Hartung's thick-fingered hands which, in some obscure association of thought, led to the wife who was being forced to suffer, a thought quite inappropriate at this moment. 'I wanted to ask your advice in another matter, Herr Kommerzienrat.' He flushed like a boy caught red-handed, having at once realised from Hartung's smile that it was the first time he had used the title.

'I am at your disposal, Herr von Adrian.' The 'von' was underlined.

'May I smoke?'

'Help yourself.' Adrian lit one of his own cigarettes.

'As you may have heard, I own a factory,' he began, after a little pause during which he kept his cigarette in his mouth longer than necessary. 'During the War it was a munitions factory and made a lot of money. Afterwards my father tried to manufacture agricultural machines and closed half the works; he couldn't put enough capital into it.' Hartung listened attentively, neither interrupting nor encouraging with a single word.

'Do you advise me to sell?' asked Adrian.

'If you can, certainly.'

'Would you be able to obtain capital for me?'

'I thought you wanted to sell?'

Adrian wanted to jump up, but controlled himself. 'I have no definite plan,' he said. 'I came to ask your advice.'

Hartung liked the way he held himself in like a startled colt. 'That's not altogether easy, my dear fellow,' he said. 'To put money into something that brings in nothing isn't what everyone wants to do.'

Adrian's thoughts turned suddenly to the woman he had forgotten for a few minutes. If the child had its father's skull it would lacerate her womb. A murderer sat there. Why wasn't he locked up, why was he getting off scot-free? He stood up, pale. 'Then please excuse me for wasting your time.'

'But wait,' said Hartung calmly. 'Sit down.' Adrian stayed standing. 'You know I'd like to help you. Just let us think the matter over.' He stuck out his lower lip for a moment. 'Agricultural machinery – there's nothing in that. Very good people have come a cropper there. By the way,' he said, after a moment's thought, 'is the original machinery still in existence?'

'I think so. It will still be in store.'

'Well then, one would be able to turn the works over to munitions without too much difficulty.'

'I don't understand what you are getting at,' said Adrian.

Hartung paid no attention. 'One would have to modernise, of course. Come to that, do you think one could make aeroplanes if one enlarged the works?'

'Is that supposed to be funny?' asked Adrian with unconcealed irritation.

'No! I'll come and look round the factory. If what I have in mind proves possible, the money will be found.'

Deeply gratified that Adrian's confusion allowed him to take on the delightful role of instructor, he said: 'In Germany, my dear Adrian, arms are a going concern. If not today, then tomorrow. It's in the blood. They'll be needed again and those who have them will get the business. Do you see my point? I don't know much about it, but I do know that.'

'So would you like to buy the factory?' asked Adrian rapidly.

'I didn't say that, my dear fellow, for the business can only work with your involvement. You have the contacts in military circles and connections with the Reichswehr. You can very easily see to it that the factory provides the necessary patriotic associations. In that way you will gain the reputation both of being a patriot and a far-sighted industrial leader, while I will obtain connections which are important to me. For that I am ready to pay. You see, I have put my cards on the table.'

'So you'd buy the factory and me as well?' asked Adrian in a low voice.

'If you want to put it like that,' replied Hartung. 'It's one of those deals where no one is going to be out of pocket and for that reason is absolutely fair.' Adrian said nothing. A revolting bargain, he thought. To exploit his connections seemed the same as dealing in his friends. But, strictly speaking, there was nothing tangible behind his disgust; commonsense was on the side of Hartung's proposal. In fact, he might be of some use to the people he knew: he could introduce them to Hartung as a source of unlimited finance, they could use him discreetly and get rid of him when he had served his purpose. However, before he had articulated an opinion, the telephone rang. Adrian saw Hartung reach for it white-faced.

'Yes,' he said hoarsely, 'yes?' Someone could be heard speaking. The words seemed loud and distinct; nevertheless Adrian, however much he strained to hear, could not make them out. 'I'll come at once,' whispered Hartung, and since he had spoken with difficulty and doubted whether he had been heard, he repeated loudly – 'At once.'

He no longer seemed to be aware of Adrian. His cheeks had become flabby, his chin had fallen, his head was slumped on his breast like a puppet's which has slipped out of the guiding fingers of the puppeteer. This sudden transformation was alarming and astonishing, and so disconcerted Adrian that even his curiosity as to what news could have provoked it became of secondary importance. It was as though a toad, whose warty skin he justifiably felt to be loathsome, had suddenly begun to weep, thereby laying claim to his compassion. Ignoring Adrian, who for the moment was no more important than a piece of furniture, Hartung went across the room with lowered head, like a blind man whose stick has been taken away, without picking up his hat or gloves. Before Adrian could put a question, express regret or offer help, the door had closed behind him.

* * *

'Push, and again, well done,' said the professor, bending over Hilde. 'It will soon be over and your troubles will be at an end.' He patted her cheeks, down which ran a mixture of saliva, sweat, and tears. Then he bent over the huge uncovered belly and listened to the baby's heartbeat, his ear pressed to the flesh. And again he patted her damp hand with all the professional tenderness of a gynaecologist.

'A little patience. Very soon, very soon . . .' An attempt at a smile lifted the corner of her mouth, which was pale and anguished. The midwife's back provided a protective screen as she lay on the white expanse of her bed. Hilde was not supposed to see the instruments she was busy sterilising but they were reflected many times over in the mirrors. The doctor too had gone white, the only thing that was red was the face emerging from the depths of her womb. The skin on her enormous bare white belly, which felt as if it belonged to someone else, was stretched so tightly that her navel protruded. It hid her legs, which the midwife had parted and tied to the bed. Her belly was a volcano from which flames of pain flickered – pricking, pulling, cutting, pressing, ever mounting pain. At the same time, there was something like pleasure about the pain which held her in its grasp. It had taken over to such an extent that all she could do was lie there and endure it. Hilde was in pain at one remove, as if another woman lay there with whom she was physically united, a twin-sister whose suffering she experienced without it somehow being her own. Of the baby who was struggling to come out, tearing at her womb, she had no picture. She had endured carrying it as if she was a mere receptacle into which something had been put, and in the same way she endured the emptying of the receptacle and the violent way this happened. A ringing in her ears, the deep vibrating sounds of a bell . . . Her body was a bell and a malicious devil rang it . . . Everything was damp, her face with tears, her mouth from saliva, her body from sweat, her thighs and bottom stuck to the rubber sheet.

'She's passed out, Sister,' said the professor, 'her pulse is weak. Sit down here a moment, I must talk to the Kommerzienrat. I'll be back immediately.'

In the sitting-room Hartung was pacing up and down; his face was grey and sweaty. When the professor came in, he rushed up to him and took hold of his hands in his own damp and icy ones. 'How is she, is she in danger? Tell me, for God's sake.'

'Her heart is very weak,' said the professor, withdrawing his hands. 'An anaesthetic is a gamble, but I must risk it. Should there have to be a choice between mother and child – I hope it won't come to that – you know it's my duty to save the mother.'

'So the child is lost?' asked Hartung very quietly.

'I don't hold out much hope and it's my duty to prepare you for the worst. Have courage, my friend, have courage! I must go back to my patient.' Quickly he crossed the room, shutting the door to stop Hartung going in. He went onto the verandah, from where he could see a quiet street of gardens where, on this warm spring day, the ice-cream man was riding along, followed by a crowd of happy children. Laughing, greedy, lively, healthy children stretching out their little tanned arms, chubby fingers holding up their coins. He, he alone would have no son, nothing to perpetuate him and give his life meaning. If all went well, dear God, if all went well, if Hilde and the child survived, he would give 20,000 marks to charity.

What use were vows, the baby would die. Hartung knew it would, as if it were already being taken away in a coffin. A line of people, a procession. He, Hartung, wearing a top hat, in their midst. It is raining and he is weeping. White horses with white plumes on their heads draw the carriage covered with white wreaths. The whole town has turned out: government officials, the best people, murmur their condolences, kid gloves press his. What a terrible blow, Herr Kommerzienrat, an undeserved blow. If only it were over and done with – let it be a daughter for all he cared, if only it were over.

Along the street went a cart laden with vegetables, coming from the market-garden opposite. Vegetables – who was buying vegetables today? What use were they? No sound from the nearby room. Quiet, deathly quiet. It was unbearable; he must at least find out for sure. Perhaps it was all over and the professor had forgotten him.

Softly he opened the door of the next room, walked across it, went into his bedroom, ventured as far as the other door and pressed his face against the white paint.

'Ether, Sister,' were the first words he could make out, and simultaneously he smelt through the keyhole the strong, sweet, revolting odour. And he heard a noise completely unlike the sobbing or screaming of a human being, something hollow, terrible, continuous, a howling deeper than a woman's, that sounded like the death-bellow of oxen in a slaughter-house, but not just of one but of an entire herd's mingled terror and agony when the axe tears through their throats. The cry drove Hartung from the door with the force of a blow. He ran, hands over his ears, although the tones were now higher and softer, like the long-drawn-out bleat of new-born lambs.

Even in the other room he dare not remove his hands from his ears in case he again heard that terrible cry.

So he sat numb, overcome with blind and dumb despair, a despair which was inescapable and not negotiable. No efficiency, no native wit, no experience protects against it, no ransom can buy his release, no titles are respected, no connections are of any use. He was not the employer now; he was in the waiting-room, exposed to the whim of a stranger who would perhaps never let him go in.

He did not move, as though he could cheat fate by keeping still, so that it would pass him by, or his stillness could stop things happening, feigning death as a beetle does, cheating death by pretending to be dead. And he lost count of time so that when the professor entered he had to call Hartung twice before he lowered his hands from his grey face and shot him a blank glance.

'Congratulations. Everything's fine. It's a boy.'

Hartung stood up. 'Say that again,' he begged in a low voice, and the professor, astonished at this, repeated: 'A boy. Very small, weighs only four pounds, but healthy. Your wife's still unconscious, but out of danger.'

Hartung stretched out both his hands, without taking hold of anything. 'But, my dear friend . . .' The professor stared, at a loss, at this giant who suddenly wept, not ashamed, not silent, but with the heaving sobs of a child. He embraced the professor and kissed him on both cheeks. The doctor stepped back and patted him on the shoulders. 'Nerves,' he said. 'I think we should both have a whisky.'

'Can I see him?' asked Hartung.

'Who, the baby? You must be patient for a little while longer, he's being washed. And then only for a second, his mother is very tired.' Hartung suddenly dashed to the sideboard and fetched a whisky. 'You don't know, Professor, it's the most wonderful moment in my life,' he shouted, laughing and weeping. 'A boy! And she's living!' While he poured the drinks with hands that still shook so much that he spilt the whisky, the professor walked up and down.

'It wasn't easy, I can tell you,' he said, taking the glass and drinking. 'It did not look good. But your wife was terrific, she was only restless during the anaesthetic. But she probably didn't know what was happening.'

Didn't know what was happening! So that frightful scream could be discounted and forgotten.

After the second whisky Hartung felt restored and completely himself again. 'Tomorrow I'll send 10,000 marks to the hospital,' he said. 'That's capital of you, Hartung,' said the professor, shaking his hand, 'and now I'll see if things have got far enough for the nurse to fetch you.'

Drunk with joy, Hartung walked up and down the room. Opening the verandah door he noticed, for the first time, that the afternoon was warm and sunny and that the trees in the market-garden opposite were in blossom. He leant over the parapet, proud and self-satisfied as a sultan before his rejoicing subjects – Max Hartung, he whose affairs prospered, whose son was born miraculously healthy, he the strong man whom fate protected, he was proof of the mysterious law: to him that hath shall be given.

From the market-garden along the street came a cart laden with flowers, piled high with heaps of red and cream tulips, countless bunches of narcissi, irises, and wallflowers, and, gleaming through the straw baskets in which they were carefully packed, white and purple lilacs, roses, and pinks. Suddenly Hartung wanted to have all the flowers, every single one of them, to adorn the house. After all – he had a son! And he shouted to the young driver who was lazily holding the reins, 'Bring up everything, all the flowers! All of them!' And then, since Sister was beckoning him from the door, he followed her, heart pounding, to see his son.

CHAPTER 11
MOTHERS AND BABIES CRY

'He's drinking very well for his first time,' said Sister Mathilde, who had put Anna Müller's three day-old boy to his mother's breast. The baby's small red head, with its tuft of black hair, pressed against the large white breast held by the woman; milk dribbled from his sucking mouth and ran down the little purple neck into the frills of his white gown. At that moment, every woman in the ward was holding an identical white-wrapped bundle of humanity to her breast. Only the bed opposite was empty.

Very gently Anna passed her large hand over the soft, fluffy down on the baby's small head, over the fontanelle where his pulse beat unprotected against her finger. 'My little mouse,' she said. The child choked a little, milk spurting from his mouth. Anna lifted him up, cradling his head in her hand. He screamed. The puckered face, like that of an old man but no larger than a fist, turned scarlet with rage. Cautiously she returned him to her breast and the wailing immediately ceased; the lips sought and took hold of the nipple and the baby closed his eyes, sucking, gulping, satisfied. Over the little wrinkled face glided something resembling a smile.

'My tiny boy,' Anna said softly. She was wearing a yellowish washed-out hospital nightgown, the second and third buttons of which were undone. Her hair had been plaited by the nurse into stiff short pigtails which lay on the pillow beside her round face. She felt happy. Not to have to get up, not even to be allowed to! And this helpless little softness in her arms!

Three times before she had experienced this. It never became ordinary, but belonged to her, was a tiny scrap of warm, breathing life. There was plenty of milk in her heavy breasts. She would be able to feed the boy for a long time; it would be good for him and would not cost time or money, neither of which she could afford. But she had milk, and love: new love, which must not be taken from any of the three she already had, nor from her husband, who might never find a job again. But she would not worry about that now. She was so tired, and was so pleased to be in bed.

Through the window the last of the evening light fell onto the next bed, where Sister Mathilde was standing, making her hood seem like a purple halo. A man's voice could be heard in the corridor. It had a foreign accent, a sing-song intonation. 'Just for a moment, Sister.'

'It's not visiting hours.' Sister Mathilde's voice was stern.

'But my wife – my name is Meirowitz – my wife has been here for two days. It's simply impossible that it isn't over yet!'

'That can happen with first births,' replied the Sister. Then she went back into the ward and removed one baby after another, even though almost all the women begged to keep theirs a little longer. Wiping the babies' mouths, she laid them in their baskets and pushed them outside. She fetched Anna's little boy last. He was peacefully asleep, his puckered cheek against his mother's white breast. The Sister picked him up, putting one practised reddish hand under his head, the other under his bottom. She bent her sallow face over Anna for a moment. Her nose was sharp, her mouth narrow and she smelt of carbolic. It was a pinched and tired face but Sister Mathilde would do her duty until she collapased. Anna did not ask to keep her child for a few moments longer; it was against the rules and Sister Mathilde would not allow it. So she just followed him with her eyes as he was pushed away like the four others, disappearing into the white pillows of the basket like a rabbit in the snow.

The ward filled with shadows, the window with darkness. Sister Mathilde came and lit the lamp. The women lay in the smoky, flickering light, some with plaits framing their faces, others with short hair; all, despite their differences in age, looked the same in the shapeless yellow hospital gown with their expression of profound peace and deep wonder at the strange thing that had happened to them. On the wall behind every head hung a sheet with the woman's name, the sex and age of the child, and a temperature-chart.

The sister gets the empty bed by the wall ready, shakes the pillows, fills a hot-water bottle, fetches a sick-bowl. The women go on talking to each other in low voices, incoherently, about the same things; several words can be heard, the same words. My little one. Milk. At home. They discuss the afternoon's visits, for every day between two and four their menfolk come, embarrassed and helpless, twisting their hats in their hands, sitting on the edge of the bed and feeling superfluous. Some bring older children, awkward and somehow scared, or a mother or sister comes to give the advice drawn from long experience. But the visitors have the feeling they are intruders, strangers who are not wanted, since women live here who are oddly detached from their family, isolated from marriage and their usual routine, alone in their narrow beds, women who are not the same as at home and seem detached from everything but the red, melancholy, wrinkly creatures shown off in the nursery to the departing visitors.

The door of the ward is pushed open and a nurse wheels Lea in on a trolley. The damp hair sticks dankly to her cheeks; her nose is pale and pointed; her half-closed eyes twitch. On the white sheets her beautiful slender hands lie waxen and ghostly. Leo Meirowitz steps on tiptoe into the room, paying no attention to Sister Mathilde's insistence that the patient required absolute rest. He strokes her hands, wipes her forehead and prevents the nurses from pushing her to another bed.

'Are you feeling better, Lea, sweetheart?' Lea, lying quite still, her eyes closed, did not answer. Perhaps she did not hear Meirowitz's voice. Perhaps his voice wasn't loud enough to summon her back to life. The long black lashes did not lift from her colourless cheeks, the pallid lips said nothing.

'Speak, dear heart,' begged Meirowitz, 'just one word! Open your eyes! She looks so awful!' he moaned. 'And after all that it's a girl.' Then he grabbed hold of the nurse who had wheeled Lea in. 'Are you sure it's a girl, Sister, did you have a good look?'

The young sister laughed. 'Yes, it is a girl, a very pretty child.' But now Sister Mathilde's patience with the intruder was at an end. Icily, she said: 'You'll get no special treatment here. In Germany there's such a thing as regulations, you know.' Startled, Meirowitz passed his bowler hat from one fat hand to the other and, anxiously turning to go, bumped into Dr Heidemann as he came into the ward in his white coat. But before he could grab hold of him, Heidemann pushed him aside. 'Everything's fine. You should be going.'

Then, although he saw Sister Mathilde there and knew nothing more could be done for Lea, Ernst Heidemann sat down beside her bed, holding her thin hand in his and waiting. Sister Mathilde's bright blue eyes looked at him in astonishment. She did not understand it, and nor, completely, did he. Because, in the fortnight since his wife had had her boy here, with every confinement he had experienced something of the awe and terrible agitation of that endless night; that dark hour when, as assistant to the professor, his unshaking hand had held the ether-soaked sponge over Hanna's face as she smiled at him before lapsing into unconsciousness. That smile was an offering which still held him enthralled. She continued to smile even when she was unconscious. And again a few hours later that smile illuminated her face, which was transformed by an extraordinary serenity. Something of that experience, not deadened by the familiar hospital routine or the mechanical activities of the days that followed, leaped at him afresh over and over again and made his otherwise sure hands tremble. And now, sitting by Lea's bed, overtired and over-stimulated, he saw, in spite of the hard light falling across the women's faces, something of Hanna's smile on all of them. And though he knew that she was lying at home, and her pillowed head resembled none of these, it seemed as if she lay in each bed and as if he ought to sit beside each woman and take her

restless hands off the sheets and into his; and that all the newly
born children, pulled with forceps from female bodies or
helped out with rubber-gloved hands, were his too.

Lea's lips were forming words soundlessly. Heidemann
bent over her, put his hand on her forehead and held a bowl
to her mouth, but she shook her head, pushed the bowl aside
with an unexpectedly powerful movement, and said distinctly,
half opening her eyes, 'The child.'

Sister Mathilde brought in the baby. Gently she held it out
to its mother, but Lea snatched it from her hands, kissing the
little red face, the tiny fists, the closed eyes, with her pale lips.
Unable to hold it, she would have let the child fall if Sister
Mathilde had not caught it. When she was about to carry it
away, however, Lea began to weep – the child had to be left
with her, it mustn't be taken away. Too weak to sit up, she tried
to grasp the lace of the baby's cushion and the Sister's skirt.

'Give me the baby, please, Sister,' said Dr Heidemann.
Sister Mathilde obeyed without a word. Only the lifting of her
fair, icy eyebrows and the compression of her thin lips showed
that she disapproved. Lea looked at Heidemann with a weak
smile, passed her hand stiffly through her hair, and looked
with half-closed eyes at the child lying in his arms. Suddenly
her eyes darkened and filled with tears. The nascent tufts of
hair, the shape of the ears, the corner of the curved little
mouth all tore aside the vanished time that lay like a dressing
over a wound, struck down the fragile bridges of those days
and let them collapse into the murky river of past experience.
Behind the empty little face with its yet-unformed features
stood, ghost-like, another, hardly similar, but stamped by the

101

imprint of death. She buried her face in her hands and wept loudly, just as if she were still standing beside the screaming chambermaid in the hotel in the strange Polish town, David's lifeless hand in hers, rudely awakened from her sleep and thrust utterly confused into the incomprehensible void of death.

Heidemann gave her time. He waited till her sobbing had died away. Then he spoke calmly and kindly. She must be quiet and go to sleep, or it would be very bad for her child, and she would have no milk when it was hungry. He stood up and laid the baby carefully beside her on the pillow. It seemed very weak. 'A beautiful little girl,' he said. Over Lea's swollen face glided a feeble, crooked smile. She took hold of the baby's tiny hand.

The sleeping powder that Heidemann gave her, and the gentle touch of her little girl's hand, made her feel full of peace, a peace which became a flood of happiness. Rocked on its waves, driven to and fro by them, she fell asleep.

CHAPTER 12
THE FIGHT FOR LIFE

'It's no good, Dr Heidemann,' said Sister Mathilde. 'You must try and get some sleep.'

Heidemann sat in his office, to which he had had Lea's child brought in its basket. It lay on the pillow, yellow and sickly with the wrinkled face of a shivering little monkey; the waxen hands were cold, despite there being two hot-water bottles in the basket. 'I must have a proper rest, too,' said Sister Mathilde. 'We do our best, but there's not enough staff for extra duties; you must know that, Doctor. And the night sister has no time for them either.'

'I know, Sister Mathilde. You go and get some sleep.'

'And you?'

'I'll stay here.'

'Even the professor thinks it's hopeless,' she said with growing annoyance in her voice. Here was someone who wanted to outdo her in dedication, or force her, at the expense of her health, to sacrifice a night's rest. Heidemann did not move.

'Good night.'

'Good night, Doctor.' Sister Mathilde shrugged her shoulders, and went out with tightly compressed lips. Heidemann stayed. It was the second night he had not gone to bed, as he fought doggedly against the expiring, the fading away, of the emaciated body that seemed to be rejecting both its milk and its life; a life that could not be seized and bandaged or sewn up like a torn tendon or put in splints like a broken arm. From under its black tuft of hair the sad little face looked reproachful at being disturbed. Why was he interfering, why didn't he let nature take its course? He could have been in his own bed with his wife and son two hours ago instead of worrying her by not going home. But in a way he found hard to explain his not going home was to do with his wife and son, with that smile of hers while she was giving birth, the smile that he had seen on all the other faces.

He should walk about a bit, smoke a cigarette, or he would certainly fall asleep. He stepped into the semi-darkness of the corridor, where the feeble night-lights mirrored themselves in the handles of the ward doors. He did not see anyone. The night sister lay fully dressed on her bed waiting to be called. A child cried in the nursery. Heidemann threw his cigarette away – it tasted sour – and entered the bleak white room where the babies, hardly distinguishable from one another, lay in little basket-prams. A larger ear here, a darker lock of hair there, a flatter nose. He had a strange thought – supposing that their destinies had been packed away somewhere in the basket, like the red water bottles at their feet? And that one of them could be taken out and another put in its place. All had pink faces with sparse and mostly dark hair which would fall out later, and then more would grow, fair curls or smooth black hair. How much of what they were going to be was already in them? How much of what they would experience later was born with them? Was their destiny determined, like their sex? Was it inevitable, in the same way that this almost bald child at whose little bed he now stood would become first a girl and then a woman, and that the darker one with the broad face next to it would become a boy and a man? Who decided these things? Who kept destiny's books?

An endless factory producing Life, Bodies and Flesh. Was that what he was working to preserve? Was it simply for this that he had struggled for the last two nights? It must be something to do with his deep dread of a merely physical existence, a dread that had grown in him from year to year, in slaughter-houses, in hospitals, in the War, on the street; and with this a growing feeling that there must be something else, like muscle beneath the skin, like bones beneath the muscle, even if undetectable by a scientist – there must be something of the unique, the personal, in each human being. He was fighting for the vast potential that lay within every nascent existence, a potential which had not yet been stifled out of them; and however muddled and indefinite the train of thought Heidemann was pursuing, the vision and experience that lay behind it were quite clear.

Steps approached along the corridor, loud in the stillness. The night sister opened the door; over the sterilised milk bottles she looked in surprise at Heidemann, who nodded and went back to his room. The baby's little yellow head had slipped off the flat pillow and hung crookedly as if her neck were broken. The pulse was barely perceptible, and the natural course of things no longer in doubt. There was only one last thing he could try, a daring experiment condemned by the professor, which would at worst bring about what must otherwise happen inevitably in the next few hours: this was a camphor preparation, almost never tested on the newborn and quite possibly much too strong. But Heidemann did not hesitate a moment longer. He prepared the solution, sterilised and filled the syringe, then pushed up the sleeve of the little jacket and stuck the needle into the flabby arm. The small body gave a frightful jerk, reared up, writhed, stretched itself. It was not going to work. He took the floppy little head in his hands and touched the drooping cheeks with the balls of his thumbs. And then something extraordinary happened – the eyes opened wide and looked at him with a long, melancholy, human look which struck a blow to his heart so painful that it might have been a sudden wound. He was filled with an immense, almost painful tenderness for the baby. It was like his own, he was holding his nearest and dearest. The child must not die. He summoned up all his powers to prevent it slipping away. The veins at his temples swelled, he looked like someone tugging a rope against an opponent a thousand times stronger than himself, his muscles aching and cramped; minutes passed in this terrible battle of wills.

In the next few seconds very little happened, yet a tiny tremor of movement showed him everything. The little head still lay on the pillow with eyes closed. But now, all at once, this twilight between existence and non-existence seemed only a slumber. The mouth moved a little, lost its rigid pucker. The opening and closing of the tiny fingers no longer appeared to be just a weak reflex, but a genuine movement. Heidemann jumped up, warmed the bottle that had already been filled with tea, and held it to the tiny mouth. The baby still could not drink, but for the first time the lips made sucking movements, for the first time the mouth came under the body's control, the throat moved and a few drops were swallowed and retained, not dribbled back. This was an over-whelming joy for Heidemann. He knew how deceptive such things can be and yet, against all reason, he had the feeling of danger overcome.

Fatigue, after the struggle, began to go to his head like wine and his thoughts scattered like hunted hares. He sank into a half-sleep and although he was not altogether uncon-scious of the outer world, to which he could return at any minute, his joy in what had just happened was lifted into a wonderful lightness and brightness. Unending sun-kissed seas lay before him, the sound of which was penetrated only by the drip of a tap. A gigantic net had been lowered into the water and, as if he were swimming with the fish, he clearly saw the knots of rope, strong in the clear tide, and felt the terror which all the gleaming, speckled, blue and golden fish could not feel. All at once he was lifted up and washed into the net. But at the same time the little girl stood on the shore beside him, her large eyes fixed on his with their candid look, surprised, as if she could not grasp how it was he still did not understand such a simple thing. 'The net only holds the fish, not the wave: the wave is free. Do you understand?' asked the child, her voice high and clear as a bell, countless bells chiming together, soft and loud.

But then the fabric of the dream was torn to shreds, and Heidemann woke up, startled. The loud ringing continued – in the stillness of the night it sounded very shrill and frightening. One of the women in the ward. It wasn't his night on duty. He opened the door. Outside, the night sister ran down the corridor and he saw her disappear into the women's ward, the ribbons on her cap streaming behind her head.

The ringing had stopped; a woman's scream was heard. From the corridor Heidemann could see part of the ward – the edge of a white cabinet and the sister's striped skirt – framed in the doorway like a picture. A head was thrust forward; Lea's burning face was almost covered by her brown curls. She was tearing off the bedspread. The hospital night-dress reached down only to her knees, and her little naked feet were thrust out of the bed. 'She's dead, I know it, I want to see her.' Like manacles the sister's hands fastened on Lea's legs, pressing down her body with gentleness and power while soothing words came from her lips. But Lea, with unexpected strength, tore herself from this grip, and had almost managed to jump from the bed when Heidemann came in. At once her tears and struggling stopped, and like a child she let the sister put her back to bed. Anxious and pleading, her eyes did not leave his face. 'She is dead,' she whispered, 'I dreamt it, I know she is.'

Heidemann went up to her. 'No, she is alive. She is better.' Lea did not answer at once. Her puckered, tearful face was unbelievably like that of her child.

'I want to see her, I do so want to see her because she's all I have, for example.' The words 'for example', meaningless and with their odd, foreign inflection, made the sentence so heavy that it sank into his heart. He glanced at the sister and they silently came to an understanding. 'Just for this once,' she said, and went away.

All the women in the ward were awake, roused by the bell and the screams, but not one was annoyed at having been torn from her sleep. The sister's return, carrying the little girl, was an event not only for Lea. All of them looked at the delicate, scarcely breathing creature, and were touched by the accident of fate that could so easily have been theirs. While Lea kissed the child's tiny hands and talked to it passionately in a strange language, they whispered to each other.

'Doctor,' said Anna Müller's deep voice from her bed. 'I would like to feed the little thing, if you will allow me. Perhaps it would help. My boy has more than he needs.'

For the second time that night Heidemann ignored hospital regulations, and accepted the offer without hesitation. The sister, surprised but not disapproving, made preparations to give the baby to a strange mother. Lea sat up in bed.

'You are so kind. If only I could, if only I had milk!'

'We're both the same, you and me,' said Anna, holding her hands behind the little dark head just as if it was her own baby's. This simple sentence expressed the understanding between all the women, uniting the white islands of their beds like a branching stream. All eyes were fixed on Anna's large breast. There was no sound, for the sister was shaking the baby to wake it up. Its eyes did not open. The little head, as if disgusted, turned slightly away. Once more Anna pushed her nipple between the child's lips and the mouth puckered up a little, and whimpered. Whispering excitedly, the women gave advice. Again the child was lifted up, patted on the back, put down. It moaned a little but its mouth did not open. With the greatest patience, time and time again, Anna went on trying.

All of a sudden the tiny mouth snapped, the stubborn lips held fast, gripped, sucked; and a child's sighs, gurgles and swallowings were audible in the quiet room.

'It's drinking,' whispered Lea, 'it's drinking!'

The happy news was passed from bed to bed. Heidemann looked at the red face on Anna's breast. The open eyes no longer had any of that sad human quality he had glimpsed, but were a blue void, like water and sky. On Anna's broad face was the smile he recognised, Hanna's smile, which was reflected on all the faces in the ward: a light, as in old paintings, which gave an inner radiance to the most homely and ordinary face. Everything was bathed in the strange clarity of his dream. Again he saw the net in which the fish were caught, that let the wave through. The drowsy waking-dream made the ward seem very far away; great golden stars circled in front of his eyes, flowing apart and together into a wonderful cloudscape of golden lakes, purple hills and green shorelines. Though his eyes were closed, he could see it all. All his senses reinforced each other, becoming whole, sight, hearing, as well as feeling, more than each individual sense and yet combined as one, not divided into image and sound, but integrated, so that he looked with this wonderful new sense as though he were a single eye; heard as if he were only an ear; felt as if he were entirely heart. Innumerable faces had left their imprint on one face alone, and that became a mask on which lay the infinitely strange smile. And from the mask spoke countless voices of those who had been and were to come. It was like a prayer not said before an altar, a song that he heard all the deeper and stronger because it was not audible. In every cradle-song is heard something of this eternal melody:

110

Not I, but you.
We must die,
But it cannot be that you must die.
Men do not grow like flowers;
They are open from the beginning,
And it is Life that closes them.
When they die they are hard and empty as a nut.
But you will open like a rose
And Death will bring you into flower.
From us Life slowly drips
As from a pail without a bottom,
And what remains are only dreams.
But our tomb is a door
Through which you go into splendour.
Stones shall be soft to you and winter not cold,
Whatever has happened to us will not touch you.
What has to be, you will reverse.
Not I, but you.

Now the net of his dreams was stretched out over the cloud-scape from whence sounded the angel choir. A different melody, not a lullaby to sing at a cradle. Perhaps the voices of the fathers. A silent, harsh male song:

Never will Life be soft, or caress as rain in the Spring.
It is not for dancing and nor will you dance.
Like a wedge Death is driven into us.
Every day he demands more from you and you must
    pay up,
Without any other reason except that you are human,

111

Both very little and a great deal.
You will be like the fish in the net,
Caught, breathless, bloody and snapping.
And waves not held by the net of life,
Which break through, break free of every mesh.

'Doctor . . . ! Dr Heidemann, don't you feel well?' The Sister shook him by the arm. Passing a hand over his forehead, he saw her startled face and all the eyes in the ward fixed on him.

'I'm all right, Sister. Why?'

'You've been asleep with your eyes open: you're making yourself ill. The baby's drunk almost a hundred grammes. You must go home.'

'Yes,' said Heidemann, and the face before him became once more the soft and elderly night sister's. With childlike pleasure he grasped the two gifts she had held out to him. The baby had drunk, he could go home.

He followed the Sister out of the ward, which was dark and quiet behind him.

PART TWO

CHAPTER 13
FRIEDA AND THE
GREAT INFLATION

Little Franz Meissner was screaming: by night and day, for no particular reason, he would begin to cry; he spoke very few words, while children of the same age were already forming sentences; instead of jumping around happily he would, when he wasn't bellowing, squat pale and ill-tempered on his small chair or crawl about on the floor; and he still soiled himself, although his mother beat him for it.

All this Frieda attributed to the times they were living in, the lunatic inflation which took away the ground from under one's feet and whirled people about like scraps of paper. The inflation was to blame for Frieda's headache, because the columns in her accounts book didn't add up. Millions for milk and bread, billions for butter and meat! She had been used to calculating in pfennigs, had looked hard at each one. She had given up life and sleep and little luxuries to save these pfennigs, so that, when added up in the large household book, the items should tally with her housekeeping money. Millions – that was something one read about in novels, an idea in dreams. He who spent millions had no worries, yet here in her accounts book stood figures that represented millions – just for bread and milk; so that she, Frieda Meissner, had possessed and had spent millions and yet was poor, poor as a beggar, poorer than when she used to enter up pfennigs in her book. There were no pfennigs now, no marks either, not even in hundreds or thousands. One spent billions and was still poor, and hadn't enough to feed the boy properly; and that was why he looked pale and cried.

Frieda pressed her hands to her low, lined forehead, which ached because her book would not add up and the boy was yelling and they were playing the gramophone in the flat opposite, the flat with the large balcony where people could sit in the evening and get cool, and where flowers flourished, whereas in Frieda's gloomy courtyard flat they died. And the people there weren't fine people, with a right to such a flat, but a quite ordinary town councillor and his wife. November criminals, Meissner called them. They had a maid and an American lodger who paid them in dollars. The woman wore clothes fit for a duchess, had a perm, smelt of French perfume and plucked her eyebrows.

'Will you be quiet?' cried Frieda. But little Franz, sitting on his small chair near the open window, a wooden horse in his hand, was quiet only for a second and then bellowed all the louder, while the gramophone next door played a strident jazz tune. The girls could have taken the child with them instead of running round the streets all afternoon . . . Tilde already had breasts, larger breasts than Frieda ever had . . . And nothing on her mind but hair ribbons and face powder.

'Be quiet,' she said, although it was just as futile as if she had said 'quiet, gramophone', since both went on making their din, and trapped between the two millstones of this ear-splitting noise, sitting thin and sad over the accounts book, over the millions whose six and seven figures were only a malicious and confusing lie, Frieda was worn out.

The door bell had rung several times without her moving, for in the music, which Meissner bluntly called nigger-whining, she could distinguish no kind of melody and even the jangling of a bell could have been part of it. Only when the tune became plaintive and low did the noise of the hall bell detach itself clearly from the child's screaming, and Frieda went to the door. She never opened it without first looking through the peep-hole: in these days there were innumerable beggars and she had nothing to give. Also, in her heart she despised those shipwrecked souls who carried their misery to strange doors and were not man enough to get on in life (although actually Frieda Meissner had no idea how this was to be done). But this time it was not a beggar but Anna Müller, the washerwoman, and Frieda would have preferred to have surreptitiously closed the peep-hole and crept back into her room, because the washing in the cardboard box had to be paid for and she had no money. Reluctantly she opened the door. Anna's face was red with the heat; beads of sweat stood on her nose. 'Good day, Frau Meissner, it's hot isn't it?'

Frieda did not reply, for she was cross and did not want to talk about the heat, which placed everyone on an equal footing and seemed to be a part of that democratic spirit which, according to her husband, was to blame for everything. Anna put the washing down on the chest. 'Here's the bill,' she said, holding out a sheet of paper.

Frieda held it close to her face, as if she were carefully going over the different items. In reality she was simply staring at the seven-figure amount.

The child screamed.

'Why is the little boy crying?' asked Anna.

'He'll soon stop,' replied Frieda.

'He must have a pain. My youngest plays for hours without a sound.'

And again! Anna Müller, the washerwoman, also had a child. Also a two year-old. Once again that equality between them. The blatant lack of respect. And here was the seven-figure bill and, although it had no obvious connection with the child or the bill, Frieda almost said: I've been to a grammar-school.

Anna dipped into her large apron pocket and brought out a little packet of biscuits. 'Perhaps he'd like to have one; I got them from the people opposite for the children . . . There!' she cried, stepping into the doorway. 'Look, I've something nice, look!' Little Franz stopped crying and reached out his hand, and Anna was about to go towards him when Frieda stepped angrily between them, grabbing her arm.

'We don't want anything from them. We have our pride, even if others haven't,' she shouted.

'Please, please,' wailed the child, starting to cry more angrily than ever. Anna's perspiring face became even redder, her plump figure almost filling the small stuffy hall into which she had retreated. Frieda, in the doorway, looked like a scared fluttering hen, with her long melancholy nose and out-stretched arms whose extremely white skin was covered with large freckles. For a second the pair looked angrily at each

118

other, and as they stood silently with lips pressed tightly together – the child's clamour absorbing all other sounds – roughly the following conversation took place, though not in words.

Anna: Stupid pitiful specimen. You may slave away and have children; but others slave away too for their children. Who do you think you are?

Frieda: Who do you think you are? You're an uneducated woman!

Anna: She looks old, her husband's a brute; she's anxious and worried.

Frieda: Everything's topsy turvy – millions just for milk. Why is the child always crying? What shall I do? How do you manage with your four?

Anna: People who are having a bad time should stick together, not isolate themselves because of their silly pride.

'You need a lot of strength to get by nowadays.' Anna spoke these words aloud and Frieda nodded. Something of the silent conversation had been understood. And, as the child fell silent and the nearby gramophone played a modern symphony very loudly, she said vehemently: 'Those people over there have no worries.'

'No, they're all right,' replied Anna.

'A woman who shaves off her eyebrows and paints on new ones instead!' shouted Frieda. And, incoherently appropriating some of Meissner's words, she said: 'Those are the sort of people who rule over us now.'

'My husband's against them as well,' said Anna. 'He calls them traitors who have sold themselves. But I don't understand much about politics.'

'Your husband's right,' corroborated Frieda. 'They've betrayed Germany.'

'Müller says they've betrayed the working class.'

'That too no doubt,' conceded Frieda, since for a moment it was pleasant to ally herself with Anna against the flat opposite; and as a result the social gap between them disappeared. She would almost have asked Anna to come in if it had not been for the still unsettled matter of the bill.

'But I shall have to be going, the children are waiting.' With this Anna forced Frieda to make a decision.

'*A propos*,' she said, entrenching herself behind the foreign word, '*A propos*, Frau Müller, I shall give you the money next time.'

Anna looked at her. 'That won't do, Frau Meissner,' she said quietly. 'You know I shan't be able to buy anything with the money next time.' Frieda did know that.

'My husband's not back yet,' she said, breathing heavily. 'He's got an important job in a bank now. Here's the dirty washing, I've counted it.' She seized the parcel from the hall chest and pushed it towards Anna. Best to proceed as usual. But Anna did not pick up the washing to put it in the basket as usual.

'I can't do the work for nothing,' she said firmly. 'My husband's out of work again and I have four children.'

'For nothing!' shouted Frieda. 'Of course I would never allow that.' Wretchedness swamped her like water. The large articles, so heavy to lift and impossible to wring out and the child dirtying the bed almost every night too, and in this heat and din! 'But I can't do the washing myself.' She swallowed the tears which choked her, her long miserable face twitching.

Anna Müller considered things. Generosity was no easy gesture. This was not a case of renouncing luxuries. This was giving up sleep, the butter from the children's bread, the rare moments when she was able to sit down in peace, having nothing more to do. But, although she had nothing in common with this wretched woman, the urge to help wherever possible was so strong that Anna, calling herself a fool, a completely stupid fool, stowed the washing in her basket and took it away.

When she had gone Frieda remained standing in the small hall, her freckled hands resting on the chest of drawers with the cardboard box full of laundry on the floor beside it. She was staring at the pattern of red embroidered lilies on a green ground which flaunted itself to left and right of the mirror. Tears choked her but she could not cry, just as if her eyes, hot and sunk into their sockets, had sucked up all the moisture.

Somewhere in her life, as in her accounts book, there was a false entry. Something or other in what she had learnt and experienced did not add up; something or other had not been explained to her. Yet it seemed to be precisely this that she needed. It was as though life, just like a crooked salesman in the War, had talked her into buying substitutes. For everything that Frieda had expected of love, of marriage, of motherhood, was as different from reality as bad-smelling, rancid war-fat was to real butter, or saccharine to sugar. Her son, the boy she had so longed for, who should have changed her life – there he lay crying, the disturber of all her nights; nor had he brought back her husband's love. Frieda felt herself cheated and stupid, empty as a leather bottle in which a tiny hole has been cut, through which the wine slowly and imperceptibly drips out until there is none left.

And now she heard voices in the well of the stairs, where Anna's step was slowly fading. She could make out a deep male one and the high clear voice of the enemy, the woman opposite. This provoked her as much as the smell of meat does a dog. Frieda tore the door open. 'Monday, then, Frau Müller!' cried the clear voice, 'and my regards to the children.' Then the woman turned so that Frieda saw her face, the closely-cut waved hair beneath the elegant little hat, the painted, smiling mouth speaking gaily to the tall young man coming up the stairs beside her, his arms full of parcels. She wore a light grey summer dress (and Frieda knew how much those sort of clothes cost) and grey deerskin shoes (of course she did not clean them herself) and she was talking to the young man half in English, half in German, and he said: 'Yes, Lily,' and 'Thank you, Lily' – which seemed to Frau Meissner a proof of quite unlawful intimacy. A few paces from the open door, where Frieda stood unnoticed by the couple, one of the many parcels slipped from the young man's grasp and fell on the stairs.

'Oh, I'm so sorry,' he cried in English, alarmed. The woman laughed with an undertone of annoyance. 'My perfume, of course.' A cloud of overwhelming scent hit Frieda's nose like a fist – it was as if what had been spilt was exactly that fragrance and glimpse of beauty which had been stolen from her life and imprisoned in a little bottle and was now smashed on a stone staircase. Clumsily, the young man stooped, whereby the remaining parcels in his arms fell down too. The young woman shook with laughter.

'Oh, Jimmy, you are hopeless.' The more the young man tried to recover his obstinate parcels – holding those that were slipping, picking up those that had fallen – the louder the woman laughed, her head thrown back as she did so. And this cooing, feminine laugh made Frieda frantic. She dashed out onto the stairs, an apparition which struck the woman dumb on the spot. Frieda was enraged. That same hatred which stemmed from the way life had short-changed her now gave her a glorious feeling of strength so long denied her. Here was what was to blame for everything that had gone wrong.

Frieda attacked. Frieda screamed. And since her own rebellion had never been put into words and she had so often dumbly listened to the outbreaks of her husband's, his words mingled with hers without her knowing it. 'You'll soon stop laughing. You'll live to tear out your hair, and the permanent waves too, blood-suckers, Jewish scum, taking baths in champagne, putting diamonds in your ears, using foreign perfume by the gallon. And where does the money come from? Sucked from the marrow of the people!'

The fair American was still stooping over his parcels, as though frozen in that position by the unexpected attack. Now he stood up straight and took a step towards his frightened companion. 'What does she want?' he asked, puzzled. But Frieda had not finished. No one else was going to have the chance to speak. The fiery energy which carried her along was not at an end yet.

'You shameless . . . with a young man . . .' Here she could not find the words to condemn what she meant, and in its place there came two of Meissner's. 'Race pollution.' And, breathlessly, even more quickly and more agitatedly, she went on shouting, for she sensed that her energy was disappearing and saw an ironic smile appearing on her enemy's face; by now she was listening to her own words and their sound confused her and their meaning seemed doubtful.

'And that nigger music, a disgrace to our civilisation, and the rent gets paid in dollars, Germany is being handed over to foreigners and in any case anyone can see that you're over forty. Sold! A German woman selling herself to the enemy!' But suddenly Frieda's voice became lower, like a gramophone running down.

The other woman had regained her self-possession. Putting her finger to her forehead she turned to her companion. 'She is completely mad,' she said in English, and the American nodded. 'Too bad.' She did not even bother to give Frieda, who was still shouting, an angry reply but calmly took her key from her bag and nodded at the young man to follow her. Both disappeared into the flat, leaving Frieda standing there. Her sentence broke off; and she was like a rubber animal at a fair, hugely blown up and now slowly collapsing on its side with a thin rattling sigh. She would have liked to cry, but she was too tired. The whole staircase smelt of perfume, the overpowering smell of the thousand flowers which someone or other had torn from Frieda's life and trodden underfoot. Now that she no longer heard her own voice, the silence was ghostly. Then she heard the child crying again in the flat.

CHAPTER 14
FANTASIES IN A
CLOUD OF TOBACCO

At the back of the beer-cellar owned by a friend of Meissner's, where he sometimes spent his evenings after the bank had closed, was a small club-room with a large table, smoky walls, dirty window, a coat-rack and a door with the notice – 'Gentlemen'. Round the long table sat about ten men, almost all in their shirt-sleeves, for the heat was oppressive and the window could not be opened because someone in the courtyard might hear what was said. Stinging clouds of cheap tobacco smoke hung in the air and something of the frenzy and disorder of the era, here twisted almost into the grotesque, gripped this excited group of men. Sweating and uncomfortable in their collars, they bent their heads over a single piece of paper that was surrounded by empty and half-empty glasses of beer.

'Everything will be clear once Meissner brings the plan of the bank,' said a fair man with a jagged scar on his forehead.

'Where is he then?' asked a haggard fellow, whose large Adam's apple twitched beneath his yellow skin.

'He might easily be late, the Jews are always on their guard,' replied his neighbour in a low voice, a man with a scarred cheek. 'Of course their days are numbered.'

'Perhaps we ought to talk it all over once more,' whispered

a gaunt man with thin hair. But the one next to him who, in spite of the heat, was wearing a grey army tunic and looked different from the others – grim, burnt out, with deep-set eyes – banged the table with his artificial right hand. 'There's been enough talk – now we need action! The hands which took revenge on Liebknecht, Luxemburg, Erzberger and Rathenau – have they suddenly become useless?'

'No, no,' the thin man next to him said quickly.

But the man in the army tunic had lost patience. 'Has every single revolver been delivered up to the Völkerbund?' he yelled, raising the wooden and rubber hand in its black glove, so that everyone was obliged to look at it. 'Or must I get my hand back from the Vosges so as to ensure there's someone left to shoot down all the scoundrels who have taken the good jobs?'

'No, no,' said his neighbour very humbly again, his head wobbling on his scrawny neck.

'The Social Democrats and the Jews have brought the French into the Ruhr,' shouted his neighbour on the other side, infected by the fervour of the man with the artificial hand who, however, insisted on going on speaking. 'We must take power,' he roared, and then broke off abruptly, for the landlord appeared in the doorway, finger on his lips, whispering that the bar was full of strangers and they must be careful: at any moment someone might want to go to the lavatory and then he would have to come through. One of the men quickly put his hands over the sheet of paper and they all looked nervously at the door which the landlord, as he went out, had left a little bit open. Two men peeped in inquisitively, but the landlord pushed them away and said something about a stag-party.

'Spies,' whispered the fellow with the Adam's apple hoarsely. 'We're being watched.'

And now, conspiratorially, so that they all brought their heads even closer together, the man with the artificial hand burst out passionately in a hoarse voice: 'To take power, we need money. Not devalued paper money, but gold.'

'Like the Jews have in their safes,' replied his neighbour with the scarred face.

'Gold,' cried the speaker, but, growing alarmed at the resonance of the word, repeated it in a whisper. 'Gold and foreign exchange, for the reconstruction of the Fatherland.' Gold and foreign exchange. All hung upon the words. Ecstasy and magic lay in them; unlimited wealth and power seemed already a certainty; an existence ruined by war and inflation, and now without either sense or meaning, became filled with splendour, with things to do, with adventure.

* * *

Meanwhile, Anton Meissner was walking the short distance from Hartung's bank to the beer-cellar more slowly than usual. He had carefully kept it from his friends that he was just the porter there (even if it was only for the time being, as Herr von Adrian had assured him), one who, mute and resentful, his hand raised to his cap, saw the powerful pass by, and who had never said anything else to Hartung but 'Good morning' or 'Good evening, Herr Kommerzienrat.' He stood and saw people fetching their money from the bank in laundry-baskets and vans. Paper money, inflation money, worthless bits of paper; whereas underground, as Meissner knew, there was a Nibelungen hoard hidden in steel vaults, real glittering gold guarded by an ogre that looked like Herr Hartung. He would have liked to be the Siegfried who snatched it away, but Anton Meissner knew what dreams were and what life was really like for someone who had not bathed in dragon's blood. Curse as he might, and make barbed remarks when it was safe, Meissner humbled himself wherever power lay. When the plan of breaking into Hartung's bank had been hatched in an atmosphere of melodrama and the smell of beer, Meissner had at first been as enthusiastic as the others. But, once sober, he had seen the impossibility of the idea and hoped that the others too had dropped the plan, as they had dropped so many of the foolhardy proposals that rose like soap bubbles from their overheated brains. It would be very disagreeable and difficult for him to be forced to spell out the plan's extravagance and absurdity, well-nigh impossible without his losing the prestigious position of being the only one who worked in a bank and knew about its organisation; it would be unpleasant entering into a disagreement with the grim spokesman, of whom he was secretly afraid. Therefore he walked very slowly and his fingers hesitated on the door handle. Finally, someone going into the beer-cellar drew him in too.

His comrades greeted him boisterously and made him sit down at the table. Before he could say a word the piece of paper was pushed towards him.

'That's the town map,' explained the fair man with the scar on his forehead. Meissner felt uncomfortable. All the heads were close to his, the hot temples nearly touching him, beery breath in his face.

'Here is the sewer system,' whispered the fair man, running his finger along a black line. 'Here is the bank, the cross here, do you see?'

'Yes, I do,' replied Meissner, vainly moving his arm to try and get space and air.

'In that spot the sewer is about six yards under the street,' the man went on whispering. 'It's quite easy to get from there into the strongrooms.'

Meissner grinned. 'It certainly is,' he murmured. The young man with the Adam's apple seized his hand in hot fingers.

'We'll dig the tunnel by day disguised as navvies. And we'll chloroform the night porter,' cried the small man with the balloon head, speaking so rapidly that Meissner was sprayed with his spit.

'Once we've got the plan of the bank and can mark on it where the alarm wires are, then it's the easiest thing in the world,' said a large man, whose blond beard tickled the bald part of Meissner's head.

'It'll be child's play,' said Meissner sarcastically, without any of the others noticing his tone.

'The lorry will be parked on the corner all night; we'll get in – and, hey presto!' the balloon-headed man cried shrilly. He bent over Meissner, beads of sweat from his hot face dropping again on his hand. Still more irritated, Meissner drew his hand back and, digging his elbows ruthlessly into his neighbours' ribs, stood up.

'What stupid ideas you all have!' he cried. 'The whole thing's idiotic.' His annoyance both with the heat and the proximity of the sweating bodies made him foolhardy. Almost instantaneously the faces round him changed. The man in the army tunic, who had not yet said anything to Meissner, fixed his evasive glance with grim eyes.

'That's enough talking,' he said; 'now hand over the plans.' Meissner glanced at the filthy window, so as not to have to look him in the eye. 'We must not be careless,' he said conciliatingly, 'otherwise we'll all be in the soup; the Jews are very cunning.'

'That they certainly are,' said the small man with the thin neck sadly. But the man in the tunic would not allow Meissner to take refuge in rhetoric. 'Where are the plans, Meissner?' he asked quietly but firmly, looking at him even more intently. Since there was no getting out of it, Meissner gathered all his strength and replied rudely: 'I thought the whole thing was just a joke. For heaven's sake, we were drunk!' His shirt stuck to his back, heat and fear making him sweat at every pore. All at once the lean fellow with the great Adam's apple had – as if playfully – a knife in his yellow fingers. No one had seen him pick it up.

'So you don't have the plans?'

At that moment fate granted Meissner an adjournment. In the midst of the calm before the storm that was gathering in the room, a loud voice could be heard from outside. 'Stag-party or no stag-party, I have to go to the lavatory.' The door was pushed open impatiently and a man in a brown suit hurried across the room, opened the door with the sign 'Gentlemen' and remained behind it, so it seemed to everyone except Meissner, for an indescribably long time; as long as the man was sitting there, Meissner was safe.

His impudence reasserted itself. 'A pint of bitter,' he cried out to the barman, and, since the landlord did not come immediately, took a step or two towards the other room. But before he could reach the door the fair man with the scar and the lean one with the Adam's apple barred his way. The knife had gone.

'Do you know the story about the regimental commander?' cried the one with the scar, for the longer the intruder stayed the clearer it seemed that he was a spy and they therefore had to deceive him. The deceiver stood behind Meissner, who was enjoying his beer, smacking his lips with relish. 'Have you heard the story about the commander? The old man had the habit of saying after every address to his officers: "Thank you, gentlemen." He had a very young and very beautiful wife. Well, one morning he called his officers together, and after the official address he said: "My wife gave birth to a boy today." And concluded as usual: "Thank you, gentlemen."'

The others had heard this story many times before, but they obeyed the narrator's grimace when, winking and with his head pushed forward, he indicated that they should laugh. The big fellow with the beard laughed hugely and the others joined in. It was such loud, neighing laughter, and was so terrifyingly unnatural, that it was as if barn-stormers were performing a play about devils and lunatics. The man in the brown suit dashed out of the door, cast a frightened glance at the snarling faces surrounding him and hurried out of the room.

Only two of them did not laugh: the man with the artificial hand and Anton Meissner, on whose nerves this piercing laughter grated like the sound of knives being sharpened on

a grindstone. Fear clutched at him and, as once or twice
on the battlefield, and at other critical moments in his life,
he was seized by violent stomach-cramps. In the next room
the man could be heard asking if the gentlemen were on the
stage. Then the laughter died away, and everyone turned to
Meissner. But before the storm could burst, before a word was
spoken or a threat was made, Meissner hurried to the back
door, his hands pressed to his stomach.

'One moment,' he stammered, and disappeared. The tall
man with the beard and the one with the mutilated face
laughed, and this time it was a genuine laughter, bringing
tears to their eyes.

'Open up, open up!' they shouted. And since Meissner did
not reply and did not unbolt the door, the others came up too.
'Traitor, cheat!' they shouted. 'Toady to the Jews! Coward!
Open up!'

Meissner did not come out. There was no reason for him
to leave his hiding-place, a barricade which gave him courage.
'Idiots,' he yelled. 'You'll only get put in jail; just listen to
yourselves.' And, infuriated by the blows, thumps, and kicks
which shook the door, he too began to hammer on it. 'What
have you got to lose, then, you hooligans, you riff-raff?'

The blows from outside became more violent. Meissner
recognised the voice of the man with the artificial hand; it cut
through him like a knife. 'We'll count up to three, then we'll
break down the door.' The voices chanted: 'One . . .two . . .
three . . .' Then fists, chairs and glasses were all hurled at the
wooden door. Meissner held onto the bolt. Another second
and the door would burst open. Once he was out of this

cramped, evil-smelling lavatory, once he was back home with
wife and children, he would be good to them, patient and
kind . . . Suddenly the hammering stopped and he heard the
landlord's angry voice. 'Gentlemen, this simply will not do.
Please listen to reason. Do you want to bring the police down
on me?'

This made an impression.

'That coward Meissner has shut himself in,' yelled someone. 'He's afraid, so he's hiding.' Once more someone beat on
the door so that it shook. But the little landlord, now that he
was protecting his own property, was firm: 'I can't stop them
any longer, gentlemen, they don't believe it's a stag-party, they
want to fetch the police. Meissner,' he said through the door,
'be sensible now, come out.'

Thereupon Meissner pushed back the bolt and stepped
into the room. He saw the wild, flushed faces of his friends,
panting from their efforts, and, through the open door, could
see laughing people who did not want to come in, but were
nevertheless enjoying the scene. The room looked like a
battlefield. Two chairs were broken; the little man with thin
hair held the handle of a broken beer-mug, fragments of
which lay on the floor. Anton Meissner's eyes were full of tears.
Gulping, and without looking at anyone, he said in a low
voice: 'What did you expect then? Where am I going to get
the plans from? I'm only a porter in the bank, I've got a wife
and children.' He stood there pathetically, his sallow face
trembling. Then the man with the scar spat and the spittle hit
Meissner on the arm; but nobody touched him as he went out,
pursued by the jeers and laughter of those at the bar.

They shut the door again and sat deflated, as if doused with water; it took a few minutes before a fresh little flame of hatred burst through the lethargy of their disappointment, invigorating them enough so that rhetoric laid itself like a surgical plaster on their wounds and, in place of the bubble that had burst, a new one arose from their brains – feverish, glittering, and unstable.

CHAPTER 15
CASTLES IN THE
AIR AND A BUTCHER

Since Leo Meirowitz did not have enough on him to pay for another cup of coffee, and the waiter was glancing at him angrily because he had been sitting there for several hours with a pile of the café's newspapers, and in particular because the business columns of the newspapers only contained things which depressed him, he got up and walked slowly home. He went through ugly streets full of noisy, dirty children and barking dogs, where the kind of people lived whom he did not want to have anything to do with, if it were not that he lived in this disagreeable part of town. He had once dreamt about somewhere very different from the home he was now approaching; but everything was completely different from what he and Lea had planned when they came to this country four years ago.

He had tried many things in those years, but nothing had worked. He had numerous debts, but no one left to lend him anything. Like everyone else he had juggled with figures which had no meaning and were only figures in name. Company promotions, speculations . . . And all at once, instead of bogus sums, real money was lost. There had been stability; and then overnight one became a swindler. How was it possible to find one's way about in an age revolving like a merry-go-round to which, too giddy to get off, one was forced to go on clinging for ever?

He sighed, and pushed his way through the children squabbling on the pavement. Of course his children played in the street as well, getting in the way of passers-by, since Lea – who was still undeniably beautiful, more beautiful in fact than ever before – always left the children to their own devices.

Slowly he climbs the staircase to his flat. It smells of cats. He thinks about the children: Manja with her enormous eyes, three-year-old Munio, and the baby; he tries to feel happy about them, but the spark does not catch, as if he was trying to light a fire with a spent match. Perhaps Lea would be more friendly today, maybe she is in a good mood; yet thinking about her does not provoke a spark of joy either, it simply leaves him downcast and gloomy. Mechanically he gropes in his pocket for the key, and opens the door. It's dark in the little hall and the flat is very quiet; the children must be downstairs in the courtyard. Perhaps Lea was with them.

'Lea!' There was no reply, but it seems to him as if there is a noise in the bedroom. 'Lea, are you there?' Again no reply, but now there was a more distinct sound, hurried, suppressed, a whispering, a rustling of clothes.

'Lea!' Meirowitz rattles the door. It is locked. He bangs on it with his fists and, uselessly and painfully, bangs his head against it. 'Open the door at once!' He bellows so loudly and makes such a pandemonium that for a few seconds he doesn't hear what is happening within. When the door suddenly opens he staggers into the room, knocks against the chair which has Lea's and the children's clothes on it and falls over them. While all this is happening, and he is awkwardly getting up, he looks round the room. The bed is unmade and the door leading to the kitchen is half-open. Standing up, he takes a step towards Lea, who faces him with folded arms. Her not very clean pink silk blouse has been hastily put on, only one button is done up; in her haste she has put on her skirt back to front. Her face is flushed, her hair dishevelled.

'Where is he?'

'Who?' Lea asks. She tries to smile. Her lips are pale, she has not had the time to touch up her lipstick. She looks afraid. Meirowitz grabs her arms, his flat face crimson, the little brush of his moustache twitching.

'Who is it?' he pants, 'who?' Lea tries to turn her head away from the hot face and the foaming mouth so close to her, to twist her hands out of his grasp. But he doesn't let go.

'I want his name, do you hear? I'll kill you if you don't tell me.'

'Kill me then.' Her head slumps forward and she begins to weep, so that her face is soon covered with tears. 'Kill me, it's the best thing anyway.'

That disconcerts Meirowitz a little. He lets go of one of her hands but grips the other even tighter and, looking at the half-open door through which the fellow must have just run away, bawls: 'I want to know the name of your lover.' Tears trickle down Lea's face, not just a few drops, but two torrents making large damp patches on her blouse and his shirt. Meirowitz's anger lessens and he has to harden his heart to stop his fury vanishing entirely.

'It could be anyone since you paint your face for all and sundry. But in the middle of the day, you, the mother of three children!' His voice is just a whimper now. He too could easily have shed tears on the scratched, discoloured floor-boards. Lea has still not said a word, but gulps, and from time to time utters a high-pitched, plaintive wail like that of some small beast whose paws have been trodden on. Meirowitz puts his hands over his eyes, cradling his head between his hands. 'While I'm slaving from morning till night to earn money for my family, my wife amuses herself in bed with her lover.'

At this Lea suddenly stops sobbing, as if the tears have been cut off. She lifts her head and shakes back her hair, eyes flaming with anger. 'Do you know whom I was with?' Meirowitz drops his hands from his face and looks at his wife, who looks entirely different. 'But I've been asking you who it was all this time,' he says, timidly.

'With the butcher.'

'With the . . .' His mouth gapes.

'Yes, with the butcher. He's already been round six times with the bill and he wasn't going to leave till it was paid.'

And there she should have stopped, for Leo Meirowitz was so crushed, so overcome with shame, bereft of every word and gesture, that he was paralysed; but she went on speaking, savouring her moment of triumph, the moment which broke down the dam and allowed a dirty grey torrent of anger and disappointment to flood in.

'How successfully you slave from morning to night! All you provide us with is debt and misery. You promised me a marble palace and silk dresses; but we dress in rags, the children and me. If it wasn't for me they wouldn't get enough to eat.' This exaggeration infuriated Meirowitz anew. He had made similar reproaches to himself countless times; but now her remarks were like stabs in the heart, and because she blamed him with such hate and exaggeration, he rallied all his instincts of self-preservation and tried to exploit the weak spots she exposed.

'And you,' he shouted, 'a model wife, her husband's other half, you simply lie in bed till noon!'

'That's not true,' shouted Lea.

'No,' shouted Meirowitz even louder, 'till the afternoon. You don't clean the house and you leave the children on their own.'

'The children? Me?' And she began to cry again. The angrier he became, the more she acted the injured party. Had he forgotten what she'd been through when the children came, and how she had nothing, nothing of the kind of thing a young woman wanted? No distractions, no theatres, no clothes, nothing but worries and work. She called him unfeeling and incompetent; he called her a lazy slut. So they stood there insulting one another, making caricatures of themselves, playing on each other's shortcomings. And while their angry words tore to shreds the few things that held them together, the children came back from playing in the court-yard, and drummed on the door with their fists. Meirowitz broke off in the middle of a sentence and hunched his shoulders.

'The children,' he said. His fury burnt itself out, leaving a feeling of complete misery. His large head hung down like a pumpkin. He went on sitting on the chair, hands clasped on his shabby trousers, while Lea opened the door. At once the flat was full of the children's noise and chatter. They were talking about the dog in the courtyard, they asked for something to eat, the baby was wet and screamed.

Meirowitz heard Manja's earnest little voice. 'The dog was nearly going to bite baby, but I forbade him to.' And without stopping, alarmed: 'Have you been crying, Mummie?' He heard Lea say no and saw her hurriedly tidy the beds, still unmade from last night, take off the baby's trousers, leaving them in the middle of the room, and carry him outside. Meanwhile Manja unbuttoned her other brother's coat and trousers. 'You scratch me when you undress me,' he grumbled.

'I didn't scratch you,' replied Manja.

'Yes, you did,' he persisted.

Through the gap in the door Meirowitz saw Manja holding her small hand in front of her brother's face. 'So, have I got claws like a cat?' Then Meirowitz, raising his head, bent forward in his chair; once he stopped being as still as a piece of furniture the children noticed him and rushed forward – the delicate, large-eyed girl with the elfin, flower-like face, and the thickset boy with the large, curly head. Both children climbed on his lap, and little Munio tried to pull his nose, upon which, according to an old tradition, Meirowitz had to emit a gurgling, indignant, croaking sound, like a main-spring being pressed, a joke which had been repeated endless times and never failed in its effect on both father and children. However, today, like a toy that's been broken, Meirowitz did not work. The little boy pulled his nose even harder but there was no funny snorting; his father only turned his face aside, didn't laugh, didn't grin, didn't grab hold of him. There was something wrong with him. And the little boy would have begun to cry if Lea hadn't come in carrying the baby and a plate of bread-and-butter. Shouting, 'For me!' Munio sprang down from his father's lap and hurled himself on the food.

Manja stayed on Meirowitz's lap, watching the large, sallow, sadly-drooping face. 'Why didn't you croak?' she asked.

Meirowitz gulped and did not reply.

'Have you got pains in your stomach?' the child asked. And since he shook his head she sought for some other cause, appropriate to an adult.

'Haven't you got any money?' From Meirowitz's mouth came a sound similar to the croaking she was waiting for. He took Manja's hand and pressed it to his eyes, held it to his mouth; her little fingers stroked his unshaven cheeks and played with his moustache. That helped and calmed him. This angelic child was his, caressed him, loved him, and was his flesh and blood; if he had such a child he couldn't be as bad as Lea made him out to be, but must just be unlucky. Everyone, even the most gifted person, was unlucky sometimes, so he wasn't a complete failure. 'Do you love me, my jewel?'

'As much as a mountain.' With her arms stretched wide she showed him how much. Then, since Lea was calling her, she slid down from his knee. 'Aren't you coming too?'

Meirowitz shook his head.

'I'll say good night to you later.'

He went on sitting there without moving, and through the door watched the children eating – the two boys in bed, Manja in profile at the table – and in spite of his bitter sadness his heart was heavy with tenderness for the pale little girl. Then Lea went out, got the wet sponge, wiped the children's hands and faces one by one and shut the door. That shut off from his field of vision and his consciousness the soothing, re-assuring image of the child. Then, sponge in hand, she came and stood before Meirowitz. Meanwhile her blouse had been buttoned up; but her skirt was still back to front and her anger had not gone.

'We can't go on like this,' she said, squeezing the sponge so that water dripped on the floor. Meirowitz watched the drops ooze into a crack in the floorboards. 'Turn your skirt the right way round,' he said.

Shrugging her shoulders Lea did so, her lip curling. 'Do you remember how you promised me the children would eat with silver spoons?'

'And you?' shouted Meirowitz. 'You promised to be a good wife!'

'And what have I got from it?' cried Lea. 'Three children and a dog's life.' Once more she wept unrestrainedly, shaken by self-pity. Meirowitz kept his head lowered. He was groping for a thought from the past, which kept slipping away like a heavy, slippery beam that has been in the water a long time.

'Mummie, come here, come!' Manja called from the next room.

'Go to sleep, Manja.'

'Come, please, come!' The child's voice was high and excited. Lea wiped her eyes with her sleeve and, giving an angry glance at Meirowitz, who was to blame both for her tears and for her having to hide them from the child, went out. And while the child and Lea were whispering in the next room, Meirowitz pulled up the submerged thought, that became increasingly heavier and heavier to lift, was becoming a burden which began almost to crush him. Lea's betrayal, the fact that he could not pay his debts, were nothing compared with this terrible thought, this awful weight on his heart.

'She wants you to say good night to her.' Lea stood in the doorway. She did not look at him. Her expression reflected the happy moment she had had with the child.

Meirowitz went towards her. He would have liked to put off or swallow the question, nevertheless he asked: 'Lea, why did you come to me that time?'

Lea knew immediately what he meant. 'When?' she asked.

'To the shop, before we were married.'

'Father, come and say good night,' urged the child in the next room, sounding anxious now. Meirowitz, his hands pressed to his ears as though Lea might reply too quickly and too loudly, groped his way distractedly towards the voice and shut the door behind him. He would have liked to lock it.

Manja was sitting up in bed. The cheap lace on the collar of her nightdress stood out from her thin little neck; the nightdress had slipped over her left shoulder, which was sharp and distressingly thin – the collar-bone rose like a slender ridge between deep hollows. She gazed into his face, looking up at him with her lovely eyes; they made her thin face beautiful; yet it was much too thin for a child's, seeming tiny between the large ears which peeped through her straight, soft hair. Meirowitz put his head on the warped edge of the old cot.

Its bars were loose and stretched; Lea had put the sides up and inside the child looked like a tiny plucked bird in a cage.

'Put down the side,' pleaded the child. Meirowitz's clumsy fingers shook as he did so.

'Sit down here.' Meirowitz sat on the edge of the cot. The child put her thin hand on his, and he was reminded of the first time Lea took his hand. And here was this thin, sweet, strange child, so different from the two boys lying flushed in their cots, fingers clenched as if, even in sleep, they wouldn't let go of anything; greedy, noisy rascals who were always dirty; and this fastidious little girl, whose voice and eyes were looking for something in him which he perhaps did not possess at all. She was surely a living excuse for her father, giving him a sort of charter for his existence, since no ordinary person could ever have had such a child. Yet could this perplexing, sweet, melancholy creature be his? Could Leo Meirowitz be her father? He squeezed her little hand; Manja winced, but did not remove it, and he kept it gently in his.

'Today you don't need to do any silly stuff.' Silly stuff belonged to the ritual of saying good night, consisting of the kinds of jokes and nonsense which made her roar with laughter. 'Do you know any stories?'

Meirowitz shook his head.

'It doesn't matter, tomorrow will do,' said Manja. Meirowitz's head went on shaking like that of an old man no longer able to control his muscles.

'Not tomorrow either?' she asked. Meirowitz gulped. The child was deeply touching, she was kind to him. And that she was so kind hurt him painfully. Was he, Leo Meirowitz, kind, then, or was it Lea? From whom did the child get her kindness? Had he been like that, once, a long time ago? Or had she got it from someone else, someone who was a better person? He could not hate this other person, he could only suffer like a dog.

Manja picked up her small bear which lay on the blanket. 'He's cold, tuck him in.'

Obediently Meirowitz put him on the pillow next to her and covered him up. Satisfied, the child lay down beside it. Meirowitz betrayed none of the tenderness and torment which he was feeling; once or twice he started to speak, and was about to hug her small body to his and squeeze her face and her thin arms and tiny little hands to his twitching lips; but he said and did nothing. With one hand he stroked the bear, with the other the child's fingers. Helplessly, he put everything off to a time which he sensed would never come; his large ugly face, on which even signs of suffering appeared as comic as on Punch, was quivering with emotion.

The child lay beside the bear on the pillow. She was fighting against sleep, having the feeling that something unusual, something alarming had happened, something she did not understand. From under half-closed eyelids she looked again at the melancholy buffoon beside her bed, then took the bear and laid it on Meirowitz's hand. 'Tonight he can sleep with you.' And as a smile crossed her face she fell asleep. Meirowitz took the bear and tiptoed out of the room.

Lea sat turning over a newspaper. She did not look up when he said, without making a gesture or looking at her: 'Now let's have the truth.'

Raising her eyes she thought he looked rather like an ugly, worn-out pair of nut-crackers which the children sometimes played with. But her disappointed hopes, the horror of all the nights lying beside him, created a pitiless iron wall. Without hesitating she said: 'Manja isn't your child.'

And Leo Meirowitz said no more. He left the house and walked aimlessly through the streets. After some hours his grief and anger were alleviated by the thought that he would not be at home tomorrow when the bills of exchange fell due. And he did not go back.

CHAPTER 16
REVENGE IN THE HAY

Walter von Adrian was paying his first visit to Bucheneck, his family's estate, since he had been forced to sell it to Max Hartung. He had often put off going back to the house, where he could remember every tree in the garden and every piece of furniture inside the house, where each brick and stone was part of his life; it was unbearable to think of Max Hartung in the brown leather armchair in which his father had died; terrible to imagine other people walking along the garden paths and going across the meadows where he had played with his brothers and sisters. He felt a strange mixture of anger and relief when Hilde led him through the house, which appeared quite different from that of his childhood, when it seemed gloomy and austere and furnished to last for ever. Walls had been built round it, the roof was flat instead of pitched, new groups of trees had been planted and there was a fountain in the middle of the wide lawn, which had been closely cut like an English one and was no longer covered with flowers and long grasses, a summer meadow waving in the wind. It was a relief that strangers had not desecrated something meant for his sons and grandsons; nevertheless it was an outrageous defilement.

Although he kept all this to himself, and dutifully praised everything Hilde showed him, he still felt depressed and upset when he sat down to eat alone with her – Hartung had not yet returned from town.

She was wearing a blue dress the colour of her eyes, which seemed even bluer than usual in her lightly tanned face. Light from the terrace through the open door gleamed on her black hair. The lovely summer garden framed her through the doorway.

But Adrian was irritated and distracted by the still life of flowers on the wall, that was hanging there instead of the antlers of a royal stag which his great-grandfather had shot in the neighbouring woods, and which he had looked at during every meal he had ever eaten in the house. Then he became conscious of her gaze on him, imagined that he read reproach in it, and pulled himself together.

'I'm afraid I am very bad company today, so absent-minded. Please forgive me.'

'But what for?' replied Hilde in bewilderment. 'I have nothing to complain about.'

He looked away from the annoying still life towards her face. She was livelier than he had ever known her. Suddenly he realised that he had come here, in spite of the humiliation, in spite of all the house meant to him, because he wanted to see this woman sitting in it, wanted to see her walking in his grounds.

'It's wonderful here, don't you think?' he said warmly. 'A magnificent piece of land.'

'Do you really like the house?' asked Hilde. 'Or did you prefer it as it used to be?' How could anyone so angelically

148

beautiful be so stupid, Adrian asked himself angrily. 'I expect you can't get used to it,' she went on, and, since an awkward pause resulted from his silence, she said with a disarmingly childlike glance from her splendid eyes: 'Everything in life is a matter of what you are used to, isn't it?'

'It certainly is,' he answered quickly. 'And the house is charming, in very good taste . . .' He broke off, for it seemed pointless to finish what he was saying. But to his surprise Hilde did so for him.

'Of course it isn't the same as when you were a child.' That made him feel better and seemed significant; it was a bridge from the purely conventional to what he wanted to find out.

'And you,' he asked, 'what was your childhood like? Tell me.'

'There's not much to tell,' she replied, looking at her plate. And again she slipped away from him, as if she were sailing away on a boat and the seconds were pushing themselves between them like waves.

'A quiet country cottage with a little garden, I can see it all. Until one day the black-haired Prince Max appears with his well-filled pocket book and wakes up the Sleeping Beauty.' Adrian was astonished by the rudeness and aggression of what he had said.

'Unfortunately we didn't live in the country at all,' replied Hilde placidly. And once more Adrian stared at her. Had a blow been parried in a clever manner or had she not noticed that someone had struck?

At this inconvenient moment little Harry came onto the sunny terrace with his governess. Hilde had turned away, but Adrian saw, against a backcloth of bright green beeches, the awkward, pitiful little fellow with his sallow face, pointed forehead and thin black hair sitting like a bad wig on his pear-shaped skull. He wore a white sailor suit with a blue collar, that emphasised all that was least appealing about him, and held a net with a red rubber ball in his right hand. The tall, emaciated governess, carefully cut out of an English comic strip and stuck onto a blue sky, was carrying a green bucket and shapes for making sandcastles.

'Come along, dear,' she said in English, but the child stood still and looked at his mother in her blue dress.

'Mummie!' he shouted and ran up to her, a smile of enchantment on his plain face. Hilde turned her head towards him.

'Mother is having lunch; come along, dear,' repeated the governess.

'He's only saying hello, Miss Hopkins, I'll send him to you straightaway.'

'Very well, madam.'

Adrian watched Hilde as she talked to the child in a friendly, disinterested manner, but without that look of intensity and rapture with which mothers usually try to lure other people into admiring their children. She does not love him, he thought. Indeed, how could she? An appalling little chap. Repelled, he turned his head away, and looked past the governess at a rose bush in full bloom, concentrating on the perfect beauty of the crimson flowers glowing in the sun.

'Have you eaten yet?' Hilde asked, and the boy replied, 'yes'. Adrian looked at Hilde's lowered face with the same devotion as he had looked at the roses. She ought to have had the purplish-blue cloak of the Madonna round her shoulders and have been holding a child as beautiful as an angel; rather than that pathetic unfortunate, who leant against her like an ugly gargoyle, his fingers gently stroking her knee.

'Would you like a peach, Harry?' asked Hilde, stretching out her hand to the fruit bowl.

'No, thank you, I have eaten already. I had vegetables and I drank the milk, as well.' Every word prolonged the precious moments in which he could be here, could gaze at his mother and touch her, postponed being sent back to Miss Hopkins.

'That's good, and now, my boy . . .'

But he gained yet another second by saying: 'I fell down this morning . . .' And pulling down the sock from his thin little leg he pointed out a small red patch of flayed skin.

'Oh, dear!' said Hilde abstractedly. 'But it's better now.'

'It hurt very much,' said the child, trying again.

'Well, my little one, go and play now. It's such lovely weather.'

If a strange man had not been there Harry would have wept loudly; as it was, his eyes filled with tears, his underlip pouted, his head hung down as though it had suddenly wilted on the thin neck, and he walked away on his slightly bandy legs, their long shadows hurrying in front of him over the sun-drenched terrace to where Miss Hopkins was standing under a tree.

'Coffee?' asked Hilde. Adrian, suddenly irritable, declined. It was too hot for coffee.

'Yes, it is hot,' replied Hilde, standing up. 'You'll excuse me for half an hour, won't you? Make yourself comfortable;

cigarettes and cigars are on the sideboard.' She gave Adrian her hand, which he brushed with his lips. 'I shan't be long. And then we'll go for a walk, shall we?'

'That will be a great pleasure,' he said mechanically.

* * *

She's like a sleepwalker, thought Adrian. He lay in a deck-chair under the verandah awning and smoked. The first person to confront and arouse her would bear a great responsibility. Did he want to? No. He wanted the woman; but he would not have her; and that was that.

The air shimmered with heat. Thoughts fluttered through his mind like a swarm of white butterflies over the rose beds. Sheer affectation to leave him alone. That must be an English habit. Was she really sleeping? The thought of her stretched out on the bed, naked in the heat, gave him a jolt. What was Hartung up to, not having come home? Was that a sign of confidence, a gentlemen's agreement? He ought to know perfectly well that agreements like that were only valid precisely between gentlemen. And looking at a fat bumble-bee greedily forcing itself down to the stamens of a rose, he was tortured, as so often before, by obscene images of Hartung and Hilde's married life. A satyr, a paunchy faun, the lecherous embodiment of obscene sexuality. When he thought of her, white and helpless in his clutches, then he hated Hartung with a burning hate, loved her like a dreamy schoolboy and wanted her like a prisoner under life sentence. The bumble-bee flew off covered with pollen. How ridiculous to be thinking like this. What business of his was Max Hartung's marriage? She had sold herself, she knew what she was doing. These quixotic thoughts were pointless. Hartung was a clever man, an exceptional businessman, and would be a dangerous enemy.

In the garden the child was crying. Then there was nothing but gentle rustling sounds, a soft humming, the splashing sound of the fountain that disfigured the beautiful expanse of grass like a raw scar. Weariness blunted his irritation. With his eyes shut he lay in a contented half-sleep, the familiar sounds and smells deluding him into thinking he was at home. But he woke up completely when he heard Hilde's footsteps. He was filled with uncontrollable joy that she was standing there and that they were going to walk through the woods together.

'Rested?' he asked gaily.

'Yes, very well rested.' Her face seemed softer after her sleep, like that of a little girl, candid, relaxed, expectant.

'Isn't it too hot for you?' he asked.

'I love the heat.' Side by side they went over the lawn, past the herbaceous border, where everything grew in disordered profusion: larkspur, scarlet and white poppies, late, almost black tulips, yellow and speckled carnations, marguerites, bushes of white and red fuchsias and innumerable flowers that Hilde seemed to see for the first time. Adrian knew all their names; Hilde repeated and then forgot them. They stood and looked at a wonderfully scented wisteria, and Hilde was surprised by the tenderness with which Adrian lifted the dull blue racemes to show her how to touch the butterfly flower so that it opened like a mouth. And he told her how all these flowers were planted and Hilde listened to him with delight, thinking of Max Hartung who only knew roses and daisies by their names and for whom every tree was a beech.

Then the garden came to an end and the wood began, an unusually beautiful beechwood. For Adrian, going into this golden-green coolness from the sunny garden had always brought the same emotion: as a boy he thought that God withdrew from church in the summer to live here, beneath the wood's luminous green dome. He felt this again now as Hilde chattered away innocently and happily.

'I hardly ever come here alone, and Max never takes a walk, of course.' The word Max sounded, at this point, like something pornographic shouted out in church and Adrian gave a start. 'What's the matter?' she asked, looking round to see what could have surprised him.

'Nothing, nothing.' Even the sacrilege did not make him angry, so peaceful was the wood, so bewitching the translucent, silky green of the leaves and the light pouring down over the tree trunks in honey-yellow streams, dancing on the moss in a shower of golden coins. In a very low voice he said: 'It is so beautiful, but the wood only stays alive within us if one is silent.' Hilde looked at him, surprised by a tone she had not heard from him before; she kept silent like an obedient child. As they walked along her hand brushed against his; he took it and held it tight.

'Now the wood is alive,' she whispered. 'I have never been so happy in my life.'

'And usually?' he asked, coming to a stop. 'Are you usually sad?'

'Not sad and not happy, just nothing.' She looked down. For a few seconds they stood listening to the rustling of leaves, the noise of twigs snapping, and the sounds of birds. Adrian gave her time; he had endless patience; he could wait.

'Things have always just happened to me,' she went on, her gaze on the green oval where a lily of the valley had faded. 'At home we were very poor; that often used to depress me. Then Hartung came and took me away from all that and into society. But – perhaps you won't understand what I mean – wherever I am I feel as if I'm just a visitor.'

Adrian stopped. 'That's been my feeling ever since I met you,' he said excitedly, 'that you've never been yourself, that you still don't know who you are.' He was gently holding her hand. He was deeply moved that she was speaking to him like a human being, for the first time in the five years he had known her. None of the smooth gallantries he usually employed with women were appropriate here, and he was shy and helpless. Suddenly he wanted to kiss her, to touch her cheeks, her mouth; but just then she turned her head away and began to talk again – so he would have had to interrupt, snatch her to himself. When she stops talking, then I'll kiss her, he thought; the words were a refrain running through everything she said.

'Perhaps if I had someone who lived only for me . . .' She was cracking a twig with her hands. Adrian looked away from her fingers as they mechanically tore off leaves. He felt awkward. When she stops I'll kiss her . . . But her voice rose above his silent refrain, forcing him to listen. 'If I had a husband who lived for me, all the time, day and night, who gave me books to read, so that I could read them and discuss them with him . . .'

When she stops . . . But the refrain stopped and Hilde's voice went on . . . . 'And read the papers to me, because otherwise I have no idea what goes on in the world, and made me go to museums, because I don't have the energy on my own, and never left me alone. But he doesn't exist.'

She stood there, her eyes half closed, her curved lips partly open, a woman wanting to be kissed. But now Adrian had not the least wish to do so. It was ridiculous to have had such half-baked feelings; his tenderness, and his restraint, was stupid.

'Quite a programme, dear lady,' he said, once again using the conventional tone behind which he had concealed his irritation at lunchtime. Hilde looked at him, disconcerted. Without understanding why, she realised that something had been spoilt, that the tender and intimate mood had been broken.

'It's not just a *grande passion* that would be needed, but a good deal of time and money,' said Adrian. She understood now what had annoyed him.

'I did not mean it like that . . .' she said awkwardly. But she sensed that, like words carried from one's lips by the wind, what she said did not reach him. If she had touched him, taken his hand, then the golden moment might have been restored. But she felt tired and defenceless. Something beautiful had come and then gone again. She had been given something but it had been taken away.

'I think we must go back,' she said.

It had become sultry; the sun had gone behind thick clouds. Adrian led her along another path, shorter than the one they had come by.

'We must hurry, my dear lady, otherwise we will get wet.' Obediently Hilde tried to walk more quickly, but they made slow progress, since she was wearing patent leather shoes which had become tight and painful in the heat, while the high heels slowed her down on the stony path. With malicious pleasure Adrian saw that they were torturing her. Anyone sensible did not put on patent leather shoes for a walk, nor wear shoes that were too small out of vanity. His mother and his sisters had worn low-heeled shoes when they went for walks here.

They passed the red-brick cattle sheds on the right-hand side of the path and could hear the cows' frightened bellowing as they sensed a coming storm; already the first drops were falling from sulphur-yellow clouds, splashing warmly on their hot skin.

'Come along,' cried Adrian, dragging her with him. 'We'll take shelter.' At the first hurried step she lost a shoe, which he picked up without stopping and kept in his hand. 'There isn't time to put it on.'

She bent down, the rain splashing on her silk dress, and snatched off the other one. And now, free of the hot, hard shoes, she laughingly ran the short distance to the cowshed door. Adrian caught her up and turned the handle; and their wet hands touched; both withdrew them at once. The rain ran down their hair. Hilde stepped into the dark cowshed. Coming out of the dazzling light before the storm, they were almost blinded and could only see the tethered cows in silhouette, the whites of their eyes turned towards them. The heat in the shed was even more oppressive than outside, made worse by the acrid, stable smell of mingled cow-dung, animals and the pile of hay left in the corner. Hilde crossed the dirty floor and sat down, digging into the hay with both hands, breathing in the smell of the newly-cut red-and-white clover. Adrian, still standing at the door, with his face turned away from her, her shoe in his hand, looked like a guard with a strange weapon. Lunatic, breathtaking excitement had attacked him like a wild beast, clawing at his chest. This had all happened before – the drumming of the rain on the wooden roof, the smell of clover and hay and manure, the cows' long tails swaying to and fro over their dirt-encrusted hind parts. Twenty years ago. He's fourteen. The fat farm-girl with the red arms . . . bad teeth, fair, wispy hair, and the large hips. He had seen her days before in the fields, her body quivering at every step, plump beneath her tight skirt as she worked in the fields. They went without a word into the hay. And all the time the dirty hind parts of a cow in front of his staring eyes, its heavy, repulsive pink udder, and then, when her skirt fell open, her splayed thighs. He sees it all, although he stuffs both hands in front of his eyes while strange fingers undress him, until, passive, trembling with horror, he sinks down into the softness and warmth of her thighs. That was love. She was called Irma and soon afterwards she left. But his fear and shame remained: not able to look at anyone or speak, avoiding his mother, keeping his sisters at arm's length, all women, everything to do with the udder, was wet, soft, disgusting. But in his dreams she was still there. He had forgotten the episode, pushed it out of his mind, but it was still there, a secret forced into a dark pit through a trapdoor. And now extraordinary chance, hidden desire, or simply the same stormy weather drove him twenty years later to the place – and what had been buried arose again.

Three paces away from him the woman sat quietly. It was a crazy thought – that one could grab her and fling her into the hay just as the farm-girl had done to the fourteen year-old boy. He gripped the door while rain from outside splashed on his face. A cow bellowed in terror; for a moment a dazzling flash of lightning lit up its horns, its wet, trembling jaws, the protruding eyeballs, white with fear, the quivering flanks.

Hilde screamed as the glaring light flashed across her face. 'Where are you?' Above the clap of thunder which rocked the cowshed she cried out in real terror, 'Close the door, for God's sake!'

For a moment he went on standing there and did not move. Then his hands fell away, dark against the grey. She herself had wanted it.

He shut the door. Now it was completely dark. It was not a cowshed but a cave in which animals moved, the air filled with the smell of dung and their bodies. He stood rooted to this piece of hot, damp, sheltered ground, and lost pride and fear like a snake its skin; all at once he felt peace, joy, resolve – no hesitation, no scruples. Who wore evening dress in a thunderstorm, who was gentlemanly in a place where graves gaped open? He saw her dark outline, went across and sat down beside her in the hay.

'Are you frightened?' he asked her very quietly, putting his arm round her shoulder. She leant against it, reassured by his touch. The animals shuffled and pulled at their chains.

'Not now.'

'It's lovely, Hilde,' whispered Adrian, 'beautiful, listen!'

159

The rain was beating more quietly on the roof and the grimy windows, a murmuring sound like the ebb and flow of waves. He pushed her very gently, so that she lay down, and made a bed for her in the hay. The unbelievable was the easiest. He was like a rider on a splendid horse that, by itself, flew over ditches and bushes. A miraculous, rapturous, intricate game, played with love on every instrument, on seductively tender flutes, with all the most enchanting sounds, for it wasn't enough simply to take her, to satisfy his lust – an even more delicious power lay in bringing her to a final, unimagined peak of joy. He was the one who revealed ecstasy.

Hilde lay quietly under his caressing hands and listened to the rain. A stranger lies beside her and caresses her body. One dreams, one feels strangely detached, one lies in the hay; yet none of it is real. Darkness covers one like a cloak. But suddenly the cloak holds one tight, clutches, demands. Someone was calling, tempting, telling the lame to walk. Someone was asking that she, who was locked in fear, should open the door. Someone wants to wake her up, to make everything as bright as that terrible flash just now, wants to take her heart from her. A burglar with a dark lantern, creeping in . . . Terror sprang into her throat like a dog leaping up.

'No, no, what are you doing?'

'Nothing, nothing at all, just to be with you, know you. Let me.'

'I cannot.'

'You must, you shall.'

The magic flute played. Thus the rat-catcher played his pipe when the rats crept bewitched from every nook and cranny and followed him; thus he played when the children danced after him along the endless sunny road from which they never returned.

'Love, love': the 'Open Sesame' for every door in the world, the rope-ladder by which one can climb out of the prison of loneliness.

'This hour belongs to us.' There had been nothing that awoke her, nothing that made sense, yet he called and she ran after him, in her nightdress and bare feet, following him, going to the limits for this moment.

She began to sob desperately. Adrian stopped her crying with his mouth. No tears, no sympathy, no commitment, only the unearthly sense of freedom, the soaring flight, bringing the ghosts of the past along with him so that instead of bringing him to a stop they raced along beside both of them.

He enjoyed the moment to the full, without giving a thought to the farm-girl who took him as brutally as Hartung had taken his house. He did not realise that he had taken his revenge.

* * *

There was now only a gentle dripping from the gutter into the barrel outside the shed. The rain, which had shut out the world like an impenetrable wall, had stopped. All of a sudden Adrian noticed that it was quiet, that the cows were shuffling and the sun shining behind the round window. Gently he pulled his arm from underneath Hilde, who lay completely still with closed eyes, and took his watch out of his waistcoat pocket. It took him a few moments to make out the time. Six o'clock. While he was wondering how to wake her and what he should say, and how, he heard the clear notes of a song.

'Quick, someone's coming!' Although she was sleeping lightly, she did not want to wake up. The song came nearer, every word was distinct; Adrian could already hear footsteps, and buckets clanking together. In a few steps he got to the door and opened it as a servant-girl, a pail over her arm, took hold of the latch. 'Jesus Mary!' she screamed. But Adrian, standing in the doorway so that she could not enter or look in, said in a tone which allowed for no questions or surprise: 'Madam and I have been sheltering from the storm; go quickly to the house and fetch a coat . . . Come along, Hilde, we don't want to stay here a moment longer.'

He pulled her up and towards the door; she removed the straw from her hair and smoothed her dress and he held the mirror while she combed her hair and powdered her nose. He did not say any of the words for which she was hoping, and avoided her demure glances, simply hurrying her out of the cowshed, where they might be discovered at any moment.

He kissed her hand and held the door open. Everything would be better if they didn't stay a moment longer in the shed. He felt wretched, words seemed impossible. He saw himself as someone who crept out of the back door in his socks to avoid the landlord to whom he owed rent. He looked past Hilde's face, transformed by a profound beauty that tortured him. She had gone outside without a word. Without touching each other they slowly started to walk. The meadow was bright in the early evening light; raindrops fell in showers when they brushed past branches. It was only a few hours since that afternoon's sunshine. Although she felt giddy in the sudden glare Hilde did not dare to ask for Adrian's arm. Gradually the last golden trace of happiness faded from her, but she still hoped for a word, a gesture, to bring it back like the afternoon sun. Adrian started to speak a few times but stopped because every sentence horrified him.

'It was a dream, Hilde,' said Adrian, 'an unforgettable dream. But now we must be sensible. Now we must go on with everyday life.' But suddenly he noticed that she had a round mark on her neck.

'Tonight you must put on a shawl or a dress with a high collar.'

The woods on either side of the path thinned out. They were approaching the lawn.

'You're not angry with me . . .' He broke off in the middle of the sentence, for down the steps leading to the house, flooded in sunlight, came Max Hartung, gigantic in tennis flannels, a black coat thrown over his shoulder like a scarf. Only the lawn separated them. Adrian's first impulse was to pull Hilde back into the shadow of the trees. But Hartung might have seen them and then the action would have been fatal.

'Did you see?' he whispered agitatedly.

'Yes.' Hilde's voice was quite calm. Did she realise what was happening? Hartung looked as though he was waving to them. If he was waving, then they would have to wave back. Perhaps he was only moving his arms as he walked. Adrian tried to think calmly. She is like a sleepwalker, he thought in horror.

'Hilde, you must pull yourself together,' he whispered, although they were still well out of earshot.

The lawn was like a chessboard on which three living figures moved about. What a disaster! The white castle was coming nearer. An elephant with a panama hat. Hilde's face as she walked towards Hartung was like a calf to the slaughter!

'Hilde, dear Hilde, don't stare like that, Hartung isn't a ghost!' And, suddenly angry, he said loudly: 'Don't behave so stupidly.' She gave a start. Oh God, she would start to cry soon. 'Hilde, don't be angry. I'm sorry. Don't you understand?'

Hartung could not hear them yet over the fountain's splashing. But he could see them.

'You must put your coat on while I'm talking to him.' Damnation, why had he bitten her? If they ran back to the woods, the fat man would not be able to catch up with them, he would get caught in the brambles . . .

Now that the battle was at hand, in which it was so important to be clever and quick-witted in the face of the enemy, a murderous army of thoughts assailed him: serves you right, young man, you'll pay for your springtime dream; thus did the Greek gods look on those who enjoyed easy love. Swindler, embezzler, you'll be sorry . . .

Hartung approached, his long, blue shadow slanting in the evening light; now they were just able to make out his features. Adrian was forced to smile, and he did so while saying to Hilde, rounding his vowels in his mouth so that Hartung realised he was talking: 'Don't forget, we got drenched and took shelter in the cowshed – admit that much. Don't lose your head.' And then, forgetting to round his vowels in his haste: 'It will all be fine if you're sensible.'

'The fountain is wonderfully refreshing in this heat, a magnificent idea,' said Adrian loudly, for now they were within earshot. While he was speaking his mind was racing. First he would say, 'Good evening, Herr Kommerzienrat,' then, 'Glorious weather now it's cleared up again, unfortunately we were caught in the rain.' Then he would reach out, but not too quickly, to take Hilde's coat and help her into it. It was bound to have some sort of collar, some sort of lapels. But he had forgotten to go on talking. It didn't matter, they still couldn't be heard. Hartung was exactly at the right distance for a bullet wound to be fatal – in the forehead, or the middle of the shadow cast by the straw hat, or in his breast pocket with the silk handkerchief in it . . .

'Hello!' Hartung flourished the coat like a bullfighter. Join battle! But then the coat would be red. He hadn't answered yet.

'Hello, hello!' bawled Adrian. Why twice? Why so loudly? Go up to Hartung and keep Hilde half hidden. Another two steps. But why should he, why should he hurry? Quietly, calmly.

Hartung seemed to be in a good mood, but Adrian could not make out his expression properly since his eyes were dazzled by the light reflected in the windows of the house. Their three shadows met and merged into one; they touched as if their owners were kissing.

'Good evening, Herr Kommerzienrat,' and put out your hand. Now, what had he been going to say?

A beautiful evening. What was the script? He had to hide Hilde, but she had gone on while he had stopped. 'Glorious weather after the storm, though it was far from glorious then, completely unexpected.' What was he babbling on about? Probably Hartung hadn't noticed anything. If only the sun didn't dazzle so much, so that he could see him.

'I very much hope madam has not caught a chill.' Now try and seize the coat.

But Hartung was not listening. He had stopped, holding on to the coat and looking at Hilde. His glance probed her from head to foot, and it was as if his blood slowly poured out from under his thick neck in its white collar and rose up into his neck and cheeks and from there to the straw hat, which was also red. But that was from the sun.

With great relief Adrian felt that all was lost. It was better so. No more dissembling, he would pay, he would answer honestly. If Hartung wanted to have it out, he would be only too delighted. And suddenly, without being at all nervous, calmly and with his head held high, he said: 'I am at your disposal, of course.'

'Really?' Hartung turned his head to him and seemed to smile. He knew nothing. That sentence had betrayed everything.

'That's very civil of you, Adrian, we have a lot to talk about. Your coat, Hilde.' The voice was perfectly calm, his expression obscured by the glare from the windows. But the large hands holding the coat appeared to be trembling, although he wasn't sure. Such pretence wasn't possible, was inhuman. Hartung was a blind fool; he had seen nothing, and the coat did have a big collar that covered Hilde's neck up to her chin. If only she would say something. But silently, very slim in the black coat, she went across the lawn, as though she were alone, without speaking, without looking round, as if she had forgotten the two men existed. Perfectly insane. Adrian did not dare look at Hartung as he walked slowly behind her. Ought he to walk behind him, stay beside him, talk to him, keep quiet? Everything was impossible. He would have given ten years of his life for it to have been an hour later.

'So you have passed the time agreeably, Adrian?' Hartung went more quickly and Adrian fell into step with him.

'Yes, thank you, very agreeably.' Had that a hidden meaning? Terrible, this cat-and-mouse game. Better come out with everything, straightforwardly, whatever happened. But supposing Hartung knew nothing, or didn't want to!

'Herr Kommerzienrat,' began Adrian hurriedly without knowing how he was going to finish his sentence.

But Hartung interrupted him. 'But I beg you, Adrian, between old friends there's no need to say a word. I am pleased that you feel so much at home here.' His tone suggested he was smiling. Adrian, his eyes fixed on the black figure that had almost reached the steps, allowed himself a quick sideways glance at Hartung's half-closed eyes and crooked mouth. What should he say? The truth? Dear Hartung, everything is quite all right, I don't love your wife, I've just had a roll in the hay with her. It's quite unimportant.

'By the way, Adrian,' said Hartung as they approached the fountain, 'I shall want your signature today in the matter we discussed.'

'I told you I could not put my name to that document,' replied Adrian softly. 'None of the figures are correct; the whole thing is a fraud.'

He made a point of speaking sharply. It would be an enormous relief to fall out with Hartung over his methods of obtaining credit, to go over every item on the balance sheet, knowing himself in the right, and to feel contemptuously superior to him. But Hartung would not oblige him.

'You are always so scrupulous, Adrian,' he said in a quiet voice, watching the slender dark figure which was just disappearing through the doorway.

Silently they walked towards the house with its windows glowing in the sun. Their long shadows glided over the lawn, touching one another in fraternal embrace, merging as though they belonged to two friends talking intimately to each other as they walked home in the evening.

CHAPTER 17
THE MAN ON THE BRIDGE

Heavy rain, deluging the street with bright puddles and driving people into their houses, drummed on Hanna Heidemann's umbrella as she walked home over the Marienbrücke with her son, whom she had been to fetch from some friends. He had his arm through his mother's, his cheek brushing against the smooth coolness of her raincoat as he walked. Everything he saw, heard and smelt – the rain on the umbrella, the piers of the bridge gleaming in the deep water from the faint lights on the embankment, the thin band of light from the street, blurred by the rain and gleaming in the water – everything enchanted him.

'Do you mind the rain?' he asked, pressing his mother's arm. 'I like it.'

'Me too, Heini. Are you all right under the umbrella?' 'Yes.' He raised his beaming, wet face and Hanna stroked his cheek with the back of her hand. It was so good to walk along with her son, whose steps fitted in with hers, and to feel his head nestling against her. The bushes on the bank, the raindrops on their black twigs gleaming in the lamplight like diamond catkins – it was all magical! The ancient statue on its plinth at the end of the bridge was oddly alive; rain streamed down from the cross held in the delicate clasped hands; it dripped down over its head and collected in the granite folds of the cloak. And at almost exactly the same moment that she was thinking the same thing, the boy said: 'He's crying.'

She felt moved and happy. He was so close to her, so much part of her – she felt almost as if she could peel off the years and grow up with him. A headlamp close by, white and glaring, a glistening tree trunk as green as in a wood on stage – it was all wonderfully exciting and intense, like taking a few steps into a wild storm or leaning out of the security of one's room to look at trains flashing past.

Just then Heini tugged violently at her arm. He had stopped and was staring across at the balustrade of the bridge.

'A man's standing up there,' he said. And Hanna saw in the feeble light of the nearby lamp a figure which looked at first like one of the dripping statues – a man leaning against the parapet, his hat pulled down over his face, rain streaming down it. What had frightened the boy so much was his standing there like a pillar, like a part of the bridge, like a tree – and yet he was a human being who had drawn pictures on the roadway of a blue sea and a boat which, together with the blue, was now drenched in rain. Underneath, in dissolving letters, it said: 'Grateful thanks.'

'A beggar, Heini,' said Hanna soothingly. She knew it was only her adult callousness that gave her a bland calm and that the child was right to be horrified. She opened her handbag and dug out all the small change she had on her. 'Do you want to give this to him?'

The child did not move. 'Why is he here?'

'I don't know, Heini.'

'Where does he sleep?'

'I don't know, sweetheart.'

'Ask him, Mummie.'

'But, Heini, be sensible. I can't ask a complete stranger . . .'

'Please, Mummie.'

'He would only be angry, Heini. Come along, angel, you're getting soaked.' That was a foolish thing to say because of course the boy replied:

'So will the man. Can we take him with us, Mummie, can we?' What was she to say? Was she to poison his mind with tales of theft and murder? Or was she to give him the easiest, but least honest, answer, that he doesn't want to work? That's what most people said to children. Heini, who was waiting impatiently for her answer, said, 'We'll take him with us, shall we? Mummie, do say we will.' He had taken hold of her arm with both his hands and lifted his wet agitated face to hers.

'Darling,' said Hanna heavily, 'we'll give him all the money I have on me. You'll see, he'll be very pleased.' She filled the child's hand with coins and took him up to the man, who stood there without moving, like a figure on a fountain. The lids covered his eyes as if he were asleep and he did not look up at the sound of footsteps. Only when the first coin rattled into the little flat cup in front of him did he half open his eyes. 'Many thanks.' And as each coin rattled down he said 'many thanks' like an automaton. His shielded, wet, hairy face, his large body leaning forward, were so hostile and alarming that the child did not try to speak to him but let himself be dragged away without protest.

They walked on. But they were no longer in step. Hanna had to pull the boy along after her. His hand was still in hers but before his fingers had been warm and tight round his mother's, and now his hand was stiff in hers. The umbrella had become too small for both of them, the rain was cold, her shoes sodden. It was their first disagreement, as upsetting for the adult as for the child. It spoilt all the familiar and happy little everyday rituals: his bath, supper together, bedtime, even the moment of saying good night, which had never been overshadowed before. Heini's last waking glance, before exhaustion finally closed his eyes, was at the window-panes on which the rain still beat unceasingly . . .

Eight o'clock. Another four hours before Heidemann came home from the hospital. They seemed an eternity, although usually Hanna loved these evenings of quiet waiting.

Then came the sound, above the splashing rain, of a car stopping, and voices could heard through the half-open window – one familiar and loud, and Heidemann's very low. It was nothing, it was ridiculous for her knees to shake. He had come home early for some reason or other. But her body gave the lie to all soothing interpretations; her skin, heart, limbs and breath burnt in fear.

She ran down the stairs, which gave way under her and felt as soft as butter, down to the door. A second before she had pressed the push-button to turn it on, the light in the hall went on. She heard the lift coming down. Heidemann stood under the light. With his right arm he supported himself on a small, dark-haired man – Dr Birnbaum. Heidemann turned his head towards her. There was no doubt any longer. That white face, old and at the same time shrunken as a child's, that nose which looked as if it had been sharpened by a file, both made things quite clear, apart from what Heidemann said reassuringly: 'I didn't feel quite well, Hanna. I've come home a bit early.'

She could not manage a reply, only a painful smile. Dr Birnbaum opened the lift door, said goodbye and wished them well, closed the lift, and left quickly and nervously. Hanna pressed the button and they went up. She fought down her worry and concern – neither her words nor her hands must betray that she knew what he wanted to hide from her. She did not scan his face anxiously but merely stood quietly beside him in the lift holding his feverish hand.

'Did I frighten you very much, my darling?'

In spite of all her self-control she kissed his pale cheek with that expression of effacement and absorption which is sometimes seen in very young lovers, when the headlight of a car suddenly lights up the darkness of a rustic bench. But, sharply, he wrenched his head away, the brim of his hat striking her on the face. 'Don't kiss me.'

Hanna stood rigid, her throat constricted, choked with unshed tears.

'It might be flu,' he said hastily. The lift rose slowly to the third floor and stopped with a jerk. Although she herself almost fell, she supported him getting out. His illness hung in him like a leper's bell and he was warding her off with it.

'Hannalein, will you come and help me?' His voice was feeble and sad. She ran to him, took his coat from him, followed him into the bedroom, and helped him undress and get into bed.

When he was lying quietly on his back, his head on the low pillow, the lamp burning at the bedside and Hanna sitting at the end of the bed, Heidemann felt all at once rescued and at peace. His thin hands lay still and brightly-lit on the sheet and his eyes sought Hanna's, who was looking at his hands with her head lowered.

'There it is, darling.'

That helped Hanna to lift her head and look at him. It was a glance which reached out like strong, kind hands, and not until they had embraced with that glance did Hanna say: 'I must know what it is. When I know, then it's ours; when you hide it, then it separates us.'

'It's the old thing, darling.'

Hanna gulped quickly. 'Your lungs?'

The lowering of his eyelids confirmed this and, although she had known it, it hit her like a blow. Her smile disappeared, her face turned pale and looked defeated. 'Is it dangerous?'

'It's hard to say. It may go away, it may return.'

'You've been overworking in the last few weeks. You must have a complete rest and get well again. Since you've had all the operating to do on your own you've been ruining your health.' The long sentences, the familiar thoughts calmed her wild anxiety. He shook his head; his eyes glittered, red patches burnt on his prominent cheek-bones.

'No, it's not the work, it's this catastrophe, this inhumanity.' His voice was loud and angry.

'Don't talk so much, darling.'

'It won't hurt me, Hannalein.' Heidemann smiled at her for a moment. He looked happy and almost well for a moment, but old and wasted at the same time. The fever had made his usually expressive features more animated than ever. 'Poor Birnbaum was the cause of it all.'

'I don't know whether I should allow you to talk.' Hanna laid her hand on his forehead.

'Who's the doctor here, madam?' If it were not for the feverish patches on his cheeks, which made his face gay and young, she might have been deceived, but even as she was looking happily at his cheerful smile, it changed. He frowned; his voice became angry and upset.

'I must tell you about it. I'll speak softly. This morning a young lad was brought in with dangerous stab wounds, a very young fellow, hardly twenty, Nazi. He was unconscious and had lost a lot of blood.'

The word blood sent shivers through her. 'And?'

'Dr Birnbaum was on duty. As usual he was frightfully over-excited, made everyone jumpy, but everything he did for the patient was quite correct. I was not on the ward. Everything I'm telling you now, I only heard about.' He licked his lips and continued, despite Hanna's anxious look: 'Birnbaum realises that he has to carry out a blood transfusion and sends for one of our donors, an unemployed man who lives locally. While Birnbaum is running hither and thither telling the nurses to hurry up, the lad being at death's door, the two brown shirts who had brought him in suddenly stop Birnbaum. They had been standing about all that time, their comments louder and louder. Wasn't this a municipal hospital, weren't there enough good German doctors? Then they attacked Birnbaum directly. They solemnly complained, on behalf of the wounded party-member, that he was going to be operated on by a Jewish doctor. Birnbaum was enraged, there was no time to be lost, he shouted, they had no right to give orders, if they didn't leave at once he would have them thrown out. The result was a disgusting storm of abuse, the patients became alarmed, the nurses ran out of the ward. Sister Mathilde, who's now on the surgical side, came in. Naturally, this was grist to her mill. A big argument. But you know her. And you realise that all this time the boy is lying on his stretcher and the volunteer is waiting in the operating theatre. Not until Birnbaum, quite beside himself, shouted that they were murderers and he'd make them responsible if the patient died, not until then did they allow Sister Mathilde to take them to the professor. And then, instead of throwing them out, the professor sent for me and asked me to take over the patient. I declined. He insisted. I refused. He accompanied me to the operating theatre. Birnbaum, white as chalk, was leaning against the wall. His strength had vanished. He could barely speak. "I think you had better do the operation, my friend." I felt terrible about it, but the condition of the patient was such that every further word threatened his life.' He took a breath and Hanna put her hand over his mouth. 'No more, my darling.'

'Let me speak, Hannalein! I did the transfusion. When it was over I lost my temper, insulted the professor in front of everyone, threw the two Nazis out of the hospital, and told Sister Mathilde what I thought of her – a real battle.'

Hanna, too upset to interrupt, gripped his hand even more tightly.

'Then something happened that was too grotesque, too indescribably comic. The donor, a Communist, had heard what had happened. He was having a meal and out he rushed, still chewing, and started to shout. A stinking shame, him giving his blood for that dirty bastard, the blood of a decent proletarian. The biggest swindle on earth. And he stood there, his arm bandaged, a plate with half a beefsteak in the other hand, shouting: "My blood gone into a Nazi, my blood in a Nazi!"' Heidemann laughed at the memory, but then went on in quiet anger. 'You know what upset me most?'

He stopped, exhausted, incapable of speaking all his thoughts at once, flushed by illness.

'After the war, you know, when we came home, I thought that what we had been through was finished, and wouldn't come back, that it had gone forever, like a fire that has destroyed part of the world. People were burnt-out and sad, but at one time it looked as if the country had changed, had become wise and more humane. I don't believe that any more. It wasn't true. Things went on smouldering. And now, slowly, it's creeping back from all sides, now voices that were silent for a while are making themselves heard again, terrible frozen trumpets blasting out appalling tunes. I'm sorry if I'm alarming you, I've got a fever. But while I stood there and shouted, the faces around me were grinning with delight at the spectacle of me losing my temper rather than them. And I couldn't make them understand that a hospital is unpolluted ground, that it's not enough just to wash and sterilise one's hands. Sister Mathilde's witch-like face, the coarse, stupid, scarred Nazis, the furious professor, Birnbaum all of a tremble, suddenly it was all ghastly, like a cloud of poison-gas hanging over the whole country, over the world. And in the middle of this gruesome vision everything went round and round and then I haemorrhaged.'

'A lot?' asked Hanna faintly.

'Enough,' answered Heidemann, calmer now and almost smiling. 'More than I took from the young Communist for the Nazi and which he wanted back.'

Suddenly the ironically tender smile was blown out like a candle. The colour left his cheeks; his nose looked very big and pointed; exhaustion descended on his eyes; only the fingers in Hanna's hand moved, gently, reassuringly. She leant her face against his hand and stroked it with her cheek. 'My darling.' It was quite still in the room; only the irrepressible, unstoppable rain beat on the window.

And then, from the next-door room where the child was sleeping, there was a sound, at first as if someone was groaning in a heavy dream, then the patter of bare feet on the lino. Hanna remembered that evening's incident which, a few hours ago, had seemed disturbing, significant and a real sorrow, and which was now as if it had happened weeks or months ago, so removed was it compared with the here and now. Anxiously, she looked at her dozing husband, but he had already opened his eyes. 'What's he doing?' he asked in a low voice. Whispering, she quickly related the incident with the man on the bridge.

'Probably the rain's woken him up and reminded him of it.'

'Heini.' He called his name softly, and immediately the noise in the next room stopped; light footsteps approached the door, which opened and the boy appeared. His hair was tousled and fell over the warm, sleepy face; he had put on one shoe, the other foot was bare. Under the blue dressing-gown, hurriedly pulled on, unbuttoned and askew, could be seen a white nightshirt with his naked chest showing through. His eyes were heavy with sleep and dazzled by the light; and at the same time defiant. But when they took in the room and his father lying in bed, something he had never seen before, since his father was always up and occupied with something or other, never prone, never so completely still, indeed he never imagined that he could be like that, the defiance in his eyes turned to fear and amazement.

'Were you going out, Heini?' Even the voice was different, did not come out of his mouth in the way it would from someone standing up, but was choked, as if coming from the bottom of a well.

'Are you ill?'

'Not very, only tired. Come here, my little one. But not too close.'

Again he turned his head away, because the child had approached, twisting round and covering his mouth; and again it seemed to Hanna more unbearable than anything else she had ever experienced. She pushed a stool towards the foot of the bed for the boy to sit on. He hesitated. A moment ago he had a definite purpose, he wanted to go out, but now it did not seem so terribly important.

'Well, where did you want to go?'

'To the bridge, Mother knows about it.' The incident assumed huge proportions.

'A man's standing there, you know, like a tree and he's in the rain.' The words tumbled over each other. 'I dreamt about him; I know he's still standing there and it's still raining terribly, and so I wanted to go to him.'

He fell silent, moistening his lips; for a moment the tip of his tongue was visible. 'One can't just leave him standing there, do you think?'

Heidemann and Hanna exchanged glances. The boy's face looked very grown-up. His fair eyebrows were puckered in a frown. He was talking to his father man to man.

'So you want to fetch him?'

'Yes.'

'And where will he sleep?'

'In the sitting-room, on the sofa.'

'And how long, do you think, ought he to stay here?' The child hesitated. 'A few days,' he replied.

'And then would he go back to the bridge? You would not have helped him at all, then.'

The child thought about it again.

'Perhaps he can sleep on the sofa always. Of course if there are guests then he can't go to bed. And when you're at home you'll disturb him. So perhaps we could push the sofa into my room.'

'Did you like the man on the bridge so much that you want to have him with you for ever?'

Momentarily a vision of the unshaven face, the low forehead, the sinister eyes appeared to the child. 'No,' he said slowly. 'I didn't like him at all.' And, with renewed strength and confidence: 'But he shouldn't stay in the rain.'

Heidemann's head tossed to and fro on the pillow. His face was so hollowed out with weariness that Hanna said firmly: 'You mustn't talk any more. Heini, Father's too ill today.'

The child looked up and saw the fear in her glance; crimson rose from his neck into his forehead, his whole face. His eyes filled with tears so that his father, his lips pressed together, said: 'Leave it, Hanna, it doesn't matter, I can sleep later.'

Hanna was paralysed. Sleep later. When? What did he mean? She listened with desperate attentiveness as Heidemann talked to the boy.

'If I get better . . .' Not, when I am better. Her heart stopped. What lay between the future and the conditional? His life and hers.

Heini and his father talked man to man. Their words were terse and unrevealing, black sign-posts in a landscape covered with snow. Underneath lay hidden valleys, meadows, and rivers.

'They must build houses for people to live in.'

'That's true, Heini.'

'I should like to build houses when I'm grown up. Is it very difficult?'

'It takes many years to learn it.'

Silence. Then the boy went on hesitantly. 'I'd like to be a doctor too. Can one be both?'

'Perhaps, if you work very hard.'

'I very much want to be a fireman as well, but that's probably too much, isn't it?' Heidemann avoided Hanna's glance and replied gravely: 'I think so.'

'Have you helped many people?'

'Not all I wanted to – not nearly enough.'

'If I work very hard and become an architect and a doctor and a fireman, will that be enough?'

'Certainly it will.'

The child looked at him searchingly. His feelings were hurt because for the first time during their talk his father

181

had not given an honest answer. Conscious of the unspoken reproach, Heidemann added: 'You'd need to be very strong and you'd require a thousand hands when you have only two.'

He raised himself up a little; the effort seemed enormous. The next question stayed unasked and Heini screwed up his face so as not to cry and pretended that his nose itched. 'Does everyone want to help?' he asked.

After a moment's hesitation Heidemann answered truthfully. 'No, not everyone.'

'You're ill because you've done too much helping.' This, for once, was not a question but a diagnosis, announced with triumph. The rain had quietened down; even when they were all silent it could barely be heard.

'I'll be like you,' declared Heini solemnly.

Heidemann found no answer to this. With his fine and utterly open face the boy suddenly looked so sensitive and delicate, so unequal to the times in which he was to grow up. For a moment Heidemann wished that he was different – robust, vigorous, crude.

Gripped by thoughts he could not grasp and by the distress behind them, the boy stood up. His cold, agitated hands seized the hot and restless ones plucking at the bedspread. 'Don't worry, everything will be all right.'

The adult self-confidence of this seemed to embrace everything he couldn't express, and although the phrase sounded so comic that Heidemann had to hide a smile behind his hand, there was so much earnestness, affection, and strength behind the words the boy had picked up that Heidemann was inexplicably calm and reassured.

'And now jump into bed! Or do you think we're going to talk all night?'

Casually, so as not to spoil things, Heini said good night to his parents, let Hanna kiss him, and went out in the remarkable costume he had arrived in, one foot bare and the other with his shoe on.

When he had quietly shut the door, a tear rolled down Hanna's cheek for the first time that evening. Neither said anything but there was great harmony between them. Anxiously Hanna's thoughts wandered through the future, but she was caught in its impenetrable undergrowth.

Heidemann stroked her hand. 'There's nothing in our sort of language which those who are luckier than us call praying for someone,' said Heidemann very softly.

'I understand that . . . so well.' Her voice was very quiet – and because there was an abyss of farewell and of surrender behind each word (although her entire being refused to acknowledge this) she whispered, with tearful eyes, the child's words: 'Everything will be all right.'

Then she stood up abruptly and went to the window in long, masculine strides, hands clasped behind her back. She stood quite still, without saying anything.

When, after a minute or two, she turned round, Heidemann was asleep, his face very peaceful and like his son's.

Hanna sat down and looked at him serenely. It seemed to her that this sleep was an amnesty which even death could not infringe, and that stillness covered him protectingly as snow does a landscape; a bolt of iron had been pushed between him and fate so that it could not reach him. She felt safe and was not afraid.

CHAPTER 18
CONNECTIONS

Samuel Hamburger sat in the room which had been allotted to him when, now that his eyesight was so bad, he had arrived a few weeks ago to live with his son. Days would often pass without his leaving this room. His son rarely ate at home; the boy had his meals with his governess; and his son's wife in her room. Only when guests came and the house was full of noise and talking was there any pretence at a happy family life. But he was excluded from such occasions on grounds of his ill-health. At first he insisted that he enjoyed company, that it would be a pleasure for him. Then, deeply ashamed, he had stopped his son from giving a reason. He knew what it was. He knew that, despite his new clothes, he would seem dowdy among all these rich people, would show himself up with his halting German. With some bitterness he realised that for them he was a ghost from the ghetto and a reproach to his son's conscience. In his old room he too had been rich, when his dream was still alive, and even richer when he was travelling towards it, squeezed for a day and a night between surly fellow-travellers in an overheated carriage; he had felt nothing but happiness during the long railway journey, the approach, the travelling towards his goal as if towards a mountain that grew ever larger.

But now he was poor, the weeks living in his son's house having destroyed his dreams of him. On the other hand, he himself was not destroyed, nor was he angry. He sat very still, his dim eyes almost closed, his yellow hands motionless on the table.

Noises could be heard above the quiet. From the nursery above him, a noisy voice which was not that of the grandson he adored; a tumbling about and a disturbance, things knocked down, wild boyish play. Footsteps in his son's study and, as clear to him as a sound, the silence in his daughter-in-law's room – no footstep or noise. The house felt like a prison with many cells, where everyone lived walled in by impenetrable loneliness, connected only by sounds that penetrated walls.

A footstep came along the corridor. His ears had not yet learned to replace his eyes, telling him who was coming to his room. It was not the child, who often came running to him, nor his son who looked in for a few minutes every day to ask how he was. It was probably one of the servants. Without turning his head he responded in a low voice to the knock; not till his visitor came in did his head jerk round in the direction of the door. 'Who is it?' he asked, excitement making him irritable. The answer did not come at once.

'It's me, Hilde.'

The old man stretched out his hand. In his intense effort to see the visitor's face his eyes filled with tears and failed him utterly. Her face was but a white empty circle, coming nearer, not decipherable. Into this white circle he attempted to fit the features he had stamped on his mind over the years from the photograph in his possession. He did not manage it.

A feverish hand was laid in his. Shyly he patted it with his finger-tips.

'It's nice of you to come, my child,' he said. In that moment she too spoke, hurriedly. 'How do you feel today?'

'And you, how are you yourself? Better?'

'Yes, better, thank you.' Her voice was as revealing as a face brought up close. He saw this as it really was: pale, the mouth half open, a restless look darting over everything and holding onto nothing. Her fingers moved in his, twisting and turning with the panic of someone walled in. He let go of them.

'Is the food all right for you, Papa?'

The unexpected question astonished him so much he obediently replied: 'Yes, my child.'

'And the bed?' she asked. 'Are there enough pillows?'

He still felt paralysed with surprise. And then said, 'Did you want to say something to me? Do you want anything?'

She made no reply. The words appeared not to reach her. He could not stop himself from stretching out his hand, gropingly; the space round him seemed so empty that he feared she had gone away, although that could not have happened without his hearing it. He touched her silk sleeve, but she twisted away from him.

'Are the servants helpful?' she asked.

Drops of sweat caused by agitation and fragility stood on the old man's forehead. Since the soul of a human being could not be taken to pieces like a watch, and the trifling cause of why it did not work be so easily discovered, it was difficult to know how to put things right, to give her help. He did not reply to Hilde's third pointless question but raised his head and said very gently:

'You have some worry or other, my child. Tell me about it. You wanted to unburden yourself. That is surely why you came.'

He waited, the palms of his hands turned upwards. There was no reply. The silk dress rustled a little.

'You are not happy, something worries you. Perhaps I can give you advice. An elderly person has a great deal of experience.'

He waited but again there was silence. He was talking to himself in an empty room where nothing echoed back. The woman next to him turned her head anxiously. The old man upset her. What did he want to know? Why was he asking her things? She had wanted to talk to someone, but words once spoken are like doors that bang shut behind you. You're trapped and things are only made worse.

Then her restless glance fell on the mirror which, stupidly enough, had been left in the blind man's room. She saw herself in it and began to tremble. Like a bird of prey the old man's troubled face thrust itself at her.

'I must go now,' she said.

The old man, who had been just about to speak, fell silent again; his final, kindest attempt to express himself went unsaid. It seemed as if the hollowness that was in her had caught him too in its net. He heard her steps go slowly and uncertainly to the door.

'Where are you going? Stay here, my child.'

She seemed to hesitate, but a noise from outside drove her on.

He went after her, not fumblingly as usual, but quickly and without stopping, and then stood for a second or two framed in the doorway like some tragic picture. He reflected that it was foolish to follow her; but nevertheless took a few hesitating steps into the passage before hearing her scurry away like a wild animal. Conscious of a very slight sound, he turned his head to one side. As the old man's glance met his, Hartung pulled back his heavy body, which had been leaning dangerously over the banisters, and advanced stiffly downstairs.

The meeting of the two men was for the first time openly antagonistic. Max Hartung felt his father had caught him out. And for the old man the way his son was behaving was the key to his wife's behaviour. This key was fear. Fear had sealed the lips that wanted to speak, fear had driven her through the house. And while he had been forgiving on his own account, his indignation at the injustice he believed the woman to be suffering rekindled his own unhappiness, inflaming his resentment.

Max Hartung was the first to speak. 'What was Hilde doing in your room?'

'Visiting me,' replied the old man coldly.

'What did she talk to you about?'

But his father, trembling with indignation, was not inclined to be cross-questioned. 'You keep a prisoner in the house, not a wife; fear of you has made her ill, fear of you will kill her.'

With a gesture Hartung warded off the words as being absurdly exaggerated. 'It's not quite as bad as all that,' he said ironically. 'So my wife has been complaining about me?'

The old man let his hands fall. And his angry voice became very low as, instead of replying to the remark, he said with closed eyes and between his teeth, unexpectedly: 'You are evil, my son.'

This sentence, which was spoken very softly by the unmoving lips, with no melodrama whatever and as if involuntarily, had a terrible effect on Hartung, penetrating through all his layers of self-love. But the shock changed abruptly into anger at the injustice done to him. How could the foolish old man know what it cost him to keep silent? Anyone else would have thrown her out, but he put her in the spare room, thus giving her no chance to justify herself. Was that wrong? Wasn't it his right to do that a thousand times over?

At this moment, when Hartung was close to breaking out in anger, there came a child's piercing scream, so loud that both men, fearing an accident, forgot their quarrel and rushed upstairs to the room from which came the cries of distress; groping his way up the banisters, galvanised by anxiety, the old man managed to reach the child's room not long after his son.

Little Harry lay doubled up on the blue linoleum, screaming. Kicking his legs in the air, he pressed his hands – covered with boxing gloves – to his stomach. In front of him, with a scarlet face, stood the victor, Franz Meissner, whose expression, with the arrival of the grown-ups, changed from triumph to uneasiness as he remembered his mother's warning him to behave properly when he visited such fine people. And now the coward was lying on the ground yelling and thereby inflicting on his visitor incalculable unpleasantness. Harry's swollen eyes had thrown a sideways glance, swimming in tears, at the witnesses of his injuries; and his sense of weakness made him intensify the bawling, which was both an accusation against the enemy and a claim for sympathy.

'What's the matter?' asked Hartung loudly, his glance passing from boy to boy and resting for a second on Franz

Meissner's red, healthy face lifted to him half shyly, half defiantly. This lad, whom he had seen waiting outside the bank a few days ago and whom he had invited merely to disconcert Meissner, this powerful, cheeky-looking lad had knocked his son down. Franz, seeking salvation in the lead he had over the blubbering Harry by being the first to report, answered clearly and without hesitation: 'We were boxing and I beat him and then he started to bellow.'

'He kicked me in the stomach,' sobbed Harry on the floor.

Franz felt himself completely alone, a stranger surrounded by three people who were related to each other and whom he had heard described by his father in far from flattering terms. He had to defend himself and felt entitled to any help he could get. 'It's not true,' he shouted. 'I beat him and he's lying.'

'You're lying,' said Harry, still sprawled on the floor. Unable to believe what Franz had said, his sobbing stopped. The thin, triangular face was stained with tears; there were drops from the big curved nose. He was so upset that the dark blue pupils in his short-sighted eyes wavered about, giving him a squint. This pathetic vision embittered Hartung all the more against the fate which had fulfilled his desire for a son but had then deprived him of the joy he might have had in him. Fury at what had happened went on smouldering and was building up to an explosion. However, it was possible that he would have come out in favour of his son and overruled the stranger had not his father come into the room and immediately gone over to the lad and tried to pacify him; he, spurred on by sympathy, cried even more heartrendingly.

Hartung was thus conscious of two distinct groups – the woebegone child with his lamenting grandfather, and little Meissner, standing alone, erect and vigorous, next to him. That turned the scales.

'Come here,' he ordered. His son did not obey at once, but clung to his grandfather's arm. More forcibly Hartung repeated the order. Only then did the boy let go of the arm which in any case could not protect him.

Franz Meissner felt safe enough by now to look with open scorn at the old man, who looked as if he had been cut out of the comic magazines his father read and laughed over. Then he glanced at Harry, the embodiment of grief, who, with sagging knees and hanging head, was walking towards his father's gigantic form.

'Stop howling,' said Hartung. 'A real boy does not make such a row over a little pain. You will now box another round with your friend and I will see that everything is fair and square.'

'No!'

'No?' Hartung stepped close to the boy, who had raised his head so high that the swimming eyes were looking not at him but at the ceiling. With his large head, slender little neck, long beak-like nose and thin tousled hair, he resembled some wretched fledgling fallen from the nest.

'I don't want to box any more, Papa,' he implored.

'Prove you are not a coward. Go on.'

Reluctantly the boy removed his gaze from the ceiling and looked into his father's angry face. 'No, Papa,' he repeated. 'It's not a game. It hurts a lot. I don't like the gloves either. I'd rather play with my train or my box of bricks.'

Hartung looked from Harry's puny hand to Franz Meissner's, a red broad-fingered boy's hand with prominent thumb-balls. 'Put your gloves on again,' he cried to Franz. 'Harry will box.' And taking his son by the shoulder he pushed him forward.

'No, Papa.'

'Go on!' Hartung said.

Harry straightened himself and took a breath. 'No, Papa.'

'I ask you for the last time, Harry. Will you do what I tell you?'

'Not boxing, Papa.'

'Very well then,' replied Hartung in a low voice, 'I will cure you of cowardice.' He seized the boy's hand. 'Come along.'

Harry let himself be dragged away without resistance, but at the door he suddenly understood what was about to happen, turned his feet in and planted himself firmly, terror in his contorted fingers and stiffened legs. 'Don't shut me up, don't shut me up, please don't.'

'Then do what I tell you.'

'No, Papa.'

There seemed no solution. Language had no further words. Hartung took another step to the door, dragging the boy's rigid body behind him. And now Harry's desperation led to the most extreme exhibition of despair, to a hysterical attempt at conciliation by doing the opposite. He banged his head against the door-frame, his hands convulsed, his face turning blue, his eyes glassy.

The old man had done his best to refrain from all inter-ference, since that would only make things worse for the boy. But now he could not control himself any longer. 'Leave him alone, you're making him ill,' he cried. But Hartung replied from between clenched teeth: 'Leave that to me, please.' Then, with both hands, he took hold of the screaming child and carried him out of the door, a struggling, kicking bundle.

On the stairs the crying abruptly stopped. Franz and the old man, suddenly left alone, could only hear Hartung's steps and voice. Ill at ease, Franz looked at the peculiar old man, like a raven in his black coat-tails, his head thrown back as he listened. Not until Harry's crying could be heard again, very low this time without yells or sobs, did he relax his efforts to listen and his thin hands hold his forehead. Franz was already hoping that the dismal figure would leave the room without remembering his presence, when the old man turned round and looked at him.

For a second Franz was abashed by the thoughtful glance in those unseeing eyes, which showed a bewildered sadness but no anger. Then the old man nodded, and for the first time in his life Franz saw a human being with a smile that was not because of happiness, but was there only because of the creases at the corners of his mouth, while his eyes retained their melancholy. With growing disquiet he endured this, till the old man, repeatedly nodding as though he found it quite natural, indeed only to be expected, that the small stranger should stand there as victor while his grandson wept outside, slowly left the room.

* * *

Once he had shut his son in the attic and locked his study door, Hartung sat quite still, his head in his hands. This hour at home was the first break in the tension he had been living in for weeks – a wild voyage past ever fresh rocks of scandal. One required unbelievable tenacity, superior intelligence, untiring energy. For what? For whom? He stopped thinking for a few moments and looked at the objects on his desk without being able to identify them. How he longed to rest, to relax, to be private like other men, to have something to come home to, something in which one could fully rejoice, like a child, like a human being.

The outline of a square white patch on the table became a letter, and this brought amusing memories of Adrian's intrigue and his dark plots with Meissner. Hartung was aware of every step they took, was privy to their conversations almost verbatim. Meissner, putting on a self-important air, watching Adrian with conspiratorial eyes, the fool! And yet he was obviously afraid that their venture might cost him his job and his livelihood. None the less, he would never have found the document if Hartung had not been so inexplicably careless as to put it in the drawer of his desk, which was continually wide open in front of Meissner when he brought in the post; even the most hopeless detective could not help but see the envelope and Meissner had fallen into the trap. Hartung could imagine the conversation between him and Adrian when Meissner triumphantly delivered the document, at the bottom of which Hartung had written in Adrian's sloping handwriting: Always at your service. The original, secure in Hartung's safe, was a list of the stock in Adrian's factory, with the figures inflated by Hartung in order to obtain capital, and it had an exaggerated importance in Adrian's eyes. Hartung had not so far used it, for the document performed its most important and immediate purpose by simply being where it was.

And here his train of thought ran into a fog of unhappiness. Words became meaningless, frightening signals, forming sentences like an indecipherable telegram. At this moment he heard footsteps approaching his door. The servant knocked.

'A lady, Herr Kommerzienrat.'

'What lady?'

'Frau Heidemann. She says it's urgent.'

The name meant nothing to Hartung, but since solitude had no charm, and only fifteen minutes had gone by out of the sixty which the boy had to stay in the attic, he unlocked the door. 'Show her in.'

Hanna had hastily pressed her hat down over her face, which looked very tired and sleepless and had been rapidly powdered and rouged. Hartung noticed the patch of powder on her right nostril, the lipstick that outlined the contours of the mouth but left the corners white, and the brown eyeshadow. He remembered having met her at a reception at the hospital.

'Won't you sit down, dear lady?'

Sitting down on the armchair, it seemed to Hanna as if she fell into it and might immediately go to sleep. She sat very upright and began to talk, quickly and softly, with clasped hands.

'Excuse me for dropping in on you like this, it's outrageous – we hardly know each other.' She put a hand up to her forehead, which had begun to ache badly. 'May I take off my hat?' She had done so before Hartung could answer.

'Won't you take off your coat as well?'

She shook her head. 'No, thank you.' The hair falling over her face made it even paler and thinner. Brushing it back, she unbuttoned her coat collar.

'It would be really quite shameless,' she began with a shy twisted smile, 'if it weren't so terribly important. Only for me, of course.'

The smile was now in her eyes which, wide open, were very clear and speckled with shining, golden lights. For the first time Hartung saw the great beauty of her face: it had little charm when impassive or uncertain but was now lit from within like a lamp.

'Won't you tell me what I can do for you, dear lady?'

'I'm afraid you'll ask me to leave,' said Hanna.

'I hardly think so.' Hartung spoke more gently than usual. He felt suddenly better, as if a glass of good wine had put an end to his dull wretchedness. 'You want to go on the stage, you need a patron, you'd like to know how to invest your money. Tell me . . .'

Hanna's lips tightened and her eyelids twitched. Hartung's noisy good cheer was startling to nerves which had not known peace or sleep for three weeks. To flirt or charm, yes, but it didn't seem possible to sit and listen to that rumbling laughter. This expedition, carefully planned and kept secret from Heidemann, was utter madness.

'Did I startle you?' asked Hartung. 'I'm a bad-mannered brute, you'll have heard that before now.'

Hanna shook her head. 'No, it's not that, only it's so hard to speak. I'm extremely tired, I haven't slept properly for so long.'

'One can see that,' said Hartung, and felt a burning curiosity to know more.

'My husband's very ill,' said Hanna. She put out her hand and touched his. Another step, and she would be prostituting herself completely, it was a tiny difference in degree. But her scruples had vanished. The bent fingers, in which she held her head, expressed the same undisguised suffering as her face.

'Do you love your husband very much?' asked Hartung. Hanna did not reply. She could not manage a single word; but she lowered her eyelids. Hartung was suddenly depressed. Why had this woman come? What was it all to do with him? Who had the right to rub salt into his wounds with such blatant happiness?

Her chin on her clasped hands, and concentrating on holding Hartung's attention with her steady gaze, she went on: 'Absolute rest and twelve months in mountain air would restore his health. We're poor. The hospital could only give him four weeks leave at the most. That's not enough. I know I have no right to come to you. What are our concerns to do with you? All the same I implore you, as I have never implored anyone, to help us.'

Hanna had stopped talking. With a slight feeling of giddiness she looked at the big, blurred face. Why was she doing this, exposing herself in front of a stranger? She could read the answer on his lips. I regret, dear lady, but at the moment I have enormous obligations. Or perhaps he wouldn't even bother to say that.

And at that moment Hartung was close to using the very words that Hanna had put into his mouth. Why should he help? Who did? Why make others happy when one's own happiness was irreparably ruined? He was not a fool, or a philanthropist. People were beasts of prey mutually devouring one another. Everything else was humbug. You are evil, my son. Which one of them was evil, you old dreamer? If he offered help, for no good reason, without any personal gain – would he still be evil? Could a man be a hard-hearted beast, an unkind father, a bad son, a brutal husband, who did that? And all at once he saw the possibility of showing that what had happened to him was undeserved misfortune – unhappy, perplexing fate – not guilt, not failure.

On the wings of this deed he could soar up away from the wretchedness of his personal life.

'How much do you need to live abroad for a year with your husband?'

Hanna, with an abrupt gesture, put both hands on her knees and bent forward till her head almost touched them, a gesture from her childhood.

'You want to . . . ? You're going to. . ? No!' Her eyes almost closed, she raised her face, her lashes keeping back the tears. For a moment her lips moved without forming a word. Then she said quickly: 'We would have enough from a small annuity to allow for twenty marks a day. I should have to leave the boy with my sister. It could be done for eight hundred marks.'

'You have a son?' asked Hartung.

Hanna nodded. 'Yes, he is almost eight.'

'And you don't want to take him with you?'

Hartung grew with his role. He adopted it wholeheartedly. He adored it.

'Want!' she said with a sigh.

'Listen.' Hartung stood up abruptly and moved towards her. He touched her hair. 'I don't do things by halves. You'll go to a decent hotel in a good resort for the tubercular. You'll take the child and find somewhere for him nearby. I'll give you a cheque at once for ten thousand marks. If you need more, write to me. Agreed?'

'Agreed?' Hanna jumped up. She walked over to him while he wrote out the cheque. 'I don't understand why you are doing this,' she said, very moved.

'I make only one condition.'

Hanna dropped her outstretched hand. So there was a condition at the very last moment! 'Yes?' she said heavily, looking past him.

Hartung laughed. 'Not that you must come to my villa naked beneath a fur coat, you silly girl.' He lingered for a few seconds on this agreeable thought, and then reluctantly abandoned it. 'I'd like you, when you're back, to let me know how your husband is and to bring your boy to meet mine. Do you accept that?'

Hanna had gone very red. 'Forgive me,' she said softly, and seized his hand. 'At this moment you must feel like Fate itself. I really can't say anything more. I can't thank you. It's all too much for me.'

He took Hanna's hands between both of his but let go of them at once. He wanted to play the part of the disinterested friend. Handing her her hat, which she put on without a glance in the mirror, he watched her take out her compact and powder her nose, again without looking at herself, and gave her the cheque she had almost left behind on the desk. Opening the door for her, he turned over her hand in its glove and kissed it on the palm between the first and second buttons. 'You have done me a great service. I must thank you. My very best wishes, dear lady!'

* * *

Old Hamburger had sat listening in his room for a long time before making up his mind to take the difficult and adventurous step of going to his grandson, up the steep attic steps he had never climbed before. He found the big key in the door and the boy huddled up behind a trunk – small, quite still, no longer crying. But in spite of his fear of the darkness creeping round him from all sides – groaning, creaking, sniggering, gagging him, clawing at his neck and stealing into his ears – Harry obstinately refused to leave before his father came to fetch him and had merely implored the old man to stay with him.

Side by side they sat on the large trunk, his hot hand lying peacefully in his grandfather's dry one. This contact, this closeness to another being, had annihilated his fear. Darkness lay quietly at their feet, like a dog.

There was a smell of dust, leather and wood. Harry felt a little giddy as if after an illness. It was a nice feeling. The old man had cheered him up and told him stories, but the more the boy's fear disappeared the harder it became for him to speak. Old Hamburger's thoughts, confused and adrift, searched among the memories of the past for an error. Somewhere or other a stitch had been dropped, a false step had been taken. And he could not work out how this had happened, despite all his efforts. Memories rushed in on him and became more and more indistinct instead of clearer, assailing him like objects which he could only just see. But perhaps his perplexity would be removed just as incomprehensibly as it had come, and some footprint be seen, some light.

The boy's hand lay warm and soft in his; for a moment all he wanted was that some miracle could safeguard the child.

'Did you lock up my Papa too when he was a boy?' asked Harry after a silence.

'No.'

'Why not?'

'There was no place to shut someone up in,' replied the old man hesitantly.

'A pity!' cried Harry passionately. His voice, still weak and hoarse from sobbing, became firmer. 'If you had locked him up then he would not have locked us up. Do you know what I shall do when I'm big?'

'No,' replied the old man almost soundlessly.

'When he's old and stays with me I'll shut him in the cellar.'

The old man trembled. He opened his eyes wide – they burned and had filled with tears. He saw nothing. Light was a long way off, and he was as afraid as the boy had been earlier.

* * *

201

When Hanna had gone, Hartung plunged headlong from the skies through which he had soared, back into the armchair at the desk. He felt the emptiness around him all the more acutely because of the contrast between Hanna and what he had lost. Again a knock on his door tore him away from his thoughts.

'Herr von Adrian wishes to see you, sir.' By the servant's tone Hartung knew that Adrian was standing near him.

He did not reply and did not open the door.

He would open it. He wanted this man to visit him. But let him stand there and taste the humiliation of not being admitted, of waiting like a dog to be whistled for or kicked.

Steadily Hartung walked to and fro. Then he slowly opened the door. 'Come in.'

The man was out of countenance. The one thing he possessed, his *savoir faire*, had suddenly been mislaid; even his clothes did not seem to fit.

For the moment it was Hartung who was the more powerful, as if the tables had turned. 'To what do I owe the honour of this second house-breaking, Herr Adrian?' he asked. But the sarcasm glanced off Adrian. It wasn't any longer a question of one's sensibilities, of shame and notions of honour, but another anxiety, a state of siege.

'Stop your nonsense, Hartung,' said Adrian unruffled. 'I couldn't find you anywhere, I have to talk to you.'

Hartung shrugged his shoulders. 'You know that these last few weeks I've been enjoying undeserved attention with people involving themselves with my financial affairs. That takes up a good deal of time.'

'I've been asked to report to the police tomorrow morning,' said Adrian slowly. 'Probably I'll be the next to be locked up, if all goes according to your plan.'

'That will depend on you.'

Adrian began to walk to and fro. Without looking at Hartung he threw out his questions. 'Why are you having me watched? Why am I being spied on? Do you want to send me to prison or what do you really want?'

Hartung laid his fingers together and waggled their tips. Thumbs and forefingers formed a heart. 'May I, since we both have very little time, return the question?'

Adrian approached Hartung in two strides. 'That's quite simple,' he said. 'I want the original document.'

'Really?' Hartung stopped playing with his fingers.

'I am accountable for what I have signed,' cried Adrian.

'True to your traditions you stand at my disposal.'

'But,' said Adrian, quietly and distinctly as though Hartung had not spoken, 'I don't stand for what has been extorted from me. I won't leave here without that document.'

'You have no sense of humour, Adrian,' said Hartung quietly. 'You do not understand that a man can have obsessions, things to which he clings for some reason or other. Not because he wants to use them, merely out of obsession. There's nothing that could make me give up the paper.'

'Nothing?' asked Adrian. He put his hand in his pocket as if to bring out a cigarette-case and, pulling out a pistol, stepped back half a pace and took aim. 'I have nothing to lose, Hartung, I too have my obsessions. That paper or I shall shoot you.'

'Well, well,' said Hartung, his mouth set.

'Blackmail for blackmail. I am waiting.'

But Hartung showed no fear whatsoever. His fat face didn't twitch as Adrian had expected nor did his big hands tremble. He spoke with genuine relief when he said: 'That's a good idea, Adrian, as a matter of fact I too have nothing to lose.'

Adrian hesitated. This unexpected turn of events confused him. This wasn't one of Hartung's tricks. Here was an unmistakeable willingness, a genuine desire to die, which made death a gift and turned the murderer into a friend. While Adrian stood bewildered before the part that had been allotted to him, throwing off the straightforward one of simple hatred, Hartung began to speak. 'Keep the revolver in your hand, although I shan't try to ring for anyone or telephone. If it's all the same to you, let's postpone the matter for a few moments. I'm conceited enough to want an epilogue.'

Adrian silently lowered his pistol.

'Your sentence would be very lenient, most likely a plain acquittal, since the motive is honour. One doesn't murder a money-lender, one metes out justice to him. Wait, Adrian. I'm not cheating you out of your fun. You can shoot because I helped you – in a way – but helped you none the less, and because I gave you an existence and work and because honour demands that you shall not owe anything to a man without it. And you can shoot because your honour demands the illusion that I've ruined you. You would see tomorrow that that wasn't true. If the facts had been properly checked they would still have tallied. Business morality isn't your aristocratic morality. That's why a bank's there, so as to direct money into another channel and obtain credits that will bring dead capital into circulation again. That's no more a fraud than high tide and low tide. The great knack is to have the high tide there, when there's an inspection.'

'Give me the document,' said Adrian almost imploringly. Although he was holding a pistol, he felt on the defensive against the unarmed man. He was desperately anxious to put an end to this ridiculous situation. But Hartung ignored the interruption.

'There is one thing for which you can't forgive me, Adrian.' He held the other's gaze firmly. 'Namely, your stealing from me. The second time it was a silly scrap of paper. You will find me a hostile witness if that is what you need to save your honour. Shoot me and you haven't stolen anything. Go on, I don't like being kept waiting.'

There was no meaning behind the words now. Hartung was already a long way from the dark water into which he had looked without terror. Every sentence was a leap from those depths, a leap into safety. But, once more, he was seduced by this flirtation with danger.

'Wait a minute. Perhaps you won't be acquitted. Perhaps you'll have bad luck and the jury will be riff-raff with no notions of honour. They'll find perhaps that you had an interest in my death, one not solely ethical.'

His life hung by a hair. The revolver that had become a foolish plaything became a weapon again. But a second before the other could fire, Hartung hurled the pistol from his enemy's hand with one sentence.

'Perhaps too,' he said slowly, 'the staff at Bucheneck, the maids and the farmhands, will be summoned as witnesses. May I offer you a cognac?'

Adrian put the pistol on the desk. It almost slipped out of his hand as he did so. Abruptly he had been thrust from the high drama of the revenger into the comedy of the burglar. No word was possible, no gesture came naturally. He turned to go.

Hartung got up. 'But wait. First of all, please take your pistol with you. Secondly, I'll give you the document. It doesn't amuse me any longer. As far as I am concerned, it has served its purpose.'

He went over to the safe in the wall, opened it and held out a sheet of paper to Adrian. He had to go up to him and put the sheet in his hand before he took it.

'Yes, yes, it's the original,' he said, as Adrian turned it over. There was no longer any satisfaction in having what he wanted. It was like a belated encounter with someone beloved or hated whom one has been looking for for years; once they are found their presence provides nothing more than surprised disappointment. He wanted to get out of this room without another glance, leave this house, this town, the world, wanted to be somewhere where no act of fate could bring him into contact with the man he left behind here.

Hartung stood at the table, leaning on his hands, and saw Adrian go as a man walks along streets in a dream, between motor cars tearing by, over bridges that break in two, below falling roofs. And he felt a melancholy anger at this flight along impassable streets and, at the same time, an acute unbearable pain which drove him to snatch Adrian back out of his dream into the realm of the actual, the yoke in which they both were harnessed.

'You haven't asked after my wife.'

Adrian, his hand on the door, stopped.

'She's not very well. We are expecting a child.'

We . . . Adrian grasped the handle but did not open the door. We . . . that word hammered them together like the two bars of a cross, made them into Siamese twins grown as one, attempting in mutual loathing to speed away in different directions, two whom nature had pitilessly riveted together by the spine, so that they could not destroy each other except as a pair.

Adrian stared at the wall as if he had just seen a ghostly hand writing something down in vanishing letters. And Hartung watched his sickeningly white face with that feeling of compassion the soldier has, looking on the boyish face of an enemy he has killed in battle, who goes to any lengths to bring back to the sorrowing mother the pictures and possessions of the dead, respectfully lowering his gaze before her weeping eyes and speaking with sincere warmth about her son's outstanding characteristics.

CHAPTER 19
HOUSE-MOVING

Anna Müller came down the stairs with her youngest boy, or rather behind him, because Karl slid down the banisters like lightning on the enormous patch on his trousers, while she, carrying a large basket of laundry, walked down carefully. Bending over the shaky banisters she cried warningly and not too loud: 'Karli, walk down.' But it was too late: just as the boy sprang to earth in a great curve, with a pleasant tingling in his legs and bottom beneath the fiery patch on his trousers, the caretaker's door opened and a scrawny woman shot out. With her thin fingers reaching for the boy and her greyish-black printed cotton dress, she looked like a hungry spider that had waited impatiently in a corner of the stuffy little room until the signal came that the prey was there.

'Caught you again, you brat! Ruining the banisters so that they fall on respectable people when they come downstairs. People might be killed by it, you little devil, you.'

Karl, in the clutches of those scraggy hands, twisted this way and that, trying to free himself, but couldn't do so because he wished at all costs to avoid the sight of that ugly, hairy face, whose hot breath passed over his cheeks like some malignant wind. 'Let go,' he growled angrily between clenched teeth, trying to dig an elbow into her stomach and kick her, all of which only redoubled her panting efforts to hold him tightly in her grip.

At that moment Anna Müller appeared on the bottom landing, flushed from her swift descent. 'Let the boy go, Frau Reuter.'

The woman turned her face, which was sallow in spite of the rage that consumed her. 'Someone has to keep an eye on the brat even if his own mother doesn't,' she hissed. And, having turned towards Anna, her fingers loosened their grip on the boy's wrist, which allowed him to free himself with a swift fencing stroke and take shelter behind his mother's skirt. The women eyed one another. Threateningly, the sharp angry bird-like head of the far taller Frau Reuter towered over Anna's round, ageing but childlike face.

'I can punish my children myself if it's necessary,' said Anna.

Frau Reuter sniggered. 'Oh yes, you can see how well they've been brought up. The girl knocks around with fellows and the boys are quite out of hand, street urchins.'

Anna's broad face flushed up to the roots of her hair. Gazing at the other's flat chest she said quietly and maliciously: 'What does a woman like you know about children?'

For a second Frau Reuter was speechless, as if the words had cut like a knife through her cotton dress and the flat board of her chest into her heart. She knew all about the barrenness of her body, the leanness of her limbs, the desolation of her heart, and like a wild beast could at that moment have happily torn the plump feminine flesh off the bones of her antagonist. Then, washing away shame and humiliation in a flood of abuse, she shouted, jeered, cursed, and accused simultaneously.

Anna, holding the boy's hand, went to the street-door, but Frau Reuter blocked her way, and it would have been impossible to escape had not her attention been distracted by something else.

From the courtyard came the noise of a cart stopping, the excited almost tearful voice of a woman with a foreign accent, a man's angrily abusive one and the chatter of children. Frau Reuter pushed the door open and ran out. The arrival of new tenants was an event which called for all her attention and left no spare energy for quarrels with Anna Müller.

In the yard stood a large cart harnessed to a bony horse, whose bridle was held by an angry little man. 'Either you pay me what we agreed now or you can carry your rubbish up yourself and I'll fetch the police.'

The woman was wearing a shabby blue velvet suit and high heels so worn-down that she stood lopsided and unsteady. Her head was lowered and she fumbled in her bag. 'That's all I have. You can fetch the rest . . .' – she hesitated a moment – 'in a day or two.'

'In a day or two!' growled the man, but putting the money in his pocket and letting go of the horse, he went up to the cart loaded with shabby furniture, untidy bundles, and trunks tied up with rope. In the midst of a heap of iron bedsteads three children sat on a mattress as if surrounded by railings, protected from the trunks and boxes by pillows – a girl and two younger boys, who followed events from their shelter with eager eyes.

Her arms folded, Frau Reuter, with a hostile sneer, stood and looked at the miserable furniture, the dark-haired children, the slovenly, agitated woman. Anna too, standing on the doorstep, watched the pitiable group and repeatedly glanced at the pale, wide-eyed girl sitting quietly between her fidgeting brothers; the delicacy and sadness in this face awoke in her the wild desire to carry the child away, to take her like a small bird in her large hands, warm her and protect her somewhere.

Between the disgruntled man and Frau Reuter an immediate contact was made. He unloaded a wardrobe, the door of which fell open as he put it down, the edge hitting him, and he swore. 'What can you expect of Poles?' Frau Reuter, coming closer to the cart, echoed him. 'Classy people we're getting! Not one piece of furniture that isn't broken, a piano and three children!'

The girl climbed down slowly; the smaller boy began to cry, and cried all the louder the more his mother, anxiously pressing her hand over his mouth, tried to calm him with an imitation pearl necklace she was wearing. Frau Reuter aired her indignation to the removal man. 'They oughtn't to be allowed in. They'll bring bugs into the house.'

The newcomer turned round, and tried and failed either to prevent the screaming child from smacking her face or to defend herself against Frau Reuter. Anna, seeing the flushed highly-strung face and brown curls, tried to remember where she had seen her before. Something about the full mouth, the mane of hair, was familiar. But she could not place her. Only when the dark eyes filled with tears and closed for a second, did she see that head on a stretcher, the long eyelashes above

211

the pallid cheeks, and the hair falling down; saw that face covering a tiny head with kisses. The little girl forlornly standing there with her thin naked legs and a too-short dress was about Karl's age. Nearly eight. And now certain about it and moved by the coincidence of this meeting, she went up to the gulping Lea with a smile so full of warmth and pleasure that her tears dried up and she gazed in astonishment at the stout woman with the peculiar black cloche hat.

'Don't you remember me?' asked Anna in her deep voice. 'Anna Müller is my name. We were in the same ward when we had the children.' And she put her arm round Karli and Manja so that the pair, who had been watching one another, shy and embarrassed, were suddenly pushed together, which was unexpected and funny. They both smiled.

'Oh, yes,' cried Lea, enraptured. 'I do remember.' And before her eyes appeared a picture too; a grey stiff little plait on each side of a broad face on a pillow, a face which, when it smiled, became young and showed the magnificent teeth she now saw before her. She remembered the evening when Manja had been laid on the stranger's breast.

'You were so good to us – I've never forgotten it! Do you live here too?'

'Yes, on the fourth floor,' said Anna.

'We're on the third.' Lea glanced at the house, grey and cold in spite of the sunshine; all at once it seemed a home, promising peace, even happiness – if there was such a thing.

'You'll be fine here,' said Anna. 'When you've unpacked, let me give you some coffee. And, if you ever need anything, come to me.'

She gave Lea her hand, patted the dirty tear-stained cheeks of the child in her arms, and the elder one on his woolly head, and looked round for Karli. He, however, was not beside her any more. He had climbed onto the cart with Manja, both of them kneeling before a box and trying to peer through the cracks and reach something inside it. Anna went up to them.

'I've got his ear,' rejoiced Manja. 'He's quite big and he used to squeak before when you pressed his stomach. Now he's too old for that. He's got one glass eye like the blind men who go in the streets with their dogs, you know.'

Karl nodded. 'Of course,' he said with curt manliness.

'My brother Munio scratched out his other. That's why I have to take care of the bear now.'

Karl stuck a finger through a crack in the box.

'Terrific,' he said. That was his big brother's favourite word when he wished to praise something as quite out of the ordinary.

Anna was amazed by the way the girl's face had changed, how lively and merry it was; and she had to laugh at the expression of ecstatic admiration in her son's bright blue eyes.

'Well, Karli, it seems to me you'd rather stay here and help unpack till I come back.'

The boy turned crimson. 'If you don't mind,' he said, his head a little to one side.

'Of course I don't mind. Help properly. I'll be back soon.' And, nodding to Lea again, she departed.

The man came back and lifted down two boxes from the cart. 'This is too much!' he muttered, going indoors bent double by the boxes on his back. Lea, nervous and doubtful again now that Anna's broad back had disappeared, grabbed – without putting down the child – an extremely full basket, from which a dented saucepan fell on the ground with a crash. Karli and Manja both bent to pick it up.

As if enchanted, little Munio stood behind the horse, whose tail thrashed restlessly to and fro. Longingly he stretched out his hand to this attractive black whip, and at once withdrew it, frightened by the slightest contact. Manja stroked Lea's sleeve and looked into her worried face. 'You just go upstairs, Mummie. Karli and I will look after things here, eh, Karli?'

'All right, Manja, perhaps I will.' The last word was questioning, as if she was waiting for an answer. Suddenly she said: 'Well, then,' and hurried into the house.

'She's very tired,' said Manja quickly, looking at Karli to see if he thought there was anything odd about her mother.

'Of course,' replied Karli. 'Moving is very tiring.' Then he got hold of a fully-laden bucket, far too heavy for him, and lifted it off the cart with his lips pressed tightly together, and a purple face.

'Good heavens, how strong you are,' said Manja.

'It's not at all heavy,' he said, breathlessly.

At this moment Manja's glance fell on her brother, whose hand was reaching out for the horse's tail with the clear intention of grabbing it. She pulled him away quickly. 'You mustn't do that. The horse might kick out, isn't that right, Karli?'

Proud to be consulted, he confirmed this. 'Yes, it can kick out.' And added: 'With all four hooves.'

Munio bawled. He wanted to tug at the horse's tail and he

was angry that Manja was talking to the strange boy and not him; he was only mollified when she asked him to help with the unloading. Carrying as much as they could they went into the house, panting with the effort. Manja had the wash-tub, Munio the scrubbing-board and the clothes-line, while Karli had made a pile of all the bed-clothes, which hid his round face up to his nose.

When the man had gone, threatening once more that he'd come back and inform the police if he didn't get his money, Lea knelt down before the half-opened boxes, taking something out of first one, then another. Despite her gloom, despite the depressing effect of the dirty walls and scratched floor, something like a party sprang up round her because of the children's happiness. Manja jumped and danced about and climbed delightedly on the upside-down chairs.

'A lovely house, a good house, a good lovely house. This is where my bed is going to be.' She ran to the corner and, with Karli following her spellbound, dragged the little iron bedstead to the window, lay down on the bare iron springs, and let her head fall back so that she saw the window from below as a blue square cut out of the sky. 'And when I go to sleep I'll be able to see the moon and one hundred and fifty thousand stars of pure, pure silver.' Springing up, she took Karli's head between her hands and showed him a big bright cloud hanging high above the roof.

'It's a swan, do you see, a swan!' And because he was looking in the opposite direction, she shouted excitedly: 'Don't you see? Don't you see the neck and the wings? There, now it's dissolving, now it's a mountain, a very high mountain.'

'With snow on it,' said Karli, his head still between her hands.

'Now it's a fan,' cried Manja.

'A ladder,' shouted Karli.

'Oh, it's lovely here, lovely here, lovely.' She let go of his head, ran away from the window, danced, turned a somersault and strutted towards the pile of washing like a cockerel, her thin little legs turned inwards, her mouth screwed up into a beak; with a haughty sideways movement of her head and shoulders she imitated it so exactly that the other children cried out with delight, even before she climbed onto the bed-clothes as though they were a dung-heap and uttered a deceptively natural cock-a-doodle-doo. Lea stopped in the middle of what she was doing and laughed too.

'She can do a pig and a cat as well,' shouted Munio.

'Do the cat!' yelled the smaller boy, 'do the cat!' And Manja, crouching down with her knees against her elbows, humped out her back, crept insinuatingly from one to the other, rubbed her head on the children's knees and on Lea's arm, purred, miaowed. There was so much noise and laughter, merriment and shouting, that Lea pressed her hands to her ears, frowned and suddenly looked tired and upset. The other children continued their noise, but Manja stopped imme-diately, going up to Lea and stroking her cheeks.

'We've made a terrible noise, haven't we, Mummie? Have you got a headache? Hadn't I better take the children away so you can unpack in peace?' she whispered, bending down. Lea nodded. Karli, who had followed Manja like a shadow while her two brothers were still rolling on the floor, said eagerly:

'I'll show you something, it's not far, a house that burnt down. There are only the walls left and you can see the whole town. I've made a cave there. There's also a cherry tree, wild cherries, but they're quite good. Do you want to come?'

Manja was enchanted. 'Oh, do let me, Mummie, we'll take the children and leave you in peace. Do say yes.' She pressed her face against Lea's cheek.

'But don't be long,' begged Lea. 'It's late.'

And Karli, quite the man and protector, declared: 'I'll look after the children.'

In spite of their loud objections, Manja washed her brothers' hands and faces, whispered to Lea that they would be back quite soon and, urged by Karli, they crept quietly downstairs. He was burning to show Manja his trick with the banisters, but for reasons of prudence postponed it.

They walked down a street of ugly houses and turned into a muddy path leading through fenced-in fields. At one point the barbed wire was trodden down and here they slipped through and stood among the old foundations of a house, which now looked like a wild garden: bricks piled on top of one another, broken bottles from which Manja carefully pulled her brothers away, and beautiful old trees. In front of them the ground fell away and they saw the river with its barges and factory chimneys, a sea of rooftops out of which church steeples towered and, over all, a great milky-blue evening sky.

On the slope overlooking this scene stood the wall, the last relic in the charred ground plan of the house. Manja stopped. Her eyes were large and brilliant; they seemed like pearls soaking up the light, holding and reflecting it. Her mouth was half open, her head back a little; the arched nostril of her slender nose twitched, she breathed deeply and with joy.

'And where is the cherry tree?' asked Munio.

Karli led the children to the little tree growing not far from the wall; in the highest branches hung very small greenish cherries in pairs.

'I've never seen them grow before,' said Manja, delighted.

'I've already picked the lower ones,' apologised Karli. 'If I had known you were coming I would have left them.' Then he showed them the cave he had constructed from stones and a bent stove-pipe, thus managing to divert the disappointed boys' attention. He climbed onto the wall with Manja; here one could sit as if on a broad stone bench looking down on the river. The sky turned purple and the sun, unequally divided by a factory chimney on the river bank, sank slowly and disappeared.

'I so much wanted it to fall in the river,' said Manja sadly.

'Next month,' Karli consoled her, 'it sets farther over there, towards that white house, and then it falls in the river and later still it disappears behind the timber-stack.'

'You know such a terrible lot,' said Manja. Karli did not contest this.

While the other two were gathering tin cans, stones and broken glass, the boy and girl talked about all the games they could play and things they could make here. A proper garden if they planted seeds and pips. And perhaps a hut of stones in which they could live later on, if they put in beds of straw and moss and nailed a few planks together for table and chairs.

'I couldn't do it by myself,' said Karli apologetically. 'My brothers and sisters are too old and I didn't want to show the wall to the other children I know. But you are different, I wanted to show you!' he said flushing and not looking at her. It was a declaration of love.

Karli's cheeks and Manja's hair were purple in the evening light, but they had forgotten the time and their promise to return soon. It was so pleasant, sitting there while the fields became darker and the trees bluer, talking about all they could do together now they were living in the same house and perhaps would be going to the same school and would have the same holidays. If the younger boy had not cut himself on the finger with a sardine tin and begun to cry when a little drop of blood oozed out, they would both have forgotten to go home. Now, torn from play and from her dreams, Manja sprang from the wall, soothed her brother and, alarmed because it was so late and already getting dark, left quickly with the children. She almost had to drag the little boy, who was suddenly frightened and tired. She didn't mind. She was happy. 'We'll come again tomorrow,' she said to Karli, 'and every evening till we're big.'

And Karli, going in front of her protectively to show the way, said joyfully and at the same time with the gravity of a promise: 'Every evening till we're big.'

Silently they went between the barbed-wire fences behind which lay the darkening fields and along streets where the houses were no longer ugly and glaring in the sunlight but looked into the darkness with bright windows like eyes. And it was wonderful to wander along without a word in the light glittering white on the roadway, as if along the Milky Way.

INTERLUDE
FIVE CHILDREN AND A WALL

At the wall where they had been meeting one another every Saturday and Wednesday evening for nearly four years, Karl, Franz, Harry and Heini were waiting for Manja, who was coming today for the last time: tomorrow she was moving with her mother and brothers to another town. Her father had sent for them because his business affairs were going so well.

Karl and Franz had been working since mid-afternoon to prepare a farewell party, planned as a great surprise for Manja. Round the tree trunks they had wound paper chains, hung red and green lanterns on the branches, worked out the different places from which rockets were to be fired and where the Bengal lights were to go off in three spots at once – the blue one in the subterranean hole which they had turned into a mysterious labyrinth, the green one beneath the oak tree from which hung the swing they had made, and the red one on the wall itself so as to make it look as if fire suddenly swept over it.

All this had been discussed often and at length and nothing now remained but to wait for the whistle by which Heini, keeping watch on the slope, would announce Manja's arrival. He had begged for this job, rather than setting off the fireworks, because he hoped to talk to Manja alone, if only for a moment. Harry had set out paper plates on top of the wall and had put the ice-cream wafers on them. If Manja did not come soon the ice-cream would have completely melted.

Karli took hold of an oak branch, pulled himself up by his two arms and, keeping a watchful eye on the paper chains decorating the tree, climbed up.

'Is she coming?' asked Harry from below. 'The ice-cream is melting.'

'No, can't see her yet. Shall I quickly go to her house and fetch her?'

'You must be able to hold out another five minutes,' jeered Franz. 'Do try. Then we can start the celebrations.' They were quiet for a few moments, the splendour of the coming festivity overwhelmed by its momentousness. It was a sad celebration, the winding up of something final, and none of them could picture the weeks, months and years that were to follow. Harry stood with his back to the others. His face was in the shadow of the swiftly falling darkness and his hands were over his eyes.

Karli turned his attention from these gloomy thoughts to a red lantern, lifted it down, wrapped the candle in a little strip of paper and bent the metal points of the holder closer together. 'If Manja isn't here in five minutes I'll go and fetch her,' he announced.

'Why you?' asked Franz.

'Why not? You wouldn't have known her at all without me.'

'I knew her before you. She'd had a meal with us at home.'

'In the kitchen,' interrupted Karl. 'And you didn't notice her. She wasn't classy enough for you.'

'Who knows?' was all Harry said. His thoughts had been distracted from the present, which faded away like some-thing in the past, while the past stood clearly before him, more real than his surroundings. The evening when he had come to the wall because Franz and Karl wanted some stamps and had promised to show him something marvellous in exchange. The thrashing he got because he didn't think the wall or the cave anything special and wouldn't hand over the stamps which were the fee for seeing them. Vicious blows. Both setting on him at the same time. And then all at once a clear indignant voice: 'Shame! Two against one.' Unexpectedly rescued, he had stood up, grabbed at his glasses and recognised the girl who sometimes had something to eat in the kitchen. His stuttering embarrassment and Manja's smile. 'We know one another,' words which made an old friend of him. Walking through the streets in the evening when Manja collected the laundry for Anna Müller. Chasing after the ice-cream man whose bell Harry had never taken any notice of before. The happiness when his pocket-money was enough for them all to have wafers. The streets being no longer just narrow passages between houses along which he was afraid to walk to the school where he didn't want to be and back to the home he didn't want to go to; they had become full of life, excitement, games.

'It'll be strange without Manja,' said Franz.

'Very,' agreed Karli.

Franz started tapping with the stone again as though he could smash the thoughts which pained him. What did the

223

others know? It was easy for them. But he had had to suffer because of his friendship with Manja. The Jewish kid – the Polish girl – how often had he had to hear that! He himself had once called Manja that to Karli, when he saw her for the first time in the school-yard, handing him the bread-and-butter he had forgotten through the railings. Franz hadn't known her then. How many beatings he had endured when he disappeared in the evenings and didn't say where he was going, for the wall was a secret no adult was allowed to share. But a beating could be shaken off like a dog shakes off fleas. Tomorrow, when Manja had gone, his father would thrash him – and what a thrashing – for disappearing from home at midday, even though he was taking him to a shooting-match that evening. Tomorrow the blows would hurt and tomorrow he would howl about them.

'I'm glad she's going to be all right, but I don't want her to become a real lady – ladies are awful,' said Karl. It was terrible, her going away, her not going to be there on the way to school in the morning or during afternoons in the courtyard and the street, her head bent over some task, sliding down the banisters faster than the porter's wife could swear, so much more than a sister – a comrade, a friend for more than three years. His Manja. They had come into the world in the same building, almost on the same day. He had found her and the wall too, and he had brought them all together; they had shown Franz the wall and Franz Harry and Harry Heini, and only then had they become friends, through Manja and the wall. Otherwise, girls were ninnies, giggling and howling for nothing. When she grew up he'd marry her.

'Why the devil doesn't she come?' he shouted. 'Heini! Are you still there? Can't you see anything yet?'

'No,' answered Heini's voice. 'But it's dark and I can't see very far.' He stood with his back to the river, leaning against the chestnut tree from which one could overlook the slope of the hill, the fields and a part of the street. Only a word here and there reached him from his friends. He wasn't listening and he didn't move. Now that he knew Manja was leaving he was not actually sad. It was inexplicable. It was just as if one had only one hand or eye. Manja was necessary to him, had grown up with him, here and for ever. However much he tried he could not imagine that this relationship could stop. Today Manja had gone to fetch rolls and milk and when she stood in front of the house with her large bag, hesitating because she could not invite Heini up into the confusion of packing in a dismantled flat, at that moment both children had felt the grief of parting very keenly. Heini saw Manja's eyes fill with tears and her head droop forward on her chest.

'It's nice that you are going to be with your father,' Heini had said in a low voice, 'and you won't have to worry about things any more.'

At this point Manja had looked round to make sure there was no one near enough to hear and, her distressed face very close to his, had whispered, 'I'll tell you something, Heini, that I haven't told anyone else. Meirowitz isn't my father. But no one in the world must know, only you.' Then she disappeared into the dark hallway.

Her secret filled him with the deepest anxiety. He couldn't understand it and didn't have anything to turn to for help. To draw on those details of natural science that he knew, to connect the union of sperm and egg with Manja's secret, was as irrelevant to him as the laws of geography. This was something quite separate. Manja's father was dead and the man who was supposed to be her father wasn't. But this disquieting and incomprehensible fact seemed to be connected with Manja's going away, with the business of a person who belonged to one suddenly vanishing into darkness.

'Now I'm going to go and get her,' shouted Karli. But just then Heini saw her coming towards the slope, waving her arms and leaping wildly. He almost forgot to whistle, then, giving a brief shrill warning, he ran towards her. Then the blue and green lights blazed up simultaneously, and a minute later the red, so that the familiar slope with its trees and fences was transformed into a marvellous dream landscape which had the magic of unknown gardens and the splendour of bright theatre wings. Meanwhile Manja leaped and danced in the three-coloured light, throwing up her arms, shouting, singing, and rejoicing.

'We're not going. I'm staying. I'm staying!'

'What?' bellowed Karli. His mouth was wide open, the tip of his tongue a light green like the illuminated round globe of his face.

'Hurrah!' shouted Harry and beat on his knee and swung his cap. In the reflection from the Bengal lights he appeared like some small furious devil. Franz was now lifting himself out of the cave where he had been tensely watching the light travelling through the labyrinth of passages, and the magical gleam of the wax stalactites which, over the years, had been made out of coloured candles and stuck on the roof.

'Good,' he said.

Heini said nothing. His heart was beating violently.

Manja danced. She was weightless, she flew. 'How lovely the fireworks are – wonderful! My father sent a letter instead of railway tickets. He says his business has gone bankrupt again. My mother cried, that's why I'm late. I'm horribly wicked but I'm so happy, tremendously happy.' In the dying glow of the red light she did a somersault in the meadow and the others followed suit. Suddenly the planned celebration was a real one, lit up by a thousand candles of delight. Karli on one side and Franz on the other began to light the lanterns they had stretched from tree to tree with such trouble. Now they had plenty of time, they didn't have to stretch out each moment. What they didn't say and do now they could say and do later, tomorrow, the day after, any time. It was marvellous. Now the globes and cylinders of the lanterns burnt above the covered table, glowing green, yellow, red, blue, white with many-coloured flower-patterns.

'Do you know what, boys, it's a farewell feast without farewell.'

They all felt the same. All five sat down on the wall, swinging their feet, and eating.

'I don't know what I should have done without the wall and you,' whispered Manja.

'One always finds someone or other,' growled Karli, embarrassed.

'We've still got some fireworks,' shouted Franz.

'I'm so happy, Manja. Do you know, I could not really believe it the whole time,' said Heini. Manja looked at him. Her long eyelashes were wet, her large eyes shone.

'It was so terrible when the letter came. I took it in and then, when we opened it – oh, Heini!'

Harry felt left out. 'Did you like the ice-cream?' he asked. 'I brought it all the way from home.'

Manja turned to him immediately. 'My favourite,' she said smiling at him, 'strawberry and vanilla.'

Just then a rocket went up and they stopped talking. It scattered in a golden shower, divided into sheaves and bundles of light.

'How lovely,' rejoiced Manja. 'How wonderful!'

'That's nothing,' shouted Franz. 'Wait for the next one.'

The next was even more beautiful. From the slender sheaf of fire, which flew straight as an arrow into the sky, red globes parted, whirled through the air, danced like flaming balloons, before they were extinguished, dissolved in purple tufts of radiance.

'Now comes the last one, it's the best of the lot,' cried Karli. 'It cost most, too.'

Heads thrown back, the children waited on the wall, while Karli and Franz whispered mysteriously. The whispering grew louder, they lit a couple of matches but nothing happened. The best rocket of all didn't go off.

'How annoying,' whispered Franz. 'It must have been damp. I'm going to ask for our money back,' he grumbled.

'It would have to be the best one,' complained Karli.

'It's not true,' Manja cried. 'I can see it.' And holding Karli's head between her hands as she had so often when she was showing him something only she could see, she began to speak quickly, emphatically, each word a spark of bright colour. 'It sails up like a great blue fountain. So blue! Hundreds of little blue rays spring from it; now they join and it's a large, enormously large, toothed star and in the middle a deep blue globe turning round. It makes you feel quite dizzy, it's turning like a top. Do you see? You see it, don't you? That's the best of the lot.' She looked up at the starry sky, head thrown very far back. Her voice grew quieter. 'It has left five stars up there.'

And the other four saw clearly above them the great W of Cassiopeia.

'Can you see it now?'

They had seen it and since the other two were just as extinguished as Manja's blue rocket there was no difference now between the one she had painted on the sky and the two previous, real ones. Hers in fact seemed more vivid and lasting because it had left behind the constellation which none of them had seen before. Each of the four boys would have liked to say something special to her but none could find the words. They were awkward and embarrassed by their affection for a girl who could stand there so simply with uplifted face and rejoice without shame, so that everything about her was filled with joy. And with a deep emotion against which Franz and Karli fought, while Harry savoured it and Heini abandoned himself to it, they felt what it meant that Manja was staying. The evenings on the wall, that island where they played, where they had their own language, a secret language meaningless to adults, like the mysterious counting-out verses with which their first games had begun, verses in which every word was a key-word with deep intimacy and hidden meaning for them.

Engele, Bengele, Sickerle, Sa,
Ripperte, Rapperte, Knoll.

Nonsense, mysterious and ancient nonsense, fascinating
gibberish. Children's games that grew up with them. 'Poor
Mary sits a-weeping.' Manja sat and combed her hair and held
her hands in front of her face. 'Poor Mary, why are you
weeping, weeping?'

'I'm weeping because I must die!' And then the wicked
brother Karl came and stabbed Mary in the heart. And Manja,
her hands pressed to her bosom, fell slowly from the stone to
the grass. How much sadness did Manja put into these foolish
children's verses, and how absorbed she was in every game!
How, when everyone was on the other side of the meadow and
one of them ran forward threateningly to catch them and
shouted, 'Who's afraid of the big black wolf?', how she cried,
'No one,' in her clear, strong voice, flung her hair back from
her forehead and flew past the wolf to the other end of the
meadow.

Life went on between these games. The children grew up.
It was a long time since they began to dig a hole in the earth
to see if there was a fire in the centre and to find the mysterious people called the Antipodeans, who lived on the other
side of the world. They had learned and experienced much
since they changed the maze into a stalactite cave and pretended the sandhill was Vesuvius. Adulthood attracted and
threatened them; already they were beginning to be told,
when they were arranging something, that they were too big
for this and that. But as long as there were two evenings a

week when they were free to do just what they wanted, to play and be together on their piece of land, then nothing else mattered.

'Can we play Red Indians?' asked Franz, 'or are we too old?'

'Of course we can,' said Manja joyfully, 'but with a real camp-fire.'

'Two fires!' cried Karli. 'A small one for the robbers and a large one for the chieftain's camp.'

Two big piles of dry twigs were heaped up and carefully lit according to the precepts of the *Wandervögel*; then, following the rules of the game, Heini sat down beside the chieftain's fire and, while he was eating with a Red Indian's appetite, Manja performed a harem dance. She let her hands swing loosely at the wrists, twisted herself like a snake, fearfully resisted something that came out of the sky, pushed away something crawling towards her, collapsed as if struck by an unexpected arrow, fell with outstretched arms and extended fingers before the chieftain, and lay there without moving. Karli and Franz had smeared their faces with burnt matches and had painted snakes and arrows on their arms, but instead of creeping off on all fours from their own fire they remained still on the spot. Not until Heini's cue came – 'You have danced very well, Leaping Spring' – did they creep soundlessly from their fire through the dark jungle near the unknown camp, just as the chieftain announced to his wife that he had to leave her immediately and could spare only Hassan to guard her. As soon as the chieftain clapped his hands Hassan-Harry appeared, a handkerchief tied round his head, and received the order to saddle the Arab mare. But it was not until

Manja-Leaping Spring gave the animal a lump of sugar on the palm of her hand that it really stood before them, snuffling with its warm lively mouth and stretching out its neck beneath the chieftain's caressing hand.

Then he could be seen swinging himself into the saddle and Leaping Spring running beside him, her long thin legs taking great strides until she couldn't go any farther but stood slender and bent, waving a weary hand and covering her face with her hands and sobbing only when the rider could no longer see her. The faithful Hassan succeeded in calming her down a little. It was he who now stroked her head and cheered her and finally prepared a bed for her by the fire, where, after many sighs, she fell asleep while Hassan kept watch. How much easier it was for Hassan to express the care and love which Harry was ashamed of showing. He was genuinely enraged when the two intruders threw themselves on him, and fought them off with all his might.

Then the robbers seized the chieftain's sleeping wife and dragged her through the jungle to their camp. With war-like yells she was bound to the stake. She endured this without complaint, but waited for death with bowed head while the villains discussed cannibalism.

'I'll eat her legs,' said Karli, noisily sharpening the knife on a stone.

'They're for me,' replied Franz.

'She's got two,' said his fellow-cannibal placatingly.

'What's left over will be pickled and put in the larder,' persisted Franz the robber.

'Red Indian larders?' jeered Karl, forgetting his part.

'I like the little toes best.' The cannibal conversation started up again.

'Me too,' replied Karl.

'I'll eat both, though,' shouted Franz. 'They're sweet as sugar.'

'One each,' bellowed Karl, adding a sentiment rare among cannibals, 'Equal Rights for All.'

The fight that followed was very convincing. It gave Hassan, who had been tied up, the chance to break free and fetch his master, Flying Spear, who arrived at exactly the right moment to knock down the villains and release his wife. While Manja was playing the scene of release like an actress in a provincial theatre, accentuating embrace and kiss, she whispered to Flying Spear so that the others couldn't hear: 'We're really too old for this now, aren't we?'

The fires had died down, the lanterns were out. They stamped the sparks out carefully. Only the lights from the river and the stars still shone faintly. In all of them a certain fatigue and sadness had arisen, a reaction to their game, an awareness of the real world.

Manja sat on the wall, with lowered head. The four boys watched her as she sat quite still, much more still than any one of them could ever have sat, her eyes closed. They felt the unrest and jealousy which lovers have when the beloved withdraws from them into sleep, seeing things from behind closed lids, excluding them. Manja was looking at a series of dark, confused, frightening images that put a stop to her happiness. Her mother, her brothers, life beginning again, the caretaker, the gas meter man, the debt collector, the bailiff's seals on the furniture, scolding mouths demanding what one hasn't got, toothless, snapping mouths like bad dreams.

A shudder passed through her. Heini seized her hand, divining the sort of picture she saw. 'Manja, don't you worry, we'll all help you.'

'We'll be together,' said Karli with great confidence. 'Then it'll be all right.'

'You can get money, Harry,' cried Franz. 'If your father doesn't give you any you just take it. He's a parasitic enemy of the people anyhow.' This was said in a friendly way and was so taken.

'You're staying here,' comforted Karl, 'and we'll exchange the rocket and have it for next time.'

Next time . . . And with the future suddenly not so overwhelming, Manja lifted her head and shook back her hair with the spirited gesture of a horse beginning to trot again. 'I'm stupid,' she cried, 'and a coward. I prayed and prayed that we shouldn't go and now we're not and suddenly I was anxious. Fear always starts here,' she said pointing to her stomach with a laugh. 'And stops here!' And she put her hands to her heart. 'But now it's gone, completely gone.'

A great calm fell on all five of them, the strength of being together. And in all of them there was the desire to confirm this, hold on to it, rule out the unknown.

'We'll take an oath,' said Manja. The boys agreed. All five stood solemnly on the wall. Manja thought: it should be a vow against death, like all oaths of love and pledges of faith, a promise that the present moment should last for ever and tomorrow never come. Like a commander-in-chief who, after a battle, receives the oath of loyalty to the colours, Manja stood, her thin arm lifted against the dark sky, with index and middle fingers spread out, a gesture of inspiring dignity that the four boys imitated.

'We swear,' Manja said in her high, singing voice, each of the boys repeating her words first alone and then together so that they turned them into a song, 'we swear that we shall never leave each other,' said Manja. 'We are not alone, there are five of us. We swear that we won't leave each other even when we are grown up, even if something happens, even if things are different, even if the grown-ups want us to.' She hesitated for a moment, looking for the words. 'We swear that we shall always help each other more than anyone else, that nothing, nothing, nothing shall change things, we swear . . .' she concluded softly in the foolish, eternal formula of all oaths, 'that everything will always be the same as it is now.'

'It must be signed and sealed!' cried Harry.

'In our blood,' suggested Franz.

'Or carved on the tree with a knife.'

But Manja shook her head. That wasn't the right way nor was it enough. Then her face lit up. She took a deep breath and could not say it straightaway. Then she cried out in passionate excitement: 'It's been done already!' And she pointed again to the constellation of Cassiopeia. But since the boys did not understand, she counted as though the heavens were a blackboard and as if the stars separated by infinite space were in reality only the dots forming a letter.

'One, two, three, four, five!' Her voice climbed up a triumphant scale. 'My star is the one in the middle. Heini, Karl, Manja, Harry, Franz. It's written in the heavens.'

The boys did not look at one another. The moment was so intense that they felt a little ashamed and almost said something stupid so that the others shouldn't notice their feelings.

'Everything's all right now,' said Manja with a little sigh.

Then, holding hands, they ran down the slope. Now that the future had been exorcised by a spell, they were able to shake hands in an adult, if slightly self-conscious way, as if nothing had happened, as if the evening had been like any other, and say matter-of-factly: 'Next Saturday, then.'

PART THREE

CHAPTER 20
MAGIC LANTERN

Women and children lined the streets. Torchlight flickered on their excited faces. With open mouths they sang and shouted, their raised hands glowing red in the torchlight. The music – hard, shrill, rhythmical – hammered into them. Men marching four abreast, the band in front. Youths with lean shining faces, in brown uniforms. And after them more figures, heads lifted to the light of torches, their faces scarred, rapt, red. Their black shadows marched beside them to the same music, monstrously magnified, silhouetted on the walls and over the crowd that stood as if bewitched.

The houses were only white walls; the windows were frames to hold the flags that fluttered out over the street. Nothing else mattered but what was happening in the street.

An old woman with a headscarf, from which her white hair fell onto her wrinkled, shining face, lifted up a small boy who was waving a flag with a swastika.

'Look, look,' she whispered.

Frau Reuter elbowed the people on either side of her. Let people go into the house if they wanted to! She had battled her way through to the first row, where the sparks from the pine torches flew into her face, and the smell of leather, puttees, and uniforms filled her nostrils. She was singing, drumming her fingers on her chest as if it were a shield. Every one of the marchers was a Siegfried walking through flames for her.

Heil!

From the first floor of a house a girl threw down flowers. She leant out as far as she could and when she ran out of flowers picked the leaves off a plant standing on the window-sill. She even threw down the stem and the little stick to which it was tied.

Heil!

The landlord from the beer-cellar on the corner stood in front of a broken window pane. He was waving a napkin, which turned into a flag in his excited hands. Suddenly he felt as if all the marching men were his customers. Barrels would be opened, beer foam in the glasses, money be slapped on the counter. New window panes instead of broken ones – the tide had turned, prosperity would come.

Heil!

The little boy dropped his swastika flag. As it fell to the ground it touched the old woman's callused hands.

'You'd throw the flag away would you, I'll give you . . .'

Her voice was high and rasping. She smacked the child on his head, three times, in time to the music.

An old man with an artificial leg banged it on the pavement in step with the marchers. It was as if he had got back the flesh-and-blood leg lost in the War. Once more he was marching in a column behind the drum. His toothless mouth was open.

'Heil!' he shouted. 'Heil!'

Anna Müller and her daughter were wedged in the crowd. Hede's face shone. She waved to the young man who was marching near the front. None of the other marchers mattered.

'Did you see him, Mother?'

'Yes,' said Anna. In the midst of all the waving hands and arms, fluttering handkerchiefs and flags, she alone was thoughtful, she alone was silent amongst the singing. 'It's like the outbreak of war,' she said.

Hede didn't hear. She was waving. Across the road, wedged between two pairs of legs, stood her brother Karli whistling on two fingers. His face was distorted with the effort, but his whistling was lost in the noise. He scowled at his sister.

The beating of drums, piercing yells, slogans in chorus, wind instruments, flags and boots, boots across the entire country. Had war broken out or were they celebrating some strange carnival? Men and women were torn out of their everyday lives into this tumult. The poor would be rich, the weak strong, dried-up women desirable, the blind would see, the lame walk. Everything would be different; now there was hope. They shouted and waved.

'Heil Hitler! Death to the Jews! Germany has woken up!'

Suddenly rubbish was thrown out of a window down onto the procession: egg-shells, tin cans, kitchen refuse. A jet of dirty brown water hissed on a marcher's torch and put it out. Rubbish fell onto collars, faces and caps. While those in front sang and marched on, the row that had been assaulted came to a standstill. Lifting an angry face, the man whose torch had been extinguished tried to identify the culprit. But the façade of the house gave nothing away. Some windows were closed and people peered down from others.

'Dirty dogs,' bellowed the next man in the column, wiping the filthy, greasy water off his collar. 'It came from up there, the third window along.'

'Enough talking,' bellowed the fourth in the row angrily. 'We need action.' He stretched out his right arm; it had no hand, only a black clenched prosthesis. And with his left hand he swung his torch so violently that the chain of little paper flags hanging low down caught fire and rushed in a sheaf of flames towards the house. Screaming, a few women drew back their heads. The man with the artificial hand dashed forward with his blazing torch.

'Burn them out,' he yelled. 'Burn out the whole gang of Red murderers.' His gaunt, sallow face was lit up between the torch and the mutilated arm. But his neighbours dragged him back. 'Discipline, comrade. Don't leave the column! We'll soon return.'

In step with the music, which was dying away, they march on with huge strides; only the torches, not so festive now but more like dangerous firebrands, threaten the grey house-fronts and the darkened windows with the reflections scurrying across them.

* * *

This night has no end. Time stands still and won't move on. It doesn't get lighter. No dawn comes. No day. Fragments of trampled flags lie in the street where the column marched the evening before. Dust-bins seem to be crouching in front of locked doors. Round them slink two thin dogs growling at each other.

The street is empty and dark, crushed and trodden down by boots, like a meadow where the trampled grass cannot straighten itself up again. Houses are grey, there is no light in any window; and yet they are not houses that sleep. Doors creak, voices whisper, half-strangled breathing sounds like the rusty needle of a sewing machine stitching thick cloth.

People lie cradling their pillows like embryos in the womb, the blankets pulled over their ears. They sit fully dressed on their beds, staring at the locked doors, starting at every sound. Husbands and wives lie next to each other in bed, hiding their fear from each other, pretending to be asleep, until their eyes meet the other's wakeful, frightened glance in the darkness. In breathless haste a man burns papers in his kitchen stove, his wife passing them to him in silence. He stuffs the piles into the flames and scatters the ashes with the poker. Only the sparks and glow of the hungry stove light up the kitchen.

It is a bad night for those not included in the celebrations, for those not in the beer-cellars among the dancing and laughing and drinking, for those who stay silent and stay awake.

Two dogs bark at each other ferociously but no one opens a window to chase them away. That night no one notices if their sleep is disturbed. No one heard anything that night. The night was deaf. Even when a shot rang out from the wood no one asked who was shooting.

When someone suddenly screams in the public gardens – no one has screamed. The sky is dark and starless. The night gropes slowly along like a blind man without a stick, making very little progress.

The dogs have run away, the wind softly stirs up scraps of paper and abandons them again. Stillness; and then suddenly singing in the street.

A happy troupe of dancers comes round the corner by the lamp. Two tall fellows in brown, with a small man in a shirt and no hat between them. They are arm in arm, in unison. Behind them someone lifts his legs up high and from time to time hacks at the back of the hatless man's knees, in accordance with a rhythm of his own. Those helpless legs are forced into a rhythm, as in a tango. Three of them are merry, their singing getting louder and louder. But the man in the middle does not join in. His face is sunk on his chest. All at once, underneath the lamp, he jumps forward as though trying to do a somersault, spreading his arms wide. But those on either side of him heave him up again. Just as children drag a nervous beginner with them onto the icerink, his two neighbours stop him from falling, pull him in a curve round the corner and disappear. A long merry slide to the woods.

No one moans. It's the wind. There's no blood on the bushes – it's red berries from last autumn. No murder's been carried out tonight because there's no one to name the murderers. No one is lying face downwards on the frozen ground. No one asks what is happening that night in all the streets, alleyways and remote woods throughout the country. It is a night without law. There is no crime because there is no witness, no outrage because no reprisal. The night shuts its ears, pretends to see nothing in the dark. Tomorrow does not come. Dawn does not come. There is no daylight.

* * *

'The day of reckoning has come, throughout the country there is a new dawn!'

The voice came loudly and clearly from the Meissners' new three-valve wireless set in the dining-room of the flat which they had moved into shortly after the night when the Reds in the flat at the front of the house did a flit across the border. Frieda stood on the balcony, bright sunshine playing on her arms, while she planted pansies at even intervals in the window boxes, the lovely green window boxes the enemy had left behind. Over the border with husband and child, under cover of darkness. Because Germany had woken up. That was why.

Frieda leant over the balcony as far as she could. She could read half the name of the dairy and see the door to the chemist's shop and everyone walking about below and everyone leaving the house and everyone entering it. Yellow and blue pansies alternately – or was it better to have blue pansies in one box and yellow in another? It would be neater, more systematic. With her thumb she pressed down the earth on both sides of the delicate little plants and watered them. A breeze played with her thin bun of hair and tugged at her skirt. Nowadays Frieda was able to enjoy sun and breeze without having to go out for them. Wind on her bare head and sun on her freckled arms.

'A new age is beginning,' said the threatening voice on the wireless, and Frieda felt this in her fingers touching the painted wood of the window boxes and in the warmth of the sun caressing her yellow scalp under her thin hair. The flat at the back had been dark so flowers wouldn't grow. They grew here. First pansies, then forget-me-nots, then begonias. A garden had suddenly been laid out round Frieda's life, a garland of colour and beauty. She could drink coffee in the open air as they used to in the country on Sundays; as in the days when the cherry trees were in blossom and Anton held her hand under the table.

Now the boxes were filled with the limp little plants. In a fortnight they would flower. Her hands clasped over her skinny chest, Frieda stood holding up her wrinkled face to the warm light. Suddenly she saw her former neighbour in the street below, looking up at her enviously with craning neck and popping eyes, just as Frieda, during all those years, had looked up at her antagonist's balcony, the one where she now stood as mistress. This gave her a deep and unfamiliar joy, like a gentle stab in the breast. Her eyes, with their thin, fair lashes, became damp, the tip of her tongue slid over her pale lips, and she clasped her hands together.

The voice on the wireless ended to thunderous applause. 'Much has been done, much remains to be done. But we are confident – because the man who has led us so far will lead us further. Heil Hitler!'

And Frieda stood, like an ecstatic saint in a Gothic church, her long nose lowered and thin arms bent like wings, dazzled by the radiance that had suddenly come into her life. A balcony with flowers growing on it! A balcony that was like a hand with which she could pick up everything going on in the street, that was like a wide-open eye following every movement. A balcony on which they could drink coffee. Full of emotion and gratitude she repeated, like an incantation, 'Heil Hitler!'

* * *

'Heil Hitler!' Leo Meirowitz said to the SA man who had come into his clothes shop. Why not? In order to survive you had to move with the times. With his head on one side, he waited while his customer came towards the counter and took a parcel out of his leather bag.

'I bought myself a suit here.'

'I remember,' said Meirowitz delightedly. 'A brown, casual suit with stripes on it, isn't that so? I remember these things.' He looked expectantly at the customer, but he did not reply, only opened the parcel and put down the suit, the one button left on the jacket clanging on the counter top. The trouser legs sprawled across it.

'The cloth was cheap.' He lifted up one of the legs. 'It's worn out at the knee.' Then he held up the waistcoat and pointed out the stained armhole. Meirowitz picked up the sleeve of the soiled suit and, rubbing it between his thumb and forefinger, examined it.

'What do you expect for 20 marks?' he asked sadly.

'I want to exchange the suit.'

'Exchange . . . it?' Meirowitz's mouth fell open. 'But you've been wearing it for three months. The suit is ruined.'

'I want to exchange it,' the man in the brown uniform repeated, and went over to where the casual suits were hanging. Meirowitz ran after him in a frenzy.

'But, Officer,' he stammered, 'you can't be serious.'

There was no answer. In front of him a broad, brown back pushed a grey suit, a brown one and then a dark one impatiently to one side and finally grabbed a blue one and took it out.

'I'll take this one.'

'That's not the same price,' said Meirowitz. 'That's the best suit I have, English cloth. It cost me 100 marks.'

'Someone like you should thank his lucky stars he's not being thrown out of here and into prison for fraud.' The blue suit hung over his arm like a drooping woman. The sight of it stabbed Meirowitz in the heart.

'But ...' he began, 'that is ...' He didn't finish his sentence. Suddenly a gesture from his customer made him aware of five men in brown walking slowly up and down the alleyway outside his shop. He understood.

'So, we have a deal,' said the visitor.

Meirowitz smiled. He went on smiling while he carefully packed up the blue suit.

'Come and see me again,' he said as the door closed. Then he sat down on the stool by the counter and wiped the sweat from his forehead.

'If I bought myself an undertaker's, people wouldn't die any more.' Then, when the footsteps had died away and he couldn't see anyone any more, he closed the shutters so that no one could come in. God help him, he might as well hang himself. This was the end. To be shutting up shop, keeping out customers in broad daylight, at eleven o'clock in the morning!

* * *

It was thirteen years since Anton Meissner had last been sent down the stairs of the firm of Gottlieb & Co. In those thirteen years he had not been back to the grey building. He had waited. Now he slowly opened the big wooden door; it squeaked on its hinges just as it used to do those mornings when he was late and crept in like a furtive schoolboy.

But today he did not wipe his worn-out shoes on the mat, but strode briskly across it in his gleaming army boots, that were tightly wrapped in puttees, and climbed the creaking wooden steps. The Meissner of the shabby trousers and full sample-case was left behind. Nothing now connected him with that miserable individual, whose every step on the stairs brought some fresh humiliation. He wasn't here as a private individual. He was on official business: he had been asked to conduct an investigation into the affairs of Gottlieb & Co. and to take proceedings against its owner on the basis of unanswerable evidence. Now it was Stormtroop Leader Meissner walking up those creaking stairs. There were still five steps and then a landing . . . But feet shod in military boots don't remember that rhythm.

He was going to be tough, make an example, put a stop to things! Break the tyranny of Finance-Capital! Burn out corruption! These were the words to whose rhythm his boots marched loudly and unhesitatingly. Suddenly, from the banisters, something sprang, something black and crouching, so indistinct and startling on the dark landing that Meissner stood rooted, his hand on his revolver, not even capable of firing blindly at it. Then with rage and relief he saw the stony, green pupils and realised it was the cat. He kicked at the wall and the animal hissed, sprang into the darkness, dashed down the stairs, crossed the yard, and disappeared into the safety of a doorway. That used to happen so often. It was a bad omen, the unexpected leap across his path by that damnable beast, and his self-confidence was dented; now he carried with him the old shabby Meissner, he with the frayed collar, who, when he slunk up the stairs, would stumble over the cat, and about whom the cat's owner complained to his boss, calling him an unfeeling monster without compassion for dumb animals; he to whom Herr Gottlieb, shaking his head and softly tapping on the table with his pencil, would say 'If I have to hear that once more, Herr Meissner . . .' Tap, tap, tap on the folder lined with green blotting-paper. The shrivelled yellow finger with its white nail . . .

And then all at once the downtrodden Meissner of the old days no longer slowed down the official tread of the police officer. The officer was winning. As if possessed by the cat, he rushed up the stairs so that the Meissner in uniform had trouble in following him. Now he could smell the fug of stale tobacco in the rooms upstairs and hear a typewriter and Rosenstock's voice dictating – his 'Hm . . . Have you got that, Fraülein?' – and could see the faded English prints in Gottlieb's room, the tear-off calendar, the red pencils he used for underlining, and the wrinkled, yellow neck between the pointed ends of his collar. And he wanted to spring blindly at it, as blindly as the cat had sprung into the darkness, dig every nail deeper and deeper into the dead twitching flesh, choke the whistling breath between his fingers, smash every window-pane in the stuffy room, fling the inkwell at the wall and the typewriter at the window, tear off all the days from the calendar at one go, right down to the papiermâché sheet after which there were no more days to come.

But the uniformed Meissner stopped him, grabbed him by the arm and shouted that he must pull himself together, behave decently, please, like an official, not like a slovenly civilian. This was not a question of revenge but of justice.

E. GOTTLIEB & CO. was written in large, imposing letters on the brass door-plate. It was new and shiny. Anton Meissner straightened his cap, dusted the collar of his uniform, and rang the bell.

* * *

'Open the door, Karli,' Anna Müller whispered. 'It's your father.'

The kitchen was nearly dark. Anna sat in the corner, Hede at the table, both of them busy with something which only provided an excuse for them not to wait about for hours – uncertain whether Müller was coming or would send a message – because for two days he had been in hiding and sleeping away from home. Karli pulled back the bolt, opened the door and bolted it again.

'Hello.'

Anna hastily pulled the curtains across. Only then did she touch him. 'No one's seen you?'

'No one.'

'Sit down,' she said in a low voice. 'Will you have something to eat?'

'If there is anything.'

'Let me, Mother, I'll see to it.' Hede jumped up, brushing

against her father's arm, her touch implying a request he could not grant.

'They're good at chasing one, your Nazi friends,' he growled.

Anna tugged at his sleeve and nodded towards the girl, who had gone to the fireplace and whose shoulders shook as she broke eggs into the pan.

'Oh, well,' he muttered, 'it's true anyway.' He had sat down. His face looked sallow and old. Karli, his hands on the table, stood looking at his father, who, in the last few days, had grown enormously in his esteem.

'Are you going to sleep here tonight?' he asked softly. Müller shook his head.

'I only want to eat and have a wash, then I'll go. The big ones aren't here?' Anna shook her head.

'I have a list of addresses for Hans.' As Hede put the plate of food in front of him, Müller covered the paper with his hand.

'I don't betray things,' screamed the girl, beginning to weep. It was the first loud sentence. Until then everything had been said in a rapid whisper.

'Be quiet, girl.' Anna put her hand over Hede's mouth. 'Pull yourself together. Give me the note, Father. I'll put it away.'

Müller gulped down his food and bit into the bread, eating like someone who didn't know when he would get his next meal.

'I can't come back any more,' he said in between bites. 'They caught Walter today.'

'How?' asked Karl breathlessly.

'They lay in wait for him in the street,' he answered, chewing rapidly.

'Where are you going?'

Again Müller hesitated for a moment, his eyes on his daughter, who was crying softly into her hands. Then he gave the name of the comrade.

'Karli, take some water into the bedroom.'

While the boy was filling the tin jug and letting the water overflow in his burning eagerness to help, Anna laid her hand on Müller's sleeve for a moment.

'When will you sleep in a proper bed again?' Müller shrugged his shoulders, trying to thank her and to smile at her.

Suddenly her heavy arm began to tremble on his. Müller lifted his head. Footsteps could be heard outside, through the splashing of the water in the next room.

'It's nothing,' whispered Hede, 'we've imagined things hundreds of times already.'

No one got up. Karli came in with the empty jug, saw the faces of the other three, rigid and alert, and ran to the window.

'Don't show yourself,' said Müller, barely audible. Without touching the curtains Karli looked out into the yard.

'They're there, are they?' asked Müller softly. The boy ran to him, yelling: 'Run down the back stairs, hide yourself, hide yourself!' He tugged at his father's arm. Still he did not get up, but only wondered calmly whether there was a chance of escaping. It was too late for the back stairs, they would be bound to be watched. Jump down from the window? A comrade had done that, and from the fourth floor. Müller had seen him afterwards. No, not that. Hide in the flat? You couldn't hide a notebook here, it was so small. Quietly Müller got up.

'Are the papers burnt, Anna?'

'Yes, the little ones have burnt everything,' said Anna tonelessly.

'You've got the addresses?'

She pointed to her breast, letting her hand remain there.

'It can't be anything much, Anna. They've no evidence against me. But I'd like to know who's fetched them now. No, I know, Hede, don't cry, little one.'

The next moments seemed endless. It would have been better for the door to have opened at once, Müller to have been led away and everything to be over, than sit still like that, choking with everything left unsaid, all the sentences which one could not finish now, nor for that matter begin either. Better to have it over, better a known horror now than waiting for the unknown.

And then everything happened too quickly. The blow on the door, a second's stillness, then someone outside shouting: 'Open up!' When they come in, two seize Müller, four ransack the flat, empty out drawers on the floor, pull pillows off the bed, rip mattresses to pieces, tear off loose tiles from the stove, saucepans from the cupboard. Everything was done systematically, swiftly, almost silently. And strangely enough in semi-darkness, since no one had thought to turn the light on.

Then, quite unexpectedly, Anna lit the lamp and turned nightmare into reality. She stood beside the table, her pale furrowed childish face lifted up, her arms planted on her hips.

'And now get out of here. I won't have my kitchen messed up like this. And leave my husband alone, he's done nothing.'

'Only thrown rubbish on our column when we marched through,' said the one kneeling in front of the chest without turning his head.

'No,' said Müller. 'I didn't.'

'Our windows don't even face the street,' shouted Hede in a shrill voice, and running suddenly from the stove she clutches at the man who is kneeling by the chest investigating a laundry basket and tugs at his sleeve with both hands, trying to pull him up. 'Look, you can see, our windows look on the yard, all of them.'

'We have witnesses,' he replied indifferently, not getting up.

'But the windows! Look at them for yourselves!'

'Be quiet,' cried Müller angrily, 'don't talk to them.' He stamped his foot. 'Can we go?'

'All in good time,' said the one holding him. Müller looked at Anna. 'Don't say anything, Mother, for my sake.'

The men had finished, all the household things were on the floor. But Müller was not going yet. Suddenly it seemed that much valuable time had been wasted, no decisions made, no farewells spoken. He turned his head towards Anna, unable to take her hand because his arms were gripped on each side. And for the first time a terrible fear seized her and she clasped his hands across those imprisoning arms. 'You'll be back in a few days?'

Müller nodded. He was gnawing his moustache and looking at the wife who all these years had been the one who didn't give in, the one on whom he had leaned. Now, as she stood before him with growing horror in her face, beginning to understand that frightful danger threatened him whether she spoke or was silent, whether he had done anything or not, Müller for once had the opportunity to make it easier for her. 'Of course,' he said, 'it's all a misunderstanding, Mother. It'll be cleared up in a few days, I expect.'

'A man who hasn't done anything, they can't . . .' she said like a child.

'No, no, of course they can't, Anna.' And by not speaking, not pressing her hands, he paid off the great debt he owed her. By denying there was anything unusual, not even kissing his wife, not even patting the boy on his head or saying a word of reconciliation to his daughter, by this he took the whole burden from her shoulders to his.

'Let's go!' The little band started to move off. Only Müller's legs, in their unpressed trousers and unpolished shoes, did not march in step with the others.

Just then the boy sprang out with the poker from behind the stove, where he had been standing all the time with burning eyes. Anna held him back. But he flailed about savagely.

'Let me go!' Anna's hands had him in a vicelike grip but her voice was quiet.

'Do you want to make things even worse for your father?' And she passed on the gift she had just received, the kind deception that was like a legacy. 'Father will be back in a few days. Put the poker down, we need that for the fire.'

The boy obeyed, letting himself be reassured and allowing his mother to put her arm round him because he realised she was unable to move. Now the light was on they could draw back the curtains. Anna, Hede and the boy stood at the window and saw the men going away, as they had come, across the yard. Only now Father was between them. And they saw the light in Frau Reuter's window and her inquisitive face and how one of the men touched his cap to her.

'Mother,' whispered the boy hoarsely, 'did you see that?'

She pressed his arm, standing without moving and looking at Müller crossing the yard towards the square, black gateway which swallowed him like a cavern, into the darkness.

* * *

'Light, turn on the light!' Hartung beat his fists against the door of his cell, but nobody heard.

He heard everything. Everything. It was only dark, not quiet. A darkness that was full of noise and voices. Footsteps, shrieks, curses, an indefinable clamour which seeped through the walls like moisture.

Days and weeks, weeks and hours had run into one another like inkstains on blotting paper, no longer separated from one another or measurable. He had been forgotten. No one knew these days who was dragged off to the barracks or where. Who was locked up somewhere, or why.

There was a sudden silence. No one moved. Where were they all? An order to march at night, the barracks empty. Why was no one cursing? Why did no one scream so that at least he could know someone was there beating someone? Anything but stillness.

There was the sound of a door, voices in the corridor. Good. One had to try and think about simple things, about a chair for example, an arm-chair, the square of the back that tapers off into the seat, about the triangles on cut glass and the star shining through the polished edge. But his thoughts were disjointed. One couldn't think in the dark, one couldn't grasp what was happening, remember landscapes, faces, tunes. Darkness, like a rat, devoured everything.

They were going to kill him. Not shoot him. He would be taken to a slaughterhouse like cattle. Some time or other, in one of the moments during these long days and nights, an axe would hiss onto his neck and between his head and body there would be a bleeding red gash. Like calves in a butcher's shop.

Why did nobody come, when one called them? Far better for the flap in the cell door to be opened, to have a face, eyes, nose, even if one only heard insults, was spat at.

Tapping started, three taps . . . two . . . stop . . . and again. This tapping on the wall was horrible. Frantic, pointless Morse signals. Who would understand them? What could the prisoners say to each other?

Light! Sunlight. Columns and spirals of yellow dust, glittering honey-coloured circles of light on the lawn. Diagonal evening light on a meadow, white moonlight, dazzling snow. Why didn't they invent spectacles against the dark? Electric light – press a metal switch and it streamed from every bulb. Candle flames, red fire flickering on the wall. Someone had switched off the entire switchboard of light, every single light was turned off at the mains.

It would come on again one more time, for that last moment between the cell and the courtyard. It would gleam on the lime-pit in which they would bury him. Everything ended, one couldn't defend oneself against it, paralysis came slowly and from everywhere, beginning at the tips of the toes, gripping his stomach . . . Cowardice/courage . . .

There were no heroes in the dark, battles had to be fought during the day. One fought one's enemies when one could see them. Other people made one brave, because no one wanted to be seen to be a coward in front of others. But not here, not alone. The ground gave way, his legs crumpled, he was dragged down, grew smaller and smaller. He could no longer shout or beat his fists on the door. In another second he would not be able to stretch out his hands, move his lips or know who he was. Slow extinction.

But, just when he was barely conscious, the cold light of a carbide lamp was brought in. Two men stood in the doorway; he stared at them without seeing them.

'Out!'

Hartung did not move till someone pushed him. He did not understand, either, that he was meant to go through a brilliantly lit room into a corridor, but simply moved like an automaton. The two men had burning lanterns instead of heads.

'Hurry up!' His legs took things in more quickly than his brain. They stumbled through the doorway and carried him, even though somewhat unsteadily, past a group in the corridor without his knocking into them. A man stood there who was smoking and spluttered an insult at him. Hartung appeared to take no notice of him.

'He's still stuffed to the guts, the sow, the food's good here.'

But the words went home. Sharp and exact, his sense of hearing delivered them to his brain; however, no wincing, no sign, betrayed that he had heard. Without raising his eyelids or relaxing his glassy stare he looked at the narrow corridor, much spat in, the besmeared walls, the electric bulbs on their primitive wiring, the faces of people who were hurrying along, cigarettes hanging from their mouths, wide-open with laughter. But light, whatever it shone on, was a blessing; walking, wherever one was going, better than being shut up alone with oneself.

From a side corridor a fresh group came out with a man who looked as if he had been torn down from the crucifix of a country church – his face revealed such exaggerated suffering, was so unreal in its pallor, the blood plastering the forehead looked painted on. For a moment Hartung's step faltered. The figure slowly crumpling by the wall was coming from the place to which he was being taken. Then the corridor turned to the left and the picture lay behind him.

But this was no painting. This was how he too would return. Yet the men went on laughing, talking, spitting as if the figure were a ghost that no one but Hartung could see. If only he was back in the cell, in the darkness protected by a door which did not open! He looked at the faces of the two men leading him. Oh, to be able to open their skulls so as to know what lay hidden behind that expressionless face! He was expecting to be blindfolded, to be pushed somewhere from behind, and trying not to go through the door first, turned round to the two who had stiffly come to a halt, stumbled forward and saw Adrian in a grey suit, cigarette in his mouth, his slim profile towards him. At the table near him was a stout man in uniform, the Iron Cross on his tunic. But he was only background, even though perhaps the commandant of the barracks. Adrian sat there looking at him, and Hartung saw himself with those eyes, his cheeks stubbly up to his eyebrows, a filthy gorilla behind whom the two warders grinned. He was being shown off before he was taken back to his cage. And once more that which wasn't happening, the darkness, even the rack, seemed better than that which was.

The conversation at the table broke off. The two looked at him, the commandant with a certain satisfaction that no brutal injuries were to be observed on the prisoner. Adrian's eye glided away, avoided Hartung's face, left his hands and lingered on his shoes, the only things which were the same. His voice was uncertain and flurried.

'I'm glad I've found you, Hartung; it wasn't easy. How are you?' The embarrassed voice jerked Hartung back into reality. Abruptly his emotions became perversely mischievous.

'Oh, thank you, thanks, dear Adrian, not too bad.' He saw the background, the Herr Kommandant, smile.

'Sit down.'

Hartung took the chair, pointed out by the arm with the swastika band. 'Many thanks.' The friendly commandant was probably going to offer him a cigar, a bath and the use of his lavatory.

'You are no longer under arrest,' said Adrian, without looking at him. 'I have stood guarantor for you.'

'That's very good of you.'

Conversation was not easy. Adrian held out his cigarette case. A smoke! A pleasure he had done without for a long time. In a gesture of uncontrollable greed his dirty fingers leaped forward. The case was pulled back slightly from his grasp, but he'd got a cigarette and with every puff took possession of his life.

'If it's agreeable to you, we can go.'

Oh, yes, very agreeable, exceedingly so.

Suddenly the room turned round, the electric light twirled, the faces were doubled, the walls collapsed. Only for a second, while he leaned against the chair-back.

'Do you have to fetch anything?' asked Adrian.

Hartung thought of that moment when his pocket book, watch, and overcoat were taken from him.

'I have all that's most important on me.'

Once again the friendly man next to Adrian appeared to smile. 'Will you confirm that for the sake of regulations?' And he pushed over a sheet of paper which Hartung read. He was being asked to say that he would vigorously deny all slanders. Without a moment's hesitation or the flourish of his signature being spoilt by any memories, he signed.

* * *

'KOMMERZIENRAT HARTUNG – IN GRATITUDE FOR HIS HELP.' The memorial plaque on the wall of the hospital hall already hung at a slant, for the young nurse on the ladder had removed three screws and thrown them into Sister Mathilde's apron pocket.

'There we are.'

'For twelve years that name has contaminated the hospital,' whispered Sister Mathilde. Hastily, as though her triumph might even now be stolen from her, she dragged the heavy plaque into the storeroom and leant it in a corner with its inscription against the wall. A gravestone without a name.

'And now let's hang the pictures.' With her short finger-nails she swiftly untied a brown cardboard box – even in the flurry of excitement she would not cut a piece of string – and took out ten framed portraits of Adolf Hitler. Rummaging in a tool-box for hammer and nails she gave her young colleague exact instructions, so that no one had to stay in the sick wards longer than necessary.

A few minutes later a loud hammering resounded round the calm of the hospital. Frightened, the patients sat up in bed or, if they were too weak, raised their heads anxiously. At the doors the nurses on duty stood and whispered. No one dared to criticise the all-powerful Sister.

From the large female ward she went into a room where there were only five beds, the dangerous cases. Fortunately she didn't have to use the hammer here because a print of a guardian angel bending over a child had, years ago, at the request of a patient, been hung over her bed and had remained there after her death. None of the women seemed to be worried when the angel disappeared and in its stead there appeared on the wall the stern face of the Führer. They were too far gone for that, engulfed by the coarse, yellowish-white sheets. As she was leaving Sister Mathilde noticed that the chart over bed No.3 was for some reason or other hanging crooked and set it right, so that the patient's name, 'Hedwig Müller', and the words 'veronal poisoning' were parallel with the top of the bed. But the sudden rustling over her head woke the sick girl from her light slumber. Opening her eyes she saw the stern, reproachful face in the portrait directly in front of her.

'Go away! go away!' She tried to sit up. Her emaciated, outstretched arm fell back on the sheets and she began to cry. The young nurse, who had already opened the door into the corridor, turned round in alarm and looked at Sister Mathilde with her round blue eyes.

'Shall I take the picture down?' she whispered. But Sister Mathilde shook her head.

'The girl's hysterical. She's always making scenes over this or that. She had a visitor today, a fine young man from the SA. She wouldn't see him. When he'd gone she cried.'

The patient's sobs became louder, she was even more upset.

'Stop crying,' Sister Mathilde said firmly, bringing the full force of her authority to bear, but the girl cried even harder.

'Go away, go away,' she said insistently.

Just then Heidemann, who had been talking to two students, came along the corridor and heard the noise through the open door. Coming into the room he saw at a glance what was happening.

'Take that picture away, Matron.'

'No, Herr Doktor.'

'You can see, it upsets the patient. It reminds her of the very thing she needs to forget in order to get well again. In her condition it is endangering her life. Be so kind as to take it away.'

'The girl's hysterical,' said the Sister angrily, not moving. There was a pause, during which the girl's quiet weeping could be heard. Then Heidemann said sharply, 'I was not aware that the nursing staff did the diagnosing here. Will you please do what I've said?'

Like fermenting wine forcing the cork out of a bottle, so the opposition she had held in check for years now tore down all barriers of self-control and obedience. Without bothering about the patients torn from the apathy of suffering by the increasing disturbance, she screamed:

'I'd rather have my hands cut off. And you, Herr Doktor, I warn you, you cannot give orders here. The authorities have been told. Your views are well known. We also know what sort of friends you have and on whose money you travelled to Switzerland.'

Heidemann took her arm. 'I don't think that the patients are interested in any of this,' he said quietly.

'This is a new era, whether you like it or not.'

Heidemann let her shout and, turning his back, took down the portrait. Sister Mathilde fell silent and stood still as if expecting a thunderbolt. The nostrils of her thin nose quivered. Her white lips had barely enough breath to be able to whisper:

'You'll be sorry for this.' Then she gripped the frightened young nurse's arm, fiercely, and dragged her outside.

With the portrait in his hand Heidemann left the room, which was now quite quiet, as if the noise had never happened at all rather than only just stopped. The patients were again wrapped up in themselves, each bed an island. Hede Müller, too, had her eyes closed, although her eyelids were still fluttering a little. Gently Heidemann opened the door and went, carrying the picture, to his room.

For the first time ever Ernst gave his full attention to this face, which was no longer an individual's face but typified a whole epoch. There could be no more turning away from this newcomer, no cheap irony. He had shirked reality for too long. While Sister Mathilde's ideal was becoming all-powerful, he had been passive. He thought of the students whose faces he saw every day in front of him at lectures, those eyes which challenged his or in some cases turned aside. The thousand anonymous faces, not the poor but the needy, women whom he had examined, the greedy, the disappointed, faces which he knew down to the lace over the thin breasts, the flinching when he put his ear down to listen to their heart.

The portrait was not of the hero of the oppressed, the ruthless and mighty leader of a victorious revolution, but of a narrow fanatic, the hero of the little man, the ideal of the mediocre. And yet, to hell with the insularity and over-valuation of the intellect which so undermines one that in the end a man cannot stand on his own two feet, not even on his big toes. They were not all raw young men or frustrated women, they were desperate, enthusiastic, starving people who could not wait any more, young people who had been promised a future. Had he forgotten what it was like to come home from the Front to a conquered country?

Searchingly, he looked at the face he had ignored for so long.

But something came between Heidemann and it. Another picture. Disturbingly at first, then in answer. He knew that face, knew it unforgettably. Sergeant-Major Bönicke in the same company as himself. Not the classic tyrant, the sadist of the comics – although in moments of fury they were as one. Bönicke spoke the language of the times. In his mouth its phrases and platitudes sounded like revelations. Homeland, Soil, Fatherland were concepts he had discovered. He had gathered a group of men round him who believed passionately in his inflammatory talk. Heidemann had never hated anyone as much as he hated Bönicke. He did nothing to provoke him but Bönicke felt himself observed and Heidemann's presence made him uneasy.

And then one quiet evening in the trenches Bönicke was speaking. Most of them listened to him. Only a few were reading or writing letters. The voice rumbled on, pouring out everything like hot broth. Heidemann had an irrepressible feeling of physical repulsion. It was dangerous to go outside, but at that moment he preferred to risk an enemy bullet rather than stay. He went over to the exit. All at once Bönicke stood before him, trembling all over.

'You'll stay here!'

'I want to smoke a cigarette.' For a moment he thought Bönicke would knock him down. 'We'll have a talk later,' came the wheezy voice behind Heidemann as he crept out. 'We'll have a talk later.'

And now it had come to this. Alfred Bönicke's voice was everywhere. All other sounds were silenced by it, his ideal had been declared correct. A perpetual barracks, a country in uniform, a nation standing to attention, levelled down to the lowest common denominator. He had gathered up the husks of ruined truths and had changed them into glittering goods for mass consumption.

Here in this hospital alone, in every ward, there lay people gashed as if torn by wild beasts, punished by the Bönickes because they were not Bönickes. On the charts over their beds stood no names; their illness was called 'Accident'. Nobody asked where they came from. When the night bell rang, some-one would be found lying in front of the door who had been brought by no one.

Alfred Bönicke was the stronger. A fist was stronger than a hand, the man who kicked stronger than the man who walked, the bullet stronger than the heart it pierced. His own impotence was vast, as vast as the collapse around him. It was a form of the disease that was killing Germany, which had as many diverse forms as tuberculosis. The one form – the galloping consumption, the megalomania, the lust for power of the Bönickes; the other – latent, insinuating, the wish to be subordinate; and the third – to bear no responsibility, which had infected himself and led to paralysis and numbness.

At the end of the War, when the soldiers mutinied and tore the officers' epaulets from their tunics, one didn't see Bönicke then; his face had vanished as if wiped from the face of the earth . . .

The guilt of inaction, the crime of letting things drift, weighed heavily on Heidemann's shoulders and placed him in a vacuum, in a place of enormous loneliness, the place between two Fronts, that strip of land under fire, riddled with shell holes, bounded by barbed wire, and belonging neither to friend nor foe – No Man's Land.

CHAPTER 21
THE BARREL-ORGAN

Manja stood with her brothers in a merry group of children who were gathered round a barrel-organ. A small monkey, shivering despite the sunshine and his little red jacket, pulled faces, put his thin fingers in his miserably twisted mouth and held out his hand for money. The children laughed and shouted with delight. Grown-ups, too, stopped and watched the little animal, who at one moment clapped his hands and bowed and at another scratched himself despairingly. He took a coin from a fat woman's hand, making her laugh so much that her breasts shook.

Feeling in her shopping bag Manja broke off a bit of bread; with his delicate hairy fingers the little monkey picked up the crumbs from her palm.

It was fun – the merry tune, the barrel-organ, the man with a blue heart tattooed on his hairy arm who was turning the handle. Every face was distinct in the strong light, which showed up every little wrinkle and line and patch of stubble.

Manja imagined the fat woman with the swinging breasts putting out her hand, with its broad gold ring, to her neighbour with a pipe between his teeth; and him putting out his hand to the girl with the blue ribbon in her hair beside him;

and they would dance and not let go of each other for as long as the barrel-organ played its cheerful song. Now Manja's brothers wanted bread to give to the monkey and the smaller one's plump little hands felt in her bag; but Manja held on to it.

'We must go home now.' The words sounded as though they were sung to the lilting rhythm.

'No, no!' the two boys screamed, and they were part of the tune as well.

'Then I'll go by myself and you come later.' Once more she stroked the little monkey with her finger and then went on down the street, smiling happily, the tune still playing in her head, her legs moving of their own accord as if they were walking along a picture-book street. A window-pane gleamed, a wall outlined against the sky looked as if it was made of sugar. Tall grass and a perfectly star-shaped daisy grew between the stones. The street, with its walls and gutters, was beautiful today, and it was lovely looking over the fences at the blackthorn in bloom.

She put her head back and looked up at the sky. It was like a blue balloon, a bell of silk muffling every sound. She could no longer hear the tune but it went on inside her head, merrier and more beautiful; other tunes came in waves, mingling together, little resonant bells of joy, the deep joy which has no reason and descends suddenly from the sky, weightless, like a leaf.

The dark stairs did not dim this joy and their creaking was less loud than the tune. As she put down her basket and took out the key – this was the day her mother went out cleaning and came home late – she heard Lea sobbing and talking. The tune stopped; her chest heaved like the barrel-organ and she went in to the reality of the untidy room. Lea crouched weeping on the unmade bed, her puffy face in her hands. The room smelt of brandy and unaired sheets.

Manja's legs stopped dancing. She went over to the table, took away the brandy bottle and opened the window. There was a patch of sunshine on the floor but it looked like a puddle of broken eggs. Then she went over to her mother.

'Has something happened, Maminka?'

Lea looked at her, her head a little to one side, as if she had first to make sure who was talking to her. She had stopped crying.

'Fat Jewish sow he called me.'

'Who?'

'That scoundrel Hammelmann.'

He was the owner of the bar where Lea cleaned twice a week. Manja tried to recapture the tune. She thought about the barrel-organ and the pathetic fingers of the little monkey, but they were a long way away.

'Am I fat, sweetheart?' began Lea again.

'No, Mummie,' said Manja softly. She lowered her head and stepped back to avoid her mother's breath. She began to make the bed, smoothing the sheet and shaking out the blanket, while Lea talked.

'I used to be exactly right, he couldn't have enough of me. And who do I do it all for? For whose sake do I allow that swine near me? One's children don't thank one. He didn't even pay me. He said he'd chuck me downstairs.'

Her mumbling became incomprehensible. Manja made her brothers' beds. Everything was dreamlike again, but a heavy, evil dream. Her mother did not know what she was saying when she was like this, she spoke like someone asleep, who babbles secrets which he knows nothing about when he's awake. One oughtn't to listen. They were not real words, meant for her and spoken to her: they were strange, ugly words from a nightmare.

'Men are all bad, they always leave you on your own, completely alone, even your father. Come here,' she said, 'you mustn't leave me on my own as well.'

'I'll make you some coffee,' Manja said quietly. She had put water on the gas cooker.

'I don't want any coffee.'

Manja pulled off Lea's patent leather shoes and made her lie down so that her head lay on the pillow; then lifted first one leg, then the other on to the bed. Lea did not stir. She seemed to like lying down; she even took the cup obediently and swallowed the hot, weak coffee. Then she lay quite still while Manja dipped a flannel in water, and allowed the child to wash her face and put the wet cloth over her forehead. 'I'm no mother to you,' she said tenderly. 'I know I'm not much use to you, but if Hammelmann hadn't got me used to the brandy . . .' Her voice grew fainter, and the room felt unreal to Manja, as did the window, the scratched door, the bed, her mother, herself. Her voice seemed to come out of the walls and clouds:

'He said you would walk on marble and eat off silver but it hasn't been like that, I don't know why.' Lea fell silent, her eyes were closed and Manja thought she had gone to sleep. But suddenly her lips moved, her eyes opened, and to a strangely primitive tune she sang:

Who dances with the lame?
Who walks with the blind?
Who sings with the dumb?
Where can we him find?

Manja seized Lea's hand. 'Maminka, what song is that?'

'Don't know any more,' mumbled Lea, holding the child's hand firmly between hers. 'You're not angry with me?' she pleaded, half asleep. 'You won't go away, will you? I'm not a fat Jewish sow, am I?'

'No, of course not,' said Manja tenderly. The song went on inside her head, reawakening other tunes, louder than them all, melancholy and beautiful. It united the gay barrel-organ tune with what had followed it; it joined the happy and the dark dreams into a whole. She stroked Lea's hair and hands, no longer repelled. She looked at her face kindly and intently, noticing the sagging cheeks, the sharp furrow from the nose to the corners of the drooping mouth, down to the double chin, the swollen twitching eyelids, the low forehead. She was not surprised that beneath this ruined face she could make out another, smaller and more delicate, similar to that of her brothers when they were asleep, but more beautiful and finer, the face of a little sleeping girl.

In the silence, in which nothing could be heard except Lea's quiet breathing, Manja heard her barrel-organ song, not in a dream but in reality, and she knew that the man with the

monkey had come into the street surrounded by children and
that her brothers were running behind him, that the monkey
was doing his comic leaps and that the sky was blue as a
bell of silk. She saw everything as though she stood in the
centre of it all.

The dark and the bright tunes flowed into one another. Joy
slowly rose within her, bringing life into her body, moistening
her dry lips. It was not merely a dream happiness but the
amazing joy one has when the heart of reality is felt beating
beneath one's hand.

* * *

That same evening Manja waited on the bridge for her friend
Karl. As if she was part of the railings, she sat with her arms
hooked through them, high above the river running silently
below. Circles of light swirled on the water, rainbow coloured
from the oil of the boiler factory opposite. Nearby was a flat-
bottomed boat, roofed on one side like a small hut; light
shone from a round window where a large flower-pot with a
little flower stood darkly outlined. On a rope that went
diagonally across the boat hung a white petticoat and two
pairs of knickers. Blown up by the wind, they looked like a
headless lady trying to jump over a rope with her children.
Manja imagined to herself that she lived there with her
mother and brothers, watering the pot in the window and
hanging up the washing in the wind, while the tree-lined
shore with its villages and meadows drifted slowly past, until
they came to the sea which she only knew from pictures and
thought of as the sky with boats on it. But in the midst of

visions of large seals with funny wet beards was the face of Herr Hammelmann saying 'fat Jewish sow' to her mother, and there was no sense at all in having travelled so far if suddenly, amidst seals and dolphins, there arose Hammelmann's face with its wet snout and protruding moustache. With that snout he had kissed her mother once, a long time ago, when he came for coffee and brought the children sweets. That was why that snout had the right to insult her mother and she could do nothing but weep about it . . .

Karli arrived. Manja heard his footsteps and turned her head to him, anxious to hear the news he brought. He had been to a Nazi barracks to ask about his father.

'Is he there?' she asked.

'No.' Karli sat down beside her at the railings. 'Hede's boyfriend was on guard.'

Manja nodded. Her thin face was feebly lit by the arc-lamp in the yard of the boiler factory.

'We could only talk for a moment, he says my father isn't there.'

Both were silent for a moment, listening to the water beating on the pillars of the bridge.

'He's going to fetch Hede from the hospital in his car the day after tomorrow.'

'What if she doesn't want to see him?' cried Manja.

'It would be a pity because it's such a good car,' said Karli with a sigh. 'I'm to let him know tomorrow.'

'Was he sad?' she asked.

'Sad?' Karli scratched himself behind his ear. 'Why should he be . . . oh, about Hede. He looked the same as usual.'

'Grown-ups often don't show it,' said Manja.

'No, that's true. My mother doesn't show anything either. Today a note came from my big brother asking her to send him his suit. Mother was to put it in a laundry basket and wait at the street corner. A chap fetched it but he didn't say anything. Not how he is or where. Then we went back home with the basket and when she thought I wasn't watching she looked like . . . like. . . .'

'Like she was crying inside,' said Manja.

'Yes, just like that. How did you know?'

Instead of answering she said, 'I like your mother very much.'

Karli felt the conversation was taking a turn which was a bit too much for him. 'Let's walk up and down the bank for a while and then home,' he suggested. 'You can't talk properly here.'

Manja looked across the river at the dark bushes and the great plane trees on the bank, the boat with its bright window and the dimly-lit factory. 'It's nice up here,' she said. 'When the river's so still it looks like a street.'

'If you'd rather stay . . .' But she had already got up. 'Is something wrong?' asked Karli. He did not often notice when something was the matter with people.

'Oh no,' said Manja hurriedly.

'Something to do with your mother again? The Reuter woman was gossiping downstairs.'

'You know the way she talks. One day she'll fly through the roof on a broomstick, because she's a witch,' cried Manja.

'She can't look me in the eye at all,' said Karli. 'When

Mother goes by she hides herself; sometimes she says good day though and grins. She never used to do that.'

They walked along the narrow path on the bank, parallel with the street. It was dark and smelt of water. Only when a tram or car went past up above did a shaft of light spring across their path like a cat. Manja was silent. It depressed her that she had lied to her friend and that he knew it.

'Karli.' She stopped and took hold of his arm.

'Yes?' He bent his round head to her. In the gleam of a car headlamp they each saw the other's face.

'Do you want to say something?'

'I'm fonder of you than of my brothers, Karli. But you mustn't tell them.'

'And I . . . and I . . .' cried Karli. He choked with eagerness. 'I'm fonder of you than of anybody, even my mother and father.' Suddenly, without having meant to, he bent forward and kissed her. In the light from the street lamp Manja saw his plump mouth and it reminded her painfully of Herr Hammelmann's snout and all that had distressed her the whole day. She turned her head away quickly, knocking her chin against Karli's nose.

'Ow,' he said crossly, rubbing his slightly turned-up nose back and forth with his fingers.

'If you don't want me, I can . . . I can . . .' Manja could hear him furiously tearing at the twigs as he went by and letting them fly back.

'Karli.'

He kept his back turned to her and did not answer.

'Will you always be my friend?' she asked hurriedly.

Karli half turned his head. He let go of the twigs and forgot about his nose.

'Won't you desert me one day because I'm a fat . . .' It was hard not to say the three words which buzzed about inside her. 'Because I'm Jewish?'

'You must be mad. I'm a freethinker.'

The pain in his nose wasn't so bad now, it was almost pleasant once he knew why Manja had turned her head away. 'When we're grown-up we'll get married, we've agreed.' He put his arm round her and led her up the embankment. 'Of course, you won't get married in a wedding dress. My father says that's bourgeois. Or do you want to?'

'No,' Manja reassured him. 'That's quite unimportant.' Though the only thing she could imagine clearly was a wonderful white dress with a train.

'I'll be a gardener or a pilot and we'll have a house in the country.'

'With a garden?' asked Manja, imagining the strange splendour of houses hidden between the trees.

'What d'you think, if I'm a gardener?'

'And it won't just be for vegetables?'

'Whatever you like. Flowers, trees, fruit.'

'Peaches on the wall!' shouted Manja, 'and a border with flowers growing really high along it.'

'Do you like chickens?' asked Karli.

'When they're very small and like pieces of cottonwool with legs I love them. The big ones look too much like Frau Reuter.'

Karli laughed. But with Frau Reuter's name Manja had destroyed their house. It no longer stood there as if they only had to go through the sunny garden to get to it. All of a sudden it was a castle in the air.

Karli too had returned from his excursion into the future. The bubble had burst, pricked by Frau Reuter's name. 'We'll have to see about all that, but I'll always look after you and see no one hurts you.' He shouted as loudly as if he were defending her against all the enemies who tried to dispute their right first to the house with the red roof, then the garden, then the chickens.

'It'll be nice, Karli, when you protect me and look after me,' she said in a very quiet voice.

They were on the street now and in the lamplight Karli saw Manja's eyes, and their strange, sad expression was such that, embarrassed by the emotion he felt, Karli spat resoundingly on the ground like his elder brother and rubbed at the spittle with his foot, casually and expertly.

'So that's settled,' he said.

CHAPTER 22
ERRAND OF SACRIFICE

Irma Reuter left the porter's lodge before the children came home. She had on her best hat and coat and was carrying a parcel with both hands. She walked with slow, short steps so as not to slip and risk breaking her precious burden. It was a jar of home-made apple jelly. The sugar formed a thin layer like very delicate paper over the thick reddish preserve, forming a natural seal under the water-and-greaseproof lid, round which she had tied string three times. The jar was concealed in newspaper. She had waited until it was dark because she hoped not to meet anyone on the way, and kept her prying, restless eyes lowered, taking no notice of the passers-by so that they in their turn should take no notice of her. For this errand was not like going shopping, when one talked and listened and noticed as much as possible. This was something that concerned only Irma Reuter and her own conscience, a sort of expiation, and for that reason she was walking as though she were holding a candle between her cotton gloves. She had put an end to the dreams which tortured her and kept her awake, that muddied her heart's hitherto unsullied pleasure in doing harm, that made her greet Anna Müller and smile at that street urchin Karli. She sidled along by the wall and if anyone had asked her, 'Where are you going, Frau Reuter?' she would not have replied and would have looked straight through them. Not till she had turned into the street at the end of which was the Nazi barracks, well known to every child in the district, did she hold herself upright and go up to a young fellow in brown standing in front of the entrance smoking a cigarette. Without explanation or question she handed him her parcel.

'For Eduard Müller,' she said and, as sole explanation for the man staring at her speechlessly, added: 'Apple jelly.'

Then, not giving him time to reply or question her, she left him open-mouthed, holding the jam jar. She ignored the laughter that rang out behind her as she turned the corner. It was of no consequence, it concerned her as little as the question whether Müller was in fact in that barracks or whether he would ever get her gift. A sacrificial candle has fulfilled its purpose and its meaning in the moment that it burns on the altar. Müller was banished from her dreams; Irma Reuter would no longer have to think about him again. Her guilt had been wiped out by home-made apple jelly, and that fat Frau Müller would have to wait a long time before Frau Reuter greeted her again when she came downstairs.

CHAPTER 23
STRAWBERRY PUDDING
AND LOVE

When her husband put down his fork Frieda Meissner, out of habit, was about to get up from the table to fetch the next course from the kitchen. Then, as she remembered that all she had to do was press the bell, newly fixed under the table, to summon Lina to come and clear away, a smile crossed her face and she threw her husband a grateful glance that first detoured via the new china. Happily she looked from the intertwined wreaths of little roses between the puddles of gravy to her husband's uniform and up to his face. Since he, however, had his eyes on Lina coming in with the sweet, she lowered hers again to the little roses and garlands on her plate.

'Ah,' said Meissner as Lina put the fruit pudding on the table, 'delicious.'

The two girls pushed their plates towards Frieda. They were dressed the same, wore new white blouses, and both had their mother's long face, her fair eyelashes and mousy hair. Franz held on to his plate, fiddling with his fork in the gravy, until Lina took it away. He gestured with his fork towards her plump, pinkish arm, which she managed to draw back in time, putting the plate which Frieda had served first before Meissner.

'I don't want any pudding,' announced Franz, although his mouth watered.

'No strawberry pudding!' wailed Frieda. 'I don't know what's been the matter with the boy the last few days. Just a little bit,' she pleaded. 'It's so good. Got so much bigger recently,' she added, referring not to the pudding but to the boy sprawling pale and glum in his seat.

'If he doesn't want to eat, he needn't. You don't have to beg him,' said Meissner, munching with enjoyment, strawberry jam clinging to the corners of his mouth and his moustache. The boy put his hands over his plate, almost on the point of bursting into tears. It was his father, from whose lips the juice was spurting, who ought not to have had any pudding. The day before yesterday, while his mother and sisters were out, he had had Lina in his room. Franz had stood at the door and seen nothing because the key was in the lock, but he had heard abominable noises and words. Then Lina had come running out with burning cheeks and ruffled hair while his father stood in the doorway in his shirt and suspenders, looking as if strawberry sauce had been poured over his face, throwing a kiss after her with his fat thumb. For a moment the boy had hoped that his father might see him pressed against the wall, and strike him. Then, however, when the door was shut, he crept on tiptoe out of the flat, waited a few minutes and rang as loudly as though he had really gone out when his father had sent him and had just come back.

And now his father was sitting there gulping down pudding, his mother filling his plate and Lina carrying it from one to the other and he getting none. His sisters were guzzling too. Tilde was having her third helping already. Her cheeks were puffed out and her breasts, lifting her blouse, seemed to be made of the pudding she had bolted and wobbled to and fro every time she moved. How they sat, the women, gazing at his father like so many sheep! His sisters were not even wearing make-up – no powder, no lipstick, German girls don't paint themselves. They looked like fish too, with their freckled faces and pale mouths snapping at the pudding.

'Have you learnt some songs, Tilde?' Meissner asked his elder daughter. 'After the meeting I'll bring the gentlemen across for a while.'

'Yes, but . . .' began Frieda, taken aback.

'Just sandwiches and biscuits and a cosy evening at home,' Meissner reassured her.

Tilde swallowed nervously. Franz wished fervently that a large piece of pudding would stick in her throat for a long time.

'The *Heideröslein* song,' she proposed.

'Splendid!' said Meissner approvingly.

'I can recite something,' the younger girl suggested eagerly, 'new battle poems.'

While she told him the titles Meissner pushed back his plate, wiped his mouth and looked at his son, whom he had ignored before so as not to spoil his pleasure in the food.

'And you, my boy, what can you contribute to the entertainment?' he asked.

Franz met the piercing gaze of his little round eyes. He had only to remember how his father had stood in the doorway, suspenders on his fat hairy legs, and all fear and respect were nipped in the bud.

'I'm going out.'

'Where, if I may ask?' inquired Meissner, standing up.

'Out.'

The two girls listened with open mouths; both raised their fair eyebrows halfway up their foreheads.

'There's coffee,' implored Frieda. But Meissner went over to his son. He had eaten very well, was replete, the whole day had been pleasant and now there was the prospect of an agreeable evening. It was difficult to whip up the rage he ought to have felt, and he was prepared to be more patient than usual.

'I asked you where you were going,' he repeated.

Franz did not answer. Behind her husband's back Frieda made frenzied signals.

'I have an appointment,' Franz murmured.

'With whom?'

Once again Franz conquered the fear in his bowels by mentally undressing the man he feared.

'With Harry,' he lied.

'You know that's against my wishes. You must give up all Jewish connections.'

'Harry is Protestant,' persisted Franz, pleased that he had diverted his father onto a false trail.

'You know perfectly well it's a question of race, however they disguise themselves.'

'Before,' said Franz, and his daring made his mouth go dry, 'it was a great honour when they invited me. When you were still the porter at the bank Harry wasn't racially pure then, either.' He was frightened by his own words and the pain of a violent slap across his face was neither unexpected nor unwelcome. Frieda's mouth snapped as though she was catching a fly in it.

'How can you?' she said.

The two girls stood glued to the wall with amazed expressions. Franz put his arm in front of his face. His father's second blow caught him less sharply between cheek and neck. Meissner hurt his hand as it hit the boy's elbow. The exertion after the ample meal drove the blood to his head and made his collar tight.

'It won't last much longer,' he shouted, 'with your Jewish friends. The whole lot will be smoked out, you can depend on that. They'll all be liquidated.' Automatically, as he spoke, he went on raining blows, without aim and without force. 'Liquidated, do you understand?'

Franz did not. He saw the frighteningly red globe of Meissner's face, the eyes with their bloodshot little veins, and the mysteriously threatening word reminded him of something which meant to burn flesh with a red-hot iron. In an instant he saw his father's stubby fingers ripping Manja's dress from her shoulders in order to liquidate her with a searing brand.

Meissner stood utterly exhausted. He would have liked to wipe his forehead, sit down and have a drink of water, but his son saw sparks in front of his eyes, his cheeks burnt, his ear smarted. He didn't want a truce. This time he didn't want to vanish through the door after the usual 'Get out!' leaving his father to the abject servility and admiration of the women.

'I know,' he said, swallowing and beginning again, 'I know what you do when you send Mother out.'

'Mind the new music, Anton!' screamed Frieda, as Meissner made a sweeping movement towards the heap on the piano, her eyelids twitching above her startled eyes, for Meissner looked as if he was going to hurl the first object he picked up. She was thinking more of the porcelain than of any meaning behind the boy's words, who was standing quietly and looked sick; she was also thinking of the new carpet and what a pity that would be. And yet with all this her heart ached and she would have liked to help both Anton and the boy at once. But each had for the moment reached stalemate.

At that moment Lina tore open the door without knocking. 'The gentlemen have arrived.' Here was the way out of an impossible situation. Meissner lifted his head, wiped his brow and passed his hand over his close-cropped scalp. 'Show them in.'

'And next time,' said Frieda, whose face had flushed, 'knock before you come in; that's no way to behave.'

Franz had escaped through the door and out of the house.

* * *

'You must run away with me,' said Franz, slowly walking up and down the dark path behind the houses with Manja.

'Why?'

'You're going to be liquidated*.'

'What does that mean?' she asked, stopping.

---

* the German word 'liquidieren' did not at that time mean 'liquidate' but implied branding or severe punishment.

'Burnt with a hot iron, your bones broken and your ears cut off.'

'Why?' Manja asked again. Strangely enough, the threat did not frighten her. She felt Franz's agitation made him exaggerate. What he was saying sounded like a grotesque fairy tale of which she was too old to be afraid.

'All Jews will be liquidated. My father said so.'

Manja's heart suddenly began to pound. 'I don't believe it,' she said.

'You will believe it,' he cried angrily, 'but then it'll be too late, when your nose and ears are cut off.'

Manja hid her alarm. Raising her eyebrows she asked mockingly: 'My nose as well?'

Franz became furious. 'You're just as stupid as the other girls,' he shouted, made a violent gesture, and grabbed at the barbed-wire fence separating the path from the fields. With a half-suppressed cry of pain he drew back his hand.

'Have you hurt yourself?'

He did not answer. Manja drew him into the lamplight, lifted the injured finger to her mouth and began to suck the blood. The touch of her tongue circling over the wound and the warm sucking of her lips tickled him agreeably. Franz wanted both to laugh and to push her away. The fear in his bowels returned.

'Leave me alone,' he shouted, tearing his hand free. Running a few paces away, he stood in the darkness, leaning against the fence. Manja put her hands on his shoulders.

'Where do you want to run away to? Who's going to liquidate me then?' She spoke as to someone much younger, earnest and reassuring. 'Your father only wanted to frighten you.'

Franz kept his back to her and did not answer. Suddenly she saw a bright star in the sky, past his obstinately lowered head, close to his ear.

Franz turned round. 'There's something I've got to tell you,' he whispered, his chin pressed against his chest.

'Yes?' Manja could hear him biting his nails.

'Do you know what they do with each other?' he asked. His voice was quiet and intense.

'Who?'

'Grown-ups – men and women?'

'I don't know what you mean,' whispered Manja, nevertheless seeing Herr Hammelmann's face, pictures, conversations overheard, ugly words. Franz was trying to talk about what had happened. He gulped down a few words and then spoke so swiftly and indistinctly that she hardly understood him.

'He stood in the doorway without his trousers on!'

But Manja interrupted him with a fierce gesture.

'Stop it,' she yelled. 'I don't want to listen. It's not true. It's horrible.'

Frightened, Franz fell silent. Impatiently standing first on one foot then on another he listened to her laboured breathing. He did not know how to comfort her, nor did he feel like it. His head was aching from his father's blows and there was a lump in his throat which grew with every breath he took. Manja had lifted up her head. Her profile was silhouetted against the sky, her throat trembled and Franz couldn't look at anything else.

'It's true.'

Manja did not reply. She looked at him for a moment and

then back on the ground. Suddenly Franz could not bear it a moment longer. With lips pressed together and tears in his eyes he began to tighten his hands round her neck and to shake her. Unresistingly the thin body bent backwards and he pressed more strongly against the fence. Leaving her neck his hands grasped her slender wrists. The fence cracked. He pressed tightly against her and felt her heart beating on his chest; his flat body perceived hers as being no longer like his, but that of a girl. It was treachery. She had gone over to Lina's side. She was turning into a woman. Choked by rising tears, he began to hit her. Manja did not cry. She neither wept nor defended herself. With an expression of great astonishment she looked at Franz's face, which seemed to be experiencing more pain than he caused, since his blows barely hurt her.

'Perhaps you want to liquidate me too,' she said quietly.

Franz let his hands drop and stood quite still. Tears ran from his eyes and nose, down his neck.

'No, I'll never, never liquidate you,' he shouted. 'I didn't mean to hit you.' He put his arm round Manja and his head on her shoulder and without shame wept vehemently. Manja stroked the stubbly head and burning ears. The sorrow of others always made her calm, gave her the strength they needed. But, while her hands and her words consoled him, her thoughts were far distant.

'I know you can't help it. You didn't hurt me. It's funny,' she said, 'really I'm so happy and would like to jump about all day, but always, always something comes to stop me. It's the same for you, isn't it?'

Franz had stopped crying. All at once he understood nothing whatever. Neither why he had struck her nor, even less, why he had cried. 'I'll inquire again about this liquidating business. Perhaps you are right and it's all nonsense.'

That was a hesitant acknowledgment of her superiority, and an attempt to reassure her, even at the expense of his own dignity. Manja looked past him. Now that he had stopped crying everything came back to her. Her father, her mother, Meissner, Hammelmann, the Jews, the whole muddle to which there was no solution. 'It's not nonsense,' she said quietly. 'I think it's true.'

Franz's round astonished face with its protruding ears was fully turned to her. She looked for the star which she had seen before with such pleasure above his ear. But it was no longer there.

CHAPTER 24
THE ENCHANTED WOOD

'Again, Papa,' ordered little Hans Peter, and Hartung crawled across the carpet on all fours, while the child grabbed hold of his hair as if it were reins and kicked his horse in the flank with his white leather shoes.

'Faster.'

Harry looked up from his Latin grammar at his enraptured father and at his small brother who was riding him. Taking off his glasses, which were misty, he wiped them and put them back on. The sides were always getting bent, making them slide so far down his long nose that his eyes peeped out over the lenses.

'Lazy horse, fat horse!' shouted the little fellow. Harry heard his hands smacking Hartung's cheeks and his father's rumbling laugh. This was a quite different father from the one he knew: happier, more affectionate, one for whom Harry, when he saw him with his brother, always felt an astonished liking.

This love had mastered Hartung against his will, subjugating him helplessly as the years passed. He forgot more and more often that his love had no roots, was a parasite; yet it monopolised him, had become an enormous emotional transformation, the meaning and the rudder in his life.

'Hans Peter must have his bath, Herr Kommerzienrat,' announced the nursemaid from the doorway.

'I'll come back and say good night,' shouted the little boy, winking and nodding at Hartung as at a conspirator and shaking off the woman's hand: 'There's no need to hold on to me, I can go alone.'

When the door closed Hartung looked round the room as though it were empty. Suddenly everything that disappeared when he was with the little boy came back again. Hans Peter's presence meant happiness and sleep, the two things that eluded him, even in the country. They had left their house in town because the windows had been broken at night, and threatening songs woke up the children and terrified his ailing wife.

'Papa!'

Of course – Harry sat at his desk comically hunched up in the brown tunic of the Hitler Youth, and the sight of the ill-fitting spectacles and short-sighted eyes peering over them was not pleasant compared with the small boy's angelic face.

'Yes?' he asked absent-mindedly.

Tonight was the night of the proposed smoking party. He had sent out ten invitations and had had ten excuses. The insult itself was nothing compared with the fact that everyone thought it would not matter turning down the invitation.

'It's night drill today, Papa,' began Harry. 'Marching and sleeping in the open and military gym.'

'Very good, my boy.'

'Must I go?'

'I don't understand your question.'

'I always get so tired and the others laugh at me. I'm left behind in the running. They call me 'Itzig'. I don't want to be in the Youth, Papa. The Christian children laugh at me and the Jewish ones hate me.'

From the next room came the little boy's merry shrieks. Hartung's face immediately changed and Harry took the sudden softness for agreement and understanding.

'I feel ashamed, Papa. I'm always called Aryan now, and when we shout 'Down with the Jews' then I always have to shout louder than anyone else . . . After all, we *are* Jews.'

That was all he needed. That stone round the neck. For twenty years he had been building his safe house, assimilation the magic word, stand firm, hold on. Whether a Kaiser ruled the country or the Social Democrats or the Nazis you had to adapt and persevere to stay on top.

'That is a big mistake, my son,' he said, so sharply that he made it horribly clear to the boy that he could not be his cheerful, affectionate comrade. Harry squinted, seeing the bridge of his curved nose . . . 'You are a quarter Jew,' cried Hartung, 'therefore three-quarters Aryan!'

Harry went on squinting down without answering. Hartung looked at his son's hopeless face. It made a mockery of any mathematical disposition of heredity.

'Let me tell you once and for all that it's a great privilege to have been accepted into the Hitler Youth, a privilege that was not at all easy to come by. Impress on yourself that you are a German boy and endeavour to be worthy of that.'

Harry, keeping his swimming gaze on his nose, replied: 'I don't look like a German boy.'

God knows, that was true.

Since the companionship of playing games did not and could not exist between them, Harry attempted to exploit the difficulty that they had in common to try and make a friend of his father.

'You don't look like a German either,' he said seriously, his blue eyes – brighter now – on his father. And added quietly and almost tenderly: 'I am your son, after all.'

At these words Hartung saw, as if on a divided stage, the little boy sitting in his bath, his fair hair covered with white soap bubbles, and Harry and himself, unmistakeably father and son even if not alike. But the affection which, according to the law of blood, should be Harry's, and the feelings which his words had released, turned entirely towards the little boy; only the fortunate few love that which resembles them.

Once again Harry was deceived by the expression on his father's face.

'They sneer at me because you've been in prison. I beat some of them up,' he prattled, his eyes suddenly bright with a fierce love.

'Hans Peter looks quite German, doesn't he?' The trust which he mistakenly believed he was enjoying made him magnanimous. 'He's so beautiful. I look like you, and he . . .' he considered, 'looks – not like Mamma but, do you know who? Like the picture in your room – Grandmother – don't you think?' He was amazed at the joy in his father's face.

'You've noticed it as well? Clever boy.'

Harry glowed with happiness. He took off his glasses, wiped the lenses and put them back on.

'So I don't have to go?'

'Of course you do.'

'To the night drill, I mean,' whispered Harry.

'That's exactly what I mean my boy.'

Harry felt himself dropped from his father's thoughts as if they were hands that had taken hold of something else. Not that he was asking his father to crawl on the floor with him, he was too old for that. All he wanted was to put an end to the coldness between them, as well as the coldness outside during the hours of marching.

'Papa, couldn't we leave here? Two boys from school have gone abroad; why can't we go too? Mother will never get better here.'

'Don't talk rubbish.' His father's voice was impatient. He tried to shake off the hand that clutched at him.

'And you, Papa, you're not safe here either.'

'What have you been hearing?' asked Hartung tonelessly, his eyes on the door.

'The history master gave a lecture: vengeance will seek out everyone, he said, even those who think themselves safe. He had his eye on me.'

'What else?'

'Franz Meissner's father said that the final word hadn't been said in the matter of Hartung. They're only waiting for the moment to strike. The nurse here repeats every word that's spoken at table, and passes on who rings up.'

'She can't be dismissed.'

'Why not?'

'Because it would be too risky to send her away. It doesn't take much nowadays to have one's neck broken.'

But it was better not to be alone with one's fear.

All at once his left hand slipped out of his father's. Hartung groped in his pocket and lit a cigar. A leisurely inhaling and blowing out of smoke separated them like a fog. Without looking at him the boy felt his father shutting himself off and going far away, like an express train in muffling clouds of smoke, with everything fading away in the sooty air; just as not a word comes to mind as you stand in a crowd of people jostling you with their suitcases . . . Hartung sucked at his cigar. The queer, round-shouldered little heap of misery still stood beside him, and just because there had been a moment of intimacy it was necessary to put more distance than ever between them.

They were not like each other, not made of the same stuff. No mirror in the world could make them look alike, only a caricature, a terrible photograph. And there, in the doorway, stood the little boy in his blue pyjamas, his damp curls brushed down, his cheeks rosy from his bath, bright and irresistibly beautiful. The nurse was holding his hand, that nurse who paid attention to every word and followed every movement with quick round eyes; who looked from Harry to himself and back again as though visible threads had really been spun between them.

'The drill should not be too tiring for you, my son,' said Hartung. 'And anyway it toughens you up. Another time you'd better go to bed a little earlier instead of staying out late with that little Polish Jew.'

'Manja is my friend,' said Harry, as if from a long way off.

'Those Polish Jews have invaded Germany like a plague of locusts,' replied his father firmly, 'and it's high time a stop was put to it.' Let the nurse report that to whoever it is that she reported to.

Harry did not answer. His face was suddenly very lined, very wise and very old. He knew what was behind his father's words and was ashamed.

'I want chocolate, Papa,' announced Hans Peter, impatient at the unaccustomed delay. But the unbelievable occurred – his father did not immediately fulfil his desire. With the exasperated feeling that Harry had seen through him, had despised him, he yelled: 'Get out, it's high time you got a move on.'

'Chocolate, Papa.'

'In a minute, my boy, in a minute.'

He bent down and the little boy fumbled with both hands in his pockets, throwing his handkerchief onto the floor with a shout, grabbing hold of the cigarette case, and at last finding what he was looking for. Enchanted, Hartung joined in the game, quite forgetting Harry, on whom he had turned his back. Without a sound – a sudden giddiness overtaking him – Harry fell down by the wall.

'Have you got any more, Papa?' Hans Peter shouted, putting his soft, round hand in his father's waistcoat pocket. It was not until the nurse said in her even voice, 'I don't think Harry is well,' that Hartung reluctantly turned towards him.

* * *

Harry had been put to bed with a cold bandage round his forehead. He was still very pale and the skin was taut over his cheekbones. The nurse sat at the writing table and, without taking any notice of him, turned the pages of the detective story she was reading by the light of the dimmed lamp. Hartung was in his room and the little boy in bed. Harry's eyes were half open; if he moved them they hurt. But when he lay quite still, keeping the eyeballs quite still too and making no effort to see, it felt rather pleasant to be as if asleep and yet awake enough to know that for this particular night he was safe. The pillow was soft under his head, the sheet warm over his toes.

A purple half-light came through the red cover draped round the lamp and fell softly on his hands. The oblong doorway was like a large frame in which a picture appeared from the play of light and shadow through the network of his eyelashes: reeds swaying in the wind, a cornfield in summer. But all of a sudden, in the middle of the picture, the handle turned, and although his eyes hurt violently Harry at once watched it anxiously, for it was possible that his father had come to order him to get up and go to the night drill even now. He hoped it was his grandfather. Perhaps. Dear God, let it be his grandfather. But when the door opened, his mother stood there in her white dressing-gown, her hair loose, a hand raised to her lips. Her face, lit up by the lamp, was so peaceful and so full of a secret happiness that Harry was not frightened by the sick woman's unexpected appearance but returned her smile, establishing a rapport between them behind the nurse's back. Hilde went towards the bed very quietly, yet a sound in the room betrayed her presence and the nurse, starting up, ran screaming from the room. Nothing in the world, and she had said so when she took the position, could persuade her to stay in the same room as a lunatic.

Surprised, Hilde shook her head and went towards the boy, who thought it very stupid for someone to scream and run away from his beautiful smiling mother.

'Shall we run away together?' She took hold of his hand and bent down to him. There was a mysterious happy smile on her face.

'It's dark, Mama.' He spoke very gently to her as if to a child, partly because when the doctor or the nurse took him into his mother's room they told him never to contradict her, whatever she might say: and partly out of a sense of concern, of timid affection, as if his finger-tips were stroking the soft fur of some tiny creature which the least touch might crush.

'But the moon's shining.' She glanced at the draped lamp as though it stood in the sky surrounded by clouds. Her restless white hand moved over the sheet like some little animal. Very gently Harry put his finger-tips on it and followed the leaps across the furrowed field of the eiderdown. 'You know, I'm not well, Mama, I have to stay in bed.'

'I'll carry you. In a little basket or . . . are you too big now?'

Harry's eyes filled with tears. 'Oh, no,' he said almost inaudibly. 'We can take a big basket, of course.'

'Yes, we can, can't we? A big basket. I never used to carry you much. But you're not angry with me, are you?'

'Oh, no, Mama, no.'

All at once the leaping hand was on his face, stroking his hair, hiding between his neck and shoulder.

'You can't carry anything if there's a hole inside you through which everything drops. But now I can love you.' She

300

laid her cheek on his and her loose black hair covered his face. It was like lying in the grass, blinking against the light screened by the tall stalks, and her high voice was the chirping of insects and the twittering of frightened birds. He tried not to think about the nurse running out to fetch someone but only about grass and scents and voices, holidays, summer. He was lying in a meadow, no one knew where, and the high voice was singing.

'When the moon shines we'll run and when it's dark we'll lie down on the moss. Sometimes the trees creak, but that doesn't matter, it's only the wind.'

'Yes, Mama,' he whispered, hardly breathing.

'Can you make daisy chains?'

'No.'

'I'll show you how, it's quite easy.'

'That'll be nice.' He was overcome by a heavy, painful and yet entirely dreamlike feeling of happiness.

'Can you fly?'

'No, Mother. I haven't got wings.'

'That doesn't matter. But perhaps I can't fly any more either.'

'Why not, Mama?'

'Because I love you. If you don't love anyone, then you're quite light, lighter than down.'

The next moment hurried footsteps could be heard coming closer and closer along the corridor. Harry didn't know whether he ought to warn – and alarm – his mother, who was completely wrapped up in what she was explaining to him so eagerly and so fondly. 'When you love someone you become heavy. You grow roots. You turn into a tree if you love someone and then you can't walk.'

The footsteps were very close now and the door-handle was turning. Harry would have liked to lean against the door, but his body would not move and he knew that the miraculous fairy tale would be spoilt now, the happiness changed into noise and flight; the moment of dreamlike intimacy might never return; behind his mother's face he saw the hairy hand of his father coming round the door.

'Mama,' he whispered, pressing her knee, 'they're coming.'

Distressed, she replied without looking round, 'Trees can't walk, their roots are too deep.'

Hartung was in the room and, as usual, when he was close to the sick woman he felt paralysed. There was a wall of fog in the room, a creeping ghostly threat. Once again he was being punished for his stupid sentimentality in not sending her away somewhere. It was the boy's astonished gaze which made him pull himself together.

'Hilde!'

Although Hartung's voice was very gentle she began to tremble and hid her head under the sheets. Her sobs sounded suffocated and frightened. Hartung put out his hand towards the red cover but Harry kept hold of it with both hands. It was the only thing he could do for his mother, the only way he could protect her.

'Was she very excited?' Hartung asked, mouthing the words silently.

Through his pyjamas Harry felt her wet tears and her warm breath on his skin. 'No, she was quite calm and happy.'

Hartung smiled at the accusation in the boy's voice. Calm and happy until he had come bringing terror and tears.

'Hilde, do be quiet, I'm not going to hurt you, I'll just take you back to your room, to your bed. I won't hurt you.'

Suddenly Hilde threw back the covers. Her burning face showed no more fear, she looked triumphant and malicious. 'He can't catch us,' she whispered in Harry's ear, 'he hasn't got a net!'

'Come, Hilde,' said Hartung, stung by the nonsensical words, behind which some meaning seemed to be concealed, directed at him. The transition from vacancy into actual illness had been so gradual that it was impossible to say when the illness began or when his wife had managed to withdraw herself so completely from his grasp, breaking away into a blithe childhood as distant from him as the moon.

Without taking any notice of him Hilde went on sitting calmly on the bed, her feet, in their red slippers, hanging over the edge; she sat like a child on a fence or in a tree-top, lost in a newly-discovered part of the world. Suddenly she looked at Hartung with her splendid eyes flaming with anger. For the first time she talked to him in anger, not as an invalid. 'You are the two mill-stones that have ground me between you. We are all flour but no bread will be made from us.'

The meaningless words stayed with him, her complaint, no bread will be made from us, gripping him. At the same time the word bread suggested other words: the nurse's reports, the bills from the *delicatessen*. And in the midst of all this upheaval was the growing certainty that he would have to have his wife put away, would have to break the spell of the prophetess.

'Hilde! Supper-time!' he said temptingly. 'There's chocolate pudding and stewed apples.'

She became agitated. Her anger and exaltation disappeared; her face turned into that of a greedy child. Harry held on to her skirt. Her sudden descent and transformation were too awful for him. She stroked his hand and then brushed it off.

'He has emptied me, I have to eat.'

'Stewed cherries,' whispered Hartung. 'Fruit salad with cream.'

And Hilde, now a small child with an expectant vacant smile, nodded at him, put her hand trustingly in his and let herself be led away. Harry could hear his father outside the door coaxing her with the names of other dishes.

So as not to hear any more, he put his head under the pillow. With his fists pressed into his eyes he could see the gold and green stars he had been seeing since his earliest childhood, which sometimes failed to appear however long he rubbed his eyelids. Blue sparks flew. Manja's fireworks. Purple mist, whirling circles, images carried him into an undergrowth of dream. He is standing in a wood, is a tree and all the trees round him are people; instead of branches they have faces and bend in the wind, and he is terribly alarmed when he finds that instead of legs he has twisted gnarled roots, and branches instead of arms. But his mother too is there, except that instead of roots she has red slippers. On her long black hair is a nest inhabited by tiny birds with clamouring beaks and, so that no one shall frighten them, she has put her finger to her lips. This human forest grows on the slope of a hill and at every moment Harry recognises fresh faces. Teachers, boys at school, people in the street. The cook stands in a round bush and the nurse lifts her head from a small fir tree. It gets more and more delightful to see someone he knows in every tree. Toadstools grow between their toes, butterflies play in their hair. All of a sudden a terrible panic passes through the wood. The air rumbles: a huge stone has broken from the rocky summit. It bears his father's features. It becomes larger and larger as it rolls down, and the dreaming boy feels the entire forest's horror at the approach of this avalanche. Everyone ducks. With a rush the stone comes nearer and the trees groan. All at once the little birch beside him begins to move. He has not seen her face before – it was covered with green hair – but he is not surprised that it should be Manja and that she can walk where all the other trees are rooted, that she runs, with drops falling from her green hair while she springs towards the rock. He feels fear, dreadful fear, that it should crush her! But suddenly the stone splits into a thousand little pebbles, forming a white path along which she returns. Through the singing of the birds and the swaying tree-tops she returns to her friend. But he is suddenly sad. 'I can't shake hands with you, Manja. I've only got branches.' However, Manja laughs. Her eyes are very bright, she shakes her hair and now she touches him with all her little leaves, which are soft as hands and warm as lips, and each of his leaves return the tenderness a thousand times over. The joy of this touch is so wonderful that it penetrates deep down into his smallest roots. He can never be, never wants to be, anything but a tree.

CHAPTER 25
IRRELEVANT TO THE THEME

Heidemann was waiting in an empty classroom of the boys' *Gymnasium* for his son's form-master, who had asked to see him. Nervously, he walked to and fro in the narrow passage between the wall and rows of desks. Open inkwells, grimy benches, and a map of the Battle of Salamis on the wall: the atmosphere took him back twenty years to the vexations of school life and its innumerable fears and memories, so that he started when Dr Wagner came into the room. The men knew one another and shook hands.

'Please forgive me for having asked you to come here, but we shan't be disturbed. Will you sit down?'

Since he could have sat down only on a bench or on the one chair behind the master's desk he politely refused. Dr Wagner, following the direction of his eyes, flushed, and a shy smile made his face unexpectedly boyish, so that Heidemann was immediately able to ask: 'Well, what's my boy been up to?'

Wagner's face lost its flush and its smile. 'Unfortunately it's rather serious. My colleague, Dr Höck, wanted to take action at once. I persuaded him to leave the matter to me for the moment.'

'What's it about?' asked Heidemann briefly.

'In his history lesson Dr Höck set an essay according to the new regulations. Will you please read what your son wrote?'

Relieved, Heidemann took the blue note-book, and while Dr Wagner, turning his back, looked out of the open window onto the street, he read his son's upright childish hand.

'<u>No more war means no more victory, means no more</u> <u>freedom, means eternal slavery. (With reference to the lecture</u> <u>on the World War and the Shameful Treaty of Versailles.)</u>'

There was a white space between the title and the essay. Heidemann could imagine the boy frowning as he thought, his thumb-nail on his lips, dipping his fingers into the inkwell along with his pen and beginning with determination.

'*The World War began a long time before I was born. It began in 1914 and lasted four years until 1918. It ended with the so-called Peace of Versailles.*'

Heidemann smiled, he could hear the lecturer laying emphasis on the *so-called*, which the boy had unconsciously included in his essay.

'*It was a bad peace for Germany, the kind of peace that contains the danger of new wars!*'

A new paragraph started here to show that Heini was no longer just repeating what he had learnt – this had been dealt with once and for all.

'*Even though I was not alive then, I know what war is like. My father has a book with photographs at home. I remember all the pictures and shall never forget them. There was one of two men hanging with their heads down on the barbed wire and their eyes are distorted and their mouths open and you think they are screaming but they are dead. Then there was one which I could hardly bear to look*

307

at. There was a cloth over the face and you could only see the stomach of a soldier with his intestines hanging out like snakes. I felt sick quite a few times while I was looking at it but because I want to be a doctor I made myself look at it again and again. And then there was one of a cemetery in Flanders, one cross after another, black ones and white ones, with nothing on them. Those are graves of unknown soldiers.

I don't want to be a soldier. In the old days more courage was needed in war than now, for then one enemy fought the other face to face. But since bullets have been invented which shoot a long way while one hides, and since gas and bombs can be thrown down from aeroplanes, a coward now can kill many brave men and many defenceless ones, and that is awful. The best would be if a king or president in each country, or if they are old then their sons, should fight with the king or president of the enemy country until one is defeated, then the whole country wouldn't be dragged into it. (Of course, it would not be nice for the queen.) If Germany had dictated the peace it would have been just as unfair towards France, because if you hate someone you are not just and reasonable, but want to harm the enemy.'

A little bull in a china shop, thought Heidemann. He had broken all the most treasured pieces.

'We must stop calling people heroes who have no pity and no respect for anyone. Boys who tear off the legs of beetles and blow up frogs from behind and then burst them with their feet can easily be such heroes when they grow up. Real heroes are people who let themselves be burned and killed for their beliefs, like Christ or Galileo. If you kill a man in peacetime you are condemned to death and in wartime you are given medals. I don't understand that. Why don't we prefer to learn what a human lung or heart looks like, not only from the pictures in biology? I remember my father explaining that to

*me – it's like a delicate fan, unbelievably beautiful. Or circulation of
the blood. People wouldn't be so keen on throwing hand-grenades
then. If I were the Kaiser or the Führer I would forbid people to tell
children about the War, and I would let them learn everything about
people and animals so that they get a great love for them. I don't think
either that one needs to be proud of being a German. I think that to
despise others because they are something they can't help being is
exactly like tearing off the legs of living creatures.'*

At this point the writing was barely legible in its enthusiasm. Heidemann could see how the bell had surprised the
boy when he still had a great deal to say.

*'In the future, people will think that just as stupid as that the
Huns had to ride their horses to death.*

*I believe that later when the world is more sensible there will be
no more soldiers and very few weapons. (Perhaps only for the police.)
One will be able to see the uniforms in the museums, like us looking
at mummies and armour now.'*

Here the essay ended. Dr Höck must have lost his patience
and taken the work away from Heini before it was finished. At
the bottom, in the teacher's slanting pedantic writing it said:
'Confused babble, irrelevant to the theme. The given facts
distorted.'

For a few moments before he turned round to speak,
Heidemann went on looking at the boy's writing, at individual
sentences which had moved him. Then he closed the exercise-
book and handed it back to Dr Wagner.

'Have you read the essay?' he asked.

'Yes.' He looked past Heidemann at the black frame round
the Battle of Salamis.

'What does Dr Höck want to do?'

'For the time being he has suggested a two hours' detention. The boy must re-write the essay.'

'And if he won't?'

Wagner shrugged his shoulders. 'Tougher resistance than that of a child's has been broken.'

Pause.

'Can I talk to Dr Höck?'

'If you wish. Dr Höck is an outstanding historian, and has the reputation of being an experienced teacher.'

A brief silence.

'I knew the former history-master,' said Heidemann.

'Dr Ernst has not been on the staff for two months.'

'I know. It's a great pity.'

'Dr Höck is supposed to be the better historian.'

Silence. Even after these few sentences there was a perceptible wall behind which the one took shelter as though the other were attacking him.

'It's easier to leave than to remain in one's post,' said Wagner, irritably. 'You have to co-operate if you don't want to be silenced. People are quickly passed over in the new order of things.'

'That's true.'

Something in the way Heidemann lowered his head, in the line of his greying temples, the quiet acknowledgement, changed the way the two men felt about each other in a moment. But immediately, so that the conversation that had now become possible should not take place, Wagner went back to the beginning.

'I like your boy very much. But don't make a martyr of him; he's too sound for that. Dr Höck is . . .' – is a distinguished historian, he heard himself concluding and hurriedly ran the sentence into the next – '. . . is a fanatic, quite ruthless. I can't protect the boy. Höck bases himself absolutely on the official curriculum.'

'I quite understand. But what can I do about this?' asked Heidemann.

'Don't encourage the boy's resistance. You have unlimited influence on him. If he writes the essay on similar lines tomorrow . . .' He broke off, shrugged his shoulders, and only now remembering that he could have a cigarette, dived into his waistcoat pocket.

'No, thanks.' In refusing the cigarette Heidemann's hands brushed against the other man's. None of the warm, passionate words which the moment called for came to his lips. Every declaration seemed histrionic and pointless. Everything was on the side of the other man – public opinion, reason, the verdict of the majority. He was right, and any explanation of why he was nevertheless wrong would be nothing more than a foolish, babbling sermon. There was a long silence and eventually Heidemann simply said: 'It's very good of you, Dr Wagner. I'll talk to the boy. Please forgive me for having kept you so long.'

When he had gone, Wagner had the feeling that he ought to go after him and stop him. Although he had avoided looking at Heidemann while they were talking he could visualise every line of his troubled face and he knew the kind of conversation they should have had – as candid as if between men of a similar type, as warm as if between friends. He felt deeply disappointed that he had missed the opportunity for ever. He hadn't even said that he had read the essay with breathless delight, that Dr Ernst who had been asked to leave had been his best friend and that he very much disliked Höck. He took off his pince-nez. His protruding eyes, looking naked without their glasses, stared sadly and short-sightedly at the unmoved map of the Battle of Salamis.

* * *

'When we haven't seen each other for a few days I always believe I've got such a lot to tell you and then suddenly it's all gone. Isn't that odd?'

Manja was sitting on the window-seat in Heini's room, her chin in her hand, looking out at the gleaming roofs.

'No,' he replied. It was exactly the same for him, only he wouldn't have said so.

'Anything special since Wednesday on the wall?'

'Oh, no,' replied Manja. 'And you?'

'Nothing really.'

Neither of them tried to hide the things which had pre-occupied them in the last few days, they were simply irrelevant. The room was bathed in warm light, every moment was still and heavy; through the window the sky stretched weightlessly over the rooftops; the light on the chimneys, the line of the horizon, the slanting shadow on the wall next door, the little tree in the garden, the distant sound of children singing – it was all beautiful, yet both real and unreal.

'The unimportant things are sometimes so wonderful,' said Manja, 'I'd rather remember the . . .' she sought for words, 'the moments when nothing actually happens. That sounds like utter nonsense.' She hunched her shoulders and smiled awkwardly; both smile and gesture came from a part of her that was quite separate from her glowing, eager look.

'It doesn't,' contradicted Heini. 'I know what you mean. Once when I was in Switzerland a butterfly flew onto my hand, a swallow-tail. It was lovely, so was the day, and the meadow I was in. But it wasn't only that. Sometimes, when my mother's playing the piano, I hear what she's playing and also something quite different kind of within it.'

'Yes,' agreed Manja quietly. 'I get that too with the piano. Then I want to get hold of it tightly and keep it in my heart. Do you as well?'

Heini nodded. 'You get that with reading as well!' he cried.

'When you're talking to someone . . .' said Manja.

'Sometimes when it's raining . . .'

'Not very hard, quite gently on the window,' she interrupted.

'Yes.'

They were talking about the unknown, something which became all the more unknown when alluded to: indefinable things lay behind the words, they were aware of the fleeting and the permanent, of movement and stillness, of fear and happiness. All of it would have to be forgotten if they were to grow up.

'I don't want to forget this moment, I want to keep it in my heart.'

'Me, too.'

They peered outside, listening to both sounds and silence. Special horses stood in a special street, a white cat sat on a red roof. As though the window-seat was a cloud on which one could only sit when one was weightless, the children had left behind everything that weighed them down. Every word they said was quiet and cautious, like pebbles dropped gently into the depths of their fears and griefs.

They both jumped up when noise, laughter and shouting cut into the silence. Hanna came in, her hat in one hand, a piece of paper in the other. Her cheeks were flushed, her face had lost the pale resignation of the last months.

'Mummie, has something happened?' Heini grabbed her hand and looked at her.

'It certainly has,' cried Hanna laughing and waving the paper.

'Something horrid?'

'Oh, no. We've inherited fifty thousand marks. Aunt Ida has died.'

'Who?' asked the boy, astonished.

'You didn't know her. A very old aunt from Pomerania.'

Hanna could not stop laughing, though she knew it would scare the children to think that one could be beside oneself with joy about the death of an aunt who had unexpectedly remembered them in her will. But when the tide turns unexpectedly after you have been trained on the Front of suffering, it sweeps everything away with it. Fifty thousand marks, in these times, at this moment! An elderly woman she hardly knew. It was impossible to think of it as anything but a piece of great good fortune. The children stared at her perplexedly.

'Didn't you like her?' asked Manja.

The bewildered look in those extraordinary eyes made Hanna take herself in hand and sit with the children on the window-seat.

'You probably think I've gone completely mad, you sillies. Of course I'm not pleased the aunt is dead, but – everything will be so much easier for Father. And I didn't know her at all. I was about ten when I saw her last. Every time she came to see us she promised me a doll which could say Papa and Mama, and every time she left she promised to bring it next time.'

'And did you ever get it?' asked Manja.

Hanna, her chin on her hands, shook her head with a smile. Again she felt that mad joy.

'Let the patients stay away, let them take the sick list away from Father – we don't care.' She twisted a lock of Heini's hair between her fingers. 'What would you most like to have, Manja? Quick, without thinking!'

'Chocolate cake and whipped cream, till I can't eat any more,' said Manja, immediately catching the high spirits like a ball.

'And you, Heini?'

'A new history-master.'

* * *

When Heidemann came home, depressed and thoughtful, determined to talk to his son, planning and rejecting what he would say, he walked in on an atmosphere of extravagant high spirits. His first impulse was to go away, having no curiosity about what had happened, only a dread of the noise. But as soon as he opened the living-room door Hanna rushed towards him, so transformed, so happy, looking so young and so eager to tell him what had happened that she could barely contain herself for another second, that against his will he was drawn into the hubbub and asked with the astonishment she hoped for: 'Is it someone's birthday or have we won the lottery?'

Hanna explained breathlessly, her face aglow.

Heidemann stroked her cheeks. Fifty thousand marks and a dead aunt. What had they to do with him? What was there to please him about that?

She looked at him and pulled his head down. 'Do you know what I'll do first?'

He shook his head between her hands.

'Send Hartung his ten thousand marks.'

'I'm glad about that, Hanna dear.'

She shrugged her shoulders with a sigh.

'I knew you would be. Of course I don't want to give it back.' She looked at his face, at every feature that was so dear to her; he was trying to smile.

'If you're not as pleased as I am this minute, I shall pull your ears!'

That did not sound quite right, it was too childish. But it was exactly this not entirely spontaneous smile that moved Heidemann. It was like a dress that a child has outgrown and looks funny and sad on the matured body. The face in front of him, lit up with happiness, clearly showed up the little crow's feet under her eyes, the lines on her forehead.

'I'm very happy, sweetheart,' he said.

Arm in arm they went in to the living-room. Red carnations on the table covered up the children's faces as far as the top of their heads, the one dark and the other fair. Hanna brought the tea in. 'We can be on an island for a few months,' she said softly, standing behind her husband, one hand on his shoulder. 'For the time being what others do won't have anything to do with us. It'll be more remote than China!'

'Aren't there any ships?' asked Heini.

Hanna shook her head. 'They don't come to us. It's not worth their while landing.'

'Are there palm trees and orchids?' asked Manja.

'Of course, and humming-birds and nice tame sharks. Manja will look perfect with a large red flower in her hair and nothing on.'

The tea was poured gently into the cups.

Heidemann drank it. 'Your island is nice, Hannalein, and the monkeys hiding behind the flowers are nice too, only very greedy!'

All four laughed, growing more and more high-spirited. The game they were playing to ward off their own troubles and other people's was more intense every moment and the curtains drawn across the windows of reality thicker and more dreamlike; the harmony of the quartet drowning the threats outside was beautiful. It was led by the children, two violins in tune with one another, clear and solemn.

'I wish everyone was as happy as we are now,' Manja said in her high voice, the cheerful tone standing out from the sombre one echoing softly through it.

Heini took up the low counterpart. 'Now we can help you too, Manja. The best thing is that everything's happened so suddenly; things can always happen that one couldn't imagine before.'

And he thought briefly about what was on his mind. Perhaps the street the school was in wouldn't exist tomorrow. Perhaps something unimaginable would happen during the detention.

Manja laughed happily. 'Three chocolate cakes and I practically feel sick.'

The monotonous counterpart could be heard: You ought to have taken two of them home with you. But the barely formulated thought was taken up by the second violin and made bright and tender.

'Of course you must take the rest of the cakes home for the boys.'

Then Hanna said: 'The difficult times have come to an end, darling, there's a breathing space. It shows that being able to wait is almost everything.'

Now there was no counterpoint, only a quiet joy ringing out in tender harmony with the words.

'Hannalein, I'll give up the hospital. It's undignified. I'll go before I'm sacked and get down to my own work, write my book at last. What do you think?'

It sounded very bold and strong, but there was a warning from the accompaniment. To isolate himself from the world was the last refuge of cowardice. However much you shut yourself off, the world penetrates every window, every crack.

'A wonderful idea. Then I'll have you at home again, and at night I'll make you coffee, just like I used to.'

Soft, melancholy accompaniment. At least there would be coffee, at least she could do the little things, even if they couldn't ever be as close as once they had been.

The sad, wordless complaint grew louder. Why didn't he tell her everything any more, why did he lock himself away? Then she said loudly and cheerfully:

'But I shan't let you work late. Until twelve at most!'

And Heidemann took up the sad, quiet tune. 'I'll have time for you again. I'm so happy about that. I've been so frightfully busy during the last few months.'

The accompaniment played variations on words they couldn't say. When one has no breath left even love is too much.

Very softly, scarcely breathing against his ear, Hanna said: 'I am so happy about it too; I need you so much.'

Underneath she was asking: I'm not a burden on you am I, boring and too old? You don't need anything else, something that you do without for my sake?

The good, kind, blessed tune of the reply: You mustn't think I need you any less, darling, even if I'm not tied to your apron strings. But the unspoken reproach: that she only bothered others with her own weaknesses. Wishing instinctively to spare other people's feelings, and hating the implication that she didn't sense what had been kept from her, she merely said warmly: 'My dear, we are as one, as we always are.'

The four voices came together in the evening calm filling the room. Heidemann looked at the boy's face. He was quiet and happy.

'Don't be worried about tomorrow,' said Heini in response to the silent question. Strong and clear, his voice rose above the dissonances of anxiety and Heiemann went on:

'It can't be a matter of life and death, can it?' Faintly, barely audible, an undertone began. Manja's voice picked it up and transformed it into happiness. 'Tomorrow something quite new might happen which we don't know about at all. Like Aunt Ida? Maybe?'

That 'maybe' stood like a rainbow spanning the unbridgeable distance towards tomorrow. It seemed like child's play to go towards it.

* * *

Even when there was afternoon sunshine in the schoolyard, the room used for detentions was dark: light did not penetrate the dirty window. There was an electric bulb in a rusty lamp hanging from the ceiling, a table and two chairs. Dr Höck walked slowly up and down, his hands behind his back. Straight, fair eyebrows met above his powerful nose; he had a small, thin-lipped mouth, no chin, and was slightly built with one shoulder higher than the other – though it was almost forced down level with the other. He was wearing a grey jacket on his long upper half and his short legs were hidden in worn trousers. The shadow striding along the wall in front of him was huge and powerful with a porter's broad shoulders. But he took no notice of it as it turned in the corners of the room, waited and went on; nor did he look at the boy sitting at the table. His voice had been hammering away at him for almost an hour.

'So the word Fatherland has no meaning for you, Heidemann?'

'Oh yes,' the boy replied softly.

'What do you mean by "oh yes"? Kindly express yourself more clearly.'

'It's the country where my father lives and where I was born.'

'So you love this country?'

It was said in such a way that the boy thought he had fallen into a trap.

It was annoying to have to keep turning round so as to be able to see the untiring walker. He had to keep moving his chair or twist his head round. So he was sitting half-turned away, looking down at the blank sheet of paper on which he was supposed to be writing the essay.

'Naturally I love it,' he said wearily and drew a zigzag line with his pencil. Immediately Höck snatched the pencil from his hand.

'Stop scribbling when someone talks to you.'

Behind him stood the mighty shadow, a sword in the threatening hand.

'What do you understand by love?'

The boy searched for an answer, raising his head to meet the teacher's eye, but Höck had once more begun his restless pacing with his double.

'Did you hear me?'

'Yes, I heard, I'm thinking about it.'

He felt the angry look in his back.

'You love your father, don't you?'

'No,' the boy felt like screaming but he pulled himself together and said very quietly: 'Yes.'

'What you've written in your essay, they're all his ideas. Answer me!'

'His and mine.'

'So, you too wouldn't defend your Fatherland in war?'

'My father was in the War.'

'In training, presumably, or behind the lines.' Höck nodded to his partner, whose shoulders heaved silently at this jest.

'That's not true! My father was shot in the lung. He was at the Front for two years. He has never been well again.'

'Don't shout! Kindly keep a civil tongue in your head.' Only the boy's heavy breathing and Höck's rapid, clacking strides were heard for a while.

'My father knows what war is like.'

Höck looked round to see if the one on the wall had understood the words to mean that he, Höck, only knew the War from hearsay, had been rejected for active service and had sat in an office for four years sticking little flags in maps. But the shadow stood there without moving, gigantic and inscrutable.

'If I am not mistaken, your father was one of those who stabbed the German Fatherland in the back.'

'No.'

But without taking any notice Höck went on: 'They flung themselves on Germany like a pack of dogs, a Germany that had been bled dry by the four years of war that was forced on her.'

In astonishment the boy looked at the man's angry face. He was swinging both arms, and behind him were the black, gesticulating pistons of his shadow. Nothing he could say would make any sense.

'No doubt the shame of the Fatherland didn't affect you? Answer, if you please!'

Barely audibly he said: 'I don't understand what you mean, Herr Professor.'

'You don't understand?' Suddenly he stood in front of the boy and with all his force struck him in the face. 'That's what it's like, that's how it feels, do you understand now?'

In the boy's white face only his eyes were alive. Although they were dark with pain they blazed with feeling. Höck lowered his eyes away from their gaze to the dented toecaps of his boots. Without touching his cheek which burnt from the imprint of the other's fingers, without relaxing the hands which were restraining themselves from lashing out, the boy said very softly: 'Yes.'

He had understood. It was the first encounter with evil, pointless and eternal. This was not self defence nor was it to satisfy hunger. It was pleasure in evil, the most alienating, the most dreadful experience. Like a destructive storm it scattered the boy's thoughts. It was this evil which was at the root of war, the beginning of it all. This was what the first blow was like. He trembled, sweat gathering on the translucent skin of his temples. His face expressed such horror that Höck involuntarily looked round at his ally, standing monumentally large on the wall as if on a commander-in-chief's hill, looking as if he had won a battle. The enemy was beaten and stood trembling before him, showing every sign of destruction, yet, against all reason, Höck had the paradoxical sensation that it was he who had been defeated.

CHAPTER 26
ALONE

'I can't allow this to drag on any longer! This is the third theft this month. I'm asking for the last time – who has taken Gretchen Meier's handbag?'

Anger flashed from Fräulein Huber's three gold front teeth and into the class. Manja, sitting on the bench at the back, swivelled her red pen-holder in her thin fingers. It seemed to her that the form-mistress's lashless eyes were fixed with particular animosity on the back row, which had for some time been called the Jewish bench since she and Röschen Bär, the two Israelites in the class, had been made to sit there. Röschen's fat freckled face was as expressionless and sleepy as ever, and half-hidden by her red wiry hair.

'I'm waiting for the culprit to own up.'

Silence. On the front bench a few heads with brown and fair plaits turned round and looked at the rows behind – blue and brown, round, wide-open eyes.

'A voluntary confession will mitigate the punishment.'

Complete quiet. Not a whisper. One could hear a pin drop.

Fräulein Huber stood up and her large, gaunt hands banged the table. 'If you lack all sense of honour I shall have to take other steps. It gives me no pleasure. Come up here, Gretchen Meier!'

She was a well-developed girl with a plain face and two blonde coils of plaited hair stuck to left and right of it. In her agitation the tip of her tongue protruded from her plump lips.

'Gretchen Meier, you say that you had a small grey handbag and its contents stolen from you this morning?'

'I do.'

'You are quite sure you haven't left the bag at home? Think about it. You are making a serious accusation.'

'No. I had my ticket to school, and I blew my nose in the classroom because I've got a cold. My mother gave me a clean handkerchief; it was there then.'

'Very well, close the door.'

'Excuse me – the door?'

'Yes, the door.'

With round shoulders, a question mark from head to toe, Gretchen Meier carried out the order.

'Now draw the curtains.'

Not one of them dared move. In the yellow half-light striped with shadows, they looked at each other in bewilderment. Then, although it was broad daylight outside, Fräulein Huber switched on the light.

'No one is to move. The bag must be hidden here. Come out in twos, strip down to your vest, including shoes and stockings. Forward, the first bench!'

Two girls stood up hesitantly, one an ash-blonde girl with spectacles correcting a squint, the other with curly brown hair and a large pinafore that covered her dress. They stood awkwardly by the teacher's desk. The fair girl giggled as she began to unlace her shoes, the white plaits tied with brown ribbons bouncing round her thin, flushed face. The smaller girl fumbled with the pinafore which was buttoned up the back.

'Hurry.'

Now they were standing side by side in their vests. The one bony, with thin, pathetic legs, the other plump and rosy, with rounded shoulders and dimples on firm, childish arms. While they giggled in embarrassment the mistress examined their satchels, shook out their clothes and underwear, felt under their arms and down the front of their vests, lifted up the fair plaits, felt the backs of their knees, and stopped only when she had given them the most thorough search.

'You can get dressed. Next!'

The scene lost much of its horror through repetition and the giggling grew more frequent. There were a good many comic incidents. Some girls had no knickers on, some no vest, yet others had torn underwear. Manja, her hand in front of her mouth, stared with horror at the file of girls who left their seats, stripped off their clothes, were mauled by those fleshless hands and scuttled back to their bench as in some strange ugly dance.

'I won't undress, Miss,' Liese Buchmann said angrily, standing in her dirty dress, with the usual hole in her black stockings. She looked at Fräulein Huber with furious, dark eyes.

'Why not?'

'Because I don't want to.'

'If you give me the bag you don't need to undress.'

'I haven't got the stupid bag.'

'Come forward!'

But the small, thin girl was as wild as a cat. With both hands she held onto the dress which Fräulein Huber was trying to wrench off, resisting her with such desperation that teacher and girls were convinced the bag must be hidden under her clothes, and were very surprised that Liese, once the dress had finally been pulled over her head, could be seen in a very short skirt that had once been red and was now encrusted with dirt; this grubby and comic sort of ballet costume reached only to her navel, leaving her brownish, pitiful bottom exposed like a skinned hare.

The tension exploded into laughter, foolish, provocative, insistent laughter that one only hears in a group of girls. Even Fräulein Huber's gold teeth were bared for a moment in something resembling a smile. Liese Buchmann offered no further resistance. She stood quite still, her untidy bird-like head hidden under one arm as if under a wing – an age-old gesture. So many past, so many future blows were suggested by it that Manja, in the midst of the laughter, covered her face with her hands. Next to her Röschen Bär shook with merriment. But the gaiety was shortlived, for Fräulein Huber's smile was always brief.

'I don't find the moment so very funny. Get dressed, Buchmann, and tell your mother she might give you a bath.'

Liese Buchmann grinned. She had an ugly, un-childlike, joyless expression. 'My mother's dead, Miss.'

'Then tell your father,' said the teacher, somewhat taken aback.

'Very well, he's in the fire-brigade,' replied Liese Buchmann, pulling her stained dress over the little ballet outfit. The search continued.

Two big fair girls who were the same size – twins, Frieda and Hedwig Thiel. They had spotlessly clean dresses and not a speck on their underwear, not a button missing; white and well scrubbed, they were both blonde and hardly distinguishable. It was obvious that Fräulein Huber examined them benevolently and rather half-heartedly, without pushing and pulling. She shook out the neat clothes gently, felt cursorily under their bench and did not look reproachful as she said, 'You may sit down.'

Through a mist of tears Manja saw couple after couple leave the benches, nearer and nearer to the back one, to hers. Already she could feel the hard, dry fingers on her skin, on her legs, on her breast.

'Sit down. Next.'

Only three benches to go. More than any of the others she was unable to strip to her vest. She was ashamed for everyone but especially for herself. She felt sick and giddy, her back ached. She couldn't. Three months ago, when it had come for the first time, Manja thought she had a terrible illness. It wasn't only the sense of uncleanness, it was so strange and frightening, like an earthquake tearing her body in two. She became conscious of her body in a quite different way. She was confronting a mystery which concerned her innermost self, a profound, frightening, exciting mystery. The river. She wished she was alone in the bushes by the water. She shouldn't be asked to go to the front, she should be left alone.

'Meirowitz and Bär!'

Leaving out their first names was Fräulein Huber's way of distancing herself from them. Manja stood up slowly, while Röschen Bär, her fingers in her mouth, went up to the teacher's desk.

'Over here, Bär.' No Röschen. Her first name, which anyway did not suit the plain little girl, had been taken away from her, leaving only the blunt and humiliating 'Bär'. Röschen undressed indifferently. She did not care that there was no elastic in her knickers, that it had been replaced by safety pins, or that one of her shoulder-straps was hanging down over her breast and that Fräulein Huber was lifting her things with her finger-tips as though with tongs and, in disgust, had pulled a sticky little bag of sweets out of the pocket of her pinafore.

'Hurry up, Meirowitz.'

Manja stood halfway between her place and the teacher. Her face was white, her eyes tried to find Fräulein Huber, tried to make contact with her as a woman. But all the teacher could see on the deathly pale face was guilt, and the sensation of dizzy triumph at being about to expose the thief drove her on.

'Come here!'

Manja stepped forward and and went close to the desk.

'Miss, I am unwell.'

But Fräulein Huber refused to understand her. Her hands, voice and eyes laid hold of their prey and Manja felt her fingers reach into her heart. Sparks danced before her eyes and suddenly there was a rush of waves and the murmuring of a river. She was quite calm. With fingers which did not tremble she undid her dress and unbuttoned her bodice.

Then she stood still, completely exposed, the red stain on her underwear coming apparently from a wound. Fraulein Huber stared at the stain, her face white. It was not just her disappointment that there was to be no exposure – it was disgust and outrage that agitated her so intensely. That a girl of not yet thirteen should menstruate was something depraved, lustful, unclean, and mysteriously bound up with the cynical rapacity which was part of her race.

'Dress yourself, Meirowitz. How much longer must we go on looking at your filth? It's scandalous.'

Röschen Bär hurriedly picked up her bag of sweets from the floor and went back to her place. Manja followed slowly, oddly relieved, walking like someone getting out of the water, swaying in the sudden softness of the air; all the faces in the classroom looked like soft white circles, flowers in a field, kind and good. The giggling and whispering was no more than a meadow rustling in the wind.

As she passed them, one of the twins glanced at her, and her frightened, cat-like expression reminded Manja with lightning clarity of a moment in the schoolyard when Hedwig Thiel had been standing alone by the fence while the others were changing after the gym lesson. Manja, who had not been doing gym, had walked past her. She had noticed the same expression then: annoyance, as though she had been caught out, and rage, which lasted for such a short time that, looking at the pretty red-cheeked face, one might think one had imagined it.

At her desk Fräulein Huber was not willing to admit defeat. Her face was patchy red.

'Very well, the bag has been taken out of the classroom. I shall spare no means of discovering the guilty person.'

Silence. The tension, which had relaxed during the charade of getting undressed, intensified again. Fräulein Huber opened her desk drawer. It sounded like a drumbeat and usually only occurred when she took out the register to note down the name of a wrongdoer. She took out sheets of white paper that she occasionally used to send ominous messages to parents. Slowly she went from bench to bench silently distributing the sheets.

'You are going to make a secret vote.' Solemnly emphasising every word she went on: 'Later on, when you have become German women, you will be voting like this for the good of your Fatherland. No German girl can do anything dishonourable. It is your duty to denounce the guilty. You know your fellow pupils, you have observed them, you have talked to them. Think of everything suspicious, everything you have noticed. Overcome your reluctance. Far more important things are at stake. It is a question of honour and dignity. Decide whom you consider to be guilty.'

To begin with there was a tangible sense of discomfort. The children looked at each other as if for the first time. Something new was in the air which changed the familiar faces, displaced them, put them in a new and distorting light. Eyes met, avoided one another, lips moved, the right hand picked up a pencil, the left shielded the paper from a neighbour's eye. Like posts around which the children's confused thoughts twined themselves, a few key words stood out. A German girl, duty, honour, dignity. Some of them scratched at the paper with their pencil; only a few wrote and those who hesitated looked across at others in alarm. Gretchen Meier was one of the first to write: the girl most entitled to do so, the victim of theft, took precedence. Liese Buchmann also began to write, anticipating the others. She assumed they would all put down her name, so she did not write only one; hurriedly she scribbled an entire list.

The only sound was the rustling of paper and the flimsy sheets being folded up. A third wrote. A fourth. Countless trivial murky streams emptied themselves into the large waters of the just cause. Several times Hedwig Thiel turned round and looked at Manja. Then she bent forward and wrote. Manja knew what name she was writing. Carefully she folded up her own paper. But Röschen Bär opened her eyes wide in astonishment when she saw that her neighbour was handing in a blank sheet. As Manja was putting it down on the desk beside the first three she asked quietly for permission to go out, which Fräulein Huber, seeing her pale face, reluctantly allowed. After a few minutes she returned and sat silently in her place.

Fräulein Huber was sorting out the sheets, dividing them into several mysterious little heaps. Then she picked up the largest, laid the papers on her hand like a fan, pushed them together and counted them out aloud.

'Twelve. That's more than a third of the class. Judgement has been pronounced. Stand up, Bär!'

Röschen Bär's face turned first pale and then crimson. 'Me?'

'How do you account for the fact that more than a third of the class thinks you are the culprit?'

Almost inaudibly: 'I don't know.'

'Do you think it's a coincidence?'

No reply. Sobs.

'I asked you how you account for it?'

No reply. Tears.

Fräulein Huber turned to Gretchen Meier. 'Was Bär near you today?'

'Oh, yes, before the gym class. She asked what I had in the bag; I didn't tell her.'

Another girl made her report. She had seen Bär touching the bag.

Fräulein Huber turned back to the accused. 'Where have you hidden it? Answer!'

'I haven't got it.'

'Is it in the class-room? Answer!'

'I haven't got it.'

'Where have you put it? I'm asking for the last time.'

However much Röschen Bär wanted to obey, she could not manage it. The question, which whistled round her head like a boomerang, bewildered her completely. Her plump tear-stained face quivered, her shoulders hunched, her arms moved as if they did not belong to her. She was shaken by wild, hoarse sobs.

And then Manja, sitting beside her, stood up. She did not try to touch her. She was no longer an anxious, hunted child, but a burning flame.

'Röschen Bär didn't do it, stop tormenting her! I know who took the bag!'

With her burning eyes Manja looked at Hedwig Thiel, whose uneasy profile was turned towards her. She was anxious not to look at Manja and yet not to lose sight of her accuser.

'I want her to admit it herself. It's wrong that someone else must suffer for her.'

Fräulein Huber was taken aback and disconcerted by the inexplicable change in this quiet, gentle child. The rudder had suddenly been torn from her grasp. Manja was holding it with unimaginable strength.

'The bag is buried by the fence. I saw her do it myself.'

Manja's eyes held Hedwig Thiel's staring blue ones. The class was breathless with tension, like spectators at a boxing match. Hedwig's twin began to cry. Röschen Bär stopped.

'It's not true! I haven't got it. It isn't buried by the fence. You're lying!' screamed Hedwig. The features of her round face had become distorted.

'I'm not lying.' Manja spoke calmly. Now that the decisive step had been taken, her knees were beginning to tremble a little.

Fräulein Huber emerged from the paralysis dealt her by the double blow.

'You, Thiel?' she said in anguish, going over to the twins, both of whom were weeping uncontrollably and indistinguishably. It hurt her deeply that the theft should have been committed by one of the children who occupied a double place in her heart, children for whose blonde, well-tended roundness she had a soft spot.

'If you knew the whole time,' she said fiercely to Manja, 'why didn't you say so before?'

'I wasn't sure.'

'You went and looked when you left the classroom?'

'Yes.'

But it would not do to prolong the cross examination with Manja. The guilty girl had been found and with a 'Sit down, Meirowitz' Fräulein Huber excluded Manja and concentrated on her painful duty.

'You, Thiel? I would never have thought it of you!'

Hedwig made no reply. Her blonde plaits hid her weeping face.

'Why did you do it?' Fräulein Huber put a finger on the round warm chin and raised the tear-stained face. The soft throat quivered under her bony finger. Pity is not logical and affection has nothing to do with innocence. Fräulein Huber couldn't help it if she was moved and if she would have liked to take this sweet, sobbing child in her arms and comfort her. The girl's blue eyes shining with tears looked up frankly at the distressed teacher.

'There was powder and lipstick in the bag and a German girl doesn't use powder.' It was inspired to come out with this favourite saying of Fräulein Huber's without a flicker of an eyelash.

'Look me in the eye.'

Wide open, Hedwig Thiel's blue eyes withstood Fräulein Huber's searching gaze. How could there be any deceit in them? They were pure and clear as a mountain pool. If such eyes could lie, the ground beneath one's feet would give way, and Fräulein Huber believed in them with all her heart. The characters in the drama changed. Here was a German girl too proud to defend herself, suffering the humiliation of an accusation made by a classmate who could not understand idealistic motives and therefore misinterpreted them. This was the myth which, spun with indulgent threads of emotion, she developed to the class.

Manja did not move. As the net around her grew tighter she felt Röschen Bär stroking her arm under the bench and slipping the sticky bag of sweets into her hand. Manja gently gave it back. This girl who was secretly stuffing her mouth with sweets again, now that she was out of danger, was quite unlike her. There was no affinity between her and Röschen Bär, even when they sat together on the Jewish bench set apart from the others. She did not belong with her nor with the others. For the first time in her life the child felt a kind of loneliness which was beyond justice or injustice. It was like a stone in her mouth which was too hard to chew and too large to swallow and which she could not spit out.

CHAPTER 27
FRIENDSHIPS UNDER
PRESSURE

Müller's father, he's a Red.
He eats nothing but dry bread.

The group of boys round Lanky Martin had all begun to sing the song they had recently made up. There was no particular reason for this. Karl had simply put the pencils on the teacher's desk and hung up the chart for the natural history lesson: The Composition of a Flower. But something about the loving way Karl was getting things ready for the lesson provoked Martin, who was boss of the class: he was sixteen, having failed to be moved up three times, strong as an ox and almost a grown man. A signal was enough for his gang, and he only had to hum for them to bellow. The song was still fairly new and did not fail in its effect. Karli dropped the chart at once, seized the inkwell, and without hesitating or taking aim threw it in the direction of the bellowing boys. No one was hit but everyone was splashed. In a moment he was in the middle of a heap sprawling on the floor. In the second row Franz stood up. It looked hopeless for Karl, even if he did join in.

Slowly he felt under the bench for his neighbour's poppy-seed roll. The fat boy, one of the keenest of Martin's gang, was fighting by the teacher's desk. Franz chewed the sweet roll slowly. The swine, six against one. But Karli had thrown the inkwell, and it was true about his father after all. Sauntering towards the combatants he kicked one of them in the buttocks as he passed, opened the door and looked out into the corridor.

'He's coming!' But the warning had very little effect. The entwined legs and arms did not disentangle themselves as the young master came in. He was a slightly built man who carried himself badly and his long wispy hair fell across his forehead and onto his collar. In one hand, carefully wrapped in a paper bag, he held a daisy dug up by the roots. He put this on the desk before asking in his thin, melancholy voice: 'What's going on here?'

He grabbed a flailing arm and a kicking leg.

'Stand up!'

The thin voice became thinner and more melancholy, but cracked in its effort to be loud and authoritative. A few of the boys, who had not joined in the fight because it was too risky to fall out with the gang, began to giggle. Lanky Martin got up; not because the master told him to, but because he did not want to go on rolling about the floor. It was clear he was not obeying an order from the way he stood there, his hands in his pockets, his lips curled.

'If you want to know,' he said impudently, 'Müller threw an inkwell.' And, his hands in the pockets of his dirty jacket, he went to his place.

The heap of boys disentangled itself as soon as their leader left the battle, and one after another went back to their places.

338

Karl, the smallest, stood by himself in front of the teacher. Blood was dripping from his nose, which he hurriedly wiped away, thereby smearing it round eyes and mouth with his grubby hands.

'Did you throw the inkwell, Müller?' The master's voice was simply melancholy now, all attempts at severity being abandoned. He looked at the round face, covered in blood, dirt and tears, which had lost its usual merriment.

'Yes, sir.'

Karli's grubby hand now covered his mouth, his eyes were comically wide open and his eyelids blinked unceasingly, for under no circumstances did he want to cry.

'Why, Müller?'

The answer was incomprehensible.

'Why?' the master repeated, looking round. This time he did not look nervous. He dominated the class like a lion-tamer.

Franz answered. 'They sang the song.'

'What song?'

Franz hesitated and looked at Martin lolling on his seat.

The red-haired boy behind helped him out. Leisurely he sang the silly verse while Karli, his head down, scraped the floor with the soles of his boots because he could not hold back his tears a moment longer.

'Go outside, Müller, and wash your face.'

With heaving shoulders, his hands over his face, he ran out.

'Aren't you ashamed of yourselves?' The master's eyes subdued the class like a vicious beast. The effort went to the limit of his powers.

'You are bad, mean, unbelievably mean. No animal would do that – unfortunately it's only humans who jeer at someone down on his luck. Aren't you ashamed?'

No one moved, the longest and most passionate speech the quiet teacher had ever made briefly silencing them; but then something changed. Something overdone in his indignant voice, his twitching eyebrows, the reediness of his voice, made Lanky Martin wipe his eyes on his sleeve as though touched to the heart. The fat boy next to Franz began to laugh and once the beast had freed itself there was no holding it. The gang burst out laughing and it spread to the others. Already every one of the teacher's words had become a sham and comic and he realised it.

'You will apologise to Müller.' He knew that they wouldn't.

'And if ever again . . . if I hear that song once more . . .'

It was quite impossible to find an end to this sentence. He concluded it with a gesture. A mere helpless threat which scared no one.

'And now we will discuss the composition of a flower.' He went back to his desk and picked up the plant, his thin hands lovingly unwrapping the paper in a moment of tenderness that set him apart from the others, a moment similar to the one when Karl had put out the pencils and hung up the chart and was obviously looking forward to the coming lesson. This involved him in the same fatal challenge. The composition of a flower! The phrase appeared to possess some hidden, devilish humour. A roar of laughter broke out. Lanky Martin whistled on his fingers, the fat boy banged on his desk, Meier with the white shock of hair almost fell off his seat, which in its turn did not help his neighbour and those behind him to stop laughing. Holding the daisy in his hand the teacher went down the centre gangway towards Martin sitting on the rear bench.

'You ought to pay more attention, otherwise you won't be moved up again.'

'I certainly will be moved up, but perhaps someone else will be kicked out. One never knows how the big fish . . .'

'Go outside.'

It was forbidden to send the children out of the class. The master knew this, and the children knew this; but as he was only making a guest appearance it didn't matter if he broke the rules.

'Of course, of course, with the greatest pleasure.' Martin made his exit as theatrical as possible. In the doorway he waved his hand and snapped his fingers.

'Regards to the composition of a flower.'

The master stood beside the chart and tried to regain control of his subject. It was hard to conjure up the sunny meadow where he had dug up the flower yesterday, hard to talk about the marvel of the leaf structure, its capacity to absorb light, hard to talk about chlorophyll, however much he longed to re-establish order out of the evil disorder over which he had no control. Painfully it occurred to him that he had once thought about children with the same affection, that he had once equated kindness with the light they needed if they were to flourish and because of that had become a teacher and a bad teacher.

Bitterness turned the daisy he was holding from an object of reverent love into a wilting weed.

* * *

341

It was twenty minutes later. The gang had asembled in the lavatory, by the endlessly-dripping tap: Lanky Martin, Meier, and two others who had followed them, all agreeing that the master and his Composition of Plants were impossibly boring. Franz was there too, trying to see the picture that was being passed from hand to hand.

'Show me.'

'Not for little children,' said the fat boy, holding it high.

'Why won't you let me see it?'

'Go home and sit on your potty,' jeered Martin.

'You think the stork brings children, huh?' mocked Meier.

'No. I know everything!' Franz yelled.

'What do you know then?'

'Everything.'

'What's this?' asked Martin, as, pushing his finger in his jacket and pinching the cloth together, he held the creases of the pocket together and released them apart so that the slit between them got bigger and smaller.

'So, what's that, if you know everything?'

The initiated roared. Franz stared at the fingers whose diabolic game bewitched him. He found them exciting, though he could not have said why. At the same time the laughter drove him into a corner and he suddenly burst out unexpectedly:

'My father's a Stormtrooper. My father's only got to say a word and all of you will be kicked out of the Hitler Youth.'

'I'll tell Papa,' scoffed Lanky Martin.

But in spite of the mockery Franz had gained ground. No one wanted to fall out with the sons of the mighty.

'Show him the picture, Fatty. If he sneaks he can scrape his bones off the wall.'

Unwillingly the fat boy handed Franz the photograph. It was a picture of a naked woman lying on a chaise-longue with her legs apart.

'What's all the fuss?' asked Franz, returning the picture with obvious disappointment.

'You're not so stupid after all,' praised Martin with a grin. 'Why are you friends with that idiot Müller?'

'I'm not his friend, we've simply known each other a long time.' Franz beamed at the mighty one's benevolence. He wanted to hold on to it and turn it into admiration.

'But he still doesn't know what this is,' said the fat boy, who was still carrying on with the finger game.

'Now then, do you or don't you know, no nonsense.' ordered Martin.

'I know.'

'Then tell us.'

Franz's hands were damp, his stomach ached, there was no way out.

'You take off your trousers,' he said faintly, his glance wandering over the walls, the taps, and the two brown lavatory doors. He wanted to run away.

'He's starting to blub,' neighed Meier.

Franz, crimson-faced, choking with fear that his ignorance would now be exposed, set on his attacker violently. 'Try it yourselves, you won't learn it from me.'

Martin laughed. 'Learn from you? I like that, little one. Have you got a girl?'

'Yes,' replied Franz without hesitation.

'The little one with the black hair I met you with once?'

Franz, a lump in his throat, answered quietly, 'Yes.'

'How old?'

'Fourteen,' answered Franz even more quietly.

'Have you had her properly and in bed?'

'Yes.'

'He's lying!' yelled Meier.

'Every Wednesday and Saturday she's with me.' The poppyseed roll had become a balloon into which someone was pumping air.

'She looks as if she knows a thing or two, that young lady. When you're meeting her next time, I'll come along.'

It was not a suggestion or a request but an order.

'I can't do that,' stammered Franz. 'I can't do that.' Further words escaped him.

'Why not?' Martin's face, with its small, gleaming eyes, was very close to his and very threatening.

'Next Saturday at eight in front of my uncle's bar. Watch out if you're not there.'

'I don't feel well,' whimpered Franz, his hands on his stomach. But Martin was between him and the brown door.

'Is that clear?'

'Yes. Let me go, I feel ill.' His hands in front of his face Franz rushed at the door, kicked it open and made his escape.

He had stopped being sick. The boys had gone. After a few jokes they had left him to his fate and taken themselves off to have another go at the composition of a flower. Leaning up against the cold wall Franz wept slow fat tears into the lavatory basin. It did him good to be able to be quiet, to be somewhere where there was only the gurgle of water in the pipes, not to have to control oneself but be able to give way completely.

'You're a swine all right.' Quite unexpectedly Karli's voice came from the next-door cubicle, which was only separated from its neighbour by a low wall.

'How long have you been in here?'

'A long time.'

Franz slowly went over the last few minutes word by word and he grew more and more uncomfortable.

'Spy,' he said angrily.

Karli did not answer, though it seemed to Franz as if he snorted contemptuously. Oddly enough it did not occur to either of them that now the others had gone they could come out.

'So you're bringing Manja and Martin together,' jeered Karli quietly.

'D'you think I'm really going to do that?'

'Why not?'

'Never, I tell you! Do you hear me?'

'Next Saturday at eight.'

'No, word of honour.'

'Your word of honour!'

There was a pause. Water dripped monotonously into the basin. Then Karli said provocatively: 'I don't think you'll do it because I'll break your neck first.'

Franz tried to think of an insult.

'My father says your father'll be put against the wall.'

'Fat lot your father knows.'

'My father's written everything down in a list.'

'Your father's a Brown pest.'

'Yours is a Red murderer.'

There was another pause.

Franz pulled violently at the chain so that the rush of water should drown the sobbing which once again choked him. 'Will you tell Manja?'

'Of course! I'll warn her.'

'I'll give you my penknife if you don't tell her.'

'I don't want your penknife. The big blade's broken anyway.'

'I'll buy you a new one. I can get some money.'

'Your money!'

Despite the water he could hear Franz crying.

'Aren't you my friend any more, Karli?'

'But I'm not your friend, we've simply known each other a long time.'

He repeated the words all too distinctly.

'Don't say anything to Manja.'

Karli didn't answer.

'Karli.'

'Yes.'

'Don't you sometimes say things you don't mean?'

'Mhmm.'

'Don't you sometimes say things your father says?'

'Yes.'

'But you like your father.'

'Obviously,' Karl said softly.

'Would you like to be like your father?'

'Yes, and you?'

Suppressed sobs, the gurgling of water, no reply. Then Karl said consolingly:

'Many boys are more like their mothers. I know several. Your father's a big cheese isn't he?'

'He certainly is.'

Silence.

'I won't say anything to Manja, Franz.'

'And not to anyone at the wall?'

'No, we'll shake on it,' said Karli, only then becoming aware of the partition between them and adding in surprise: 'In fact we could come out.'

'You're right.'

Both opened their doors at the same time. But they did not wait to shake hands. Without looking at one another's tear-stained faces they hurried out as though they had met by chance for a moment.

CHAPTER 28
BATTLE FOR THE OASIS

Two bare legs, a hand which lightly brushed the hedgerow in passing, a fluttering little skirt billowing out like a transparent sunshade over the half-darkness of white thighs and dark knickers: this was all Lanky Martin could see of Manja through the elder bushes as he silently followed a few steps behind her on the sunken path; while she, her face turned towards the cool breeze coming from the river, went across the stubble field to the wall – little realising that furtive glances were looking at the hollows of her knees and peering beneath her skirt.

He had already accosted very different girls from this one with thin legs and a little faded skirt. But his growing excitement made him follow her like a dog.

With every step she took into the apple-green open air Manja shed the burden she was carrying. Her hand playing along the hedge, her legs walking more and more quickly and her sense of physical well-being gave her a delicate, winged quality and an athletic power which lent her extraordinary grace. Her legs danced in front of Martin's eyes. He grabbed hold of a blackthorn bush and bent it back so that he could see over the bank, but stopped halfway up because someone was coming towards her on the far side of the field.

'Hello, Manja.'

'Hello, Harry.'

Martin slid down and took cover. The two in the field shook hands. In the slanting evening light Martin saw Harry's plain face become glowing with happiness. A lousy Jew stood there, head over heels in love.

'Are you well?' asked Harry.

'Yes, fine, and you?'

This was uninteresting, a stupid childish conversation for which it was not worth standing in a prickly hedge on a slippery slope supported uncomfortably on one leg. It might be best to come out and tell the fellow to go to the devil; he would probably run away when he saw him. But suddenly he changed his mind. The ugly boy, who was wearing a peculiar garment, something between a cloak and a raincoat, turned round and pulled a box out of his pocket.

'Here,' he whispered.

Manja took it. 'It's terribly nice of your father. I would like to thank him.'

'There's no need,' Harry assured her hastily.

Martin waited for some action after the payment. He made himself as comfortable as possible, but nothing happened. The two went on walking beside each other along the path and then across the meadow. Without revealing himself, Martin was unable to step into the field. Meissner had it coming to him. He couldn't enter the field without being visible a long way.

Heini came up from the river, up the steep slope on which few trees grew. He came without a cap or jacket, just as he had got up from the table. He had left his parents sitting in the dining-room as if they were waiting in a station. Perhaps they would still be sitting there when he got back. They never mentioned that there was not going to be another train, that they had missed the last one. That's what it had been like over the past few weeks, though they had all been trying hard – or perhaps it had been like that just because they had been trying hard. Perhaps the Wednesday evening habit, which he had only broken in an emergency, might not have mattered so much this time, perhaps he shouldn't have come. But there was Manja. He wanted to be with her, even if they didn't talk.

He heard her voice and ran up the slope by the rowan bushes.

Beside the two little trees they had grown from a cherry and a plum stone he saw Harry and Manja's dark heads bent over the wooden hutch which the rabbit lived in during the summer. He saw Manja's profile and the speckled-grey animal sitting quietly in her lap, nibbling the leaf she was holding out to it. He could hear what she was saying to Harry.

'Haven't you told your father how they torment you on the marches? He probably doesn't know. I know.' She let go of the rabbit's ear and put her hand on Harry's.

Heini felt like a thief creeping up on them.

'The boys who are stupidest in class are the worst,' said Harry. 'I have to let them copy my homework, and then they wait for me in the street.'

The rabbit had jumped off Manja's lap and hopped a few steps away from her. Harry begrudged it Manja's attention. He went on talking to her.

'I always pull my cap down over my face when I go out. Do you know, Manja . . .' He put both hands on her knee, since she was distracted by the rabbit. 'I'm glad about everything though, because . . .' – he hesitated and finished the sentence abruptly – 'because we have the same thing . . .' Heini turned, in order to go, but, although he avoided making any sound, Manja turned her head and saw him.

'Heini!' She didn't jump up, but looked so happy that Heini was overwhelmed by joy.

'What a lovely evening,' he said, noticing for the first time that the field had autumn crocuses in it, the trees were turning the yellow of late summer and the river, which before had been no more than a backcloth, was glowing so brightly that it framed Manja's slender figure as she leant towards him, her face suffused with pleasure. Harry had bent down to the rabbit and was sadly stroking its warm, quivering ears with his thin hands.

* * *

It was dark when Franz walked cautiously up the slope. He had had to wait until his father left the house. Perhaps his younger sister, who had seen him slip out, would not give him away, since that morning he had made a clasp for her belt. The elder one didn't count; she was in love and did nothing but gaze out of the window. And his mother wouldn't say anything: she was only too pleased if a day went by without his having a row with his father. Of course, he had to rely on there not being someone who recognised him in the street and would let his father know. But Franz had worked out a whole system of lies which he used with increasing dexterity. But he would not have known what to say if anyone asked him why he went to the wall twice a week in order to meet what his new

351

comrades would call the sons of a racketeer and an ungodly Liberal, a dirty little Polish Jew and his Red school friend.

It was a loyalty of a kind he did not normally feel that made him continue going, for the comradeship of the Hitler Youth, which took up the rest of his spare time and brought many new words to his vocabulary, could not take the place of these evenings; and he felt an affection for Manja that he felt for no one else, which was like a small oasis over which all the new words splashed quite harmlessly.

When a branch was pushed aside and Martin's hand crashed down on his shoulder he almost collapsed with fright.

'You weren't expecting me, eh?'

'Oh, yes,' lied Franz. He had hoped to be able to get to the wall without Martin seeing him. Up till now he had always been able to shake him off.

'I waited for you in the street.'

From the sunken path Lanky Martin looked gigantic standing against the sky.

Franz had managed to slip out of one trap only to be caught by another.

'You can't make a fool of me any longer,' said Martin. 'She was in the field with an ugly sort of chap.' Contemptuously, he outlined a hook over his own bulbous nose.

Franz did not reply.

'I thought she was your girl.'

'So she is.'

'He gave her something, I saw him myself.'

'Nonsense!' said Franz. Martin felt in his pocket, and a naked blade flashed past Franz's face into an elder bush.

Martin handled the sharp knife playfully and twigs hurtled to the ground.

'A new knife,' he said.

'Yes,' replied Franz very quietly.

'Let's go.'

Franz looked at his shoes, on which a twig had fallen; it gleamed white and sharp where it had been cut.

He climbed up the bank and walked next to Martin who, with his hands in his pockets, whistled softly to himself. Franz had a not altogether unpleasant sensation of weakness in his knees and was almost glad that he need no longer make up new excuses to avoid Martin's anger, that in the most literal sense of the word a knife had been put to his throat. And it was fortunate that it should be today, when Karl wasn't coming to the wall.

* * *

That afternoon Karli and his mother had travelled to the other end of the town to visit his father. Since the censored letter had arrived from him they had talked about nothing else but this visit. In the tram they sat opposite one another silently, Karli's eyes fixed on his mother's hands in her black cotton gloves as they unceasingly opened and closed round the handle of her black umbrella. She was looking at his scratched knees and the white scar on his calf. Then she looked out of the window opposite at the suburbs in late summer. They did not say a single word the whole way; at first because the tram was crowded, but when the people sitting next to Anna got out and they were the only passengers left,

353

they still did not exchange a word. They were sitting like this when the conductor cried 'Terminus.'

Then, in the scorching heat, looking around them as they went, they walked along the path which a man had pointed out to them. Anna opened her umbrella.

'It's good against the sun too,' she said. That was her first remark. The dry pine needles crunched beneath their feet. Anna walked heavily. Several times she had to stop and wipe her forehead with a handkerchief.

'It's hot for September,' remarked Karl.

Paper and tins littered the ground and although they had walked a long way they seemed to keep passing the same fir stumps; they looked as if they had been wrapped in brown paper in which careless hands had torn great holes.

And then all at once they were walking back along the same path. Neither of them could have said exactly what had happened in between. There were still the same brown stumps which they passed even more slowly, only in a different direction. They walked over dry ground with bits of stone, discarded sardine tins and old wheeltracks. Anna supported herself with her right hand on her umbrella, her left on the boy's shoulder.

Between the way there and the way back there was something that was still too close to be looked at properly. It split into separate images: a wall with barbed wire; splinters of glass pointing to the sky; a gate, the butt end of a rifle barring their way; and words that had to be repeated before they understood them – 'All visits suspended till further notice.'

354

Tufts of withered grass, heaps of stones, rubbish, flies. Everything was scorched, burnt, glowing with heat. Glittering spears bounced off the white stone wall into their eyes, soundlessly as if there was no one behind the wall.

And then they were going back.

'It's not so hot any more,' said Anna as they went through the wood.

'No,' agreed Karl.

Then she stopped and leaned against a tree and Karl held her, because his mother was so stout and the fir tree so slender. Anna slowly drew a large circle in the sandy ground with her umbrella.

'What they can do to people,' she said in quiet amazement, 'what they can do.'

These words, said to herself, hurt Karl more than anything else in life ever had. But he did nothing. Had he taken her hand, spoken, or looked at her, he would have burst into tears. So he picked up two fir cones from the ground and put them in his pocket.

Then they travelled the long way back in the tram. This time they sat side by side and looked out of the same window at the allotments and darkening suburban streets.

When they got home Anna sent the boy off to his friends.

'If you don't need me,' Karl said.

'I don't need you.'

He went without looking back and although he walked away from the house quickly, he felt no more cheerful than if he had been watching her slowly crossing the covered court-yard in her best black dress, supporting herself on her umbrella, the only thing upright about her being the perky little feather that decorated her hat.

He did not go straight to the wall.

* * *

'Here's Martin,' said Franz, and gave his companion a shove which was so unexpected that, instead of appearing elegant and sophisticated as planned, he stumbled and almost fell on top of Manja.

'Idiot,' he said to Franz, and 'Excuse me,' to Manja.

At that moment he revealed two faces: the thrusting head, drooping underlip and eyes narrowed into slits of a raging bull, and the stupid cocksure face of a suburban Don Juan with an embryonic moustache sprouting between snub nose and upper lip. Astonished, Heini and Harry looked at the intruder whom Franz had brought illegally to the wall. Both disliked him, though in different ways. Horrified, Harry recognised the face of one of those who tormented him for no reason whenever he saw him, and a helpless smile spread over his face like an opened umbrella. With hard dark eyes Heini looked at the broad figure, handkerchief in the breast pocket, baggy trousers outlining the powerful legs, shoes with heavy toe-caps not unlike the face; and was filled, not with gradual antipathy, but with an immediate and passionate hatred. Hands behind his back, he took a step back. Only Manja, unconstrained, pleased and curious, gave Martin her hand.

'I hope I didn't hurt you,' asked Martin, bringing his small bright eyes close to her face; they reminded Heini strangely of snails' horns stretching back and forth.

'Oh, no, not at all,' replied Manja in surprise.

'I have the honour of meeting Fräulein Manja?'

Manja nodded.

'It's a pretty name, suits you perfectly.'

Don't talk rubbish, Franz wanted to say, but he only punched Heini in the side.

'Have you been up here before?' Manja asked.

'No,' replied Martin, his small eyes observing her more closely. 'Lovely view,' he said and looked at her curving lips, soft neck, and small breasts underneath the thin blouse.

If he does anything to her, thought Franz, if he does anything! And suddenly he wanted to grab him by the collar and send him rolling down the slope.

'This is Heini,' said Manja, embarrassed for a moment, 'and this is Harry.'

She wanted to include them in the conversation, wanted to break through their silent hostility. Martin gave a fleeting glance at them over his shoulder.

'Heil Hitler,' he said mechanically.

'Heil Hitler,' Harry answered very faintly. Heini did not reply. But Martin did not bother to include them in the conversation. The little girl had got something. Seen close to, she looked even more as if she knew a thing or two. The presence of these hostile idiots added to the fun of things and the girl was worth making an effort for. Later, when he'd sorted things out with her, he'd clear things up with the gentlemen. The rabbit bounded back to the wall. Manja bent down. From above Martin could see her bare body right to the top of her knickers. Manja lifted the little animal up and held it towards Martin.

'This is Ronny,' she said.

'Ah, Ronny,' repeated Martin. He pushed his finger against the black ear standing out against Manja's throat. Slowly and as if unintentionally he touched her neck.

Heini saw him.

'Mustn't you go home, Manja?' he asked.

Martin dropped his hand and laughed.

'Why, Heini?' she said. 'It isn't late yet.' And fell silent seeing his reproachful eyes, the tormented, angry expression on his face.

'It's nine,' said Harry, looking at his expensive wristwatch.

'I make it half-past eight,' remarked Martin.

The three were beginning to annoy him. Too much time had been wasted on preliminaries for his liking. Now Manja went over to Heini. She was talking to him so fast and so softly that he could not hear what she was saying. Had it not been for the tingling in his skin, the pleasurable burning in his finger-tips, he would have left them, now that he had met Manja and could see her again as opportunity offered. However, he thought better of it.

'Can you cut whistles out of elder wood?' he asked in a friendly manner.

None of the three boys answered him. But with his new knife Martin cut a piece from the bush growing over the wall and started to hollow it out and cut out holes. Franz, though he tried to look aloof, couldn't take his eyes off Martin's fingers. He was thinking of the sunken path. Harry watched

358

Manja looking at Martin with frank interest. Taking off his glasses he wiped them on the lapel of his jacket.

Heini saw the hand doing the carving. He took no notice of what it was doing, seeing only the large fingers, the two wide red lines along the palm that looked like bulging, bloodshot veins. He saw something else – an animal, fifty pfennigs-worth of meat, something absolutely hideous. It was a paw holding out the little whistle to Manja, palm-upwards, and it made him feel hot and sick.

'Try it,' said Martin.

Manja put it to her lips but only managed a funny squeak. Martin took it out of her mouth and, putting his fingers on the air-holes, blew out with rounded lips. The sound was pure and strong.

'Lovely,' cried Manja. Heini could not bear to see the whistle pass from Martin's large, wet lips to Manja's mouth. He wanted to leave straightaway and yet felt compelled to stay, to go on watching without making Manja annoyed. 'I don't want to be nasty to him, why should I be?' she had said.

At that moment Harry asked, 'Do you know any Latin?'

'Of course,' replied Martin. 'Do you know how to treat an itch?' He looked at Harry with one eye open and the other shut and said to him: 'Wanna cura nitch/ Gettas quis fromma bitch. Do you understand it?'

Slowly Harry translated the words.

'Quis means who,' he stammered.

Martin laughed dryly. It wasn't a child's laugh, but the coarse laugh of a grown man, a deep bass. He whispered in Harry's ear. 'Wanna cure an itch – don't you know Latin?'

'Good,' laughed Franz, 'very good.'

'Yes,' laughed Harry nervously. Manja joined in, happy because one little word had broken the ice.

Heini did not laugh.

'Do you get it?' Martin asked him. He had stopped laughing and his eyes had narrowed.

'I get it,' he answered, 'and I don't think it's funny, I think it's stupid.'

'You think it's stupid?'

'Yes.'

'I'm going to have something to say to you about that.'

'What?' asked Heini, his glance blue and hard, looking at Martin unblinkingly.

Again his eyes made Heini think of snails' horns stretching in and out. But at that moment, just as battle was joined, Manja's arm brushed against Martin's, giving him the opportunity for a chivalrous gesture.

'Not in front of the ladies,' he said, turning from Heini to Manja. Again he ogled her; she was surprised and flattered.

Franz had sat down in the grass with Harry and was getting him to do his maths homework for him. The evening had been spoilt, but it might as well be usefully occupied. They both watched Manja and Martin, while Harry scribbled on a sheet of paper.

'That's the oak tree we climb,' she said, 'you can sit right at the top. There's a bird's nest on that branch there.'

'Really?' said Martin. He picked a flower and held it out to her.

'A flower for a flower.'

'A squadron of 46 war-planes bombards an enemy town. Each has 5 bombs,' murmured Harry. Franz nudged him.

'Look at that.'

Looking up, Harry saw Martin kiss Manja's wrist as she put the flower in his buttonhole. 'It was you that brought him here,' growled Harry.

'He won't leave me alone.'

'If every third bomb explodes and every twentieth causes a fire, how many fires are caused by the squadron?'

They appeared to be completely absorbed in their maths problem, but were listening to every word the other two said. Manja was showing Martin the stalactite cave and the swing and both felt that everything was tarnished and ugly.

Heini stood by himself watching the barges going along the river, the car headlamps going past and the trains rushing by. He watched everything that moved and wanted to be on it or in it, swimming, riding, driving, running, flying, anything but standing there listening to Manja behaving like a tradesman displaying his wares to a stranger.

'Franz and Karli made this bench,' said her voice, too high and too eager.

'Karl Müller? The Red from our school?'

'Yes,' replied Manja, 'he's my friend.'

'You can have quite different friends, Fräulein.'

'I don't want different friends.'

Heini stopped looking at the trains and didn't want to drive or fly any longer, but wanted only to stand and watch Manja angrily reject this alien concept. Harry put down the sheet of paper and he and Franz forgot the bombers.

'Are you the one who made up the song about Karl's father?' she asked quietly.

'With your permission. Do you like it, Fräulein?'

'No, it's horrible. I don't want to talk to you any more. Go away.'

Her thin body trembled with the impact of each word she said. Without looking at Martin or at any of the others she walked away a few steps and put her arms round the trunk of the oak tree as if to stop herself from falling. Martin found it easier to confront her trembling back than those flashing eyes.

'I'll go away when I want to and I won't be staying here long, you can be sure of that. And if you think I don't know what you do here, if you think I'm stupid enough to be taken in by the kindergarten here – wall, swing, rabbit, climbing oak . . .' He took a step nearer Manja, whose back was still turned, her arms round the tree, quite still, as if asleep.

'If you're doing it with the three of them . . .' But he got no further. His collar tightened over his throat as Heini seized him from behind.

'Go away,' said Heini, and pushed him with a strength that had been growing in him during the last few minutes, so that he staggered a few paces across the field. Franz stretched up for a branch and Harry bent down for a stone.

Martin did not come back but went away in the direction that Heini had pushed him in. They were not going to get away with it, that was definite. He went on without looking round and without hurrying, leaving behind a trail, like excrement, of shouted words echoing through the darkness. Harry wanted them all to shout something out to obliterate what Martin was saying. Franz muttered angrily, but not loud enough for Martin to hear. Heini realised with horror that at that moment he wanted to shoot at that long, dark, leaping body until it stopped moving. He wished he had a gun.

'Good night, Polish Fräulein, perhaps someone will tip the authorities a wink to tell them what you . . .' Martin could not think of the verb. 'What you . . .' he repeated, turning his head away. But as the field sloped down to the sunken path, invisible in the darkness, he slipped, waved his arms to keep upright and disappeared. Incomprehensible curses were drowned by the noise of cracking undergrowth and falling stones.

Manja was the first to laugh: it was the heartfelt laughter of spontaneous relief. But their humiliated enemy was not the only reason why they laughed. Franz and Harry laughed the hatred out of their hearts, and tingled with unashamed *schadenfreude*. Heini had seen Martin fall over at the very moment he had pulled his imaginary trigger, and was afraid; but he let himself be caught up in the laughter that engulfed them all, washing away the filth of the last few minutes. It was this laughter that brought them closer than anything else that evening.

When it died away nothing more could be heard of Martin. And they had no idea that, furiously angry, he had hesitated, his hand on his knife, just as Karl almost ran into him on the sunken path. Despite the darkness they recognised each other immediately; but did not acknowledge each other. Martin went down. Karl went on towards the wall.

He looked down at his shoes without being able to see them. He was angry at meeting Martin, at the laughter and cackling he heard coming from the wall and, avoiding the field, he went on walking along the sunken path, so that he emerged suddenly in front of the others. And since his friends fell silent on seeing him, it looked as if they had been laughing at him, at the thing that was slowly rising from his heart into his throat and nose, that burnt and hurt him.

'Here I am,' he said crossly.

Manja came towards him and took his hand.

'How is he, Karli?'

Karl put his hands in his pockets. 'What was that stupid laughter about?'

'About Martin from your school,' Harry told him.

Karl turned to Franz, who was sitting on the wall swinging his legs. 'So you brought him along, then?'

Franz shrugged his shoulders. 'Anyway, he's gone.'

'I don't care,' growled Karl, 'do what you like.'

Manja put her hand on Karl's cheek. 'Was he pleased?' she asked.

'We didn't see him,' shouted Karl, beginning to stride up and down.

She walked behind him.

'Won't you tell me about it, Karli?' she asked.

'No.' He walked faster and faster round the wall, speaking a word or two, walking on.

'All this silly stuff here, the swing . . .' He pushed it so that it flew up and hit against the tree trunk, 'and the silly games and garden and Indians and all that nonsense about the wall.' He kicked with his heel at a stone which broke into fragments.

'I'm not coming any more,' he yelled, and now his words were indistinct and hoarse with tears. 'You're bourgeois, you've got nothing but nonsense in your heads, you're Nazis, and the wall is idiotic.' For a second or two the other four heard only his panting. 'My father . . .' And then there was nothing more. Suddenly Karl bent down, broke off some stones from the carefully constructed entrance to the stalactite cave and began hurling them against the wall. In front of his eyes was the other wall, glittering and scorching, behind which were hidden gravel paths and red barracks; and somewhere in that horrifying quietness was his father. He wanted to throw stones at that wall, they were intended for that one. When he remembered that he came to his senses and stopped. For the second time that day the wall had been attacked and vilified; everything was stripped naked, everything was trivial and nothing other than what it actually was – a handful of stones, a few trees, an overgrown garden and children's silly games. Manja went up to Karl, who was now standing quietly with his head bent. 'Am I a Nazi?' she asked.

He did not answer, but this time he did not pull away his shoulder, which she had put her arm round.

'Am I a bourgeois?' she asked.

'You're not,' he said, and took Manja's hand in his damp one.

Now at last he could talk and Manja listened.

'But that can't be possible,' she said, when he had finished.

'That's nothing to them. Perhaps they've killed him.'

'Can't he be set free?' cried Heini with childish desperation.

Karl, worldly and adult, shrugged his shoulders.

'If I say something to my father he'll do something,' boasted Franz.

'My father doesn't need your father,' said Karl.

'He can stay in prison as far as I'm concerned.'

'Franz!' cried Manja, stamping her foot. 'He only wants to help you, Karli!' Her fingers dug into his shoulders.

'Hitler Youth!' shouted Karl. 'I won't stay here any longer and I'm not coming again. You come with me.' He tried to drag Manja away but she would not let him.

'No, Karli, no.'

'I'm going anyway,' said Franz.

'You can't go away, you mustn't! Don't you all remember what we swore?'

'Rubbish!' said Karl. The months since that evening seemed like years. Life had changed; they all felt it.

'I was going away then, and I stayed. We were so glad and now . . .' Her voice shook. 'Instead of helping, we're quarrelling.'

'How are you going to help then?' asked Karl, impressed in spite of himself.

'We'll find a way. Heini, you think! Harry, you've helped me, you can help Karli as well.' And while she was talking to the other two she put her arm through Karl's and Franz's and held them tightly.

'Now we're all together again,' she said, drawing a deep breath. 'We'd be so unhappy without the wall.' Again she said something that only she could say, she could open her heart without feeling embarrassed.

And once again the old magic worked on the four boys, and once more anything was possible. The river smelt of the sea, the air was full of noises and smells, there was a heightened reality about everything. The harsh outline of things changed in the gentle, unreal light so that they seemed like dream objects. In that world the barbed wire wall was surmountable.

'With a rope ladder,' suggested Heini, and no one contradicted him.

Less likely things had happened.

One of them would keep watch outside and if someone came they would knock him over, so that he fell down like a tin-soldier. What was ju-jitsu for? David had defeated Goliath without it. The white gravel alleys between the barracks weren't impassable. Oceans had been marched over before now. Nor was opening doors an insuperable problem. Either the guard could be drugged with veronal – Heini's father would be able to give them some – or Manja would lure him away.

Karli, holding a file, would climb up to the window. Of course that could be done. Prisoners had often been carried off from dungeons in the middle of the night, and young men had often climbed up to turrets using a maiden's long hair as a rope. It could be done. It was easy.

Too grown up and dignified for little children's games, they turned a bitter experience into a game and for a few magnificent seconds stole from life what life had stolen from them.

PART FOUR

CHAPTER 29
THE OVERTURNED BEETLE

The dark waters of the river slapped against the pillars of the bridge and covered up the layer of slippery green lichen and moss clinging to it like a sponge. Only a narrow yellow strip across the swirling water separated its grey waves from the leaden sky. Imperceptibly, evening was turning into night.

Beneath the gravel of the path which Manja and Franz were walking along there was a noise in the sewer. A fat rat came out fearlessly from under a stone and ran towards the river.

Franz was speaking non-stop, his voice hoarse and breathless; he glanced round continually as if someone on the bridge or the water or the dimly lit street above the embankment might hear what he was saying.

'I'm not going home any more, Manja, I've finished with my father. In any case I can't go back, he's thrown me out.'

He drew her by the arm towards the embankment. His hand felt dry and hot on her wrist.

'The barge moored over there is going tomorrow morning. There are sacks and empty crates on the bow, that's where we'll hide. We'll be in the North Sea by the time they find us.'

Manja looked at the dark boat straining at the rope.

But Franz gave her no time to ask him anything.

'I can't go home or back to school. Martin's watching me. His gang beats me up and throws ink at me and slashes my trousers. All because I won't let them near you. And the same goes for my father – because I won't stop being your friend. That's why you've got to go with me, Manja!'

'You've said all this before, remember?'

'Yes, now it's got to that. They caught one girl, cut off her hair, branded her with a hot iron and threw her into the street, all because she'd been with a Jew. My sister told us. My father's been going off at night to punish people. I don't know what they do. You must come with me, Manja. You have to go away too, because of Martin.'

'I'm not afraid of Martin. I'll come to your school tomorrow and talk to him.'

'You will not!' shouted Franz.

'I need to find out what he wants of me.'

'He wants what my father did with Lina,' whispered Franz. 'Martin has had girls already. Come on, Manja, come on the boat, you must go with me. I've got the money I took from my mother's bag.'

'But, Franz,' said Manja gently, 'I can't just run away from everything.'

'You can write to them. Come along,' persisted Franz, pulling her towards the river.

They had reached the gravel path and little waves were splashing their shoes. They had only to climb onto the narrow landing stage to be able to reach the keel of the boat.

Franz put his foot on the gangway.

'I'm not going, Franz,' she cried.

'Do you know what will happen to you?' He paused for a moment. A large wave soaked him completely.

'Come back, Franz,' pleaded Manja.

But Franz, waving both his hands, shouted, 'We'll all be branded, Heini and Karli and me, because we go with a Jewish girl. Is that what you want?'

Manja stood still; she held her head with both hands. Franz was alarmed.

'If you come, everything'll be all right,' he added. He got down from the gangway, took her hands and implored: 'You won't leave me, will you?'

Manja looked at the reflection from a car going past.

'No one will do anything to you because we're friends,' she said, strangely calm. 'No one will come and hunt us down. And if anyone does come, then I want to see them. I want to talk to them. That's why I've got such a large mouth.'

When he looked at her face, not sure if he had seen her smile, she turned away.

'The terrible things that are happening – only a few people do them and the others are ashamed of them. If I ever see . . .' She didn't finish but turned from the river towards him.

'You can sleep at Harry's tonight and if . . . What's the matter?'

'Quick, Manja, come along.' His face was so distorted with fear that she was frightened, looked back and cried out in relief: 'Why, it's only Martin, you did frighten me.'

Franz let go of her hand. There was no time to climb into the barge, no time for anything now.

'Good evening, Fräulein Manja. Are you still angry with me?' asked Martin, taking off his cap.

'Good evening,' said Manja quietly.

'I wanted to apologise for the other day.'

She looked round for Franz, but he was staring at the barge, which was so near but which now he couldn't escape on. Martin turned to him and, winking and sucking in his mouth, tried to convey that the other should make himself scarce. And, since Franz didn't obey the silent command, he said without embarrassment: 'Off you go!'

'Why do you want him to go away?' asked Manja.

'I want to talk to you.'

She lifted her head and looked at him. 'I want to talk to you too,' she said.

'There you are then,' said Martin with a grin.

'Manja!' Franz pulled at her arm. He wanted to be brave, to save her from Martin. At the same time he felt a paralysing fear which turned Martin into a monstrously powerful person who robbed him of breath and judgement.

'If you . . .' he began.

'If you don't clear off immediately, do you know what I'll . . .'

'I'm going,' yelled Franz. He wasn't brave enough, and there was no way out. He ran up the steep embankment.

'Don't go with him!' he yelled without looking round. Seeing him running like that, Manja was frightened.

'Franz,' she called after him, 'Franz!' For a moment she was on the point of following. Her heart beat up into her throat. Martin put his face close to hers.

'Frightened?' he asked.

374

Manja tossed her hair back. 'No, I'm not afraid of anyone. Why is Franz so afraid of you?'

'I'll confess everything, I'll explain it all.'

Franz stood above them, at the side of the road, yellow in the bright headlight of a car. He shouted something she couldn't hear, then disappeared as though swallowed up by the darkness which had settled on the street. Manja looked at the spot where he had been.

'He's mad,' said Martin. 'Shall I tell you now why he's frightened?'

'Yes.'

'He's frightened I might repeat something he told me.' Martin began to walk very slowly and Manja followed without being aware of it. 'You can probably imagine what it was.'

'No.'

'No?' he asked, and suddenly turned his face to her. 'What a girl! You'll get on in life.'

Up above Manja saw the bright squares of the tram windows and the sparks of the electrical current in the sky. She wanted to cling on to it and let herself be pulled along as fast as possible.

'I don't want to know,' she said. 'I want to go home.'

But a different Martin was speaking in an agitated, faltering voice. 'Why are you so cruel to me, Manja? Since the day I saw you I've been a different person. You could make something out of me. My heart yearns for you. I love you, Manja. Why do you hate me?'

Manja listened with growing astonishment; these words, taken from the *Letter Writer for Lovers*, which Martin had at home and which was consulted by him and, on payment, his friends, were new to her and sounded wonderful.

'But I don't hate you at all.'

'Will you go for a little walk with me?'

'If you want me to.'

'You make me very happy, Manja.'

Manja's fear disappeared. She felt the familiar ground beneath her feet and abandoned all thoughts of running away over the muddy embankment. When the path was wide enough she allowed Martin to take her hand so that they could walk together. Bushes shut them off on both sides – there were reeds and rotting tree stumps in the swampy ground between the path and the river, woodland with slender trees and a tangle of bracken, moss and weeds on the slope up to the street. Pale wet tree trunks gleamed in the dark. Summer still hung about bush and wood; there was a buzzing of flies and gnats; the darkness was full of the sounds of animals fleeing and pursuing, the hunted and the prey.

'I don't like walking here in the dark,' said Manja in a low voice.

'But you're with me.'

He put a protecting arm round her and drew her on, chatting and telling her stories. She said little in reply and tried to free her shoulder and hand, which Martin was stroking with the tips of his fingers.

The path became so narrow they could only walk side by side pressed closely together.

'Do you like chocolates?' he began again, pulling her closer.

'Oh, yes.'

'With cream centres or chocolate all through?'

'With cream centres,' she answered, walking faster and trying to tear herself away.

'You can have them,' announced Martin, stopping.

'Why are you trembling?' he asked.

'I feel a little cold. Let's go faster, please.'

'Don't you like it here?' he asked close to her ear. He didn't move.

'Alone with you at last. Feel how my heart beats.' He pushed her hand under his jacket, onto the warm dry skin. She resisted him under his shirt. But Martin's fingers were no longer caressing. With an iron grip they pressed her resisting hand further down, pushed it across his chest and down to his stomach which suddenly hollowed out. She clutched at his belt. Martin tore it off with his other hand and threw it in the grass. During this painful struggle he whispered into Manja's ear:

'Franz told me what you do together. That you go to bed together.'

'That isn't true. Let go of my hand, at once, please let go. I want to go, you're hurting me horribly.'

'No more fuss, my little one.'

They heard a distant voice from the street and for a second Martin let go of her so that she, with the agility of a cat, tore herself free and ran – ran like an animal for its life, with wild blind leaps in the darkness, panting and stumbling on the slippery ground.

Another ten paces and she would be out of the wood and within sight of the street. She didn't dare look round. Through the rushing and ringing of panic in her ears she heard the breath of her pursuer. Then his hand seized her leg, she fell forward, pulled herself up and fell backwards into the bushes, which scratched her cheek. Martin threw himself on top of her, tore her blouse from her skirt, not bothering about the buttons, broke the strap and, while his other hand ran up her thigh, seized her breast.

She lay quite still, her head on a damp, strongly scented shrub with rough leaves. She wanted to cry like a child, but the tears did not come. She wanted to scream like an animal, but the scream was trapped inside her. What was happening was beyond complaint or entreaty, beyond justice, it was what happened every night in the undergrowth – choking, shoving, hacking.

Not two hands but a thousand hands groped at her. 'Please, leave me alone, please.' But her mouth was no longer hers either. Something wet was pressing against it, wet, spit, a prodding tongue. And since she was lying there so quietly, unresistingly, he let go of her to strip off his clothes. In that moment Manja changed into a panther. She scratched his face, so that, cursing, he let go of her completely. She bit his hand while he was trying to grab her and ran. This time she had the advantage because he was cowering on the ground, his eyes watering; and although her knees were trembling and she felt giddy she ran and ran. There was no speed great enough to get away from him and no space large enough to put between them.

There was the light from the street. Another two steps and she could pull herself up on a bush and jump onto the tramline.

It was lucky there was no tram coming. A lorry-driver yelled at her for crossing the street blindly. Her hair was wet and dishevelled, her cheeks scratched, her blouse torn, her skirt hanging down from one strap.

Thus Franz saw her. He had been waiting, crouched behind a haystack. He ran after her without her seeing or hearing him.

'Manja, Manja, stop!' But she ran on in wild, disjointed bounds quite different from her normal, lovely swiftness.

'Manja, Manja, it's me! Franz! What did he do to you?' He grabbed at her skirt to make her stop, but with a terrified gesture she turned her head back for a second and looked past him with black, wild eyes he had never seen before, eyes which did not recognise him. Pushing him away, her head buried in her elbows both for protection and attack, she ran in a zigzag line like an animal seeking its lair, the lair where it can disappear and bury itself. For a moment Franz stood still in helpless horror; his next thought was to fetch help, his friends, Heini; and jumping onto the tailboard of a passing lorry, beer barrels rolling and rattling between him and the driver, he sat trembling and soaked through, his head on his knees, his hands on his aching temples, and in front of his closed, burning eyes he could see Manja running like a mole hunted from its burrow.

* * *

It began to rain very softly. The drops rustled on the leaves of the little birch tree and fell on Manja's uncovered hair, as well as on her face and hands that lay lifelessly on the wall. Only when she was like that, like a tree, like a plant on the ground, not flesh and blood like an animal or a human being, only then did the choking and panic start to go away. Only when she was as still as a plant did the pictures start to be ghosts. Her mind was blank, she was unaware of time, was only Manja, was no one.

She saw Heini before he, deceived by her stillness, saw her, but she didn't put out a hand, didn't raise her head, just let him go past without calling him – so that it was only when he looked round that he saw her dark outline next to the familiar birch tree on the wall. In two steps he was beside her and took hold of her wet, clammy hands.

'Manja! I've been looking for you everywhere. I'm so glad you're here!'

But Manja and the birch did not reply to the tender words; he was so moved that they were almost inaudible. Her icy hands, held between Heini's warm ones, only clenched themselves more tightly, and pushed his away.

'Manja, don't you want to see me? Don't you want to talk to me?'

She did not reply.

He sat down silently beside her. After his first hasty sentences, which he uttered spontaneously in his great joy at finding her, he couldn't think of anything else to say. He sat there, a helpless helper. She was so still, so quiet, so strange and stiff that only his fingers, gently holding a corner of her skirt, proved she was there.

It rained harder. Manja's torn blouse lay half off her naked, exposed shoulder. Heini put his coat over her. A man and woman were singing by the river; otherwise, apart from the rustling of leaves and rain it was quite quiet.

He sat there, his cold knees hunched up. Although he was alone with Manja, the person closest to him in the whole world, isolated from everyone else by an impenetrable wall of dark and rain, and although he would have been ready to tear out his heart for her, anything he could think of doing was stupid, and would make things even worse.

He gripped her shoulder.

'You've got to tell me everything, Manja. You'll feel better. We've always told each other everything, we mustn't have any secrets from each other now.'

But when she felt his strong grasp she jerked her shoulder away and sprang up so that his coat slid off her. She ran a couple of steps away and stood all hunched up, shaking her head from side to side.

'Manja, please stop it, no one's going to hurt you! Please stop.'

Though he very much wanted to, he dared not go near her in case it upset her even more. So he stayed where he was, watching her trembling and shaking only a few steps away from him. She was unreachable.

'Manja, aren't I your friend any more? Why aren't you listening to me?'

Unable to go on watching her anguish as though he did not share in it, he began to cry as he had never cried before; he didn't have to go on looking at her, imploringly, because her weeping was his, the screams she had stifled when she ran like an animal through the wood, her sobs of fear as she was being assaulted, all the tears he wept now were those she should have wept then. While he was crying Heini understood everything he had not understood before.

Then, when he was at his most miserable, a miracle occurred. As in a fairy tale his crying brought her frozen heart back to life. The person who had been turned to stone was turned back into a human being.

'Heini!' He could hardly hear her, but her first word made him unbelievably happy; then the miracle turned into affectionate blackmail as he realised that he who wept had greater power than he who was silent. He kept his hands in front of his eyes and listened to Manja's first step and then her second, joyfully felt her fingers on his cheek, and reached for her hands which stayed quietly in his. Her cold cheek touched his burning one. Thus they stood very still, listening to the rain, the wind and the sounds of the river. They were as one again, both of them carrying the burden of the last few hours.

'Manja, do you remember how we played, what did you call it . . . placing the moment in your heart?'

She nodded.

'Now we've got to do the opposite. We must hurry time up, make it pass a hundred times more quickly than usual, so that we're grown up and don't remember tonight and you're my wife and our children are grown up.'

'I don't think I want any children, Heini,' she said faintly, and shouted: 'They lied to us; being good doesn't help; and I don't believe in heaven any more.'

Heini was silent, unable to think of an answer.

'I'm not very good, Heini, but if something falls down I want to pick it up, and I don't ever want to knock something down.'

'I know what you mean,' he cried eagerly. 'A long time ago at school there was a beetle in the yard, on its back. I turned it over so it could crawl, but there were some boys who kept on turning it back to make it wriggle. Those kind of people are different.'

'But there are so many of those kind of people.'

'Yes, aren't there? There are suddenly so many,' he agreed. 'But, Manja, if we and everyone like us are cowards, then all the beetles in the world will have to stay on their backs.'

Manja said nothing but pressed his hand. 'You've turned over a beetle,' she said presently, 'it's crawling again.'

In spite of the darkness he could see her eyes were smiling and felt so happy that everything ached at once – his heart, nose, and ears – and was almost pleased when the beam of a pocket torch appeared on the slope, small raindrops dancing through it. Although much had been left unsaid, he was greatly relieved to see Karli's face under his hood.

'So here you are,' he said to Manja. 'Your mother was looking for you.'

He shone the torch down at a daisy, some grass and a few stones. He couldn't make sense of the fact that the other two were sitting here on a quite ordinary day, not a Wednesday or a Saturday, and were sitting on the wall in the rain.

'Harry came round. Franz is staying the night with him. He's ill. He said something about Manja and Martin. Your mother was anxious, she didn't know where you'd gone. She came looking for you. I promised Harry that I'd whistle in front of his window when I'd found you.'

During this muddled report he made circles of light on the field with his torch and looked at a thistle and some couch grass with enormous attention. Then he lifted the torch and it shone on Manja's legs and face; immediately his annoyance and his jealousy vanished.

'What's happened to you? Who scratched you like that? I'll kill the swine! What's he done to you? I'll show him.'

Manja gave no reply. She hunched her shoulders together and lowered her eyelids.

'It's all fine now, Karli, I don't want to talk about it. I must go home. Good night. No, I want to go on my own.' And to Heini she added softly: 'I'm not a coward any more.'

Then she waved at them, turned round quickly and walked very upright, though not in her usual way, across the stubble field. Both boys watched her till she disappeared.

Then, while Heini followed her in his thoughts as she turned onto the path and he couldn't see her any more, Karli turned to him agitatedly.

'What did he do to her?'

But mentally Heini was walking beside Manja on the muddy path. 'I don't know,' he said absent-mindedly.

'You must know, you've been here with her.'

'No,' answered Heini, now walking with Manja beside the dripping shrubs.

'You're lying,' yelled Karli.

Now they turned onto the road. They had to jump over puddles.

'I'm not lying,' he said in an unconvincing voice.

'Keep your secrets then, I don't want to know anything

about them,' Karli growled, his angry face disappearing into his hood.

Heini stepped away from Manja for a moment and held Karli by his coat. 'I really don't know.'

'Didn't you ask her, then?'

'No.' Now there was such conviction in his voice that Karli believed him at once.

'I can't understand it.' Karli scratched his head helplessly. 'And she didn't tell you anything herself?'

'No.'

Deeply reassured by this reply, Karli fell silent. Heini left him again and went back to Manja, turning into the alleyway and covering her torn blouse with her hands.

'If he's had her like people in the paper! They cut girls' throats with a broken bottle, young girls, and they have to go to hospital and never get completely better. Have you never read about it?'

'Yes,' said Heini softly.

'So you don't know what he did to her?'

'No.'

'Don't you want to kill him?'

Heini hesitated. The image of Martin had stayed oddly in the background. Manja was so close there was no room for hatred.

Karl took it for granted that the responsibility was his.

'I'll get it out of the swine tomorrow, I can tell you.'

Heini did not reply. He and Manja were going along the street, which was gleaming in the dim light; they walked in the shadows of the houses.

'You know that Manja's going to be my wife when I'm big?' said Karl casually.

Heini left Manja alone for a moment.

'No, she's going to be mine,' he said.

'We've already discussed it. We're going to be married at a registry office. We can't both be.'

'No,' agreed Heini.

'There are countries where two men can have the same wife,' went on Karli, 'but I don't think that would do for us, we'd have rows all the time.'

'When we're grown up we'll see which of us she wants,' said Heini. Being grown up was a long way off. He returned to the street into which Manja had now turned, passing the baker's, the coal merchant and the sausage shop, with its grey shutters rolled down.

'You can't marry her at all,' declared Karl triumphantly, 'because she's Jewish. Haven't you had any lessons about race?'

'Nor can you then.'

'I don't care about all that. If we have to we'll go abroad.'

Manja was walking across the yard and Heini saw her glance at Frau Reuter's window, creep up the stairs, quietly open the door, heard a sleepy voice and knew Manja was safe. He let her go.

Now there was nothing to keep them standing by the wall in the rain. He was wet through and tired. 'It's late,' he said, 'I must go home.'

'I promised to whistle in front of Harry's window.'

Together they went down the slope to the river. Wet grass squelched under their feet. From below came the noise of singing and marching. They were used to that, it was an everyday event. Silently the boys walked on.

Karli watched the procession with a gloomy face. In front of his eyes he was seeing a white wall flooded with sunlight. To Heini it seemed as though hundreds of Martins strode whistling and drumming along the street; like a shadow, Manja ran in front of them. At that moment their sad thoughts met like two hands touching and they felt ashamed, as if they were two twelve year-olds caught hand-in-hand in the street. Karl shook his plump burning face out of his hood and wished he could say something that would unite them like a declaration of love and separate them like a box on the ears, both at the same time.

'If Manja wants to love you,' he said, 'you'd better get married. Then I'll be a sailor.'

But, groaning deeply just like a three year-old, he added: 'Let's hope she'll prefer me.'

CHAPTER 30
EINE KLEINE NACHTMUSIK

'Will it take long?' asked Hartung in a low voice, pointing to the door of the next-door room, where Franz Meissner lay in bed.

'One or two weeks, if he doesn't get up,' replied Heidemann.

The light from Hartung's desk lamp fell evenly on the two men's faces, their very different hands and every object on the desk between them.

The corners of the room were shadowy. The grandfather clock showed that it was five to ten.

'Leave her alone!' shouted Franz's delirious voice in the next room.

The two men listened.

'He'll go to sleep,' decided Heidemann. 'I won't go in again.'

They heard Harry say a few quiet words. Then, as both fell silent, the clock chimed the hour.

'The shock to his nerves is more serious than the chill,' said Heidemann. 'Do you know his father?'

Hartung smiled. 'It's not very easy when one of the bosses of the new régime was once the porter at your bank.'

He spoke even more quietly than he had been, watching the door. Heidemann looked at the large, puffy face, with its sallow, wrinkled skin. I'd give him another five years at the most, he reflected, and then: perhaps he saved my life. But he didn't pursue the thought.

'You think I've changed,' said Hartung immediately. 'No wonder. My life isn't a rest cure. But I've got an iron constitution, don't you agree?'

Heidemann gave the expected answer.

He remained sheltered behind the professional protection of 'it's only the doctor', receiving confidences without having to return them; he could guess how much this lonely man needed to unburden himself. He glanced across from Hartung's restless, dishonest face at the quiet, composed one in the famous painting of his mother, lit up by the table lamp; the frank, all-seeing gaze was in harsh contrast to the self-deception of the living.

'What is grotesque is that I don't feel Jewish, that I did a great deal for the national cause long before it was the thing to do. I've always agreed with ninety per cent of anti-semitism. By the way, who said "Self-knowledge is the first step to anti-semitism"? It's grotesque that you're meant to be a martyr for a cause which means nothing to you. Do you understand what I'm saying?'

Heidemann nodded. He knew that his was only the role of the dummy, the listener whose most important characteristic is that he wouldn't ever repeat what he had heard.

'For me socialism is a childish disease and not a political movement. It was high time there was a reaction against such *naïveté* and incompetence. I'd seen it coming for a long time. I've always had a good nose for what's coming: I appealed to the German national spirit when it was fashionable to be an internationalist. I was one of the first men in Germany to build aeroplanes.'

'Yes,' said Heidemann, feeling as if he were at the bedside of an ailing man holding his head while he was being sick; mild nausea mixed with a faint sense of satisfaction that the patient must feel better.

'What is happening now, however,' said Hartung, still whispering, 'will undoubtedly end in ruin, believe me. Men like Meissner in power, people like Baron Adrian. He's a friend of mine, a decent type, but a child when it comes to business. You know, I feel like a builder who's constructed a house being pulled down by idiots. One has to watch while fools and bunglers destroy everything. I can't do a thing.'

'Shouldn't you let Meissner know his son's here?' asked Heidemann, bringing things back to practical matters.

'Oh, I wouldn't mind giving him a pain in the stomach!' answered Hartung, returning to their conversation.

'I'm not what I used to be either.' He rested his hands on the table. 'I don't have the grasp I used to have; my energies have drained away in too many directions.' He was silent a moment, his lips pressed together.

'How do you think my wife is?'

'Better,' said Heidemann. 'Quieter.'

'I'm helpless,' began Hartung again. 'Everything that's humanly possible has been done to help her. There are no sacrifices I haven't made. It's inexplicable – such a happy, carefree woman!'

Truth and untruth strangely mixed up together, thought Heidemann. Pain and guilt wrapped in lies, like lard wrapped round meat.

'Did you see the little boy?'

'Yes.'

'A splendid little chap, isn't he? A wonderful child. I want to go on for his sake, to hand on my work to him. Isn't he exactly like my mother?' He half turned round towards the picture, and Heidemann looked at it. It was as if the gold frame contained within it this man's entire lifetime of self-deception: all the shiny artificiality that stood between Hartung and a tough, honest understanding. The eyes seemed to wink at him contemptuously.

The ringing of the telephone cut short his thoughts. Hartung held the receiver to his ear. A momentary twitching of his face revealed amusement and his features became firmer, lost their flabbiness. With his hand over the mouth-piece he whispered, 'Meissner.' Heidemann could hear the bullying deep voice barking into the receiver.

'I expect you in my office at ten tomorrow.'

'Could you make it half-past ten?' asked Hartung. 'I have a conference.'

'I said ten.'

'Very well,' said Hartung submissively. 'I'll arrange it. May I ask what it's about?'

'You will find out tomorrow. I don't have time for long explanations ...' Meissner spoke more quietly, so that Heidemann only heard the end of the sentence: 'please be punctual.'

'In fact I was just about to ring you up, Herr Meissner.'

'Me?' It sounded like a snort.

'Your son is here in my house.'

Pause.

Quietly: 'Why is that?'

'He's ill, with a very high temperature.'

'Liar!'

'Hardly. I've called in Dr Heidemann.' The next sentence was inaudible.

'I'm afraid that's impossible,' replied Hartung, and held the receiver away from his ear towards Heidemann.

'Get him ready and I'll be there in half an hour.'

Heidemann shook his head.

'The doctor says it's impossible to move him.'

'I'll be responsible for that,' bawled the person at the other end.

'He's hung up,' said Hartung. 'A nice state of affairs.'

'I'll stay here,' decided Heidemann. 'I'll talk to him. It's putting you in a difficult position.'

Hartung laughed. 'It's a situation which gives me so much pleasure that I'm willing to pay a lot for it.'

He bit his lip. His face had changed; his words were no longer so confused and agitated, but forceful and curt.

'You can't afford it either, can you, to make yourself unpopular in high-up places?'

'I'll risk it.'

Hartung looked at him, no feature in that pale, thin face escaping his scrutiny. A short Swiss holiday would be good for him again, he thought, but probably wouldn't help much now. Poor woman, she's so devoted to him. All at once he wanted to be closer to this man, whom he had always liked but had never taken seriously, having dismissed him as an impractical idealist.

'And you?' he asked. 'How are you managing? Practice not busy? The rats desert the sinking ship? I know all about that.'

'I manage somehow.'

'Can I do anything?'

'No, but many thanks.'

Silence, apart from the clock and distant singing in the street.

'What good does it do you,' asked Hartung, 'not to admit that you too have had it up to here?' He drew his hand across his throat.

'And how does the opposite help?' asked Heidemann.

Hartung shrugged his shoulders. He looked old again, bent and miserable. We should unite in our loneliness, thought Heidemann, as though it were easy for all lonely people to stand together, as if the whole world didn't lie between them. The same blows hit everyone differently.

'Well, in any case the next fight we'll fight together,' said Hartung. His fingers drummed on the table. 'We're two old warriors, you know.'

The singing in the street became louder, became a roar. Hartung got up and went over to the window. Without touching the drawn curtains he peered through a narrow gap into the street, where a troop of young men had positioned themselves. One could clearly hear what the loud, youthful voices were singing:

Jews get out
From our German house,

We'll fight with sticks and stones,
Till the Jews are dead.

'*Eine kleine Nachtmusik*,' said Hartung quietly.

For a second Heidemann forgot about the painting, the lies and the loneliness and put his hand on Hartung's bowed shoulders.

* * *

Harry was sitting by Franz's bed when the singing began in the street and he frowned in annoyance and tiptoed to the window. Like his father he peered through the curtains and looked out of the dark room at the column lined up on the pavement.

'Harry!' called Franz from the bed.

'Go to sleep,' answered Harry quietly, as if his whisper could drown out the shouting.

'Have you got pistols? We've got to shoot.'

'Shh . . .' said Harry as if he were talking to a child or a fly.

'Are the others down there?'

'Who?'

'Heini and Karl.'

'They've been gone a long time. Go to sleep!' He whispered but the noise from down below grew so loud that no one could possibly have gone to sleep, so he went back to his friend's bed and sat down beside him.

'We'll put all the lights out, then they'll soon go away.' He straightened the pillow under Franz's head and touched his forehead. 'Are you better?'

The song came loud, piercing and threatening from below:

So long as Jews stay in the land,
Filth and plague will be spread around.
Get out, get out from our German house.

'My mother will be frightened,' whispered Harry.

'Don't go away,' begged Franz. 'Martin is with Manja. He's burning her.'

He threw off the cover and tried to get up. Harry held him down and covered him up.

'Please be quiet, your father isn't here, and those people in the street will soon go away if we take no notice of them.'

Max, Max, come out here,
Or else I'll scratch your eyes out

sang a voice down below very clearly; there was a laugh like splintered glass.

Franz tried to jump out of bed again.

'We must tell everyone that he's got sock-suspenders. Your father's got to take his uniform away.'

Just when Harry could hold onto him no longer the door opened and Heidemann came in. In two strides he was at the bedside. Franz shrank away from him.

'He made her go into the wood. She doesn't have a chance. I must get up.'

'No one's been hurt,' said Heidemann, 'you're a bit feverish. You're in bed at your friend's house and all your friends are asleep.'

Fight, fight, fight,
Away with the serpents of hell . . .

Just as Heidemann's words had calmed him down, Franz sat up trembling. Then, for no reason, the song broke off. Only one voice continued and then was silent.

On the balcony a woman in white had appeared, followed by a dark-haired nurse in uniform. In the silence Heidemann clearly heard Hilde's admonishing voice.

'You mustn't sing at night. The stars will fall down.'

And then the deep, masculine voice of the nurse: 'The lady is ill.'

'No, I'm not ill.'

Then it was quiet, there was an order, footsteps and complete silence.

'There you are,' said Heidemann, bending over Franz, 'now it's perfectly quiet and you can all go to sleep.'

'I'll lie on the sofa without undressing,' whispered Harry, 'I'll look after him.'

Hartung appeared in the door between the two rooms.

'Everything's all right.' The silence was an immense relief.

'Do you think he'll still come?' asked Heidemann.

No answer was necessary, since outside there was the sound of a car turning into the street, stopping, doors banging shut, loud ringing on the doorbell, all in quick succession. Heidemann glanced at the sleeping Franz and left the room with Hartung.

* * *

Meissner strode stiffly along the passage in his tightly fitting uniform as if he was on a parade ground. In vain the housemaid, wishing to announce him, tried to keep up with him. Through the open door he saw Hartung in his study walking slowly up and down.

'Thank you, I know my way.' He pushed her to one side and knocked on the door as he went in.

Hartung was standing behind his desk, as he always used to when Meissner, another Meissner, but terribly similar to this one, came into his room.

'Heil Hitler!'

'Good evening, Herr Meissner. You know Dr Heidemann?'

'I haven't the pleasure.'

'Our boys are friends,' said Heidemann as they shook hands.

'Will you sit down? Cigar?'

Meissner tried to free himself from the constraint which the atmosphere of the room imposed on him. With growing anger he perceived the advantage of host over guest. He ought to have seen Hartung in his own office, he sitting and the other standing. Walking up to the desk he was like an undefended man going towards a fortress.

'Thank you, I have very little time. Where is the boy?'

'Franz must not be moved, Herr Meissner,' said Heidemann firmly.

'I've got the car downstairs.'

'In his condition a car journey is out of the question.'

'Where is he?'

'He's asleep.'

'Then he'll have to wake up,' said Meissner loudly. 'I'll carry him down.'

'That would be a real danger for the boy,' said Heidemann.

'He was perfectly well this afternoon,' interrupted Meissner impatiently.

'And now he's extremely ill,' repeated Heidemann.

Meissner turned to Hartung. 'Perhaps you would be good enough to tell me where I will find my son?'

'Do be reasonable, Meissner.'

Meissner tried to repel the icy rebuff but it bounced off Hartung, who was quite calm. He longed to be on a parade ground, with troops whom he could command, a wall against which he could line up his enemies one by one by saying one sharp word: Fire! Not these wallpapered civilised walls, this half-dark, elegant room.

'Don't touch her,' shouted Franz from next door, to his father's relief since he could now advance directly on his goal. He opened the door and went in.

Again he wished someone would tell him what to say. He saw that they had not been lying – the boy had a burning fever.

'Make yourself ready, we're going home.'

Instead of answering, Franz sprang out of bed and crawled underneath it, pulling the blanket down with him.

'Go away, go away!' he screamed, sliding into the farthest corner between wall and bed. He wrapped himself in the blanket and whimpered with fright.

Helpless and furious, Meissner bent down and tried to reach Franz's leg. His huge, brown bottom made him look like a diving duck. But it would have been too undignified to crawl under the bed.

'Come out!' he ordered. 'Come out at once.'

The boy whimpered.

'I'm not going to beat you,' Meissner reassured him quietly. 'Do be reasonable.'

'Go away, go away!' screamed Franz.

Meissner went towards the wall and tried to approach the boy from there, but he merely crawled to the other side of the bed, moaning loudly.

'Come out at once, I'm ordering you, immediately!' Again the grotesque brown diver bent down.

His fat bottom had a provocative effect on Heidemann. It made him angrier and angrier. His uncontrollable rage increased by the minute until he could not restrain himself. He seized Meissner by the belt and, feeling as capable of fighting as someone far younger, pulled him up.

'How dare you?' asked Meissner.

'When he's well,' said Heidemann icily, 'you can put him against a wall. Until then you have to wait.'

While Meissner, his jaws working, tried to find an answer Hartung went over to him. 'You've now seen for yourself that the boy's really ill. I assure you, he will lack for nothing here.'

'I want to consult a decent doctor.'

'You can call in a second doctor tomorrow if you wish, but if I might advise you . . .'

'I haven't asked for your advice,' said Meissner.

'I'm very sorry you have been troubled for nothing, Meissner; *force majeur*, if you know what I mean.'

Meissner glanced again at the bundle under the bed, which he could not get hold of without crawling under the bed himself. He did not glance at either of the men.

'You'll be hearing from me,' he shouted, and fled down the passage without saying goodbye. His footsteps rang out as if he were on a parade ground.

'Stupid,' said Hartung when the front door had shut, 'very stupid.'

Heidemann laid Franz down on the bed – he had let himself be lifted up without a struggle – and was feeling his pulse.

'Stupidity is like blood-letting, a great relief.'

For a second he met Harry's eyes, beaming with admiration under his bent glasses.

'The blood-letting will be expensive, Dr Heidemann.'

'It's worth it to me,' he answered, feeling a boyish cheerfulness and relief.

'And to me,' said Hartung. He was pleased to see his son's admiring gaze which abandoned Heidemann and, squinting out, rested lovingly on him.

* * *

When Heidemann got back home and gently opened the kitchen door to get a glass of water, he found his son asleep at the table, his head on his arm. As soon as he came in Heini woke up.

'Is something the matter, my boy?' asked Heidemann, looking at his son's face, which had red marks from the edge of the table, as did his fingers.

'How's Franz?'

'He was quite quiet when I left.' Heidemann sat down, the white expanse of the oilcloth-covered table between them both.

'Did he say anything while he was delirious?' began Heini.

'Yes, he said all sorts of things.'

'What?'

A little surprised, Heidemann said: 'About his father, about someone he wanted to chase away.'

'Martin,' said Heini in a low voice.

'Who is Martin?'

Heini did not answer. Heidemann saw how he was trembling, how his hands held the table tightly; with its pale lips and closed eyes his face displayed strong and unchildlike emotion. It was as if the boyish face had changed, in front of his eyes, first into that of a young man and then into the grieving adult he would not know. He had the worn look of a lover standing in front of strange doorways in the darkness, the despair of people on landing-stages when the gangway has been raised and the last link broken.

'Has he done something to Manja?' asked Heidemann.

Heini wasn't surprised that his father had guessed what he could not have said. Falteringly he spoke. For the second time that day he discovered that in conversation with people close to you there are no smooth and well-formed sentences, no sequence of clear question and answer.

'You must help me. He's evil, he wants to . . . What does he really want to do?' In a flash the suffering adult face changed into that of a four year-old wanting to know why water is wet and birds fly.

Heidemann spoke slowly and carefully, preparing every step they took together into the human jungle. But he hid nothing.

The boy was very pale, his mouth and throat twitched, as though he was about to be sick. 'Did he do that with Manja, father?'

'I don't think so, my little one.'

Heini reached for Heidemann's hands and laid his forehead on them, keeping quite still and trying to control his trembling. Heidemann did not say any fatherly words. For as long as he could remember, they had always talked as between equals.

'I'd like to help you, my boy. I'd like to do anything I can to see he doesn't go near Manja again.'

Heini lifted his head and looked at him. Heidemann was seeing himself as a boy and Heini was seeing himself in the future. There was more than mere similarity; there was the same mould, character and expression. The feeling of oneness filled both of them with immense joy and every danger seemed negligible compared with it.

'Did you know, by the way, that I have known Manja longer than you, Heini?'

Heini looked at him with Hanna's wry, sideways smile. 'Why haven't you told me that before?'

'I only found out later when I saw her mother.'

And he told Heini about the night over twelve years ago when he had fought for the life of the little two day-old girl as though it had been his own child.

The boy's face beamed with joy. He forgot everything, he forgot it was night-time, that they had been talking in whispers. He shouted with delight:

'Can I tell her?'

'Of course, if you want to.' Heidemann was infected by his joy.

'It's wonderful,' shouted Heini; 'wonderful.'

They heard the living-room door open.

'Now we've woken her up,' whispered Heini.

'It's too late to whisper now,' laughed Heidemann; 'now there'll be a frightful row.'

Hanna stood in the doorway. 'You're right,' she said. 'Have you both gone mad? What are you doing in here?'

'We've been having a man-to-man chat,' answered Heidemann.

Hanna looked from one to the other. She remembered how the boy had rushed out that evening, how he had come back pale and silent and gone straight to his room.

'At two o'clock in the morning!' she scolded, deciding to allow herself a little revenge for her fright and their secrecy. 'What was it about, then?'

In their attempt to keep their secret, in their refusal to lie, Heidemann and his son were equally at a loss – as helpless as two boys caught stealing sugar.

In that moment Hanna loved the pair of them as if they were one person.

'I'm glad things are all right again.' She patted Heini's hair for a moment. Taking hold of her hands and nodding to the boy, Heidemann said:

'I wonder if there really is such a thing as a man-to-man chat.'

CHAPTER 31
QUADRILLE ON A DARK FLOOR

Things look quite different in the morning from the way they do at night. When Hartung, who had hardly slept, thought over the events of the evening before, he felt he had behaved like an idiot. Foolishness of the kind he had indulged in the previous night was amusing in better times, criminal in these.

The first thing he did in the morning was to order an ambulance and, observing the greatest precautions, see that Franz Meissner, who had had a fairly good night, was sent home. Then, since Meissner had not cancelled the appointment during his stormy visit, he went to his office at ten. He was not there and Hartung waited for half an hour in a draughty corridor, being eyed suspiciously by everyone who went by. Then he left and, used to always being in a hurry, took a taxi but didn't know what address to give. Somewhere, anywhere, through the park. No one needed him just then, no one was waiting for him. But he had a great deal to think about and there was no better place for thinking things out than in a moving car.

He had been practically forced out of his bank. Adrian had established himself at the factory and was no longer merely the nominal owner of the firm. Hartung had run things so efficiently that he would soon become dispensable if he didn't succeed in regaining control and consolidating his relationship with Adrian. Immediately he decided where to go, casually, informally, without making an appointment. Adrian had had a hunting accident and was at home, so a polite sick-bed visit away from the atmosphere of the office would be a good way of getting a sense of how things stood. He tapped on the taxi window and gave the driver the address in the suburbs that he remembered seeing at the top of letters. He had never been to Adrian's house. As the car drove down the sunny avenue of chestnut trees, where the leaves were turning yellow, he felt oddly apprehensive.

Adrian was sitting on the terrace in a deck-chair, his injured arm in a sling. Every now and then a yellow leaf fluttered across from the next-door garden and fell gently on the ground. Then the black dog lying beside him would lift its head for a moment and, bored, shut its eyes again. In the door leading to the living-room, intruding loudly on the sleepy, sunny autumn morning, stood Meissner. He intended his loud voice and his tense restlessness to contrast sharply with the other's indolence and calm. Lying as he was he looked like an outstretched dog. But Meissner was not going to allow himself to be impressed any more by his obsolete, aristocratic manner. The new Meissner was equal to anyone he pleased, an equality he would only surrender when he chose to do so.

'Hartung must be got rid of!'

It was very quiet when he stopped speaking; one could hear the sound of the leaves falling and of women's voices in the windows of nearby houses. Adrian held a leaf in his long thin fingers. The dog turned its head and yawned, showing the inside of its red mouth.

'Why bring up all that old business again?' he asked, twisting the leaf on its stalk. Looking at his weak, decadent hand, Meissner said to him grimly, 'The whole set-up's going to be smoked out.'

Adrian was listening to a bright, cheerful woman's voice from across the way.

'You'll be chief witness for the prosecution,' said Meissner.

Adrian patted the head of the dog, who was growling in his sleep. 'I haven't the slightest wish to,' he replied calmly.

'I've come to give you some advice for the sake of our old friendship.'

'And what sort of advice is that?'

'Don't try to shield Hartung. I know better than anyone what you think of him. I reme . . .'

'Wouldn't it be better if you didn't remember too much, Meissner?' asked Adrian, bending down to the dog. 'Let sleeping dogs lie.'

For a moment Meissner felt himself subordinate to the other again, felt feeble and cornered. For a second the humiliations of the past returned.

'You are perhaps unable to decide today,' he said. 'You're evidently still weak after your accident.'

'No, Meissner, now that you're here, I'd like to get things sorted out. I don't want to have anything to do with it.'

'That will be seen as proof that Hartung's quick release was brought about by a certain person's influence.'

Adrian shrugged his shoulders.

'There's nothing held against you,' went on Meissner more firmly. 'Your position would be stronger if Hartung were removed. Naturally you won't be asked any questions that might . . .'

'I've already said once that no one is going to ask me any questions.'

'So you've decided to go against the authority of the State and put yourself on the side of a Jewish swindler?'

Adrian did not reply. He examined the brownish-yellow chestnut leaf in his hand as though he had never seen one before.

'Then I shall probably not be able to protect you any longer,' said Meissner.

Adrian looked up, his eyes gleaming with an angry, scornful smile.

'Have you been protecting me up to now, then?' he asked.

Anton Meissner was crimson, and his neck hot under the collar of his uniform. But he was no longer someone who gave vent to his anger like a child slamming doors. Nowadays it was too precious to waste and he kept it under control.

'That remains to be seen,' he said curtly.

'I would have liked to have seen you to the door, Meissner, but I really feel too tired.'

Before Meissner had even closed the door of the living-room Adrian had forgotten about him, sinking back into the mood of the autumn morning, which made everything seem gentle and distant. People crawled like ugly dwarfs over the earth, noisily disfiguring it. The perfection of the dog getting up and stretching contrasted with the coarseness of Meissner, whose noise and conceit had deprived him of an hour of the morning.

He was still twisting the leaf in his hand. Perfection – leaf, dog and autumn foliage! The woods where he walked and rode, the whole world, was ruined by people. At some point, perhaps in the not too distant future, he would leave it all, and spend the days roaming through the woods before dawn, away from the sound of human voices, seeing no human face. Peace, beauty and clean air. The dog put back its ears and began to growl.

At that moment Meissner almost bumped into Hartung, who was coming up the steps. Each was surprised to encounter the other and both had their worst fears confirmed. Hartung recovered first and began to say something, but Meissner walked past him without taking the proffered hand.

A second uninvited guest intruded on the peace of Adrian's morning and could not be refused. Hartung shook Adrian's uninjured hand, overwhelmed him with solicitous questions, admired the house and, reluctantly, the dog, which was barking angrily at him.

'Come here, Prinz!'

The dog, still growling, lay down at Adrian's feet. Its presence upset Hartung. He sat down on a wicker chair some distance away and hunched up his knees protectively. He had really wanted to push his chair next to Adrian's deck-chair and talk to him confidentially, but without going closer to the dog he couldn't.

'I met Meissner,' he began, watching Adrian, whose head was against a cushion and whose eyes were shut.

'Meissner did not seem to have enjoyed his visit.' Hartung stopped for a moment but as Adrian did not interrupt him he went on:

'I should like to talk quite frankly, if it isn't too much of a strain for you.'

Adrian shook his head.

'Meissner's up to something. I don't know to what extent he's bluffing, but nowadays one must be prepared for anything. Have you . . . Did you tell him anything?'

'No,' said Adrian sharply.

Hartung scrutinised his haughty profile. 'Please don't misunderstand me. But your relationship used to be close. Meissner has doubtless obtained information which he will know how to use.'

'Those are things that happened a long time ago,' replied Adrian vehemently. 'Since I took over, nothing has happened which everyone can't know about.'

Hartung smiled. 'The present situation has in that respect been of considerable help to you. Armaments are the thing in official circles. But let's not quarrel, that's not why I came.' He put out his hand to Adrian's, but drew it back at once when the dog snapped at it.

'No doubt Meissner won't dare do anything on a large scale. He prefers small deceits, small meannesses.'

'I'm not so sure of that,' said Adrian.

Hartung looked at him silently for a moment, trying to read the thoughts that lay behind the scratched forehead.

'Did he say something?'

'How dare you cross-examine me?' said Adrian angrily, almost immediately controlling himself; and as though its master's rage had transferred itself to something else, the dog sprang at Hartung, putting its paws on his chest and its foaming mouth on his throat.

Hartung had turned pale. 'Do you want me to be mauled by your dog?' he asked without moving.

Adrian called off the dog, which at once obeyed – retreating slowly from Hartung and barking furiously. Hartung wiped his forehead.

'I beg your pardon,' said Adrian.

'A pedigree dog indeed,' muttered Hartung under his breath and then, out loud, with a laugh: 'Mutual antipathy. I want to make a proposal to you, Adrian. I have to sell Bucheneck.'

For the first time during their conversation Adrian turned his face towards him. He leant forward and a flush of excitement rose up to his grey temples.

'I've made great sacrifices to hold on to it, but as things are it's not going to be possible any longer. I should like you to have it.'

Thus was the past thrown like a huge boulder on the road of the present, and could not be overlooked. Hartung could not be got rid of so simply. Using his boulder, he broke into the world of the present. Pretending to be exhausted, Adrian thought about it. Part of him wanted to accept the offer with alacrity. He realised for the first time that it wasn't lack of money which had stopped him buying an estate. He didn't want just any estate, fields, and woods – he wanted his own estate, his own woods. Bucheneck, however, was no longer full of quiet memories. Hartung's mark was on everything, the two were entangled, connected, indebted.

410

'I don't have any money,' he said.

'I'll let you have it at a good price.'

Falteringly, their conversation edged along the abyss of their thoughts.

'There are tremendous opportunities at the moment for making money. It's lying on the streets.'

'Why don't you pick it up then?'

'It's there for the taking.'

Swift, quiet, convincing questions and answers.

'There are any number of Jewish factories and estates that can be bought for a song.'

Adrian had a fleeting image of a battlefield at night with grave snatchers creeping silently about pulling rings from dead hands, watches off wrists and money out of pockets.

'There's no need to be shocked. We're doing people a favour. Unless you think they would rather the state took over their businesses.' Hartung spoke quietly and vehemently, leaning forward without getting closer to Adrian. The dog sat between them, alert and threatening.

A chestnut fell into the courtyard, shattering on the stones with a crack.

'I'll think about it,' said Adrian. He looked through the wrought-iron balcony into the courtyard where the shiny chestnut lay.

'You'll never be a business man,' said Hartung. And, driven by a strange impulse, he said by way of a diversion: 'You won't be here much longer. I'd like to see you back in the fields at Bucheneck.'

Adrian, oddly moved by the words and their tone, let go of the dog's collar.

'Keep hold of your dog,' said Hartung.

Adrian ordered it to lie down.

'Why is it in your interests to see me at Bucheneck?'

'Perhaps I'd like you to run it.'

'I didn't think of that,' said Adrian, in a tone which immediately reassured Hartung.

'People ought to be where they belong,' he said quietly.

For a second it seemed possible that Hartung might give Bucheneck to Adrian, who felt momentary pity for this man who belonged nowhere. The second passed. He would get rid of me without hesitation, thought Hartung. He wants me to involve myself in risky deals so that he becomes indispensable, thought Adrian.

'It's out of the question that I could afford Bucheneck,' said Adrian.

'Of course I've invested a good deal in it.'

Adrian pressed his lips together and frowned. A memory which had recurred several times while they were talking but never quite surfaced, now forced its way through and struck Hartung like a blow. The little boy's face was identical in every feature to the one before him.

'Don't you feel well?' asked Adrian, seeing him turn pale.

'It's nothing, thank you, I'm better already.' And because one cannot conceal or push away a grief of such intensity, Hartung tried to drive it away by surrendering to it. He felt in his pocket and took out a photo of Hans Peter which he always had on him.

'Have you seen this picture?' he asked and, seeing how Adrian withdrew his hand and clenched his fingers, took pleasure in forcing it on him. Adrian looked at the extreme beauty of the boyish face he was holding in his hand. He had the same mingled emotions about it as he had about Bucheneck. He wanted both to preserve and possess and not to acknowledge, not remember.

'A lovely child,' he said. Once, through the garden railings, he had seen Harry and the nurse pushing him in his pram. He had seen an ordinary, round baby face, but this picture was different. The way the boy held himself, his expression, reminded him of the faded pictures of children in old-fashioned clothes in the green-plush albums at Bucheneck.

'He's very attached to me,' said Hartung. 'We're the best of friends.'

The photograph lay in Adrian's hand, just as the yellow leaf had done before; the face was as perfect and as immaculate as it had been. Adrian's fingers trembled as he handed it back, just as they had when he took it.

'If you want to see the original you are most welcome,' said Hartung, putting the photograph back in his wallet.

'Thank you.' A slender, living thread ran from the photograph in Hartung's wallet to the albums and to his estate.

'Let me know before you sell the estate, Hartung.'

'Certainly. And now I must leave you in peace; you look worn out.'

With great politeness they quickly shook hands.

The dog growled.

CHAPTER 32
AN EXCURSION IN AUTUMN

That morning Heidemann had been told at the door of Hartung's house that Franz had been taken back to his father and that the Herr Kommerzienrat was unfortunately out. They had failed to inform him earlier, having no doubt assumed that he would telephone before coming. It was the first of the day's errands, planned to help him carry out the task he had decided upon the night before.

'He was very upset,' the maid whispered confidentially at the door, and she winked at him conspiratorially knowing he was someone who would immediately understand what she meant. He walked away thinking about what he had to do that day. It was a relief to get away from his whirling thoughts and try to concentrate on something straightforward. He had to find an antagonist whose first name, he knew, was Martin, and to make sure Manja was unharmed. That was all.

He walked to Manja's house. It was a sunny autumn day. On the pavement the wind swept withered leaves along in waves. He noticed an old man in a high collar slowly and methodically sweeping a path in front of his house. The leaves covered it again almost at once; he didn't look at the trees endlessly frustrating what he was doing, only at the broom he was using to sweep so systematically. Heidemann had to smile.

It wasn't until that evening that the image of the man came back to him, and seemed more significant.

He knocked at Frau Reuter's door. Having already seen him approaching through the window she opened it quickly – men as distinguished-looking as him rarely came to the house. He asked for Manja's flat, then his glance, avoiding her malicious grin, noticed something both familiar and out-of-place: the writing on a jam jar poking out of an open parcel. It said *'Plums'* in Hanna's handwriting.

'Which floor?' asked Heidemann.

'There's no one there. A lady's already asked; she went away again.'

Heidemann realised that Hanna had been there before him; the jar was an old acquaintance.

'Second floor?' he asked.

'Third,' she answered mechanically, 'but no one will be in. Shall I show you up?'

'No, thanks,' said Heidemann and pushed past the woman in her doorway.

Nothing stirred when he rang. Nevertheless he had the clear impression there was someone in the flat. His thumb on the bell, he listened to its shrill ringing until he thought he heard footsteps. The peephole opened and Manja's eyes looked out.

'Are you going to let me in, Manja?' asked Heidemann, intensely relieved. She stood in the door, flushed with pleasure, smiling in astonishment.

'There's no one here,' she said.

'I've come only to see you.'

She stretched her hand out, asking him to come in with a graceful gesture that was in great contrast to the room into which she led him. Whatever the child might have been doing, while she was alone in the locked flat, she now sat opposite him perfectly at ease. Slowly the flush of pleasure faded away and was replaced by a laboured smile like a mask held over her face.

'How is Heini?' she asked.

'Very well, thank you, he's at school. Manja, I have come....'

'Yes,' she interrupted. 'It's not very tidy. My mother's gone out, so have my brothers.' She put these rapid sentences in his way so deliberately that Heidemann was aware of the brutality with which he had to remove them.

'Who scratched your cheek?' he asked.

Manja's face closed up. It became small and pale and her eyes disappeared beneath the lids.

'Brambles,' she said.

Heidemann felt great respect for the young girl who was making it so hard for him to help her. 'Manja,' he said without looking at her, 'I'm not only Heini's father, you know how fond we are of you. Can't you talk to me quite frankly, tell me everything? I want to help you.'

His words seemed blunt and *naïve* even to himself. He could see that he was causing her agony. His hands, fidgeting on the faded table-cloth, touched her finger. He held it for a moment.

'There's nothing to tell.'

'Heini told me you didn't feel well yesterday,' he began again. It was at once obvious that she dreaded the end of his sentence and was relieved. A smile gleamed in her eyes but was lost before it reached her cheeks and mouth.

'I'm perfectly all right,' she exclaimed loudly, throwing her hair back, then was alarmed at her own vehemence and added quickly and very quietly: 'It's so nice of you to have come.'

'I have a request, Manja.'

Her head in her hand, she looked at him.

'It may be quite unnecessary and you are probably quite right. But I want to be sure. Let me examine you.'

'But really,' cried Manja, 'there's nothing wrong with me.' She fought with her tears.

'I've examined you so often,' said Heidemann gently, 'so I'm not a stranger. I had a look at Heini too yesterday, since you were both together with Franz.' He spoke in a low casual voice. Manja had got up; she turned her back and stood with her face to the wall.

'I can't,' she said in a choking voice.

'Why, Manja?'

She turned round and Heidemann saw from her face that he had to leave her alone at once, and not exert any pressure a moment longer.

'Of course I won't, if you don't want me to. Heini has obviously worried himself unnecessarily that you caught cold in the rain yesterday.'

'It was quite some rain!' said Manja, and the mask-like smile spread over her face again. It was fragile and transparent and implored him to let it stay where it was. It was decisive. He

417

was not such a pedant as to insist on an examination simply to establish empirical facts and pay for them by a further terrible shock. Her face, voice and demeanour were proof in themselves that she had been the victim of violence even if there was no physical evidence.

'Yes,' he said, 'Heini came home wet through. I had something to do nearby, so I thought I'd come and have a look at you.'

She came with him to the door. 'Thank you for your visit,' she said, holding out her hand.

'If you need anything, Manja, you know . . .'

'I don't need anything. Goodbye. Thank you.'

It seemed to him that she couldn't hold the door open a moment longer and he let himself be ushered out by her smile.

When the door was closed he stood for a moment perplexed. He had achieved nothing, had learnt nothing he didn't already know. He'd been a clumsy, blundering fool; he seemed to have lost the gift of getting people to talk. He almost rang the bell again, but the smile in the dark doorway which had made him go was more powerful than instinct or reason. As he turned to leave he heard a noise from above. Turning his head he saw a large figure waving to him on the dark landing.

'One moment, Doctor.'

At first he didn't recognise the woman, but when he came up to her and she nodded to him he knew her but without being able to remember her name.

'Have you got a minute?'

He followed her through the dark little hallway into a room almost identical to the one he had just come from. But this one had what was so lacking downstairs: warmth, tidiness, care.

'I was going to come and see you today,' began Anna Müller. She sat opposite him in a leather arm-chair, leaning her thin grey hair against its worn back.

'How long is it since I saw you in the hospital?' asked Heidemann, looking at her greatly-aged face.

'Six months, Doctor, since I came with Hede.' All the disparate images linked up, he even remembered the name: Hedwig Müller over the girl's bed, and the business with Sister Mathilde.

'Six months,' he repeated. But the strain on the face opposite him dated from months before that.

'Isn't she well, Frau Müller?'

'Everything's all right with Hede so far, but the child below . . . You've been there?'

'Yes,' said Heidemann.

'Her mother called me during the night. The child was raving and shouting and didn't recognise anyone. Doctor, I don't know what that brute did to her, but she's covered with bruises. One can't do that to a child.'

'Do you know who it was, Frau Müller?'

'I've heard nothing else but his name since yesterday evening! Though my boy didn't tell me anything, all he said was that he's going to kill this Martin.'

'Do you know him?'

'He's the nephew of the landlord of the bar on our corner. Hammelmann he's called. Karl says he's very self-important at the school. He's very active in the Movement,' said Anna, lowering her voice instead of winking, in the way people did when they wanted to show they didn't belong to it.

'It'll be difficult to find him; I know how. . . .' And then came a frightened pause, that sudden doubt whether the person sitting there was enough of a friend, that inspection of walls and doors to see if they wouldn't betray the barely-spoken words.

'How is your husband?' asked Heidemann in a low voice.

'I don't know. I haven't seen him.' Anna bent down, picked a strand of cotton off the floor, put it on the back of the chair, and straightened it out with her fingers.

'But what's going on with the child downstairs, I won't have that. She's not the sort to get it out of her system by crying, it will tear her apart.'

'Could you give me the address of Hammelmann's bar?' Anna did so and also told him where Karli's school was. She offered to accompany him to the next street since she had something to do nearby. While she put on her coat and hat in the bedroom and they were talking through the open door about Manja and her mother and brothers – carefully avoiding any reference to Anna's difficulties – Heidemann saw twin beds, sticking out diagonally into the room: one with white sheets where someone clearly slept at night, the other looking abandoned with its forlorn, smooth green bedspread. The sight of these two different beds was sadder than any lament could have been.

Heidemann followed Anna, who was wearing her hat with the stiff little feather. They began to talk loudly about the weather until they were out of Frau Reuter's sight and hearing.

Then Anna said, 'It was she who got my husband arrested.'

Heidemann thought of the bed with the green cover and realised what it meant to have to walk past that woman every day.

'Best wishes to everyone at home,' he said when they parted.

'There are not many of us left at home, but thank you.'

* * *

Heidemann went first to the school, arriving before it closed. A lorry stood in front of the gates, decorated with swastika flags. The caretaker, tired and bad-tempered, directed him to the classroom he asked for. He went up, through the buzzing sound of pupil and teacher, and paced up and down the corridor. A young teacher in uniform hurried past him, gave him a quick, friendly look and disappeared through a door.

The school bell went and at once the buzz was transformed into a roar and babble of voices. The door opened and two or three boys rushed out before the master. Heidemann stopped the first and asked for Martin. He pointed to the large boy who had just gone by. Heidemann walked towards him and called him by his name.

Surprised, Martin stood still and looked at him. A disagreeable resemblance, which he could not place, made him hostile and suspicious. Heidemann saw Martin's face and the eyes which had reminded Heini of snails' horns. He pushed the image away.

'I must talk to you for a moment,' said Heidemann.

From every classroom boys streamed out in the uniform of the Hitler Youth.

'What's it about?' asked Martin. His small half-closed eyes avoided Heidemann's.

Instead of sensibly making an appointment for another time, Heidemann said quickly and quietly: 'Manja.'

The boy's face changed, turned red and annoyed.

'Are you a relation by any chance?' he asked arrogantly.

Those angry steel-blue eyes reminded him of something and suddenly he knew whose face the one in front of him resembled.

The young teacher in uniform hurried out of the door into which he had disappeared. He talked to a group of boys, who stood to attention while receiving his orders and then ran downstairs. They could hear him asking for Martin.

'I haven't got time,' the boy said to Heidemann. 'They're calling me.'

'I can wait.'

'Till this afternoon, if it makes you happy. But you'd do better finding out what your son is up to.' Heidemann saw a mixture of impudence and fear on his face.

'You'll leave Manja alone,' he said between his teeth.

Martin did not reply; he waved to the master and shrugged his shoulders.

'I'm sorry, I'm on duty.' Heidemann heard him talking loudly and eagerly to the master. It was to do with the arrangements for a trip in the lorry Heidemann had seen outside.

Before going downstairs Martin glanced back at him out of the corner of his eye; fear, threats and contempt were conveyed in that half second. Then he rushed downstairs, followed by a group of boys who had been waiting for the conversation to end. Heidemann remembered that Karl Müller was in the same class. He went in and asked for Karl.

He was told that he had been there but had not come back after the break. His things were still on the desk.

'Are you looking for someone?' asked a voice behind him.

He turned round to the young master whom he had seen in the corridor. His face was flushed and cheerful; his eyes had a childlike expression and looked at him with trusting curiosity.

'I'd very much like to speak to Karl Müller.'

A troubled look passed over the youthful face and it seemed to Heidemann that the good mark he had been about to earn was reluctantly exchanged for a bad one.

'He's in detention. He attacked another boy.'

'Was there a fight?' asked Heidemann, who at once understood what had happened.

'No, an unprovoked attack with a knife. Luckily he was stopped before there was a tragedy.' He stopped and looked at his watch. 'But excuse me, I'm in a great rush.'

The annoyance in his voice, the childish gesture with which he excused himself, made him both likeable and comic.

'Nevertheless, may I talk to you for a few moments?' pleaded Heidemann. 'I can wait.'

'No, come with me to the office,' said the teacher, holding out his hand in a friendly way and murmuring a name Heidemann could not catch. On the way he explained that he was in charge of the Winter Relief Campaign in all the intermediate schools, a gigantic business. The children's enthusiasm was unparalleled.

On the desk there lay, neatly arranged, large sheets covered with writing. The telephone rang. With a gesture that expressed both haste and delight the young master sprang to answer it.

'One moment,' Heidemann heard him say; then, snatching up a pencil, he jotted down numbers and names.

'The first results!' he cried, putting down the receiver. 'Prodigious! You've seen our boys, haven't you?'

Heidemann nodded.

'There's something splendid in the way the Youth is reacting as though it has been waiting for this moment. Its readiness for sacrifice is extraordinary! But you must have seen them yourself, out in all weathers with their collecting-boxes.'

Once again the phone rang, once again the teacher made notes ecstatically.

'What were we talking about?' he asked, looking up and seeming both surprised and pleased that Heidemann was there.

'We were talking about Karl Müller . . .' said Heidemann, trying again.

'There are always bad elements,' interrupted the other absent-mindedly, deep in his notes.

'The attack you mentioned was on Martin, was it not?'

'Sorry? Yes. How did you know?'

'Because I know the cause,' said Heidemann, trying to catch the other's preoccupied eye.

'We can't concern ourselves with private matters. We have a goal which we are all working towards. Personal differences will fade away, as the party spirit grows stronger.'

Someone knocked at the door. The caretaker brought in a letter at which the young master cast a hasty eye.

'One's got to be everywhere at once,' he exclaimed and as a boy came in from the next room to give him a plan and ask a question, felt his words happily justified and nodded to Heidemann with his bright, merry smile.

'There are three people who can help you next door,' he said, telling the boy what to do; he went away hastily as if on an important mission.

'On Saturday we're having a school concert in the town stadium. We're hoping to raise a large sum of money. Could I perhaps offer you a couple of tickets . . .' He held them out to Heidemann.

He hesitated only for a moment, then took them and put the money on the desk. He who loses, pays.

'Please forgive me for taking up so much of your time,' he said, and left.

In the street, once he had walked a few steps into the wind, he suddenly felt tired and stood for a moment leaning against a tree. For a few moments it was all he could do to breathe. Then he stopped a passing taxi and gave the address of the bar Anna had pointed out to him. In spite of its ridiculous ending his trip hadn't been totally in vain. He had seen Martin and realised that talking to him was pointless and that he could only confront him with force.

If the uncle to whom he was going would not help, he would go further, to the police, to the courts. He had friends – he would make use of them, scrupulously dig up everything which could be of use, surround Martin by a wall of threats, and look after Manja. Looking at the street, with the leaves blown along by the wind, he breathed more easily and collected his strength. He stopped the taxi at the corner and walked slowly to the bar. The smell of rotting leaves mingled with the sour fumes of stale beer and cold smoke. The room was almost empty; the slanting autumn light was reflected in the metal on the counter, leaving the walls and room almost in darkness.

The landlord looked at Heidemann expectantly. He had small, inquisitive eyes and a glistening smile on his fleshy, round face. Heidemann sat down in the darkest corner of the room and the landlord himself came to take his order.

When he returned with the cognac he began to talk about the weather. Yes, it was cool today and windy, agreed Heidemann. He let the man talk about the price of beer, how his business was doing, and about the difference in his takings on Sundays and holidays. The man spoke rapidly and confidingly, in contrast to his glance which scrutinised a customer who, in clothes and manner, was unlike his usual guests.

'You are not from round here?'

'No.'

Heidemann looked over at the men who were standing at the bar, deep in conversation.

'No, I've come to have a word with you. . . .' Looking at Heidemann's suit, the landlord came closer. Secret police, he thought. He was not easily taken in, he knew a thing or two.

'What's it about?' he asked quietly.

'Does your nephew live with you?' began Heidemann.

'Yes. What's he done then?' asked the landlord uneasily.

'He attacked a young girl.'

The landlord burst out laughing.

'He's a one, young Martin, always after the women. He goes after every skirt, that boy.'

'There are severe penalties.'

'Has he killed her?' asked Hammelmann, startled. His fat face was a shade paler. Heidemann did not hurry with his reply.

'No, the worst has not happened, but . . .'

'Well, then!' interrupted the other. 'Why are you making such a fuss?'

'Because she's just a child.' Heidemann's glance held the little gleaming eyes. Perhaps he could persuade the man to help, perhaps there was a touch of good nature behind the ingratiating landlord's face. He resorted to flattery.

'If you have a word with Martin and ask him to leave the girl alone in the future . . .'

'You can't say a thing to him,' declared the landlord, visibly gratified. 'Who is the child by the way?'

'She lives quite near here. She's twelve years old, her name is Manja.'

The landlord's jaw dropped so that it looked as if it would fall on the table. 'The Polish girl?' he asked. 'Do I know her! Well, that explains things. I can't understand why you. . . . Her mother is a fat Jewish pig, throws herself at everyone. Like mother, like daughter.'

He paused for breath, stumbling over what he was saying.

'That isn't true,' replied Heidemann. 'I know the child.'

'You've been sent here because of her? Fancy the police bothering with that kind of –' and in mid-sentence he realised

427

that that was impossible and began to accuse him of lying:
'You're not from the police at all!'

'I didn't say I was,' replied Heidemann, now understanding his willingness to give information.

'And who are you if one may ask? What right have you to
keep me here and ask me questions?'

'I'm the girl's doctor,' said Heidemann standing up. 'I
came to warn you.'

'Don't listen to what they say,' shouted the landlord. 'I
know that lot.'

Heidemann left.

When he was back in the windy street, among the whirling
leaves, the sun broke through briefly and the last leaves on the
small trees on either side of the street gleamed a fiery red. He
could go home, read and have a rest. But all too clearly – like
stations at night when a train passes through – the separate
stages of his mission were entered in today's timetable. Then
a name came to him as though written down in red ink: Hans
Walter, Judge . . . He remembered clearly that he had dealt
with juvenile crime for many years. At any rate, he was an
experienced lawyer and a decent man. Heidemann had not
seen him for a long time. Did he still live in the town, was he
in the phone book, was he at home . . .?

Half an hour later Heidemann walked through a brightly-
lit reception area into an even brighter room. The first thing
one noticed were large windows looking out on bare trees and
an autumnal sky, only after that the room and the books
and the table and his friend. Heidemann remembered the
open face of his schoolfriend, the eager one of the student,

428

the small head beneath its steel helmet, all came together in the calm civil servant's face with pince-nez and a forehead that was now high and learned-looking because of his receding hairline. It was not easy to bring the conversation round from the past to the present. They sat drinking coffee. Heidemann allowed himself to be reproached for his long silence, to hear his friend explain why he had not married and what amazing good luck it was that he happened to be at home that day and not in court. That gave Heidemann an opening.

Clearly and simply he explained why he had come. Walter listened to him in silence, his cigar in his mouth.

'Do you think he raped her?' he asked at the end.

'As I said, I haven't been able to examine her.'

'Any other bodily injuries?'

'She's scratched and badly grazed,' said Heidemann impatiently. 'But don't you understand?'

'Of course I do. And from the human point of view I realise why you didn't insist on an examination; but as a lawyer I must tell you that it leaves you without the slightest grounds for prosecution.'

'I've seen the fellow,' interrupted Heidemann.

'Even a murderer cannot be punished until he has committed a murder.'

Heidemann looked away from Walter, whose condescending, rather smug smile irritated him, to the leaves falling gently and indifferently outside the big windows.

'Be reasonable, Heidemann. If the affair comes to court the first thing will be for a less sensitive doctor to carry out the examination which you haven't, and if no injury is traceable on the girl's body. . . .' He shrugged his shoulders and stirred his coffee with a spoon.

'I came to ask your advice,' said Heidemann. He stood up and went over to his friend. He looked the same and sounded the same as thirty years ago when he, the cleverer of the two boys and someone Hans Walter looked up to, initiated adventures the shy model-pupil would rather not have been involved in; but for the sake of his friend participated in blindly and enthusiastically.

'There must be some way with or without legal hair-splitting. I've described the boy to you. He's a coward, one could frighten him. A summons might be enough. Interrogation would not make him talk but it would scare him and at least the girl would be safe in future. That must be possible.'

'We can summons him if you like,' promised Walter. 'I can probably arrange for the case to come my way.' He murmured a few names. The eager face was that of Walter the schoolboy. 'There are four or five of my colleagues who might get a case like that nowadays. The judges are horribly overworked, as you know.' Let him frown and wrinkle his nose self-importantly.

'I can't tell you how grateful I am!'

'Oh, it's a pleasure.' He made a shrugging movement, refusing thanks. 'I ought really to place your declaration on record. But it'll do for the moment if I make a note of the names. What is the boy called?'

Heidemann dictated Martin's name and that of his uncle. Walter entered them in a little leather book.

'And the girl?'

Once more Heidemann spelt it out. He watched the large fountain-pen between the writer's fingers. As he began to write the name, his hand stopped. 'Hm,' said Walter.

'What?' asked Heidemann sharply.

'Awkward. After all, we're not living on the moon. If it comes out that I'm acting for a Jew it might be my downfall. There are a good many waiting to step into my shoes and they'd be delighted to find an excuse. You must see that, Heidemann.'

His round eyes under the round glasses looked at the angry, white face which, since he was sitting and the other standing, he had to look up at like a child. Heidemann began to pace slowly up and down the room and to talk. He was not talking to his friend or to anyone in particular but spoke fast and quietly about the things that were breaking his heart.

'To come up against this kind of cottonwool all day long! And no opposition. Cottonwool! There's no solidarity, no resistance, one stands alone. Everyone else understands each other, everything's clear to other people. I don't know the secret language. I'm not part of it.'

His eyes focused on the startled man, still sitting there, pen in hand, and he came back to his last remark.

'I see it perfectly, Walter. For you, for us. I think that washing one's hands is action as well, just as responsible and just as absolute; that this affair is a trifle for you and that I have no right to ask you to make a sacrifice, that you think me a fool, and that primitive slogans such as Equal Rights for All, a minimal basis for civilised values, are no longer valid and attainable, and that there's nothing to hold onto, absolutely nothing if one gives up this principle of fundamental human rights. Forgive me for troubling you,' he said quietly, picking up his hat and holding out his hand. Then once again it was as it was when they were boys in bathing costumes crossing a river on a fragile tree trunk and Heidemann with the same expression on his face said:

'Don't jump if you don't want to!' Whereupon Walter would plunge after his friend into the icy torrent.

'Why are you so worked up?' asked Walter. 'What's promised is promised. You'll hear from me.'

Heidemann pressed his hand.

'Thanks very much and don't be annoyed with me!' Now his face was that of the contrite boy who had dragged the weak swimmer onto the bank and, bending over him, had rubbed his limbs till he opened his eyes.

'You haven't changed,' said Walter. 'You still take everything to heart. One doesn't get anywhere with that.'

In a very human and quite understandable way of compensating for the promise forced upon him, Walter thought that he had after all done better than his more gifted friend, who was now forty but had no job, no prospects and was obviously ill. He patted Heidemann on the shoulder.

'If one doesn't detach oneself from things a bit, they become unbearable from time to time. Whenever I have a free moment I sit down with my books and the telephone and radio turned off. That's my island.' He smiled fondly and complacently as he looked at the books on the open shelves. Pale, fading sunlight shone on the leather and gilt-edged volumes.

'The outside world has always been despicable. A little more or less doesn't make much difference.'

Heidemann looked at the bare trees outside the window. Evening gave them a threatening outline.

'There's no island for me,' he said quietly. 'The water covers everything, up to my neck.'

'Ring me the day after tomorrow before nine.' Then immediately, and without consciously meaning to, Walter spoke another sentence, which came from deeper inside him.

'I'll give you an answer myself. You know you can rely on me.'

He saw Heidemann to the door.

Slowly Heidemann walked along the wet streets in which the darkness of an autumn afternoon was falling moment by moment. Wryly he considered the questionable results of his day.

A wet leaf brushed against his cheek, and he remembered the man he had seen that morning, who kept on sweeping the pavement in front of his house although it was immediately covered again by falling leaves; and it seemed to him that he was exactly like that foolish man, sweeping an autumnal street which in spite of all his efforts was at once covered in leaves again.

CHAPTER 33
SNAIL'S TRAIL

'A friend to see you,' said the maid to Franz, who was just putting his soup on the bedside-table.

'Bring the young gentleman in,' ordered Frieda and put her embroidery down. In these happy times she had taken up embroidery – a symbol of leisure and luxury – and was making a cover for the piano while sitting at her convalescent son's bedside. They were happy days, for Franz not only put up with her presence but demanded it, and she filled his life with scrambled eggs and apple sauce. Happy days, since no one shouted, and when he came home Meissner sat down beside the boy's bed.

'Who will it be?' asked Frieda.

'Perhaps Heini.'

Franz sat up in bed, the corners of the pillow sticking out like white ringlets on both sides of his face, which had got much thinner. He was not pleased to have a visitor: for a week this bed, within four protecting walls, had been a secure world, where nothing was asked or expected of him, where the long days wrapped themselves around him broken at intervals by lovingly prepared meals for which he waited eagerly. They began with his mother tearing a leaf off the calendar with the fox terrier head on it and ended with an affectionate visit from his father who tore leaves off his past life. But that was all a long way away and it was no worse than the gentle detaching of dates from the dog's-head calendar. Now something had happened to disturb the peace of his convalescence and the visitor who had just been announced might be another disturbance from outside.

'I'll leave you alone with your friend,' said Frieda. 'I'll make the bed a little . . . it looks untidy.'

She bent over him to plump the pillow, but with unexpected vehemence the boy stopped her.

'No, you mustn't! Don't make the bed!'

Frieda, alarmed by his flushed face and inexplicable outburst, gave in at once. 'If you don't want me to . . .' she said, and decided to take his temperature later.

At this moment there was a knock and Martin came in. He nodded and stepped back to let Frieda out.

Franz stared in horror at him. He would have liked to call his mother back, but was ashamed to do so in front of her and Martin.

Slowly the visitor approached the bed and held out his hand. 'How are you?'

'Thank you,' said Franz in a low voice. His heart jumped like a fish under the knife.

'I thought I'd see how you were getting on,' said Martin amiably.

'Nice of you.'

Both were embarrassed.

'When will you be allowed to get up?' asked Martin, his hands on the brass bedrail.

'I don't know. Not for a long while yet.'

'When you're better I'll take you under my wing,' promised Martin.

'We're moving to a different neighbourhood, then I'll go to another school.'

'When?'

'Christmas.'

'That's a long way off,' decided Martin, 'a lot can happen before then.'

He paused and left it to Franz to imagine what. 'I won't just take care of you at school but on the school trips too.'

Franz shut his eyes for a moment; the lids became heavy.

At the foot of the bed where he now stood he had seen Martin innumerable times in feverish, terrible dreams. Perhaps when he opened his eyes Martin would have gone. But he was still standing there.

'But I shall want one small thing in exchange.'

Franz had been waiting for this since Martin came in.

'What?' he asked.

'Only that you shouldn't say anything about the little Jewish girl, or that I went for a walk with her.'

'No.'

'What d'you mean – no?'

'I mean that I won't say anything.'

'Whoever asks you. Word of honour?'

'Word of honour!'

The real purpose of his visit was achieved and Martin could have gone. But he still wanted to put a stop to any possibility of something being said.

'Does your father know that you see her?' he asked.

'I don't see her any more.'

'I knew she was Polish but meanwhile I've found out quite a lot more: I'd rather be dead in my grave. Have you actually known all the time that she's a Polish Jew?' he asked slowly.

'I'm not seeing her any more,' shouted Franz.

'All right, all right,' Martin said soothingly. 'I'll introduce you to a quite different sort of girl. Did you say anything?'

'No,' said Franz, 'I didn't say anything.'

His head was pressed into the pillow and he didn't look as though he could be dangerous.

'Well, get well soon,' said Martin, 'and when you're better I'll look after you.'

Franz lay with his face to the wall while Martin shut the door. Outside he heard him talking to his mother; then Frieda came in and came towards the bed on tiptoe. A flicker of his eyelids betrayed that he was not asleep.

'Are you tired after the visit?' she asked. 'He's almost a man, your friend.'

Although Frieda would have liked to know more she did not press him. 'Now go to sleep,' she said gently. 'I'll just make the pillow . . .'

But when he heard that word and when Frieda put out her hands Franz shouted afresh. 'Stop that. I told you, you mustn't!'

'But why not?'

'You shan't, I won't have it.' His voice was high and excited, his thin body trembled.

'Well, I won't. Just lie quietly.'

She sat by the window, spread out her work and, in the fading daylight, began to embroider. The boy's got a fever again, she thought. Half an aspirin in his tea and something very light for supper. Like the boy, she really wished that his illness would last a little longer and leave him to her. He was lying quite still now and seemed to be sleeping. He had Meissner's thick blood. And while she embroidered yellow stamens onto the flowers she decided she would give him semolina pudding for supper. That made her feel better. Not with chocolate though, that was bad for him.

Franz lay without moving. His right hand, hidden under the pillow, held a crumpled piece of paper Manja had sent him that morning. She would very much like to come and see him but perhaps he wouldn't want her to because of his father. She was pleased that he would soon be able to come to the wall again. Franz pressed his lips together so that his mother shouldn't hear him crying.

How nicely he's sleeping, Frieda thought. Children had no worries, and she was surprised to realise that she had no worries now either. Only that Meissner wanted to climb even higher. Now they were going to move to a larger flat in a better district. Frieda remembered the fairy tale about the fisherman and his wife and she could sometimes see herself back where she'd started, watching the golden fish swim angrily into the sea.

* * *

Anton Meissner's table was not just the large desk of an official with a telephone, inkstand, and a heap of files. It was black and the size of a battle-field, and the pen lying on the ink-stand was sword-shaped. When Meissner wrote an 'M' under a document brought for him to sign he did not scribble it hurriedly. He not only read with great care but also waited a moment like a king before signing a death warrant, and the pen in his hand became fatefully heavy. Only then, driven by a grave sense of responsibility, did he put a firm 'M' at the bottom of the paper.

From this neat, whitewashed room wires extended through the building and throughout the town. They constituted something between a spider's delicately spun web and a modern telephone network. When a foot got caught somewhere in the periphery of the net, the intricately interwoven threads in the centre twitched and then, without haste, Meissner started to act. But – and this was the crucial difference – he didn't act himself, he didn't spring upon his prey himself. From the centre he transmitted orders to the less important, who passed them on to the still less important, and the least important of all then went and did what they had been told. Gone were the days when Anton Meissner was one of those who themselves had to go; far distant were the days when, filled with rage and hatred, he had committed many acts of violence. Now it was enough to press a button, say a word into the telephone, drop a hint without exerting himself; a sensitive and powerful piece of apparatus, like a microphone, transmitted, executed, communicated.

There was a cupboard, a special cupboard, divided into compartments like a book-shelf, except that their fronts were wood instead of glass and each could be separately locked like a drawer. Anton Meissner had opened the part in which the files with the letter 'H' lay neatly in a row. Hartung. That file was so full that the metal clasp barely held the overflowing material. New and important items were added almost daily.

The net was so sensitive and so finely spun that it led to totally unexpected catches. Who could have thought that in a barracks in another town a man would, under pressure, admit, among other things, that for years he had received enormous sums from Hartung for giving the weapons being turned out from his works the official stamp of the Government Commission? The piece of paper containing this declaration was pinned to the expert judgement of a commission on an aeroplane which, a few weeks ago, had come down in flames. It threw a new and glaring light on matters that went back a long way. And then there were the recent sharp practices, the foreign transactions.

The file was heavy, and grew even heavier and larger as if it had a life of its own. Meissner put it back carefully and picked out another from the same row.

Heidemann. It was not nearly as extensive as Hartung's. But a conversation he had just had revealed something new. It paid not to rebuff an old comrade. Hammelmann's visit had been important in all sorts of ways. Heidemann, about whose dismissal from the hospital there was a detailed report in the file, had received a large cheque from the other file. Hence his pro-Jewish sympathies.

Nice little affairs. Meissner turned over the papers and put in the new sheet. Fraudulently obtaining the confidence of a man under pretence of being a police officer. Intimidation through slanderous allegations. Perhaps – one would have to see – Attempted bribery of an official.

Meissner was not dissatisfied as he locked the compartment again.

He could afford to wait. To wait until things matured, until the files were heavy like fruit in autumn which bursts out of its skin or falls from the tree, because to do so is a law of nature. Meissner would only have to put his baskets in place for the harvest to collect in them.

* * *

The corridor in the district court was narrow and had two windows. Through one could be seen a small light-well and the wall opposite; nothing through the other since its glass was frosted.

Heidemann had been waiting half an hour and could hear the voices in the room which bore the name of his friend, Hans Walter. He would be called when needed. Apparently he was not needed. Heidemann had time to weigh the ups and downs of the conversation. There was Hans Walter's voice on one side of the scales, on the other those of Martin and his uncle, Hammelmann the landlord of the bar.

First there was the quiet, deliberate official's voice of his friend, the words filtering through the door so distinctly every one could be understood. A throat was cleared, there was a pause and then words again, monotonously.

Perhaps the door muffled them and in the room itself they sounded different.

It was nothing to do with the door. One of the voices sounded sharp and hard, and the second one hoarse and vehement. He could guess every word they were saying, even though no one word stood out. The side of the scales with Walter's thin, gentle voice dipped very low.

Over the frosted window glided the shadow of a bird. Heidemann looked at his watch. In half an hour he had to visit a patient in another part of town. He looked round to see if the little usher who had brought him here was anywhere about; but there was nothing but the empty corridor which apparently led nowhere except to two closed doors before stopping.

Then, most unexpectedly, since they had gone into the room from the other side, the door opened and Martin and Hammelmann stepped into the passage.

Heidemann, who had expected to be called in but did not want to meet them if he did not have to, made a clumsy gesture of retreat that made him look as though he had been eavesdropping.

Martin took a step back. Hammelmann, ever the man of the world, raised his hat. 'Ah, the Herr Doktor is also here. But you are troubling yourself for nothing. I saw the poor victim today. Full of beans. You would be well advised to give your esteemed protection to someone else.'

'The matter isn't at an end yet,' said Heidemann quietly. He put his hand on the handle of Walter's door.

'You are mistaken, Herr Doktor; it is at an end. At least for my nephew. Not for you, perhaps. I presume I shall soon have the pleasure of meeting you again.'

And he went off with Martin, who, during this exchange, had been watching Heidemann with silent enmity.

Walter was sitting quietly in the window, as though he and his desk had been pushed into the farthest corner of the room. He did not move when Heidemann went up to him, the wooden floor creaking angrily under his feet. His round eyes gazed bleakly at Heidemann from under their glasses.

'There was no need to call you in.'

'Why not?'

'The whole thing's absurd. I was against it from the beginning. One ought always to follow one's instinct.'

Heidemann bit back a reply and waited.

'Is it true you were asked to leave the hospital?'

'Not entirely,' said Heidemann. 'I left. Probably they would have got rid of me. Have you decided to interrogate me in private?'

'I'm not in the mood for clever little jokes,' Walter dismissed him irritably.

'Won't you tell me what actually happened?' asked Heidemann, putting his hand on the sleeve of his depressed, unfamiliar friend.

'The family has a very bad reputation. The mother is a pathological drunkard and lives off men. You always were an idealist.'

'Does that also mean,' asked Heidemann quietly, close to Walter's face, 'that I can no longer count on your help?'

'I must have witnesses,' complained Walter. 'It's hopeless as it is.' And lowering his voice he added: 'He knows Meissner.'

Heidemann tightened his lips. For a moment Hammelmann's parting words came back to him and made sense; he wanted to beat his fists on the table or to laugh like a lunatic. Then, repelled by the other's superiority, and sickened as always by the stale taste of righteousness, he stepped back. A mirror which had never had a face of its own reflected the grimace that peered into it. At that moment, when the other had entirely detached himself from the associations of their boyhood, Heidemann remembered how Walter always used to follow him about to his own disadvantage. He left silently without shaming him with a reply.

* * *

In the hall Hanna was saying goodbye to her pupils' mothers, who had listened to their children playing at the piano concert and were about to leave with them. There had been two hours of appalling tinkling and hammering away and, at the end, ten minutes of breathtaking excitement.

A little while later every hand had been shaken, every compliment returned, and it was suddenly very quiet and empty in the hall, there were only their own coats and those of the children who had not yet gone – Harry, Karl, and Manja, whose voices she could hear in the living-room. However, she did not go in there, but went along the passage to Heidemann's study.

He was sitting on the table since all the chairs in the flat had been taken into the music-room for the concert.

'Finished?' he asked. She nodded.

Hanna went over to him and mechanically picked up the book he had been reading. 'Did you hear Manja playing?'

'Yes, it was incredible. The concert was a marvellous idea of yours. It's made her think of other things. Perhaps got her over the shock.'

Hanna shook her head. 'You only heard her from here. If you'd seen her sitting at the piano . . . She could only play like that because something inside her has been destroyed. A child doesn't play like that. So mature, so despairing. While I was sitting there among all those silly mothers I felt for a moment what the child had suffered and my heart stopped. She was very pale, and Heini had to get her a glass of water afterwards.'

She sat down beside him on the table.

'I'd like to take her with me and go away with the children. I don't like the look of Heini recently, either – and my husband least of all. What about Switzerland? How about that?'

'And your lessons and my patients?'

'I keep racking my brains whether it couldn't be managed somehow.'

She put her head on his shoulder and without raising it asked him: 'What happened today at Meissner's? Don't spare me, please! That's worst of all.'

'I've been accused of slander.'

'No,' said Hanna quietly.

'But Herr Hammelmann is willing to withdraw the charge if I apologise to his nephew in writing.'

'And Walter?' asked Hanna.

'Hans Walter has been sent away and removed from his post.'

Hanna's tongue felt heavy, she had to push it aside before asking: 'And what else?'

'Well,' replied Heidemann, 'I can make a report and bring an action in which Manja would be tormented, cross-examined and interrogated. My sole witness would be Franz Meissner. If I called Manja's mother it would only make matters worse. Anna Müller, who saw Manja that night, can't give evidence for other reasons. Even if we insisted on her doing so she's not a reliable witness. You see what the chances are even with a decent judge.'

'So what will happen?'

'Either we risk Hammelmann accusing me, which he probably will, and we try to tell the truth and risk the verdict – or we apologise.'

'No,' cried Hanna.

'Of course not.'

'Do you know what it's all like?' asked Hanna, looking at the ground after a moment's silence.

'It happens in so many fairy tales, that you come back, thinking you've been asleep for one night, and it was a hundred years. The same town, the same streets, but you're a stranger, you don't belong there. Where are all the people like us?' she asked passionately.

'They're silent, Hannalein. Paralysed, shouted down by the others. There are doubtless a thousand other fools like me conducting ridiculous campaigns. Poor Walter! He's not cut out to be a scapegoat.'

Hanna stroked his hand. 'It's true,' she said, 'that they're silent. Even Heini, do you know what's wrong with him?'

'He is conducting his own campaign,' replied Heidemann. 'Manja hers, Karli his. The curse of it is that we can't help each other. If one tries . . .' He broke off, shrugged his shoulders and, lifting her hand, laid it on his cheek.

'With us there's still something like a miracle,' he said smiling. 'For once the silent are having a proper conversation.'

'Go on pretending,' she whispered in his ear, 'it's so good.'

Heidemann kissed her.

'It's true,' he said. 'And true that. . . .'

* * *

In the music-room Heini, Harry and Karl had put the chairs back in their places and were standing rather shyly and solemnly round the piano. The lamp above it was lit and Manja was still sitting on the upholstered piano-stool.

Karli was the first to speak, impatiently pushing his finger down the stiff collar his mother had put on him. If it were not for his horrible anxiety about the next day – Karli did not dare to think about it and certainly not discuss it with anyone – he would never have worn the beastly bourgeois collar. But as it was he didn't want to oppose his mother. He had stood with burning ears while Manja was playing, twisting his fingers.

'You didn't get stuck once, and so fast and without a single mistake.'

It was a long time since any of them had seen the brilliant smile that flashed over her face.

'That just happens on its own, Karli, you just put your fingers on the keys and they run.'

'Not with me,' declared Karli, adding abruptly: 'I must go now.'

'Aren't we going together?' asked Manja.

'No,' he replied brusquely. 'I have to meet someone.'

Manja looked at him, turned her head away and said nothing.

There was an embarrassed silence which Harry filled with a tactless question: 'Wasn't Franz invited?'

'He's probably not well enough yet,' replied Heini hurriedly. He was holding a sheet of music and looked over it at Manja's lowered face.

'Of course he's well,' said Karli. He held his hand out to say goodbye to Heini and did not notice that he was trying to make him understand something. He had other things to think about.

He went up to Manja. In spite of all his resolutions he might have whispered something to her, but she hardly looked at him and drew her hand away. All right then, if she didn't want to . . . He left with a curt nod. Outside the front door slammed.

Harry began to talk about the concert, but Manja would not let him. 'I saw Franz today,' she said. 'He was on a lorry. He looked away.'

'He can't have seen you,' cried Heini.

'He did see me. I waved to him and he turned away,' Manja repeated quietly.

Lurking in the corner of the room was everything they wanted to hide from her. The whispers, persecution, muttering during exercises, silenced when they came, but then impudently repeated in front of them, the constant insinuations that became insults. Two fists weren't enough to hit out in every direction. They came from nowhere and from everywhere. There wasn't a day on which some little note or drawing wasn't found in their satchels. Every German boy and every German girl was called on to put an end to certain shameful nuisances. Beastly, mysterious words, cruel, poisonous, murky. The bit of paper with a caricature of a girl with a thin neck and big nose above a version of the song of 'A little man stands in the wood':

Say, who can the lady be
who never goes alone in the wood
with her frightfully long little nose?

Heini had torn up quite a few pieces of paper. Harry had replied with a haughty 'no' when asked if he knew the lady, protecting both himself and the picture of Manja at the same time. The paper was sold and systematically circulated in the school. When would one find its way to Manja's desk?

Heini looked at her. She sat looking at her hands lying white on the black edge of the closed piano, as if she was not quite certain whether they would belong to her a moment later and not be taken away by someone.

Hanna came into the room as Manja was getting up to go. She said how proud and happy she was, but there was something about the atmosphere that was muted and depressing. Harry said goodbye awkwardly. Heini's face, of which she could see only a bit, seemed restless and agitated.

'I must take Manja home.'

'No, Heini,' cried Manja, 'you mustn't.'

'I'll walk with you some of the way,' said Harry haltingly; 'only then I must go by tram because my father . . .'

'I don't need anyone!' shouted Manja. She pushed the boys aside and went to the door.

Harry and Heini followed her.

In the lamplit street she walked so fast it was as if she wanted to outstrip the boys on either side of her. Harry explained long-windedly why he had to be home early. While he was talking he kept looking round, and said goodbye hurriedly when they got to the tram-stop.

'You played wonderfully, Manja.' Then he jumped on the tram before it had stopped and waved his cap from the platform until his friends were out of sight.

The other two looked straight ahead of them at the twinkling lights. All evening Heini had wanted to be alone with Manja, but the enormous number of things which he could not say clogged the frank and intimate way they usually talked. They turned from the main road into a quieter alley.

'If I become an artist,' she said unexpectedly, 'no one would have to marry me.'

'You know you're going to be my wife.'

'But I can't, Heini,' she said. 'There's a law coming against it . . . What's it called?'

'Race pollution,' said Heini contemptuously. 'My father says it's all twaddle.'

'But if we had children they'd be bandy-legged and idiots,' she replied. 'I'm a. . . .' She hesitated a moment and then said as if it were a poem she had learnt by heart, with the solemnity induced in her by the chain of majestic words '. . . a near-eastern, oriental, central-asiatic, nordic-hamitic, negroid hybrid.'

Heini laughed but Manja continued seriously.

'Really, Heini, it has it in books and everyone says so.'

'Not everyone,' said Heini again. 'And I don't care what kind of hybrid you are. If I can't have you then I shan't get married at all.'

450

Manja hesitated. 'I'd like to very much, Heini, but I don't want to pollute your blood.'

'Manja, can't you drop that rubbish?' shouted Heini.

'Terribly gladly,' she replied with a sigh of relief. Immediately her voice changed and became strong and lively.

'Sometimes I want to climb up out of all that and sit high up, like a sparrow on a telegraph wire.'

'Did you say that for a joke?'

'No.' She stopped a moment. 'Sometimes at night when I'm in bed I make myself rigid and stiff like a doll, and then something flies out of me. Then I'm sitting on a star and it's bright, and everything's far away, just like looking through opera-glasses the wrong way. I can only tell you that.'

They crossed the road at the corner near the baker's shop, which they had to pass to turn into Manja's street.

'My father says the times are diseased,' declared Heini. 'History goes in waves, not in a straight line.'

At this moment a lot happened. The window over the baker's shop was flung open, two heads emerged, someone shouted, someone giggled, someone laughed. A bad egg flew past Manja's head, almost grazing it, and hit the ground. The revolting smell of sulphur went up their nose.

They heard the tune of 'A little man stands in the wood', with the words punctuated by laughter, then there was silence. Heini had grabbed Manja's hand. Now he let go of it and bent down to pick up a stone to throw at the window, where the light had just gone out.

'I'll show them,' he shouted. 'I've had enough.'

He was shaking all over. Manja was calm. She pulled him away.

451

'That's the Thiels,' she said. 'They don't like me. Don't be so upset.'

'Cowards,' shrieked Heini, 'come out here.'

Nothing moved. Very gently Manja led him away.

'I promise you, all that's going to stop,' said Heini. A thought, cold and hard as stone, took shape inside him and calmed him for the moment.

'They didn't dare before; now they do, that's all,' Manja said.

Heini walked gloomily beside her with his head bent.

The stone rolled and grew inside him.

'I don't worry about it,' cried Manja, stamping her foot and throwing her hair back. 'Especially not now. I can sit on a star with you and let my feet dangle.'

'Yes,' Heini cried. He caught her high spirits. They inflamed him and in that flame the thought which seized him burned hot and hard.

'Where are you sitting? I'm sitting on the shaft of the Plough.'

'I'm on the back of the Little Bear. He's lazy and he won't go, he's licking the Milky Way.'

'He can't!' shouted Heini. 'He'd have to have a tongue as long as three times round the Equator.'

'He's got it, my bear,' said Manja.

And then from one moment to the next she quietened down.

'I can walk down the street when people throw bad eggs at me if I'm with you, Heini, but only with you.'

'That's not true, Manja. It's very difficult for Harry. He's not brave, but he is your friend.'

'He told me he is a School-Aryan,' she interrupted.

'That's just piffle,' he consoled her. 'You know that.'

'And Karli? Why didn't he want to come with us?'

'Not because . . .' He broke off, alarmed. He had nearly betrayed what he had been trying so hard to conceal all evening.

They passed the lamp-post a few steps from her house.

She could see that Heini had turned crimson, and touched his cheek with her finger. There was laughter in her voice again.

'Do you think it's like me?' she asked.

'What?' he whispered.

'The picture in the paper. I do have a long nose, but it's quite different. Much nicer, not so beaky, don't you think?'

'You've seen it?'

'Of course. They put it on my desk. I wiped my nib on it.'

'Manja, I told you, it's going to stop.'

They were now standing in front of her house. She took his hand and pressed it. 'It doesn't matter, Heini. All that matters is the wall and us.' She lowered her head and her shoulders quivered.

'No one's going to abandon you, Manja. Really! Even Franz won't.'

'Will everyone be at the wall on Saturday?' she asked. 'Then I ought to be ashamed of myself.'

And without looking round she disappeared into the dark doorway. Heini knew she was crying and did not go after her to comfort her. It wasn't enough now.

Behind everything that was happening to her stood a face with eyes that pushed themselves in and out like snails' horns. He must not wait any longer or rely on anyone else to help him. What he had to do was burned in his heart.

CHAPTER 34
THE CATACOMBS

It was not yet six o'clock in the morning when someone rang at the Heidemanns' door. A pale girl dressed in black asked to speak to the doctor. Hanna took her into the waiting-room and fetched her husband.

'You won't remember,' said the girl when he came in. 'My name is Hede Müller.'

'Of course I remember you,' he said to her, holding out his hand. 'What can I do?'

'Come to my father,' she answered, quickly and quietly.

'Yes?'

'Dr Heidemann,' she hesitated. It was obviously an effort for her to talk. 'I must tell you . . .'

'No,' he interrupted calmly. 'You must only tell me what's wrong with him.'

A few minutes later they were driving through the streets which were still almost completely dark. At the wheel sat a young man in a leather jacket and a cap pulled down over his ears, who gave Heidemann a brief nod as he opened the door of the car. He drove well and fast through the badly-lit streets, where there were only a few laden carts going to market, through suburbs, villages and dark patches of woodland, past endless stretches of grey fields which, as it grew lighter, became green meadows and reddish-brown soil. Just as imperceptibly, without his asking much or being told a great deal, Heidemann gathered roughly what had happened.

Hede Müller sat wrapped up to the chin in a brown horse blanket, her eyes closed. Heidemann looked out of the window at the landscape flying past. Red streaks of dawn were separating sky from land more and more clearly. He could see the mist rising from the fields, and pictured the events into which he had suddenly been drawn so that they overlaid the landscape at which he was staring out. It was something that had been carefully planned for a long time. A warder, a friend of a friend of Hede's – possibly the back with the cap sitting almost motionless at the wheel. A builder's ladder leaning against a barn and dragged off in a single brief moment to the wall of the camp – a hidden pair of scissors, sharpened with endless effort, which don't do their work well enough so that there has to be the risk of a jump despite broken glass and barbed wire – and then a man is running for his life through a dark wood. Behind him the alarm shrieks, and it can be heard in the car at the other end of the wood, where the friend with the leather jacket or his sons are waiting. And then the car makes its first trip that night towards the village surrounded by meadows and woodland, which it is now approaching for the second time.

Little red houses, the roofs clapped on them like hats, a church spire mirrored in the pond where the ducks were diving in the morning sunlight.

The shops were just opening; women with baskets and school-children looked round at the stranger who walked among them, sniffed at by the village dogs. Heidemann did not have to ask the way – Hede had described it to him step by step – but it seemed wiser to do so since he realised that he was the centre of attention. He spoke to the baker's boy, who cheerfully told him where to go.

He turned into a side street and approached the house, in whose little front garden wet, colourless asters were fading. A dog barked when he rang and a man with an unshaven face and open shirt ushered him into the dark hall. He hastily shut the door into the parlour in which there was a smell of coffee and where Heidemann caught a glimpse of an old woman sitting in a leather arm-chair. The man led the way up the steep wooden stairs. The dog began to bark again. Heidemann entered a brightly-whitewashed room where Eduard Müller was lying on an enormous wooden double bed in which he looked as small as a child. Shyly a heavy, fair woman nodded to the visitor.

'The doctor,' said Klausner. 'Come out, Marie.'

Heidemann went over to the bed where, on the pillow, lay the furrowed boyish face with its big moustache.

'So you came,' began Müller, and drew his hand from under the mound of the eiderdown.

Heidemann held it. 'Of course.'

The woman came in with a blue wash-basin which she put on the chest of drawers. Heidemann rolled up his sleeves, washed his hands and arms.

'Does it hurt very much?' he asked, turning his head towards Müller.

'It's not too bad.' Heidemann pulled back the sheets and examined the wound, which reached from the knee almost to the ankle.

'I must put in a few stitches.'

Müller nodded. 'Go ahead,' he said.

Heidemann unpacked his bag on the chest of drawers. The fair woman with blue, protruding eyes quietly watched him as he sterilised the needle and prepared bandages and ointment. When he asked her to go to the chemist to get a large bandage she shook her head in alarm. He asked her if she had a clean strip of linen. With a surprisingly swift movement she bent down, took a towel from a drawer and in a second had torn it into strips.

From outside came the man's voice, loud and impatient: 'Marie.' She nodded and went out slowly and heavily.

Heidemann began his difficult task. From time to time he looked up into the pale trembling face, waiting for a sign – only given with an eyelid or corner of the mouth – that he could go on. No conversation other than this very intimate and fraternal one took place till Heidemann had sewn up and bandaged the wound. Then he felt the barely perceptible pulse, stood up and laid his ear on the emaciated chest.

'I'm not done for yet, Doctor,' said Müller's voice, low but distinct.

Silently the door opened and the woman came in with a glass of brandy which she put down without a word. She closed the blue-striped curtains, for it was apple-picking time in the garden next door and the lads could see into the window from the trees. Then she went out again soundlessly. Heidemann held the glass to Müller's lips.

458

In the drinking and the giving of the drink, between this helping and that gulping down – not more than the painfully raised throat could take, not less than the thirsting lips demanded – there was a certain mutual dependence which represented a more personal connection than the few words which had been exchanged up to then.

'How long will it take to heal, Doctor?' asked Müller.

'Two weeks before you can move.'

'I must leave here long before.' Müller's eyes looked uneasily round the darkened room. From outside the boys could be heard calling to one another from the apple trees.

'Aren't you safe here?' asked Heidemann.

'As safe as anywhere, but I mustn't ask it of the Klausners.'

'You can't go out till the wound's closed.'

Müller laughed. It was no more than a twitch of the brown ends of his moustache above his lips. 'You can if you must,' he said sternly. Both men fell silent, lost in the same thoughts. Flight, chase, concealment, persecution.

'I haven't seen my wife yet,' said Müller.

Heidemann had an image of the high empty bed in the flat where Müller couldn't go. He spoke a little about Anna, but in his efforts not to hurt him by commiserating the words sounded too dry.

'I'm not the only one,' said Müller. 'They won't thrash it out of me.'

Once more their conversation was punctuated with pauses, growing as long as shadows at evening. Finally talk ceased altogether, leaving nothing but these dark tracts of silence. Then, in the stillness that seemed particularly intense in the room, as if it was in part a furtive reaction to the shouts of the apple gatherers in the garden and the children's cries from below, a dialogue took place; this never happens in real life, preoccupied as it is by externals, bound up with the internal, and distracted by inessentials. The curtained room, removed from the day, separated from every sound like a waiting-room between sleep and non-sleep, was the most fitting of chambers for the unspoken debate which continued after Müller's last sentence, like a foot that lifts itself up and, without noticing it, goes on walking along.

Müller: No, they won't thrash it out of me. I'm not an idiot, I know what you're keeping quiet. But there are my sons, there are the others, thousands of them. Anyone who doesn't understand that doesn't understand what life is about, not even if he's read a million books. Everything else is futile.

Heidemann: They won't thrash it out of you, no. But there are other things beside whips and boots stamping on you. There are thoughts in chains, truths that are gagged, justice that is perverted, all of which hurt no less.

Müller: What justice? It's never been anything but a weapon against the oppressed. You deliberated, you split hairs, but your sort wasn't with us. We didn't need deliberations. During the day there was work and at night there was sleep, and when there was no work the only thought was where to get some. Our thoughts weren't free.

Heidemann: That's true.

Müller: You had time to philosophise and you could afford to wait. We couldn't.

Heidemann: That's true.

In unspoken conversation, too, there are pauses – absolute silence.

460

Then Heidemann: Thinking means distancing oneself, stepping back. Not to live solely in the moment, not to be just solely interested in the individual, means having connections with the past and accepting responsibility for the future.

Müller: We don't have time to look to the past and the future. The present drives us on. You deserted us. You've allowed them to attack us. (With growing indignation): You opened the door to them.

Heidemann, softly: No.

Müller (even more vehemently): You understood us and you understood them until there was nothing left to understand and even now, while we're fighting, you do nothing.

Heidemann, quietly: People don't only use their fists: thought is a weapon too.

Müller, shouting: If you're not with us you're against us. Better a scoundrel who helps than a saint who watches.

Heidemann, passionately: One can't build the future with dirty hands. Not because of ethics but because it won't last. Every murder creates two murderers.

Müller: It takes too long.

Heidemann: It takes less time.

Müller: Waiting and watching and understanding! (Scornfully): You see, I don't understand you.

Heidemann: Yes, I see that you don't understand me and that it doesn't help that I do understand.

At this stage in the imaginary conversation loud laughter from outside made Müller open his eyes and say to Heidemann: 'It hasn't been too easy for you either, I suppose?' And Heidemann answered evasively:

'No one's taken a pistol to me yet.'

Then the real words faded away and the silent dialogue continued.

Müller: But they've taken your work from you, so you have no money to live on.

Heidemann: No.

Müller: Then you're one of us. Why aren't we together? Why aren't we comrades?

Heidemann: I'm a poor soldier. I can't just keep my eye blindly on each step I'm taking, I can't just blindly obey; I must have an overview on the battle, I must justify it.

Müller: We need ideas too. Some of them are useful. But we don't want any that hold us up; we need ideas that are banners.

Heidemann: They are only banners if they are alive, if they wave at the head of the procession of their own accord. Once they're borrowed they turn into shabby rags. It sounds commonplace and stupid and stilted but it's true and unavoidable. Ideas die if they aren't free.

Müller: Free? Of course. So long as they help to free the oppressed, freedom against force.

Heidemann: Yes. But they only work as long as they're not constrained. Voluntarily. Otherwise when they're harnessed there's nothing left but the reins.

Müller: That's playing games. And this is no time for them. For neither you nor me, because we're risking both our heads.

Heidemann: That's true. And once the head's gone the ideas go as well, good and bad, living and dead. But as long as it's on my shoulders I'll fight for them as you fight for bread.

Müller: I can't understand that.

Heidemann: Don't try and understand too much, otherwise you're risking your head.

Again the mental conversation was interrupted. Müller rubbed his head nervously on the pillow and, chewing his moustache, burst out vaguely:

'It oughtn't to have been like this!' To that Heidemann gave no answer in words, but once more the four walls around them turned into a twilight space between waking and sleeping. With the obstinacy of a dreamer Müller took up the threads of the dialogue again:

If we have the same enemy why don't we fight together on the same front?

Heidemann: We quarrelled. Only brothers quarrel. There's no quarrel with the others, because there's no common language. There's only destruction. Brothers quarrel about every word in their mother tongue.

Müller: That has to stop, it strengthens the enemy.

Heidemann: It strengthens the enemy but it won't stop.

Müller: Everyone to whom injustice is done belongs to us.

Heidemann: Of course.

Müller: It won't be long before it's our turn. Not me perhaps, but my sons, my comrades. Then the others will be put against the wall.

Heidemann did not reply.

Müller, with benevolent irony: You won't shoot. We did the dirty work before, we'll do it again. Your hands will stay clean.

Heidemann, in the same tone: I'll be with you and I belong to you even if perhaps I'm one of those you'll put against the wall.

There came a loud knocking at the front door and the two men started, each in a different way: Heidemann was like someone torn from his thoughts who has barely returned to reality; Müller was like a hunted man for whom every sound means pursuit.

They heard quick, heavy steps on the stairs. The farmer's wife came in and begged Heidemann, in rapid, indistinct words, to go downstairs to the grandmother. The woman from next door was outside – she hadn't opened the door yet.

Heidemann followed her while the knocking outside grew more violent. The woman pushed him into the parlour he had seen on coming in.

'Grandmother's deaf,' she whispered, and went to the front door to open it.

It was very hot. The tiled stove was lit. Children's clothes hung on a line. Very little daylight came through the small window, which was obscured by a flower pot and kitchen utensils. At the back of the room was a pram with a baby asleep in it, which was being pushed to and fro by a fair girl who, with the same protruding eyes as her mother, gazed curiously at the newcomer as he came into the room.

But everything in the room was a backcloth for the old woman, sitting upright and black in her armchair, who blinked at Heidemann with hard, gleaming bird's eyes.

'She told you I was deaf,' she said, craning her wrinkled neck forward, which made her fragile, shrivelled head look even more birdlike. Heidemann could not find a reply.

'Did you say something?' asked the grandmother and bent even further forward. She blinked and giggled to herself: 'So you've come to see me.'

Heidemann nodded. The farmer came through the back door, neatly dressed and with his hair brushed. Beckoning to Heidemann he began to whisper about Müller. But a jerk of the old woman's hawk-like head made him stop in the middle of his sentence and, almost in her ear, he said loudly to Heidemann: 'It's Grandmother's legs which trouble her, and a bad cough.'

'Five years I've been troubled with my legs, and I've been plagued with the cough since Christmas,' said the old woman, screwing up her eyes, 'and they've never fetched the doctor to me.'

'He's here now,' said the farmer nervously, putting his hand between his collar and neck.

'Yes,' repeated the old lady, 'he's here now. Now I'm eighty-five!'

'You've always been well.'

The grandmother ignored these words. With a loud 'What?' she brushed them away as if they hadn't been said. Then she turned her head. 'How is the man upstairs in the bedroom?' she asked with a high mocking laugh. The farmer stood quite rigid.

'Go on, shut your mouth,' said the old woman, very pleased with herself. 'I'm not all that deaf.'

He grabbed her by the sleeve. 'Don't say a word to anyone, Grandmother, I beg you. You'll get us all into terrible trouble if you do.'

'What?' the grandmother said, turning away from the agitated man as if insulted.

'And now, Doctor, you can look at me. Take the children out and go!'

Obediently, like a dog that's been punished, the son went away, taking one child by the hand and pushing the pram outside.

It took Heidemann half an hour to examine the old lady. She seemed to have been waiting for eighty-five years for the moment when someone would listen patiently to all her complaints and answer all her questions. She related every trouble she had had in life and insisted that he write a prescription for every single ailment. Then she began to ask him about the man upstairs and what was wrong with him.

Skilfully Heidemann brought her back to her own health. She was to tell him again about her attacks of breathlessness, which she did with great enthusiasm. He showed concern and encouraged her to tell him more. She took the bait eagerly.

Then, while she still wanted to know more about the state of her health, he talked about Müller. He was his patient and he had had an accident and had been carried into the nearest house. No one must know about it, and – Heidemann was particularly emphatic about this – as long as the patient lay upstairs he would be coming regularly and would see how she was until the attacks of breathlessness were over. And it wouldn't cost anything. Cooing like a dove the old lady said:

'What you've just said is all lies. But as far as I'm concerned let him stay up there, he won't be the first nor the last the police catch.'

'You said it won't cost anything,' she called after him as he was leaving the room. He heard her shouting impatiently for her son and giving him sharp orders in the loud voice of the deaf.

* * *

It was late afternoon by the time Heidemann, exhausted and quite done in, got off the little local train which had brought him back to town. Despite all his thoughts and images, he had been tormented throughout the entire journey by the recollection that, when he had hurriedly packed his bag that morning, he had left the cupboard unlocked. He tried to tell himself that it didn't matter but kept coming back to it. Thus separate incidents can become connected in retrospect even though they are actually unrelated.

At home, when he was putting his things back in the cupboard while Hanna made coffee, he suddenly knew that something had happened even before he knew what was missing. Even before his hand pushed the bottles to one side, inanely groping in the corners of the drawer, he understood what he was thinking before it became a thought: The revolver has gone and Heini has taken it. He remembered Heini's face when he came home the previous evening and turned round in the doorway, saying: 'So the court won't help us,' and his own consoling reply.

'The coffee's ready,' cried Hanna. Heidemann came out of his room, sat down at the table and pushed his cup towards her. 'The boy's not at home?' he asked.

'No, he's out.' Heidemann wondered whether he could ask anything else without making her look up from the sandwiches she was making for him. He risked it.

'Do you know where he was going?' he asked as casually as possible. 'The coffee's good.'

'He didn't say,' replied Hanna, and began to ask questions, and at the same time to urge him to eat. While he was chewing, swallowing and talking, the thought of what might be happening somewhere at that very moment almost choked him.

'I still have a call to make,' he said.

'Now?'

'Yes, I forgot to tell you.'

'But you must eat something first and have a rest.'

'No, dearest, I must go straightaway, it might be urgent.'

Hanna did not answer.

Heidemann briefly sensed that she knew he was lying; but was not even capable of being grateful to her for pretending to believe him.

One thing was clear as he ran across the road to the nearest taxi rank: he had to find Martin. Heini would be where Martin was. The taxi drove slowly, was twice held up in the evening traffic, stood endlessly at cross-roads. He stopped the taxi in front of Hammelmann's bar, went inside and asked the woman at the counter for the landlord. He had gone out with Martin to a concert. That was all she knew. For the Winter Relief Fund.

While Heidemann's hand dived into his coat pocket he remembered the encounter with the young teacher and the notice on the wall: Concert in Aid of the Winter Relief Fund. No, he couldn't think of the address, however hard he tried, the tickets had been thrown away, and time was flying past. Perhaps there was no point in hurrying. Perhaps he already had a great deal of time. Then he made a breathlessly exciting discovery – his hot fingers found something in his pocket: the tickets.

Once again the taxi door slammed shut and, horribly slowly, he drove to a different suburb. A large, ugly sports stadium, looming over a street of dark and shabby houses, noisy, lit up with electric signs, wide open somehow like a slaughtered animal. A crowd of people, police, children, SA men, noise from inside, instruments being tuned, the disquieting buzz of a massed assembly of people.

He had to show his tickets twice before going in and was horrified to see that the circular hall, with balconies round it, was as big as a circus. It was going to be impossible to find anyone here. There was loud applause, and three girls appeared on the platform to sing. Heidemann neither saw nor heard anything.

'Sit down,' demanded a woman behind him sharply. He walked on. During the doleful ballad he pushed through those standing up.

Then, with a feeling of enormous relief, he saw Martin, who, wearing a steward's armband, walked beaming along the rows, showing people to their seats and in whispers begging those who stood to have patience till more chairs were brought into the overcrowded hall. He stood under a light, his fair hair parted and oiled. Heidemann knew that somewhere in the hall his boy's eyes were fixed on that face.

The three girls with the lutes sang something about a well that was deep, oh so deep. Heidemann pushed on through angry muttering, going on regardless of others like a sleepwalker. He could now see a part of the hall to the right of the central entrance, as far as the gold pillars. Not one face, not one profile, not one neck escaped his searching eyes. Nothing.

Martin was just showing a plump couple to their seats. Heidemann couldn't see him very well. Which moment had his boy chosen? Why here? Heidemann realised that he could not wait in the dark, but why in this hall? Would he wait for the end or for some particular moment as distinct from all the others?

A cold piece of flag brushed his cheek. Now a group of boys were standing on the platform. Heidemann heard only a few words, sounding strange and meaningless:

> The Frenchman rages on the Rhine
> Just like a savage swine.

He had made his way through to the right-hand aisle of pillars. Martin was leaving the central gangway. He saw him hand over the collecting-box to a smaller boy.

> Vengeance is ours

the children sang.

Roars of applause, clapping, talking, moving of chairs, scraping. Through a side door a drum was being pushed onto the platform and from the hall, from left and right, came two groups of ten up the side steps onto the stage. Martin was the second on the left. At this moment Heidemann saw with dreadful clarity the semicircle of boys in the background and, in front, by the drum, in the middle and target for all eyes, he saw Martin.

He sways and falls. Hands seize his son. Panic breaks out in the hall. Women scream and fall down fainting.

Heidemann raised his head to shake away these images, and then, through the carved heart cut in the wooden balcony, he saw Heini's eyes. They were not looking at him but at Martin, standing by the drum twirling the drum-stick.

Heidemann sprang up the steps onto the platform, where the song had just begun with a roll of the drum, ran through the rows of singers and climbed up the narrow iron steps leading to the balcony. Behind him thundered forth:

Rouse the men, the old and the young!
Rouse the sleepers from their beds!

A few people had jumped up from their seats, staring in amazement at him.

Rouse the maidens to come down here!
Rouse the mothers from their cradles!

Heidemann had reached his son. While the choir sang threateningly:

Rouse the dead from their graves

and the drum rolled, he touched the boy's shoulder and at the same moment his left hand grabbed his wrist. 'Come!' he said quietly.

They were allowed out without question or hindrance, for both were deathly pale and it was impossible to say who was holding up whom to stop him from falling.

∗ ∗ ∗

They did not go home, but walked along the unfamiliar streets in silence. It was mild and misty. The red and yellow lights from the suburban bars and cafés were reflected in the puddles of rain that had fallen that afternoon. The lit-up sign of the stadium was a hazy red in the darkness. Not a word had yet been exchanged between them.

They walked side by side without touching or looking at one another, Heidemann gripping the revolver in his pocket.

The streets became bumpy, the houses came to an end. They would nevertheless have gone on had not the road been blocked by a plank, behind which they could see muddy ditches and scaffolding. The rapid pace thus being interrupted, Heini said quietly without looking at Heidemann: 'I knew I'd have to shoot if you didn't come. But you came.'

They walked slowly back in ever stronger rain.

Heidemann had not walked along the street at night with anyone since he was an adult. He was numbed with a joy that was intense but unreal. As a boy he had walked along like this with friends who had then been not only comrades and peers but close allies against black walls, against the uncertain, threatening world. Now the red neon light shone down on them as they walked along the dark, narrow streets, where every now and then some domestic scene was briefly revealed in a lit-up window. Heidemann wanted only to go on walking like this, silently, but the boy's hand in his and the expectant face half turned towards him was asking something from him.

Hard on the glowing feeling of rescue followed the bald question about the immediate future: What now?

'Couldn't you have come to me?' asked Heidemann. It was a clumsy start. With a pressure of his hand he tried to give the words the intonation they had missed.

'One either does it or one talks about it,' said the boy coldly.

A slow waltz came from a wireless in a window.

'You know why?' He looked at Heidemann with dark, burning eyes.

'Yes, my son.'

In another wireless, three houses farther on, the waltz broke off.

'And why didn't you let me?'

'Because it was pointless. Your life would have been destroyed without helping anyone.'

They came to a larger street with a kiosk on the corner lit by a small lamp. The smell of sausages rose from the steaming copper saucepan. In spite of looking determinedly away, they were both savagely hungry after their exhausting day, and the evening of enormous tension. Heidemann's mouth watered, he swallowed, and in the light of the kiosk he saw his son was feeling the same.

'Would you like something to eat?' he asked.

Heini shook his head vigorously. But Heidemann went up to the kiosk.

'I haven't eaten properly all day.' He let the man fish out two pairs of sausages and bit alternately into the bread and the

473

spurting sausage. For a long moment Heini turned his head away, then he took his plate and gulped down the food ravenously, stealing a glance at his father, who smiled at him.

For a while there was no sound but that of eating, and the encouraging voice of the vendor. It was an unforgettably blessed moment that blotted out all the emotion and tension like blotting-paper. When they went on it was suddenly easier to talk.

'What are we going to do?' asked the boy.

His face was calmer and the child's use of the word 'we' had come back again, and with it a sense of responsibility that made a sharp gash in the dreamlike happiness of the moment. It made Heidemann hesitate before answering.

'You won't go to court?' asked Heini. 'I don't want you to have to stand there being interrogated so stupidly that you have to tell lies. And you mustn't apologise. That's why I . . .' He could not finish the sentence. 'It's only because of Manja.'

They had reached the river where it flowed grey and narrow between stone embankments.

'We're living in times that drive one into the catacombs. Not to hide but to survive,' said Heidemann after a silence.

'But Manja . . .' cried the boy, trying not to be engulfed by the dark shadow of the picture in front of him. The river was an enduring, murmuring link with the other side of his life.

'Manja must leave here for a while. I'll send her to the country, to friends. Her mother must move into another district where no one knows her, until the whole ugly business has been forgotten.'

'When?'

'I've already been thinking of going out there with you tomorrow to arrange everything. It might be very nice, don't you think?'

'Yes,' said Heini, and there was a short, restless, expectant, slightly mistrustful silence. A superficial suggestion had been made which skimmed the evil only on its surface but was no real, fundamental help. The reassuring answer was a trap which Heidemann set out of consideration for the boy, to spare him. But deep down he himself was hoping that his son would not allow himself to be caught in it. Heini hesitated, because he was grateful for this consolation yet wasn't sure whether his father now believed everything to be settled. But the experiences of the last few weeks had shaken him too deeply for him to be satisfied.

'But that's not enough,' he burst out.

'And if you had fired?' asked Heidemann quietly.

'That was only because I didn't know what else to do – because nothing is enough,' the boy replied breathlessly.

'I would very much like to help you, Heini, but . . .'

Heidemann was grateful that a noise in the street interrupted and ended the sentence for him.

Heini broke the silence which weighed on him as heavily as a stone. Without inhibition or any sort of self-consciousness he opened up to Heidemann, his forlorn, child's voice trying in vain to be firm and steady; stumbling, almost sobbing, and then trying to cover up his sobs by coughing artificially.

'I don't understand,' he began. It was difficult to hear him for his face was turned away towards the river.

'Why is everything different to what both of us . . . always thought it was? Mustn't one try any more to be as . . . to be as decent as one can?'

Heidemann waited.

'At school they measured my skull and wrote the figures on the blackboard. They laughed at Harry because he hadn't got the Aryan skull measurements. The newspaper, that dirty verse about Manja!' he shouted; 'and at the same time . . .'

His voice sounded queer and tremulous.

'. . . and at the same time they use our words: Freedom, and that no one shall starve and everyone must help, but not as you do. And if Rathenau was a traitor why did you tell me something different? And about Horst Wessel you said . . .'

Heidemann put his hand instinctively on the boy's arm because there were people walking on the other side of the road.

'There, you see, you do it too,' cried Heini, terribly upset. 'If you said it and it's true . . .' He broke off, shrugged his shoulders and said: 'Is that the catacombs?'

Heidemann kept his hand on the boy's sleeve. His grip grew tighter the more difficult it was to find words. Pity and love called for something different to what the deeper truth demanded.

'No,' he said vehemently in answer to the boy's question while at the same time evading another that forced itself on him. What distinguished him from Walter, from Heini's master, from all the yes-men? Was he in fact no different from them?

Beneath their feet the wet leaves rustled. Rain fell gently and continuously on their bare heads.

'I don't know how I can explain it to you, my boy. Not every problem is a knot which can be undone if one only takes trouble. If only it were! I said catacombs. I did not mean being cowardly and silent. A light and a sword – one of them protects the other one.'

'Have things often been like they are now?' asked Heini.

'For everyone who's living through it it's the first time. There have been times like ours, similarly dark times, but history is no help. Science doesn't provide an answer; we can't use the experience of another age.'

Suddenly, with a gesture which was quite unlike his normal self, Heidemann felt in his pocket, and with a wide sweep of his arm threw the pistol in the river. The boy's eyes followed it to where it vanished with a splash somewhere in the dark water.

'Why did you do that?' he asked. 'I wouldn't have taken it again.'

'I know that, Heini,' replied Heidemann. There was a heavy, foreboding silence, then almost immediately there was a flash of blinding lightning and in its brightness Heini saw his father looking exposed and very frail and realised that he had thrown away the pistol not because his son might use it but to prevent himself from doing so. Heidemann understood what his son was thinking and waited anxiously to see whether the thunderbolt would destroy the delicate illusions of youth, to see what would be left when the illusion of his father's omnipotence was destroyed. All this was compressed into the fragment of a second.

Then the dazzling light faded away, and from the ruins of the old affection arose a new and maturer love. The hand holding his was no longer the tugging, fidgety hand of a child wanting to be led, but that of a friend, calm and consoling.

The rain trickled down on them and on the bushes and the river. The damp wood had the tangy smell of resin, mould and fungi. Their happiness had the same flowing rhythm as rain and wave.

At that moment Heidemann stopped trying to weigh his words, fitting them to the boy, and was gratefully freed from the burden of being an example; while Heini stopped saying whatever came into his head. Neither could find any words good, strong, or tender enough to seal their new relationship.

Heidemann felt as happy as a child, as relieved as an actor when he can tear off the dignified white beard glued to his chin.

They ran along the river like two children.

To get home they had to cross one of the bridges and go through the old town, whose steeples were recognisable despite the darkness, but for the time being they stayed on the unfamiliar wet path by the river.

Like a dark wine in a glittering, delicate cup, Heidemann's thoughts were full of joy and affection.

'You haven't got a father leading you by the hand.'

'I don't need one,' cried the boy.

Heidemann laughed and his cup of joy overflowed.

Not far away the Marienbrücke stretched across the wide, gleaming river with its twinkling line of three-armed lamps.

'These are difficult times to grow up in,' Heidemann said as they walked towards it.

'More difficult than yours?'

'Yes.'

'Perhaps,' Heidemann went on – asking a question only possible because of their new equality – 'perhaps we've been wrong about many things? Could being a decent human just be a liberal's daydream? Perhaps Might is Right has always ruled the world.'

'We too want Germany to be free, both of us, or don't we? You know, it's not very easy to say "That isn't true!" to everything you hear.'

Heidemann laughed. 'You're a German all right,' he said, 'and I am too.'

'Do you really mean that?'

'Yes, I do.' And following these important but not always clear ideas, he said enthusiastically without being afraid of what he was saying:

'In both of us there's a piece of German destiny. Do you remember how you used to collect elastic bands when you were very small and play with them for hours? When they snapped against your hand, you still went on playing.'

'Yes,' said the boy, 'I remember. How funny.'

'Do you get the comparison? There's something similar to a rubber band within people. The more it's pulled out, the more painfully it springs back. Can you see what I'm saying?'

'Yes,' said the boy. His mouth was open in his effort to understand.

'I referred to German destiny – often the band breaks, isn't elastic any more, stretches a long way and doesn't spring back. A nation of writers and thinkers!

'A lot of words and phrases, figures of speech, are like elastic that's been stretched too far. There's no vital force left, not even the force of tension. That's how idealists lose their grip on reality. In times like these they are the first to fall by the wayside. And materialists let themselves be killed for something that no one can get hold of,' he added.

'And us?' asked the boy.

'The rubber band hasn't broken yet. It's still springing back, it still hurts.'

They were back on the gleaming asphalt of the bridge. In the water dark boats rocked and black birds slept with their heads tucked under their wings.

'Yes,' answered Heini quietly.

But Heidemann pursued another train of thought.

'Try to imagine human aspirations as an infinite series of numbers. One, two, three, four, five, to infinity. You know about that.'

'Yes.'

It was as if the child's face was becoming smaller all the time with effort and strain.

'Try to follow. It would be easier if I could write it down for you.'

'No, no, it's fine, go on.'

'Think about our rubber band again. Sometimes you used to tie things to it to see if it would break. Starting with your rubber and finishing with a paperweight.'

'That made it break,' said Heini.

'Yes,' said Heidemann, 'just as it's broken now. An enormous rock has been tied to the elastic and we've been jerked back into another era. Do you see? I do so want you to see?'

'I think so, I'm not quite sure.'

'Let's go back to the infinite series of numbers.'

Heidemann stopped for a moment and pointed to the wet railings.

'Here, one, two, three . . .' His hand moved along slowly measuring out equal distances. At a certain point he allowed his fingers to stop. 'I'll give you an example. Someone, or rather a lot of people, think slavery is wrong, they think it's wrong to cut out people's tongues to silence them. There are thousands of examples like that. Time moves on. One, two, three, four, five, six, seven, eight or a hundred. We're here, for example, and all of a sudden we're thrown backwards.'

His fingers moved along the railing.

'In the new era people's tongues are cut out, they are slaves again. Do you see what I'm getting at? It's not very clear, they're only images, random thoughts . . .'

'I know what you mean.'

They walked slowly on, Heidemann talking. 'People have the most wonderful dreams and give them the finest names. It starts with man's primitive dream of paradise. Deer and grass and flowers, people loving each other beneath a starry sky. It's hard to let go of that and sometimes *naïve* dreams take hold of people again. Some never grow up completely.'

'What do they do?' asked the boy. He kept hold of the balustrade and supported himself while he walked.

'They know,' said Heidemann, 'that one can't cook soup with the light of heaven, that prayers aren't answered, that there are no answers. Perhaps it was a part of German destiny that people should try over and over again to heat pots by the light they could see.'

He fell silent for a moment, and the river was there and waves and a gentle dripping.

'We live within two circles,' he went on, suddenly very quiet. 'They're not in the same dimension and obey different laws. That shatters us. The radius of one isn't the same as that of the other, and the most horrible confusion results if they're mixed up. At one and the same time an infinite circle of us is innocent of what's happening now, and it's also our most private shame. It's true both that Martin is your brother and that you must fight against him to your dying breath.'

During these last words Heini had stopped concentrating. He saw the rain dancing round the lamps and the railings on the bridge became fuzzy. His father's words came from a long way off and then were ferociously close. The name 'Martin' fell like a hammerblow on his head. At the same time he saw a man standing where the lamplight merged with the darkness. All this had happened once before. The figure on the balustrade, questions that had no answer.

The man's figure grew larger against the sky. This moment of walking and talking on the bridge pressed down on him and he felt imprisoned like some caged animal. He shrank and finally stopped being there at all.

'Heini!'

Heidemann caught the unconscious boy in his arms, carried him to a stone bench, swept away the puddle on it with his hand and laid him on his back.

From across the road the man who had been standing there approached hesitantly. Heidemann waved to him and sent him for a taxi. All of a sudden the world was very clear and concrete, was made up of weekdays, narrow streets and squares, was not a rain-covered nowhere. While he watched the man running off, and wondered how long he would be, he rubbed the boy's hands and temples; and from the time when the face he looked down on was still pale and lifeless, to the first twitching of the eyelids and the return of colour to his lips and cheeks, Heidemann felt how completely, how unconditionally, he would give up all that he had ever known, the paradise of a garden in bloom and grazing deer, for one single smile from that pale mouth.

CHAPTER 35
THE OIL OF THE OLIVE

When anyone came through the entrance hall on their way to the street Harry hid himself on the dark stairs and, as soon as they had gone, took up his position again between the front door and the wall. From there, even though it was nearly dark, he could watch the street and the entrance to Manja's house without being seen. He had spent a long time standing there the day before without Manja coming out and he had gone home without seeing her. He didn't know how he was going to explain to her that she had to be patient, perhaps not come to the wall for a few days more, and that he could not risk being seen with her when he was in uniform and that it had become illegal to shake hands with her, but that he was as faithful to her as ever, even more than before. He turned hot and cold as he thought about how difficult it was.

He stared at the street, where few people were about, and hoped it would be deserted when Manja came out.

A man with a basket walked across the rear courtyard. Harry saw him too late to hide on the stairs and stayed by the wall, his cap pulled down over his face, so that the man gave him a suspicious glance but walked out into the street without saying anything.

And at this very moment Harry, looking over the man's shoulder, saw that Manja had come out of her house. For one single burning second he forgot everything in the joy of seeing her and ran past the man. She was between her brothers.

Frau Reuter, visible through the archway, was feeding the hens in the light-well. The man with the basket turned to look after him. From the other end of the street he saw, with a horrible surprise, Franz slowly advancing towards her and stopping as he did. Like him, Franz must have been waiting for her in a doorway.

All this was in his field of vision; through his glasses his eyes looked into the distance.

Manja had raised her head and taken her hand from her brother's shoulder. Then she lowered her head, put her hand back and went on.

She was talking loudly and vigorously. Little David looked round at Harry but she pulled him away. Harry could hear her talking about a horse, a white horse with a rider on a red saddle. He knew that he would always hear that high-pitched voice as he was falling asleep, a voice that sounded as if it were trying to hold onto something on both sides.

She quickened her pace between her two brothers.

Harry took a few steps after her, saw her pass Franz, heard Frau Reuter say something, felt the eyes of the man with the basket following him and went, without really intending to, in a zigzag across the road towards Franz.

'You here too?' muttered Franz. He stood with a red face looking after Manja, who was now turning the corner.

'I'm not going to run after her. Are you?'

'No, I'm not.' They walked back together.

'There's nothing to stop you walking with her. You're a Jew yourself.'

'I'm three-quarters Aryan.'

'Oh, very likely, with that face.' Something had hurt Franz very much and he wanted to hurt in turn.

'You won't be among us much longer anyway. You'll be kicked out.'

'That's not true,' said Harry.

'It is. Bribery doesn't work with us nowadays. You can be sure of that.'

'I don't want to be one of you at all,' said Harry, disarmingly calm.

'Sour grapes.'

'No.' He was too tired and unhappy to think of cutting replies. He remembered how Franz had been in bed at his house and how the singing outside had frightened him; 'with us' had meant Franz and himself then.

'When you were ill I looked after you.'

'You don't have to rub my nose in it. Perhaps I ought to pay you?'

He had reached the peak of wanting to be hurtful and mean and the curve fell away abruptly. 'I'm going to be group leader' was the sentence with which he tried to break the fall and Harry did not reply.

He took a deep breath. 'We're both swine.'

'She ran away from both of us,' replied Franz. But he did not contest the 'we' that joined them once more. Both walked on silently not looking at each other.

'Doesn't your father thrash you any more?' asked Harry.

'Not since I was ill. He's very decent to me. So you understand . . .'

'I understand perfectly,' said Harry.

'I say,' cried Franz, stopping, 'can you keep a secret?'

'Yes,' said Harry astonished.

'Swear you won't say it was me that told you.'

'I swear.'

'By what?'

'Manja,' said Harry without hesitation.

Franz was satisfied. 'Your father's going to be arrested tonight.'

'How do you know?'

'I can't tell you.'

'Is it true?'

'You can take my word for it.'

Harry's tearful eyes held his friend's for a moment. 'Why did you tell me?'

Franz put his hand inside his collar like his father did when he was uncomfortable. 'You said we're both swine,' he began, but the tram spared him having to finish his sentence.

'Here comes my tram,' he cried out in relief. 'Heil Hitler!' And without looking back at Harry he ran off.

Harry's heart had begun to beat violently. He thought no more about Manja and, his cap pulled down over his face, ran faster than he ever had in his life.

* * *

When he tore open the gate he found his father and Hans Peter in the little front garden, deeply occupied with making an aeroplane fly.

Harry stood at the gate. The thing that had driven him there so breathlessly seemed no longer so urgent or so dangerous.

'I can wind it up myself, Papa,' cried Hans Peter.

Neither he nor Hartung had taken any notice of Harry's arrival.

'Papa, I must speak to you.' The imminent danger seemed as urgent again as when Franz had warned him.

'Speak on, my boy,' said Hartung gaily without taking his eyes off Hans Peter who, with head thrown back, was watching the aeroplane's flight. Hartung's adoring gaze dwelt on every line of his son's profile. Everything he had withheld from others, he fervently and unthanked offered to this child. In the same way as tough and lonely people are smitten by love for one particular thing – a dog, a picture, an antique – so he looked at Hans Peter.

'It's very important, Papa.'

The aeroplane hurtled past him to the ground and he only avoided it by quickly moving his head. Hans Peter gurgled with laughter at this and Hartung joined in. Taking his father by the sleeve Harry whispered into his ear which, because he was laughing so much, kept moving out of range. 'They're coming to arrest you tonight.'

'Where did you hear that?'

'I can't say, but it's true. You must go at once.'

Hans Peter turned round. 'Not yet,' he declared.

'No, my little one, not yet. Play with the aeroplane.' He drew Harry aside. 'Where did you hear that?'

'I can't tell you. I swore I wouldn't.'

Hartung had got over the turmoil caused by the whispered words.

'You're a coward.'

'Believe me,' pleaded Harry breathlessly.

'Not unless you tell me where you heard it.'

'But I can't.' Harry's voice was alternately high and deep. Hartung clapped him on the back.

'Do you think because young Meissner wants to frighten you I can drop everything and run away?' He was pleased at the boy's astonishment.

'I guessed right, did I? Don't you worry, I was on the phone to his father today; he was very affable.'

He thought about the conversation he had had for a moment. It had reassured him that he was in a better position now than he had been for a long time. He had bought houses, businesses and land and sold them again at great profit to himself. Bucheneck had gone to Adrian. Everything indicated that he had been right to stay, that dogs that bark don't bite, or at least not people like him.

'Papa, it's terrible that you don't believe me,' said Harry.

'Help me wind it up,' demanded Hans Peter.

'In a moment, little one.'

Harry, with the precocious, penetrating look on his face of the short-sighted, realised that his father was only concerned with ending their talk and getting back to his game with Hans Peter. Hartung turned away and wound up the propeller.

Harry's warning was rejected. He himself didn't know how seriously to take it. He no longer felt any jealousy or hurt. But a thought that had been pushed into the back of his mind by the experiences of the last months came strongly to the front of his mind; relieved and unafraid he came out with it.

'I won't stay any longer in the Hitler Youth. I've been a coward and I'm ashamed of myself. I don't belong there.' And with a determination he had never had before: 'I'm taking off the jacket and I'm never going to put it on again.'

He began slowly to unbutton it. Hartung let go of the aeroplane and looked at his son. In that moment he saw Adrian's grey estate car turn the corner and stop in front of the house and knew that Harry's warning was no childish chatter.

'We'll talk about it later,' he said mechanically.

Harry went upstairs determined to brave all opposition. But there was none, even when he came down a moment later in a coat. He was happier than he had been for a long time. Now he could talk to Manja as before, without caution, on an equal footing.

Then he almost ran into a stranger who was opening the garden gate as he ran out.

Hartung had taken the little boy's hand.

'It's getting dark, we must go in, Hans Peter.' He added a word that all of a sudden had no meaning and fluttered limply in the air. 'Tomorrow . . .'

'Why are you trembling?' the child asked. 'Give me the aeroplane, or you'll drop it.'

* * *

The three of them went upstairs, the little boy between the two men. They had exchanged no word other than a greeting.

'It's chilly,' said Hartung.

'Yes, very.'

'It isn't chilly at all!' cried Hans Peter.

He looked at the stranger, who was very pale and whose mouth and eyes were twitching.

'I'm going to be a pilot,' he said.

'Would you like to come on a flight over the town with me one day?'

'Could I?' asked Hans Peter breathlessly.

'Whenever you like.'

'Tomorrow?'

'Yes, that can be done.'

'Did you hear, Papa?'

'Yes, my child. Say thank you to Uncle,' Hartung answered in a low voice.

'Thank you,' said Hans Peter in his clear, ringing tone.

Never had the stairs had so many steps. It seemed unbelievable to Hartung that they only led to his house and not to the entire expanse of time and space. He met Adrian's glance over the child's fair head and did not seek it again. He had seen something burning and perplexed. He put his hand on the little boy's shoulder.

'You go into your room now, little chap.'

But Hans Peter wanted to play in the next-door room, with the door open. He begged to do this with the smile that was his greatest charm, and for a moment Hartung's sense of happy possession was so powerful that all other threats vanished. The stairs turned back into real steps. No avenging angel with a sword stood at the top, only the housemaid, who opened the door.

'After you, Adrian,' said Hartung . . .

* * *

When they were standing opposite one another in the study they dispensed with small talk.

'You must leave today, Hartung.'

'Has something happened?'

'Meissner called on me.'

'What about?' asked Hartung.

'The two accidents. Seven years ago with the estate car; six months ago, the plane crash. He's going to prove they weren't accidents.'

'He'll have to find proof first.'

'He's got witnesses. Workmen who say the material was shoddy, an engineer who was sacked, I can't remember his name.'

'I know,' said Hartung, 'a complete fool. What else?'

'He's arrested a man who confessed that he was bribed to put the official stamp on everything without checking.'

'That's a lie,' snapped Hartung. He looked at Adrian.

'Adrian, this is not the moment for lies,' he said pleadingly. 'I give you my word of honour it's not true. Of course I did a little greasing of palms for a time, when things were in a mess. In so-called higher circles too. But that thing about bribing to get an official stamp is a rotten lie.'

'I believe you, but who else will? Who's going to take the trouble to test every thread in the tangle?'

Half turning away, Hartung said: 'Meissner has done his work thoroughly.'

Without realising it, both men were remembering the letter which had been Meissner's starting point, the first mesh in the net.

There was a moment's silence which Hartung in his misery took for sympathy.

'What can we do?'

Adrian cut through the connecting 'we'.

'You must leave! This evening. I don't know whether Meissner's having me watched, but I don't think anyone has seen me.' He felt in his pocket.

'Here is a ticket to Paris. Your train leaves in two hours. A passport will be ready in an hour. My chauffeur will be waiting for you at half-past seven on the corner. He'll come in a taxi. Don't stop anywhere, don't take any luggage.'

'And if I don't go?'

Adrian shrugged his shoulders.

'Don't count on my being able to get you out again, Hartung. At best I'd only be keeping you company.'

'I've never yet run away from a danger in my life.'

'Do as you like; the charge is murder.'

'Murder?' repeated Hartung in a low voice.

From the next room came the clear laughter of the boy delighted by something he was playing with. Adrian heard it and felt a sudden stab of joy. Hartung stared in front of him without seeing or hearing. The reality of furniture and walls was turning into a mirage. It was faraway, like faces and voices in a dream.

He saw a courtroom with an oddly tiered church-like dome. People sat on benches as in a circus. He saw each face more clearly than his waking memory would have done. There were the faces of all his enemies. Every worker dismissed by him rightly or wrongly, everyone he had humiliated, driven to bankruptcy, every outwitted fool, every swindler he had exposed. Only the judge on the raised platform had a mask. Every mouth opens, everyone speaks, and what they are saying is faintly reminiscent of those choruses sung in front of his house, they are like a dream which is part of another dream. Everyone has a voice; everyone has a right to a voice. He alone has none. The accident on a hilly street costing five people their lives. The car had skidded on wet asphalt. The aeroplane flew into fog. There were innumerable accidents of this sort every day in the newspaper. His lips moved but his voice was gone.

Slowly the judge took off his mask. It was Meissner's face. He had known it, felt it coming. Terrible none the less.

Two cases were mixed up. The one, the real one, whose accusations he knew and could refute. And the other, mixed up with and merged into the real one like skins on an onion. And something else was behind Meissner's face, a new mask, a different judge before whom he could not exonerate himself, not even if he shouted so loudly that all the mouths which were now opened as if to sing appeared only to whisper in comparison.

'Hartung,' said Adrian, and put his hand on the reeling man's shoulder. But Hartung recovered his self-possession

494

again, except that his face was still pale and sweat stood on his forehead. He sat down and turned right round in the chair so that he could see through the open door a part of the aeroplane and the boy's cheeks and hand.

'How can I leave?' he asked.

'Don't you worry about that. I'll take Hans Peter with me. He can stay at Bucheneck.' Since that was the urgent and important point, and feeling Hartung's demeanour becoming calmer, he made haste to continue.

'I'll do everything you want for the rest of your family; you can rely on me completely.'

There was a malicious smile on Hartung's mouth.

'That's very good of you, Adrian,' he began softly, 'very cleverly arranged; you can take everything away from someone who isn't there. Only animals walk into traps. Thanks for your trouble. I'll stay. I'm not giving him up,' he whispered, covering his eyes with his hand.

And now the door from the corridor was gently opened and Hilde entered the room, calmly, as though the arrival of the lady of the house to welcome a guest was common politeness.

'You are very late,' she said to Adrian; 'we expected you earlier.'

Adrian found no words to reply. He was so shaken by this unexpected meeting that he couldn't speak.

'Do sit down,' she said calmly.

Hartung had regained his composure. 'Why have you come here, Hilde?' he asked. 'Where's the nurse?'

'I've sent her away,' she interrupted, impatient at being delayed by something so trivial. She sat down in the empty arm-chair, and with a sweet, distracted smile resumed her conversation with Adrian.

'It's not as hot as yesterday, don't you think? The leaves have been falling all day. They couldn't wait any longer.'

Adrian held his hands in front of his face, in torment. He felt Hartung looking at him and tried to hold back his tears with his finger-tips.

'Oh please, it really doesn't matter,' she consoled him in her high voice, 'they'll be washed away by the water, by the river. They can't wait.'

'Hilde,' began Hartung. But she interrupted him.

'No, I won't go to my room, I must stay here and say it all.'

Hartung stayed where he was. He was conscious of the double madness of this scene, already lunatic enough without Hilde driving it into the grotesque. Her unexpected entry coming, as it were, well after the final act, was the last straw. He looked at the clock standing on the desk.

The minutes passed, minutes during which he had to decide his fate, and here he was sitting and listening to the drivelling of a madwoman. He looked at Adrian's pallid profile and turned away from him. In the background he saw the child, who had looked up at Hilde's entry and then gone on playing.

'Even the path under the beech trees was deceiving and came to an end. But it was lovely – it was summer – and the tulips unfolded like hands – the roses were open – their inside petals held up to the sun. It happens every summer, this blossoming, when the heart of everything is exposed, and then there's nothing left but to fall off and part, isn't that so?'

Her hands and arms gliding out of her sleeves emphasised every word. Both men were forced to watch the fingers of that hand opening and spreading out its veined white surface, and neither succeeded in looking elsewhere, nor in avoiding the agony which both suffered equally yet in a different way. While Adrian's torment was increased through being forced to endure it in front of Hartung, it brought Hartung a strange and deep relief to feel their mutual yoke.

'Do you know what devilry he's been up to?' asked Hilde.

As if through a veil Hartung saw Adrian shake his head.

'He put happiness in a trap like a piece of bacon. It's still there.'

'That's terrible,' said Adrian, pushing his head forward hopelessly. This upset Hartung very much, although he did not move.

'But he trapped himself as well,' he heard her say through the buzzing in his ears.

'He's emptied and plundered everything, except one spot. Strange, don't you think?' And the glow on her face vanished just before it would have turned into a smile.

At this moment Hartung wished that Meissner, fat, red and blundering, would hurry upstairs and storm into this exhibition of waxworks.

'I knew you would come and fetch the child. He'll be ruined here. He's been planted in the wrong soil. What's permitted once is forbidden the second time. You're taking him, aren't you? Why don't you answer?'

'Yes,' said Adrian gently.

'I know what will happen if he stays. First he'll be afraid

497

and run through the corridors. Then the walls close up on all sides and he's looking in from outside with his one, dreadful eye. Your legs want to run by themselves without your body, your fingers want to hold on to something without your arms. Everything falls apart and your skin hangs on you like a sack. That's what happens where he is. Take the child, quickly. If you don't there's going to be a frightful catastrophe. Why are you waiting? Take the child. Promise!'

'I promise,' said Adrian, and could think of nothing to add.

Hartung wasn't there, Hartung was nobody. Nothing but a dark, heavy, bent shape between the arm-rests of the chair. It was easier to imagine that the chair would get up and walk and talk than the man sitting in it. Those words had struck and blasted him, they had destroyed the lies and the living nerves that had grown around them.

The child, who had now come into the room, seemed very far away. The possessiveness to which his love entitled him was no longer his. The verdict had been given. From a distance he heard Hilde and Adrian talking. The boy answered and it did not hurt.

'When's he going to fetch me?'

'Tomorrow morning, when you get up.'

'What colour is the pony?'

The boy was very far away and it did not hurt.

'White.'

Suddenly Hartung got up out of his armchair and walked across the room.

'Say good night, Hans Peter, you must go to bed.'

'I'm going to have a white pony!'

'Go along now, my child.' He felt the boy's astonished glance and at this moment the rules of the game were almost broken. Something deeper and wilder than a scream tried to surface. He thrust it down.

'Good night.'

'Good night.' The door was quietly opened and Hans Peter went out.

Hilde was sitting quietly without any interest in her surroundings. She played with her fingers, twisting them in and out of each other, shut up within herself in the dream-like confines of her second childhood. Adrian looked away from her and stood up, since Hartung had done so.

For the first time there was some intimacy between them, but it was even more divisive than anything that had gone before. They were like two people dying in the same room, who seem united but are implacably separated by everything each one has to endure on his own.

'Thank you for your visit,' said Hartung. 'I'll go by the eight o'clock train.'

'My chauffeur's reliable. He'll fix up everything for you. Have you enough money on you?'

'It'll do.'

'I'll do everything for your family. If there's anything else . . .' began Adrian, and broke off.

But Hartung did not spoil the game, whose rules still applied even if nothing else did. Conventional behaviour, which he had always despised, was his now that it was more pointless than ever, a mere thread between disintegrating bits of fabric.

'All my thanks. *Auf Wiedersehen*, Adrian.'

Adrian made a stiff, unseeing bow towards him, tried to find something to say, some greeting, a farewell; but an incomprehensible fate had confused everything so much that he felt he was saying goodbye to his only friend. They had something in common that could never be recovered, their lives were irrevocably intertwined. He had not the faintest sense of triumph but felt only a dull, throbbing ache as, deeply aware of the lie they contained, he mechanically repeated Hartung's words, *'Auf Wiedersehen!'*

* * *

When the nurse had taken her patient away, and Hartung, after the enormous stress, was left by himself, he waited in vain for the onslaught of the agony he had been repressing for so long. But the storm of despair he expected did not come. Calmly he opened the drawer of his desk, destroyed letters, wrote cheques. He even tempted fate by picking up and looking at Hans Peter's photograph which stood in front of him. He had felt dizzy and empty, as if he had had an operation. Yet something new groped upwards, as yet uncertain, towards the desolation. The release from the millstone of love. Freedom from obligation and responsibility.

He packed a few things in a small bag, and thought briefly about his resources abroad. The wanderer would not have to sleep in the hay. He felt unencumbered, a free spirit with a little weekend case travelling towards a new, unimagined way of life. In ten minutes he had settled everything he could. He had no wish to pass the remaining time with the little boy, whose laughter and singing he could hear. Oddly enough he wished that Harry was with him. But at that moment Harry stood waiting in front of Manja's house in vain. Then, on impulse, Hartung went to his father's room.

* * *

They had not talked for a long time, since they had only had arguments about the old man's compromising visitors – a procession of anxious Jews who, despite Hartung's objections and protests, went in and out and attracted unwelcome attention. Even now he saw a darkly clad stranger hurrying down the stairs.

'Are your consultations over?' he asked, going in to his father's room.

'I'm alone,' replied the old man curtly, wondering what lay behind those words. He was still wondering as he spoke. 'Every day new people come. Words are a poor plaster for wounds that burn the flesh. They pretend for my sake that I have helped them. They do so to save me from shame. But what's that to you, my son?'

Half listening for an answer which did not come, half carried away by his theme, he went on:

'Misfortune was good to them, woke them up, brought them to themselves.'

'The Ministry of Propaganda ought to give you a job,' said Hartung.

For a moment his father's eyes met his. His face was so small and wrinkled that the intensity with which every emotion took possession of it was alarming. 'Injustice is like a

501

stone thrown into the world,' he said. 'We may not understand the laws of gravity, we may not be able to calculate where it will fall, but it will fall and hit its target as surely as it will not remain in the air.'

His forehead sank onto his clasped hands. 'Many bleed from the stone of your injustice.'

'Do you think me so great a sinner?' asked Hartung. 'Believe me, there are worse.'

'The reckoning is different for you,' cried the old man. 'There's one kind for themselves and another for foreigners.'

'That's certainly true.'

'They were foreign when they said "yes" to you, and foreign when they say "no." Take their "no" and their "yes" to mean the same thing. The foreigner lashes out, but he does no harm. They say the Jew is like an olive: the more he is pressed the more oil he gives.'

'Then the industry must be flourishing,' said Hartung. But it was increasingly difficult to shelter behind irony.

'One does wrong without knowing it,' said the old man, taking no notice of Hartung's interruption. 'I uprooted you and made a foreigner of you when I married your mother. I tore up the strong roots from their darkness and you have always spun round like a leaf in the wind: if you keep still you think you're dying. It takes a stout heart to live without roots, and one has to open it wide for it to take root in the world.'

He fell silent and listened. No word, not a breath came from Hartung. The old man waited no longer for a reply. The words took possession of him and he spoke as though they might be snatched away from him before he had passed them on.

'This is what I mean,' he whispered, his lips mouthing the words: 'You travel about, never rest, never take root. But what matters is to put roots down despite their having been torn up, to make a home despite being a foreigner. I didn't understand that until I stopped being able to see.'

Unexpectedly he got up and went towards his son.

'There are two laws you have not kept,' he said kindly. 'The big law and the small. You wanted an easy life and wanted to be like the others; and you wore a coat which didn't belong to you and muddied it in the process.'

Hartung was about to interrupt but his father anticipated him. 'I don't accuse you. I don't want to close the door of your heart with angry words, I want it to open.'

Hartung, resolved not to listen to a voice which did not belong to his world – that plain, normal world of aeroplanes and wireless, not this mythical, vanished world which he had never experienced where one tended sheep on bare hillsides – suddenly found himself replying, defending himself, endeavouring to justify his life. But he did not manage to establish the superiority of the modern cosmopolitan over the blinkered superstitions of the past. His words fell to the ground, too trivial to be picked up.

'If I were strong, if I still had the power to pray like my father,' said the old man, 'I would beat on the doors of Heaven until He heard.'

'And to what purpose would you disturb the well-earned Heavenly rest?'

'So that He should take things away from you, so that He should leave you as naked as you were forty-two years ago when I saw you for the first time.'

The voice was barely audible; he had to catch his breath before he could go on. 'And that He should allow you to start again.'

There was a moment of profound silence, then Hartung spoke. 'You don't need to trouble yourself, your prayer is already answered.'

The old man got up.

'What have they done to you?' he asked angrily.

He used to stand like that with an arm raised when his small son came home bruised and bleeding after a fight. Despite the turmoil he was in, Hartung could see the comic aspect of the situation.

'But you wanted to beat on the door of Heaven,' he said in a low voice.

'That's the smaller love, that wants to close the door again.'

'I must go now, father.'

'Are you going alone?'

'Yes.'

'Far?'

Hartung nodded.

'Yes?' the old man repeated anxiously.

'Yes.'

Astonished, Hartung looked at the face that was weeping for him. The old man's grief had nothing to do with the clear-sightedness of his soul or his severity of judgement. But what he dreamed of and what he was experiencing were as one. Now that he could not see his son, he did not have one image of Hartung but many thousands strung together from over forty years; and all those thousands of images suddenly wished to depart far away and for ever.

Hartung turned round as if there was someone else for whom these tears were being shed and felt a painful affection for the old man.

'You will begin all over again,' said his father's voice, slowly beginning to declaim the blessing for travellers.

Hartung heard the words in the way one hears distant voices in the house which one is leaving in a car. They are sounds which are being left behind – the rattle of plates, crying and dogs barking – and they have gone already, they no longer exist. He left the room and with every step distanced himself from the world where there were grey faces with eyes that looked towards Jerusalem. He had an eternity of time in which to consider eternity but only a moment to save himself from its untimely arrival.

He took his small case and left the house without looking back.

CHAPTER 36
MANJA AT THE WALL

It was hard to leave and go home. On the trees the last leaves hung burning in gold and copper-red, then gently fell in the windless autumn air as though an invisible hand had suddenly touched and removed them. Reluctantly at first, they then abandoned themselves utterly and were scattered over the streets, over the grass plot and the stone bench on which Manja was sitting watching them. A golden five-fingered chestnut leaf and a fiery red serrated one from a little oak tree lay in a circle of light on her little blue skirt. No one else was on the grass, the only green spot in the unrelieved ugliness of this part of the town. It was pleasant and melancholy to watch the falling leaves. Something so lovely as a green and yellow plane leaf couldn't be left sticking in the drain. Manja picked it up and held the stalk against the spot where the leaf had been growing only a moment ago; but the bare branch and fallen leaf were now separated and did not belong together any more.

Manja looked at the familiar trees and thought of a magical game. She went through all that the year did to these trees – clothed the chestnuts with sticky buds, let the tips of the leaves unfold, made the buds stand up like candles and then burst forth in whiteness. She did this, too, with the lilacs, beginning with the first green finger-tips of bud up to their blossoming splendour, thence to the withering, yellowing and falling – and began afresh till it became ever more wonderful and not sad at all that they should now be bare. It was hard to go home.

On the way back she tried playing the game with the people she passed. She changed men and women into children, made them small and fat or slim and delicate, let the children become big and gave them beards and paunches. It was pleasant and strange though not as lovely as the game with the trees.

But the game stopped when she turned into her street.

'Where have you been for so long? You know I've got to go out,' cried Lea angrily when she entered. She was in the kitchen with her hat on, stirring beans. 'I shall be late, they want to go out, I have to look after the child.'

'Why did you wait, Maminka?' said Manja gently. 'I'll get the meal ready for the boys.'

She took the spoon from Lea's hand and went on stirring, while her mother walked up and down, opening drawers and not shutting them again, and at last stood hesitantly behind her.

'Is there anything the matter?' asked Manja.

'David hasn't come back,' complained Lea. 'I sent him out to get something.' Very carefully Manja detached the spoon from the bottom of the saucepan.

'He ought to have been back a long time ago. Perhaps he ran into Munio and they're playing together. Why aren't you saying anything? I didn't feel well, darling. Really. I felt so weak in my legs. I have to stay awake for such a long time till they come back from the cinema, I can't afford to lose the work and you can't buy anything in the shops here.'

Manja turned round, very pale.

'You haven't sent him there?' she asked in hardly a whisper. 'Oh, Maminka!'

Lea tried to defend herself. 'What can happen to a big boy like that? Our money's as good as anybody else's, and Hammelmann certainly won't recognise him.'

Her words grew more and more confused and uncertain. Unconsciously she fingered a button on her blouse and looked at it helplessly as if she were noticing for the first time that half of it was missing. Manja could not remember ever having seen the whole of it. The helpless, humble gesture hurt Manja. She drew Lea's head down with both arms.

'You mustn't be ashamed,' she cried, at once angry and pleading. Lea held her tightly and caressed her.

'You weren't there,' she said like a child, 'it was only because you were out. But, angel child, I can't go myself. You know what he says to me in front of everyone. I can't.'

Manja took hold of her hands. 'I know, Mummie, I'll go.'

Lea's lips trembled. She stroked Manja's hand.

'Maminka, you must go or you'll be late.'

She patted back Lea's hair hanging down from under her hat and gently pushed her to the door. It sounded as if Lea were saying something quietly outside the door but Manja did not move.

David might still come. She listened to the departing footsteps. No one climbed the stairs. It was quite still.

Manja took her coat and went downstairs. Perhaps she would meet him on the stairs. But no one was coming up.

The courtyard was empty as Manja went across it. Frau Reuter's hens stretched out their necks from their wooden cage and Manja looked intently at their brown beaks and their restless, beady eyes. She looked at the green blades of grass between the cobbles, the grain of the wood on the front door, the brown and yellow stripes in the paint, the blisters of varnish and the scratches and dents caused by constant usage.

Then she went into the street, looking left and right, although she could not have missed her brother if he were coming from Hammelmann's. She stopped outside Thiel's bakery, staring at the pastries and pink and green cakes on lace paper and managing to peer through a dark patch in the frosted glass. David wasn't there. He couldn't be there, anyway; he was embarrassed about going into shops. When he was embarrassed he stuttered dreadfully.

But perhaps he had gone into the sausage shop after all. Perhaps he had had a terrible longing to have a slice of the red one hanging from its hook like a snake. Despite the crowded window Manja could see that her brother wasn't there either, nor in the stationer's shop, nor in the laundry, nor anywhere in the street.

She turned into the side street. There was a wall with swastikas on it and Hammelmann's bar was at the end of the row of houses, where the sign with the foaming beer mug jutted out.

Perhaps she could stay there and read the notices and posters on the wall.

If the bar was full David would have to wait till everyone was served. He would stand in the corner, too shy to go forward.

She came to the end of the wall. And now she could hear loud laughter and an indistinct disturbing babble. One moment more – another – perhaps he would come now.

He must, he must come.

There was still the divided oblong of the door separating her from the fearful hubbub. Inside, the laughter grew louder, swelled up, became a bellow, a neighing, and in the middle of it, quite thin, a stuttering, high-pitched voice was crying; and she forgot all hesitation.

She pushed the door open and went in to the over-crowded, smoky room, saw white circles of grinning faces showing all their teeth, saw them indistinctly as one face yet saw them more than clearly, as if she would never forget a single one of them, would know for ever after each hair, each wrinkle, each filling – of all of them.

The moment was like a sack into which, with enormous speed and frightful fury, things were hurled indiscriminately.

She took in the bar-counter and every glass on it – full ones overflowing into puddles, empty ones with stale dregs – and all the faces – and one, Martin's, was for a moment the only one in the room, with his thin blur of hair over his lip and a pimple on his chin.

Somewhere or other there were pictures and chairs and scribbled-on cardboard beer mats on which the beer mugs stood. She could see nothing but heads, hands, backs, but somewhere in the hubbub she could hear a stuttering voice:

'L . . . l . . . let me go!'

That was what was going on in the room before Manja got there.

She hurled herself into it though she was not yet part of it. But then she was in the thick of it. Everyone saw her, for a moment everyone was amused by her passionate, flaming presence. But then laughter broke all bounds, became louder. The joke was going to get even better, priceless, wild, beyond everything.

Manja, pushed forward by their surprise and her own strength, had almost reached her brother, who was trying to hold up his trousers which a man was pulling down.

'L . . . le . . .' The 'let' wouldn't come from his mouth, which was twisted with weeping. It sounded like a warble, it was funny. They could not stop laughing at the dirty, puckered face of a new-born kitten. His hands were clutching at his trouser-belt, trying to cover his nakedness at back and front.

'We'll soon see if you are one.'

At this moment the tear-swollen eyes saw Manja. And, his hands being busy with his trousers and therefore unable to reach out in a gesture fitting the horror of the moment, his entire body made a crooked, abortive twist, bending forward in ridiculous supplication and almost falling down. It was funnier than ever.

Until now Manja had pushed her way forward with no difficulty: men who were paying attention to something else let themselves be shoved aside. But then, when she has very nearly reached David, she suddenly becomes part of the game. Two men seize her and hold her. Martin, with his head thrust forward, saunters over from where he has been standing by the unframed picture of Hitler nailed to the wall.

David's trousers have fallen down and his hands are too small to cover up his nakedness.

'Have a look! Have a look!' shouts someone. 'Keep hold of the girl. You can see it by the nose in her case.'

But almost in the same moment Manja frees herself from the hands that are holding her. It is not only her agility and the way she suddenly dug her nails in that set her free; it is the superior strength that total resolution has over a merely cruel game. For a second she stands without anyone's hand on her, tears the boy loose from his tormentors, then turns round. 'Swine! You ought to be ashamed!'

This is no longer a joke. She has attacked, has disturbed the monster at its sport, has attracted its furious attention. It is no use saying now, very quietly: 'I want to go home, let me pass!' For from every side the storm breaks.

'Swine . . . Who are the swine here . . . ? Who?'

Martin is quite close, his breath warm on her face.

'A teaser who picks up young men and takes them off to the woods . . . That's what you live on, showing them a thing or two.'

From the bar, in between filling glasses, Hammelmann shouts: 'That's what the whole lot's like. Mother and children. Beggarly, degenerate mob.'

'A girl like her is dangerous . . . a slanderer . . .! Killing her with a wet rag is too good for her.'

The sentences are like swiftly thrown nooses. Impossible to catch each one. Her throat becomes tighter and tighter as though it is choking inside while outside it is being throttled.

'I haven't done anything to you. . . .' is quite unheard, immediately lost in the noise.

An unequal battle, provoked and stirred up by Martin, threatens her from all sides. A tower of faces, dissimilar and similar, menacing, rising from the floor to the ceiling, hands, teeth and bodies.

This kind of moment stands outside the sequence of others and outside the chain of slowly acquired morality, it has the warm breath of the jungle, and makes a mockery of a thousand year-old lie. In the moment that follows this one people hang dead from trees and lamp-posts, lie trodden and mutilated beneath human feet and horses' hooves.

But it is not easy to set about lynching among the beer barrels. There was no room, no landscape, no street. The space was constricting, as was the presence of neighbours and acquaintances.

Someone mouths the word 'Authorities'. It immediately becomes a riverbed for the murky flood.

'The authorities must take action, we must have order.'

The magical German word saves Manja from the blind violence of the crowd. There was something else as well.

She makes a strange movement, a sudden lifting up of her arms as if they were wings by which she could soar aloft. This snatching at the heavens is so instinctive and so far-removed from her surroundings that it was as if something had arrived to carry her away.

But her angel abandoned her, the pathos of the gesture falling into nothingness and seeming funny beyond all measure. Laughter, more mocking, and angrier than before broke out afresh . . .

Manja looked round. She was searching for a face, one face, that was not laughing. There had to be one that would listen when she spoke.

There was none.

'We've done nothing to anyone, let us go outside.'

There was nothing imploring in that voice. Had she, through tears and pleading, acknowledged the superiority of the others, perhaps after one or two coarse jokes she would have been released. But there were no tears in Manja's eyes.

'One must put a stop to this,' shouted Hammelmann. A fanfare in the chorus of laughter. Other voices joined in.

Manja did not move.

Hammelmann, leaving the bar, went up to her and seized her arm. Four fat fingers on her skin and his thumb round her wrist. Behind her the little boy clung to her skirt and sobbed loudly.

They walked through the crowd, which parted in a staring line, Hammelmann pulling Manja, David at her skirt, two witnesses chosen by Hammelmann, and Martin and a few other young men behind. As in the fairy tale, the laughter that accompanied them was distant and unreal, as if narrated by a story-teller. Nothing was real. The streets, the houses, the fingers round her wrist, her brother tugging at her skirt, the cat-calls and the men behind her. It was like in a book:

'And so they went through the whole town: men and women put their heads out of the windows and he who saw them became so merry that he had to laugh.'

Hammelmann was talking and Martin was talking. They were saying that Manja would be sent to a reform school and that her mother would be made to leave the country.

The door of the police station was not made of gold. The stairs they went up were not quite the right ones. Nobody bestowed an invitation to a wedding to be celebrated for three days and three nights.

When Hammelmann let go of her wrist to make his report it suddenly hurt very much, which reminded her that she must pay attention and notice everything in the room, although it was far from beautiful.

There were two long tables between the two officials. Only one of the men was writing. His face was lean, small and green. The other man's was round and hidden behind a gigantic moustache.

'You called Herr Hammelmann and his guests, swine?' asked the man with the green face.

'Yes.'

He wrote something down with his small, stiff fingers, while Manja's glance wandered, seeking something to look at. Her name was written down and spelt out. It sounded very ugly. For a second she met the eyes in the other face, then they immediately disappeared behind the bushy moustache.

'Address and occupation of mother?'

'She goes to houses.'

'What sort of houses?'

Behind the green face was a window on which an exhausted fly attempted drunkenly to climb into the grey sky. The little man had to repeat the question before Manja replied.

'She goes to help people.'

'A very special kind of help,' commented Hammelmann.

'She cleans and sews,' answered Manja quickly. Once more, while she was speaking, she was looking for the other face hiding behind the bushy moustache like a bird in a thicket.

The man had not said anything except 'Stay outside' to Martin and the others crowding after him. Despite his not looking at her, despite his surly, indifferent expression, there was something about him that helped, helped so much that Manja even tried a few words of self-defence.

'I said "swine", because my brother was being . . .' and got no further, as though her mouth had suddenly been sewn up with sticky thread.

Hammelmann quickly explained the harmless joke, and gave further information, listened to inattentively by Manja. She was again watching the fly, enfeebled by autumn, trying to climb up the pane.

'Vagrant,' said Hammelmann's voice. Manja opened her mouth again.

'That's not true! Herr Hammelmann used to talk quite differently about my mother . . . He . . .' And once again, that gag in the mouth.

Hammelmann went on with his report, and started attacking her again. She was a dangerous liar, well-known in the neighbourhood. But Manja did not answer back, not even when the official backed Hammelmann up: reform school, penalty to be paid, leaving the country.

The other man at the table gave a kindly snort, but on his superior's asking him whether he was not perhaps in agreement, he merely pulled out his handkerchief and blew his nose for a long time as though the snort had never had any other meaning or origin. And so all help had disappeared. So had the exhausted fly.

'You can go for the moment. Your mother will receive a summons.'

Without looking at anyone, dragging her brother along behind her, Manja went as though she were walking down a garden path between hedges alive with shouting faces. Martin and the other customers from the bar escorted her. She walked with her head held high in the middle of the narrow street, and could not have borne herself differently if she had been riding in a carriage through a cheering crowd, if the filth and stones that flew were flowers and green branches, if the insults had been cheers.

She did not protect herself as her small brother did, by an arm held in front of him; she walked along smiling, a smile that seemed painted on her face, a scornful provocation. Stones and bricks flew past her, grazing her. But the words were like surging breakers which washed away, they were very loud but had no meaning.

'Jewish whore! Street-walker!'

That meant nothing, nothing at all. If only it had meant something! But it did not. The words were being sung somewhere far away, they sounded like songs on summer evenings.

517

Blue balloons floated and dissolved. There was the kind of singing, bawling voices you get in processions sometimes. Loud words, ceremonial singing.

'Lousy bitch.'

It was a litany. She was outside. She went on. If what was flying through the air were stones and tin cans and clods of earth it would have hurt very much on her cheek, on her neck. But what went past was not stones or saucepan handles. It would have hurt very much if they had been stones.

Manja did not walk quickly. And yet the house door was suddenly open in front of her and Frau Reuter stood there. And then an amazing thing happened – Frau Reuter drove the crowd angrily away and bolted the door behind Manja and David. It became a protective wall against which the noise from outside rebounded impotently.

For the first time that evening Manja wanted to cry, and she would have thrown herself into Frau Reuter's arms, so unexpectedly had she been disarmed by this help, if she, shocked at her own action, had not quickly barricaded herself behind her glass door.

Then she ran up the stairs, she fled. She had held herself back by sheer will-power, now she released her arms and legs. But she did not run like a creature wanting to save itself but like something already brought low, a leaf carried before the wind, a plank driven by the flood. Her brother could not catch up with her.

The door of the flat stood open. Little David found Munio in front of the locked bedroom door. Manja did not answer and did not let him in, so they accepted that she was not going to come out. They began busying themselves in the kitchen, talking, pulling saucepans from the shelf and in the end to fish out the cold beans from the saucepan. Then Manja came in. She looked the same as always, but was very quiet.

She heated up the supper as usual, ladling it on the plates, but ate nothing; got the beds ready and waited till the boys, rather subdued, had gone to bed. Slowly and conscientiously she washed and dried the plates. Over the hearth there hung a tear-off calendar stuck on a blue spring landscape. Saturday. The word broke away and sprang into the midst of the faces and the chaos of words which, now that they existed only in memory, had greater effect and seemed all the more powerful. The room was full of Martin's face. A thousand Martins. And in between someone whispered 'Saturday,' as if they were kind and helpful, like that face behind the moustache, which had left her in the lurch too in the end. Manja took her coat and crept out. Perhaps Karli would come with her to the wall. Perhaps it would help if Anna Müller opened the door and smiled.

She rang the bell on the fourth floor, waited, rang again. Silence. The door which she pressed her head against was cool and good.

For a moment she stood leaning against it. Then she went down, past the flats with empty milk bottles already standing outside, and opened the street door, which was still bolted. The street was empty and dark.

She went without looking round her and without fear. Everything that could happen had happened. She was walking towards a very faint light, a very faint hope. But only one. The field over which she walked was misty and damp. A single star stood in the sky.

There was nobody at the wall.

Manja sat down beside the little birch tree; its delicate, naked branches were swaying gently in the wind. She sat completely still and waited. She was no longer waiting for her friends. Nor for any special thing. But for something bright and decisive, which would halt her fate. It did not come. And she did not mind. There was no fear lurking in the bushes, because it was as if everything had already happened – one had only to go along a path which had been traced out before. Horror had disappeared. Had she turned back everything would have returned a hundred-fold, a thousand-fold. At every step, each moment, for ever.

She would have very much liked to stroke the rabbit, but it was not in its hutch, having already been taken to its winter quarters at Heini's . . . She wanted to leave a sign behind for her friends, when they came here a little while later. She couldn't find anything suitable. In the end she took out her scarf and tied it round the birch tree. It looked sad and stupid. But she left it.

She did not look again at the beloved things they had there. Parting isn't like that. There was no bitterness, no brooding about what had already been forsaken, only a careful preparation for what was to come, which called for all her strength because it was very new and very strange. She took in everything at once and, despite the darkness, saw each object clearly, in all lights and at every time of year, in the most minutely observed detail and at the same time linked to all the other similarly known things. Then she let go of everything completely and gently.

The ribbon of lights shone from along the river; the lights of trams and cars swept over the bridge. The silhouette of the town, indistinguishably dark against the sky, was however clearly visible to Manja, familiar as she was with every gargoyle on the church tower, every slope in the roofs and bend in the gutters. She could see the sun on the red bricks and chimneys and setting fire to factory windows.

It was not hard to cross the street onto the bridge, whose trembling lights were mirrored in the river. To slip through the railing was as easy as it had often been before. She saw the bushes, the dark bobbing barges on the water, which was black and dark as velvet. Only the whirls of light drawing floating leaves into their funnels showed that it flowed, was alive beneath the smooth surface. Manja shuddered a little as she looked down on it.

And then something occurred that helped wonderfully. The plane tree, slanting over the river from the bank so that in summer its shadow reached a long way across the water, let fall a golden green-outlined leaf which, as though carried by hands and visible in all its beauty, gently floated into the lamplight and, leisurely sinking like some playful dragon-fly, danced into the water.

It was quite easy. It was beautiful. It was nothing. Manja threw back her head, took her hands off the iron railings, stood upright for a moment like a candle, then jumped.

In the hundredth part of the second between the bridge and the black flood, a vast whirlpool of everything she had

ever experienced closed over her before the water did: a
rushed tangle of images turning round and round, not in any
order and as if drawn in wild abrupt strokes. Everything she
had ever had of her own, every face, the smell of bread, of
leaves, of fields; lights and stars, all whirling meaninglessly;
gleaming whiteness like a blossoming cherry tree; Martin's
mouth, chords, words out of context, snatches of a tune, a
gateway, a river, the school, the street, rockets bursting in
a night sky, spilt beer; it all mingled with dreams and with
things that had happened long ago and with images of what
had not yet been. All that had been done and all that had been
felt, being hungry and eating, sleeping and the pain of having
a tooth pulled out, the piano, chocolate cake with whipped
cream, driving clouds and wind and sky, things blossoming
and fading, voices and shouts – everything.

And now, with every fibre of her being, she fought against
the never more, holding on as though her body had a
thousand hands with countless, grasping fingers.

And then the water. It was everywhere at once. In her ears,
making them deaf; in her eyes, burning and closing them. It
clung to her hair like lead, sucked at her shoes, tugged at her
numbed skin through her heavy icy clothing. It was everywhere. It allowed no screams out of her mouth, it rushed over
her tongue and into her throat. It pulled from below and leapt
from above. It grasped, it beat, it tore, it pressed. It did not
let go. It was not black velvet. It was cold. It hurt cruelly. It
blinded, paralysed, bound, tore, beat, broke, choked.

Only when Manja was quite still, spread out, given up to
the water, was it kind and gentle as velvet, combing out her

hair, spreading out her dress, stroking her hands and face lovingly and carrying her like the golden plane leaf edged with green which slowly drifted towards her.

EPILOGUE

The scarf which Manja had tied to the birch tree was sodden after four nights of rain. It looked very small, creased and forlorn.

When the four children saw it no one dared touch it. Hanging there, torn and ragged, it was like a part of Manja.

They had come without arranging it that Wednesday evening. No one could look at the other or say anything, and no one knew why he had come, each wanting to go back, each staying.

First they sat down as if they were waiting for Manja, as if she were merely late again and at any moment a twig might crack under her foot and her voice call from the darkness.

Then Karl broke the silence. 'I saw my father on Saturday.'

Heini didn't answer him directly. 'We went to the country. To the people who were to take her.'

Harry said nothing, but looked at Franz, who turned away.

The gleaming curve of the bridge spanned the river as it always had done, dark barges rocked on it and bright ones glided along.

Since they could not talk about Manja, nor about anything else, they might as well go. They did not have to sit there like sparrows on a telegraph wire.

Yet they remained where they were. Not one of them fought against sitting there, silent and sad. They wanted to be together.

What they were looking for could not be found there.

And then something happened that had happened before during the years they had been coming to the wall. Life was transformed and a new reality came into being. Manja was part of it, alive and near.

It was very wonderful. The wall stood like a reef on which yesterday and tomorrow dashed themselves like waves. The past no longer existed and the future had not yet happened.

The river was there and so was Manja's laughter, and the one had not destroyed the other. The torn scarf was there and their happiest games.

They felt deep sadness but it was bound up with deep joy; great loneliness merging into tender intimacy.

Only the clouds were moving in the overcast sky.

Heini lifted his head and held his breath. All four of them saw a ragged cloud part slowly above the cross on the church tower, as if at an unveiling. Miraculously distinct, with its five stars, Cassiopeia stood over their heads, enclosed in a black frame by jagged cloud.

No one spoke. They felt an immense joy fulfilling everything. Stillness surrounded the birch tree and the children sitting on the wall, as if they were on a reef against which the flood of events impotently dashed itself, and then was silent.

Nothing had happened.

If you have enjoyed this Persephone book why not telephone or write to us for a free copy of the Persephone Catalogue and the current Persephone Quarterly? All Persephone books ordered from us cost £10 or three for £27 plus £1 postage per book.

PERSEPHONE BOOKS LTD
59 Lamb's Conduit Street
London WC1N 3NB

Telephone: 020 7242 9292
Fax: 020 7242 9272
sales@persephonebooks.co.uk
www.persephonebooks.co.uk